AN AFFAIR OF HONOR

Robert Wilder

G. P. PUTNAM'S SONS New York

AN
AFFAIR
OF
HONOR

To
"Mike" and Ludie Johnson.
With Devotion and in Memory of
the Short, Bright Years

AN AFFAIR OF HONOR

I

Early-morning sunlight forced its way through the slatted blinds and lay in bright stripes across the huge and untidy bed. A tangent beam struck the closed eyes of the man sleeping there, causing him to move restlessly. Finally, with a grunt of irritation, he turned away from the persistent intruder and dug his face into crumpled pillows.

With the sun came the first light stirrings of wind which would freshen later. Now it did little more than riffle through the coconut palm heads as they bent high above a white beach. It shook the lacquered branches of bayberry bushes and set the brown, flat pods of woman's tongues to clacking and nickering as they brushed against one another in their endless gossip. At this time of the year day creeps softly upon the Bahamas, flaming out across Eleuthera toward New Providence and Nassau, Andros and the Berry Islands, creating a giant's palette of the sea with its smears of indigo, pink, yellow and blue.

Within the house there was no sound, although eight servants were grouped around a table in the kitchen with their hands curved about heavy mugs of strong coffee. Within easy reach was a mound of freshly sliced bread, an earthenware pot filled with melon preserves dripping in a thick, sweet syrup. A bowl of rice and red beans occupied the table's center, and beside it was a platter of fried fish and crisp salt pork. The men and women ate steadily, hands going out to reach for bowl

11

or plate. When they did speak, it was in a whisper, although the kitchen was far removed from where Maximilian Hertog slept. The voices were muted from long habit when Max Hertog was near.

As the men—gardeners, chauffeur and a boatman—finished and slid back in their chairs with contented grunts, they dug into their shirt pockets for cigarettes. These they turned with a slow speculation between their fingers. Now and then they glanced with a sly, hopeful humor at the cook. She was an exceptionally large woman, heavily boned and muscled rather than fat. Her height of over six feet was accented by an intricately wound bandanna of bold orange color covering her head. The starched apron of gray stripes on white stood out in stiff folds. Her feet were bare, and around one ankle was fastened a thick gold chain. From it a small bell tinkled when she walked. From her place at the room's end now she stared down the length of the table with a dark impassiveness. She knew what the men wanted. Without words they asked permission to light their cigarettes here in the kitchen and smoke over the last few swallows of coffee. They were without any real hope Big Maum would relax her discipline. To smoke here would be a breach of etiquette, a violation of the unstudied dignity she maintained. That these outside servants were allowed here at all was part of the complicated system of caste instituted by this formidable-appearing black woman. There were other servants who came to Windmere by the day to work on the extensive gardens, clean the beach, paint the stables or some of the outbuildings. They arrived in a Hertog truck in the morning and were taken back to their villages in the evening. These were not permitted to enter the house, although Big Maum sometimes sent out a tin gallon container of coffee and some leftover food from the table.

There was an easy scraping now as the men arose, shifting their chairs and then moving in a single file toward the back door. They ducked their heads slightly, an almost embarrassed acknowledgment of courtesy, as they passed.

"T'ank yo', Big Maum, an' a fair mornin' t' yo'."

In passing each repeated these words as though they were

part of a ritual, and they were voiced in the soft, elusive accent of the Bahamian Negro.

"Yo' welcome, mon." The faintest of pleased lights illuminated the brooding eyes as the men passed. "Take care yo'se'f dis day." She knew them all by name but never addressed them by other than the generic "mon."

Only after the kitchen table was cleared, wiped and a place set did Big Maum take a seat at the head of the long rectangle. One of the kitchen maids brought her a cup and saucer of the most fragile and transparent porcelain. Silver was laid and a freshly brewed pot of coffee brought. These things were not taken from the household's many services. Big Maum had purchased each item with her savings from the silversmith's, china and linen shops on Bay Street. They were her own and carefully handled and put away each morning. A second girl, without instructions, put a large slice of ham in a pan and began breaking eggs for scrambling. A pan of biscuits was in the oven.

The two other housemaids now made an awkward curtsy in the cook's direction. They did this without self-consciousness and from long habit, murmuring a single word with lowered eyes. "Maum."

The cook nodded with a pleasant absentness, watched them leave, and then creamed her coffee as a girl poured it for her. The routine day at Windmere had started.

All this might have carried with it an element of almost theatrical absurdity: the men at the table earlier, their leave-taking, the behavior of the house and kitchen girls, Big Maum herself. It could have been a burlesque, an exaggerated charade of nonsense. It was saved from any of this by the unconscious and unassailable dignity of the woman herself. Watching, one would have felt the behavior of all not only had been correct but had been spontaneous. Big Maum made little display of her authority. She had no need to raise her voice or repeat a command. She was supreme here, and the household staff accepted her position without question.

Unhurriedly Big Maum finished her breakfast. Now and then her eyes strayed to an electric wall clock.

13

"Mistuh Max be ringin' soon."

One of the maids brought a breakfast tray for her inspection. She straightened a fork and nodded, touched the folded napkin lightly. Then she took a thin brown- and green-flecked panatela from her apron pocket and lit it. She smoked contentedly, moving around so she could look out of the window to the bright green freshness of the yard, where the perfume of flowers was heavy in the air. A parrot worked its way clumsily up a vine framing a window. He pecked on the screen and uttered a hoarse cry.

Big Maum laughed deep within her throat.

"Hey! Yo' theah, Sir Rupert. How do yo' do?" She called back over her shoulder. "Stella. Bring me a biskit. Sir Rupert wan' he breakfas' too."

In his bedroom Max Hertog stirred, snorted softly, kicked at the light covering until it fell away from his legs. He wriggled bare toes, watching the movement with an alert fascination as though the members were entirely disassociated from the rest of his body. He laughed and then belched with a sound of complete satisfaction.

Hertog wore only the lower half of his pajamas. He scratched now at the whorl of hair on his chest. It was the silver-black color of partly burned gunpowder.

He was a big man, slightly gone to fat about the middle, but the muscles of shoulders, arms and legs were still corded. Although the hair on his chest was black and gray, that on his head was sandy red. It was cut short and stood upright now as though the ceiling held a magnet and the hair were a collection of rusted iron shavings feeling the pull. He dug at his ears, rubbed his nose, and then blew it on a corner of the linen sheet. For a moment or two he lay there, his ears picking up small sounds in the yard, the wash of the sea on the beach, the rustle of a palm fan. Everything was as it should be, in order. He half rolled from the bed, sitting on its edge. Then he slid his feet into glove leather slippers and stood up.

The bedroom was part of an apartment in the east wing of the house. There was a large bath, a sitting room opening on a wide balcony and a dressing room. His daughter, Jan, occupied a similar, adjoining suite. The house was built in the shape of a T and spraddled a coral ridge fronting on the shore and ocean. A balcony ran the entire length of the T's crossbar, but this was divided by a series of ornamental screens into separate compartments. By this arrangement he and Jan had their private balconies. By choice they were completely insulated from each other. There were no doors connecting the suites, and there were outside flights of stairs from the balconies to the terraced porch. Both of them had a high regard for individual privacy, and they did not think the arrangement of the household was at all unusual. Ordinarily they would meet in the lower garden, in the airy, brightly decorated living room, or on the terrace in the early evening or late afternoon. But this was strictly by choice and not by arrangement. Neither felt it a duty to appear. There was no set hour. It sometimes confused the servants but no one else. It was not at all unusual for Jan to say to her father, "If you're not doing anything, stop by and have a drink with me before dinner." Or Max might suggest, "I'm having some people in for dinner. Join us if you like." There was between them a curious and guarded affection. "You are," Jan had once said, "a real son of a bitch, aren't you? Charming, but a son of a bitch just the same." He had been delighted with the description and in high good humor for the rest of the evening.

Now Max Hertog crossed his bedroom to throw open the French doors. He stood within the frame, taking deep, satisfying breaths of the damp, salt-laden air. Lying as faint shadows on the horizon were the small cays off Andros. Sometimes, when the light was right, they seemed to hang suspended between sky and sea. Below his balcony the Hertog property stretched away in a narrow white blade of sand. A breakwater enclosed part of the sea to make a sheltered deepwater marina. Gazing out on a familiar scene, he found it, as always, new and fired with a stimulating challenge, as though it and the world waited to be reshaped by his hands. Mornings invariably filled him with this sense of exhilaration. Even if he had been drinking heavily the night before, his head miraculously cleared

15

with the excitement of awakening to a new day. It sometimes set him to bouncing lightly on his feet, the way a fighter moves before the bell sounds.

Far down the beach, not much more than a shadow among the slanting shadows of the tall, slender palms, the figure of a man stood motionless. He was a Negro, Hertog could see that, but the distance was too great for him to identify the features. The man wore a faded pair of dungarees, carrying a white shirt in one hand. Idly Hertog wondered who he was. The beach was private. If it were one of the Hertog yard workmen, he would be cleaning it, picking the sand free of driftwood or palm fronds. This one seemed only to stand and peer fixedly out over the water. After a moment he squatted, sifting handfuls of the powdery crystals through his fingers. Hertog watched him with mounting irritation. He liked to know who walked or stood on the Hertog beach.

Up from a southeasterly direction now an Out Island sloop. She moved sluggishly, heavily laden, on her way into Nassau. He marveled as always at the skill of the native boatmen. In their weather-beaten craft they struck out for their island destination without benefit of compass. Always they seemed overloaded to the point of capsizing. The sails were patched, the cordage spliced or knotted. He could see three or four persons on the deck with the usual complement of pigs, a dog and a goat, and a few chickens. The trip to Nassau was an event, and families spent weeks preparing for it. Since they could never be sure the animals and fowl wouldn't mysteriously disappear during their absence, they were brought along. In the ship's well there would be fresh live fish for Nassau's market. Tomatoes, a bundle of sugarcane, a few pineapples, yams and peppers were in baskets. These would be peddled at curbside or in the open-air market. The women would go ashore to sit and exchange Out Island news and gossip with the women at the hat stalls near the piers. The men would get a bottle of cheap rum and share it on a dockhead in the warm sunlight. The children would play on the quays or deck and, if they were fortunate enough to have a cruiseship come in, dive into the clear water for small coins. For a moment

16

Max Hertog found himself envying them their easy association. He was a man without friends. Far more persons disliked and feared Max Hertog than found in him a good companion. He was convinced this wasn't his fault. He moved along roads where competition was strong and never-ending. As he disputed the passage of others, his own way was contested. Men were aware of his aggressiveness, and there was a growl of challenge in his throat. He was the predator who overlooked no weakness. The man who sat at his dinner table tonight might well be tomorrow's victim in one of the innumerable deals with which he was constantly occupied. Men were wary of him. Women found him attractive and sometimes irresistible. They sensed the latent cruelty with an ambivalent excitement. His affairs in Nassau were well known, his conquests many. Maidens and matrons came willingly to his bed. There was excitement in him. Stripped, naked in bed, they found themselves willing partners to what he made them feel was rape. Oddly enough, and this amused him, the married ones sooner or later voiced the same words: "My husband would kill you for this." The idea seemed to stimulate their desire, and they would elaborate on it, choking with their excitement.

Hertog was always astonished by these exclamations. If someone were to be killed, then it ought to be the unfaithful wife who was a more than willing partner. Max Hertog was only taking what was so easily available.

Watching the Out Island sloop, he thought of the invisible undercurrents in these sun-washed islands. The intrigues, jealousies and adulteries constantly shifted and re-formed with the participants seeking new partners or rivals out of sheer boredom. Time was in abundance here and must be used before it overwhelmed them all. They could drown in it.

Beneath the exterior of indolence, the atmosphere of everyone being on a vacation, the scarlet bougainvillaea, palms, flowers, sun and temperate sea, a small group contested ceaselessly for money and influence. The tourists were not aware of this. They saw what they were meant to see, found what they came to find: good hotels, effortless, smiling service, a charming accent, golf courses, excellent fishing and an occasional romance beneath star-dusted skies. Running as a dark and dangerous stream beneath the surface was the playground of the sharks. They fought one another silently and out of sight. Nothing must be permitted to disturb the lure of scented indolence. Blood was rarely permitted to stain the surface. The tourist never saw it. There was, in the Establishment, a tight clique of the old families.

For some three hundred years the Establishment had run things to its own advantage in the Bahamas. Early fortunes had been made in wrecking, by changing the lights so ships went aground on the reefs. The cargo was promptly salvaged and sold. These fortunes were added to by financing the fast, blockade-running vessels which did a highly profitable business between the islands and the Confederate States during the Civil War. Still later the first families, under excellent cover, were partners in the rum-running during Prohibition in the neighboring United States. The Establishment fought within itself but drew together against the intrusion of an outsider. The Crown-appointed Governor in Nassau was a figurehead. It was in the House of Assembly power lay. This the Establishment never forgot, and it managed to dominate the Assembly through the United Bahamian Party, which swept all elections. The Establishment controlled the construction industry. It held the reins of the import and mercantile trade. Thousands of acres of fallow land in the Out Islands were available for large-scale planting of produce. This was not encouraged since it was far more profitable to sell the natives a can of corn for sixty-five cents than to grow and pack it in the islands. The Establishment operated the banks, the shipping, the real estate developments. It saw to the election of only those who would eagerly further its interests. It held the hand of the Minister of Finance and Tourism, for he, more than anyone else, had the power to dictate what should and should not be done.

Max Hertog had defied the Establishment which formed the British Square against him. He charged and broke it, loosing a yell of triumph as he recognized, with a feral instinct, that the old members were soft and frightened. He bribed, cajoled, made loans to well-placed individuals, and there was little thought of payment on either side. In small pieces he began to gather a certain influence within the Assembly. He built an airport, introduced a hardy type of sheep for breeding in the Out Islands. He inaugurated an interisland flying service and began real estate development on a large scale. He acquired a hotel and a large share in a couple of banks and then branched out to purchase holdings in some of the larger Out Islands. Within a few years it was no longer possible for the Establishment to deny the presence of Maximilian Hertog. His offices on Bay Street became the focal point of power, and the man's dominant character drew those of lesser will into his service.

Hertog's daughter, Jan, had been four years old when her mother died in a cheap flat in Toronto, Canada. Max had been prowling restlessly in search of his destiny and had no time for a child. Jan had been raised in a Montreal convent until she was fifteen years old. By then Maximilian Hertog had become a stormy freebooter. Copper. Nickel. Gold. Asbestos. Oil. The great, unexplored and untapped stretches of his native Canada thrust their riches on him. In the space of a few years, through drive, shrewdness, an indifference to all the amenities and a scoffing disregard of principles, he had put together one of the great fortunes. He looked about him, and his imagination was caught by the Bahamas. He descended on Nassau, fired by the notion of conquest, and set about subjecting it to his will.

Max Hertog had no quarrel with the Establishment's theory of "a lot for the few of us." He was no wild-eyed revolutionary and quite frankly didn't give a damn about the large Negro population and the poor, inbred white Out Islanders. It was his contention that after every social upheaval someone still had to take out the garbage. There was, he knew, a political change fermenting. The United Bahamian Party had ruled for so long most persons could not recall any real opposition. Now, though, there was a ragtag association calling itself the Progressive Liberal Party, and it was making its appeal to the Bahamian Negro. The group had yet to raise one clear voice. No one had struck the spark to fire a real enthusiasm. The blacks listened with a listless indifference to the speeches and then went their way. Politics was a white man's business. With an interest of some sort in all the major islands, Hertog received regular reports on the activities and leaders of the groups which constituted the Progressive Liberal Party. These he sifted well and evaluated. He saw in the faintly murmuring opposition to the established order no threat. It could be turned into an opportunity. First, though, it must find its leader.

Hertog watched now as the Out Island sloop disappeared around a hook of land. He experienced a small twinge of envy for those aboard her and then had the grace to laugh at himself. He had been on those native craft, and they stank. There was no other word for it. They stank and were of erratic behavior in unfamiliar hands. Below him, in the Hertog marina, lay a twenty-eight-foot speedboat. Jan used it for water-skiing. Nearby was moored a seventy-six-foot Chesapeake bugeye. He had had the bugeye built especially for him on Maryland's Eastern Shore, where the design was native. She had auxiliary power, and with her beam and shallow draft she was ideal for sailing the island waters. He had spent close to seventy-five thousand dollars fitting her with every conceivable luxury, and there she lay. Once in a while Jan took her out with the crew and a company of friends. They cruised the Exuma Cays and the Out Islands, went into Miami, Palm Beach, Fort Lauderdale or around the Florida Keys. But for the most part she lay unused. He walked from the doorway out upon the balcony, leaning on the railing to study the bugeye.

"Dat yo', mon?" Jan's voice, touched with a subdued, laughing affection, came from behind her screen. "Walkin' 'bout en th' cool o' th' mornin'?" She had a sharp sense of mimicry for the Bahamian patois.

"You're up early." He could see her slender shadow against the screen.

"I'm always up early, but I don't usually speak to anyone. You're special. Want to go for a swim before breakfast?"

"You got anything on?"

"No."

"Well, you damn well put something on this time."

A week ago, at about this same hour, she had surprised him

on the beach. He was testing the water's temperature with one foot. Standing beside him, she dropped her light robe to the sand. She stood completely naked and unembarrassed until he whacked her angrily across the buttocks and chased her, laughing, into the concealing water. She swam away from him with the easy grace of a dolphin.

"I'm a nymph made of sea-foam," she called over her shoulder. "Didn't you know that?"

For a moment he stood, waist-deep, watching her with pleasure. At twenty-five she was a beautiful creature, all light and laughter and sudden humor.

"I don't know about the nymph part, but you surer than hell aren't made of sea-foam."

Now she called to him. "I'll meet you down by the point in five minutes."

Max started to reenter his bedroom and then halted, turning to yell back through the open doors. "Who's that nigger on our beach?"

"That's no nigger. That's Royal. I was watching him before you came out."

"Why?" The question was impatient.

"Because he's beautiful. Haven't you ever noticed?"

He walked back to the balcony, drawn there by Jan's words. He was vaguely disturbed without knowing why.

"Niggers aren't beautiful or ugly. They're just niggers."

"Not that one. Not Royal. He always makes me think of a big black leopard. He doesn't walk. He pads, stalking something."

"Well"—he was finished with the subject—"he ought to know damn well better than to pad on my beach. The only niggers allowed there are the ones who go to clean it."

"I suppose he came to see Big Maum."

"Then why the hell doesn't he go to the kitchen and see her?" He was abruptly impatient and inexplicably angry.

"How th' hell do I know, mon?" She was teasing him. "If he's still there when we go down, we'll ask him." Her voice rose with a shrill, waspish sound as she pretended to call to the distant figure. "Hey! You, Royal. You big, beautiful black bas-

21

tard. What you doin' on Max Hertog's private beach? Hey? Say me dat, mon."

Hertog left the balcony, walking with slow thoughtfulness to his bathroom. Did she really think a nigger was beautiful? He shook his head. He was never sure what this daughter thought or believed. Could a white girl like Jan actually be excited by a man of black skin? He had seen a lot of fair niggers, but damned few, if any, had come from a white woman. Usually the white man took the black girl. That was common enough. He had never thought it might sometimes be the other way around.

As he went to his bathroom, he was thinking of Big Maum's son Royal. What the hell was his last name? Keats? Keating? That was it. Royal Keating. The last name was probably of an early slaveholding family in the Bahamas. That was the way all the niggers got their names. There was no white strain in mother or son. The line, say, maybe three hundred years here in the islands and God knows how long before in Africa, was pure. Royal stood as did Big Maum, straight, proud and black. Now he was back home. Max knew Big Maum had sent her son from the islands to be educated in England. She had scraped all of her life for this, as had two or three other nigger families in the islands. They were people of small property and great pride. It was all a lot of damned nonsense, Max thought. After you educated a nigger, what did you do with him? You changed him so all he could do was cause trouble.

In the bathroom he rubbed some water into his spiked hair and then bared his teeth in the mirror. He was proud of them. When he had been poor, so poor he went to the barber colleges for a haircut, he had never neglected his teeth. They were his. Now he brushed them vigorously, grunting with the effort. He allowed the foam to spill on his chin. Close at hand was a bottle of clouded jade, exquisitely carved and lettered MOUTHWASH. Actually the flask held a particularly fine and aromatic Barbados rum. He poured some in a glass, sniffed it with pleasure, and then tossed it into his mouth. He sloshed it around and finally spit it out. The rum was exactly what the bottle said. MOUTHWASH. He used it for that because the perfume, sharp flavor and bite of the alcohol pleased him better than any of the concoctions he found in a drugstore. He threw a couple of handfuls of water onto his face and reached for a towel.

Jan was waiting for him on the crushed shell path which led to the docks. A rubber bathing cap swung from one hand, and she wore a simple white robe of heavy terry cloth. Walking beside her father, she came only to his shoulder, but that still made her tall for a girl.

Hertog glanced at her with pride. "Do you sleep standing up? I've never seen you looking untidy, rumpled the way most people do when they get out of bed."

"I've been out of bed for hours. Also, it's surprising what you can do with a comb and a little cold water."

"You know, I think about you sometimes."

"That's nice."

"No. I mean, I wonder. You don't seem particularly interested in any one man."

"There's no one here. In Nassau. Besides, it's something of a handicap being Max Hertog's daughter. After a while you get suspicious of people and wonder what they want. So I'm never sure whether the attraction is my beautiful body, my keen mind or Max Hertog's money and influence. Come right down to it"—she looked up at him—"who are your friends? Oh, I know we have a lot of people come to the house, but name a friend."

"Well." He gazed about the beach. "Well, there's—"

"Go on." She was encouraging.

"Well, the Mainwarings." He spoke the name triumphantly.

"Jesse Mainwaring hates your guts. He's hungry, and you throw him a bone now and then. He even pretends not to know you slept with his wife. I guess slept isn't the word, is it?"

"How the hell do you know that?"

"Polly Mainwaring told me."

"I'll be damned."

They walked through the shallows, kicking absently at the small fish which were streaks of silver and blue light as they rode in and out with the tiny swell. The waves barely curled on the beach. Jan glanced up and ahead.

"There's Royal"—she spoke with a grin—"if you want to ask him what the hell he's doing on your beach."

The Negro was standing where the first line of tall, silver-trunked coconut trees grew. When the beach had been deserted, he walked on the sand. Now he had moved off it because Max Hertog and his daughter were going to swim. The reasoning went far back into time and custom, but all three understood it. Royal made no effort to leave or conceal himself. He was bare to the waist, and his skin glistened like polished onyx. The features were clear with only a slight widening at the base of the nostril. The hair was a tightly curled cap. He did not slouch or lean against a tree in the indolent attitude most island blacks adopted. He stood straight and with an easy confidence, but he did not smile or speak until he was spoken to.

"Royal?" Hertog made a question of the name, although he well knew now who the man was. "That you, Royal?"

"Yes, Mr. Hertog." The reply was an odd combination of British and native accent.

"What the hell are you sneaking around down here for?"

"I wasn't aware of sneaking around, Mr. Hertog. I was waiting until I was sure the kitchen was through with breakfast."

"Goddamn that nancy-dancy speech of yours." There was an unreasonable anger. "Why don't you talk like a nigger?"

"Max." Jan wheeled on him. "Max Hertog, I'm ashamed of you." She turned to the Negro. "I'll apologize for him, Royal."

"That's all right, Miss Jan. People, black people, are used to Mr. Hertog."

"Well, I'm not." She put out her hand. "I—we didn't know you were back."

"No one has to apologize for me." Hertog wasn't too sure of himself. "I say what I like—what I feel. You see what happens?" He was accusing Royal. "I never knew an educated nigger yet who didn't cause trouble."

"You can damn well swim by yourself, Max Hertog." Jan turned away and ran back toward the house.

24

Max watched her. "You see what you've done?" He blustered. "Everything was fine until you came along." The words trailed without conviction.

"You know none of this is my fault, Mr. Hertog. I haven't said anything or done anything to cause trouble."

Hertog glared at him. "You've been away to school in England." He wanted a way out and stated a fact well known to them both, hoping it would lead to an exit. "When did you get back?"

"A few months ago."

"Big Maum never said anything about it."

"I don't imagine Big Maum thought you would be interested."

"Are you being smart with me, Royal?" There was uneasy suspicion in the question.

"No, sir. You know I'm not." The answer was reasonably voiced.

Pettiness wasn't in Max Hertog's nature, and he wondered to himself what perversity drove him to prolong this encounter. He could walk away. Instead, he took a cigar from the pocket of his robe and lit it.

"Now that you've come back home with an education what are you doing, portering in one of the hotels?" He was embarrassed by his question.

"No, sir. I've been working, laying out a development on Eleuthera for the Janis Corporation."

"You're an engineer?" Hertog was astonished.

"Yes, sir."

"I'll be goddamned. I thought all you niggers with an education wanted to be lawyers so you could get up and make speeches. Well"—he was being generous—"you come and see me sometime. Maybe I can find something for you to do."

"I have something to do, Mr. Hertog."

"Now I know damn well you're trying to be smart with me." There was a muted threat in the statement. "Why?"

"You're making it impossible for me to be anything else, Mr. Hertog."

"Now you listen to me, Royal." He leveled the cigar in the

25

Negro's direction. His voice was harsh. "I won't take that kind of talk from you."

"What will you do, Mr. Hertog?" There was anger here also, but it was controlled. "Have me whipped?"

Few white men and, certainly, no Negro in the Bahamas would have spoken to Max Hertog in such a manner. Royal's eyes were as level as his words.

"By God, that's not a bad idea." The agreement was quick. Oddly enough there was no bite in it.

"But not very practical, Mr. Hertog."

Now a strange thing happened. The smallest trace of a sheepish grin appeared at the corners of Max Hertog's mouth. He tried to wipe it away and then spat, pretending there was tobacco on his tongue. He looked around and then up into the trees. There was a muffled snort of laughter.

"By God, you're right. I'd have to get you strung up first, wouldn't I?"

"Well"—Royal smiled—"I just wouldn't stand around and wait for you to do it, Mr. Hertog."

"If we were in the States," Max Hertog ruminated, "I could have your watermelon and chitterlings taken away from you."

"Yes, sir." Royal agreed with a solemn face. "In the States I guess a darkie couldn't get along without his watermelon and chitterlings."

"Huh!" Maximilian Hertog peeled off his robe. "Well, I came down here for a swim, and no goddamned smart coon is going to keep me from it." The words were harsh, but there was no lash in them. "You came to see Big Maum. Why don't you go up to the kitchen instead of standing around and making talk?"

"Yes, sir." Royal was grave.

"You got me backed into a corner, Royal." There was regret and surprise in the statement.

"Yes, sir. I know."

"Don't you ever tell anyone." He started for the water and then turned. "Royal?"

"Yes, Mr. Hertog?"

"When you finish that job on Eleuthera, come and see me. I can always use another good engineer."

With a faint smile of understanding Royal watched as Max Hertog waded in and then breasted the water. He submerged with the clumsy agility of a rhino and then emerged, blowing gustily. Royal turned away and began climbing the slight rise to the house.

II

Big Maum, arms folded across her heavy, pendulous bosom, watched with pride as Royal finished the large breakfast she had prepared for him. When he reached in his pocket for a cigarette, she struck and held the match for his light. They smiled at each other.

"Yo' eat good, boy." This was a compliment. "Yo' eat like a workin'man should, an' dat a good t'ing."

"I am a workin'man, Maum."

"It ain't like nigger workin', though. Is it?" She was anxious. "I mean yo' got no one t' say do dis, do dat, pick it up, put it down?"

"No, Maum. I guess it's not like nigger working."

"Dat's good." She leaned across the table. The attitude was conspiratorial. "I never did understan' for real jus' what it was yo' learned across t' Englan' th' white people now pay yo' t' do." She wanted to be reassured.

A warm smile of understanding and affection flooded across his face and reached out for her. He put a large hand over hers, and they were almost identical in size.

"I can build things for them if they want, Maum. I'm a construction engineer. Then, say"—unconsciously the faintest trace of an island accent crept into the words—"a mon own some lan', but he doesn't know exactly how it lies. How the

28

boundaries are, what is his, and what belongs to someone else. I mark it out, an' I say, 'This is yours. That is his.' "

"Yo' tell th' white people dat?" She was incredulous, studying his face to see if he was making fun of her. "Could yo' tell Mistuh Max like dat without him gettin' mad?"

"I could if he asked me to find out."

"Hmmm!" It was an expression of astonishment.

A buzzer sounded, and a numbered indicator on a wall box showed. One of the maids glanced at it, quickly poured coffee into a nickeled Thermos, checked the tray to see if it contained everything it should, and then left hurriedly.

"Dat Miss Jan," Big Maum explained, "she don' like t' wait fo' her coffee."

"I saw her on the beach with Mr. Max. They were going swimming."

"She a pretty girl, nice, too," Maum mused. "Mus' be 'roun' twenty-five. Time she had a man her own instead of takin' off wid other wimmen's like I hear tell she do. Was some scandal talk awhile back." For a moment she eyed her son moodily. "Yo' got a woman on Eleuthera?"

"I got a woman, Maum. A girl."

"A fo' marryin' girl o' jus' lyin' en th' grass girl?"

His smile warmed her. "A for lyin' in the grass girl, Maum. Could be the other way if I want it. When I get my mind for marrying, I'll bring the girl to you first."

She relaxed. "Good fo' a mon t' have a woman. Keep him out of other mon's bed. Dem islan' girl all right. Not like dem conchie girls Over th' Hill in Nassau. What yo' doin' heah today?"

"We flew over to get some things. Have to go back this afternoon. There was a truck coming out to Lyford Cay and I rode it to see you."

"How yo' goin' t' git back?"

"Oh, someone will come along."

"Mistuh Max go in every mornin'. He take yo' ef yo' ask."

"I'll get in all right, don't worry."

"Yo' a good boy, Royal. A good man. Too bad yo' papa can' see yo'. Th' other boys gone an' I never hear from dem. I keep yo' always wid me. I worry some 'bout yo' goin' away t' school an' all. Sometime it don' do no good t' learn above yo' place. It make fo' trouble."

"Things change, Maum. Even here in the islands, they change." He stood up. "I'd better go now." He came around the table and kissed her on the cheek.

For a moment her arms enfolded and tightened about him. Then she pushed him away gently.

"Yo' come an' see me when yo' can. Long as I know yo're all right I don' worry too much."

After Royal had left, Big Maum stood by the door. Her face was a mask of dark unhappiness. She was worried about her boy, but she was proud. He walked good, that Royal did. He walked like a king, never looking to right or left.

The maid who had taken the tray upstairs returned.

"Miss Jan say she have eight fo' lunch en th' garden at one o'clock. She say for yo' t' mek up th' menu."

Big Maum nodded absently. Her thoughts were still with Royal. She had a feeling but couldn't name it, and this made her uneasy.

Jan leaned back in the high-backed fan-shaped chair and studied her father.

"You're not really mean. Why do you act the way you do? This morning. On the beach. Royal."

"I never have any trouble with niggers. They understand me." He reached down, took her coffee cup, and drained it.

"I'm surprised one of them hasn't taken a shot at you. Why do you call them niggers?"

"Because that's what they are. What should I call them? Black people? That doesn't make any sense. Do I say to Josh I want a crew of a dozen black people to clear some land? Hell, no. He'd think I was crazy. I tell him get me ten or twelve niggers, and he knows what I mean."

"I don't know." She was unconvinced. "The word sounds ugly. It's ugly the way you say it." She lit a cigarette. "I'm having some people here for lunch. Americans. I met them at the

30

Montagu the other evening. I thought you might join us, but I see you have your hunting clothes on."

This was a small, private joke. Max Hertog's favorite apparel when he went to the offices on Bay Street were riding breeches, boots, a soft flannel shirt open at the throat and an old shooting jacket with worn patches of leather at the elbows. He had closets filled with beautifully tailored clothes he rarely wore. Among the tourists with their shorts and wildly colored shirts and the soberly dressed businessmen of the community the figure of Max Hertog leaped out in its individuality when he walked crowded Bay Street. The thoroughfare was his hunting preserve, and he dressed for the sport.

"I can get back if you really want me." He wasn't too enthusiastic.

"There will be a couple of very pretty girls who are just wild to meet Maximilian Hertog. They have heard so much about him and all his beautiful money. Why don't you marry?" She asked the question abruptly.

"Why don't you?" He took one of her cigarettes.

"I would." She was serious. "I would or will when I find someone I want to spend that much time with. This way I'm free. When I get bored here, I can go to New York, Europe without having to ask anyone's permission. I like the islands. I really do. Nassau with its sophisticated gaiety." She laughed. "We have sedate luncheons. Tennis in the afternoons. The Governor's wife gives a tea. The whole thing is so bloody British, but I like it."

Hertog enjoyed these times with his daughter, found himself looking forward to seeing and being with her this way in the mornings. They rarely spent an evening together.

"Nassau," Jan continued, thinking aloud, "might be a country village in England with you the squire and the tenants tugging at their forelocks when you pass. Only, of course"—her eyes fired with amusement—"you're not at all the kindly squire but a real bastard, aren't you?"

"I try. I do my best." He was almost pious.

"These Americans who are coming to lunch. When they

31

found out who I was, they were curious to hear about you. When I said I didn't know you too well, they thought I was joking. I don't really. Only what I read and hear. Is it true, as the Nassau paper said the other day, you own a law firm? You actually own it the way another man might own a shop or a hotel? The firm's members do only what you tell them to do? It seems an odd possession."

"In a way I do, I guess. Sutter, Tracy and Longworth. They represent me."

"They don't have any other clients?"

"Nooo." He trailed the word out.

"The editorial said, and I'm sure you read it"—she was enjoying herself—"Sutter, Tracy and Longworth belonged to Maximilian Hertog. They did what they were told to do. Through them and their connections in the government, Max Hertog could ram through the Assembly any bill or legislation profitable to Max Hertog. The paper took a dismal view of this. Is it true?"

He scratched an ear, rubbed at his nose, and gazed about the room with an expression of pleased embarrassment.

Finally: "They do seem to have a way of getting things done."

"And if they didn't get things done?"

"Why"—the question surprised him since the answer was so obvious—"why, I'd close up the Sutter, Tracy and Longworth offices the way I'd shut down any unprofitable enterprise."

"Then I should think Sutter, Tracy and Longworth must lead precarious lives."

"They are better off than when I put them together. Then they had three, individual, small law practices. Now they have one large practice. I gave them jam for their bread." He looked at his watch. "I just may come back for lunch. You say the women are pretty?"

She laughed. "Pretty and, I should guess, compliant. I'll draw off their husbands' attention for you."

He nodded absently, his mind moving ahead to the day before him. For weeks, at odd times, his mind had been exploring a new venture. It would be on a larger scale than anything ever attempted in the Bahamas. The talk of Sutter, Tracy and Longworth revived his interest. He picked up Jan's cigarette, turned, and walked from the room. Already he was down in Bay Street. He didn't even say good-bye to his daughter, who watched him with a quietly sardonic interest.

The narrow road from Lyford Cay into Nassau was a lane of shadows and dappled sun, with the trees sometimes arcing overhead to form short tunnels. Jan drove it with the top of her small convertible down, her face to the morning's warmth.

She deliberately passed the walking figure and then braked to a smooth halt a few yards ahead. Turning, she waited and then called over her shoulder. "Royal. Want a ride in?"

He came to the car's side. He was still bare-chested, carrying his shirt slung lightly over one shoulder. Now he slipped it on, knotting the tails around his waist in native fashion.

"Thanks. All the trucks seem to be going the other way this morning." He started to slide into the small rear compartment.

"You don't have to sit back there. Come up here." She was a little impatient. "I don't imagine anyone will misunderstand." She was immediately offended by her own words.

Royal nodded, well aware of the rebuke. "I'm sorry. I didn't think." He settled himself on the seat beside her.

"How did you and my father get along on the beach after I left?" She slid smoothly through a change of gears.

"Well, we decided a whipping was the only cure for a smart nigger." The face remained expressionless, but there was subdued laughter in the words.

"And?" She was sorry now she hadn't stayed.

"We couldn't find the overseer with the whip. He was out with the bloodhounds chasing some runaway field hands." The amusement was a deep, throaty chuckle. "So we just had to put off whipping me until another time. I promised to come back so he could do it."

Jan was amused. "Do you know? I sometimes believe he really thinks things are that way. All New Providence is his plantation and Nassau his village."

"I wonder what it is about color that irritates him so? He has been around black people long enough for it to have worn off."

"I'll let you in on a secret. He doesn't like many whites either. Tell me"—she changed the subject—"what are you doing? I knew you were back. Big Maum told me."

"I have a job with the Janis Corporation. It is an American outfit. They are laying out a resort development on Eleuthera."

"I read a couple of your letters to Big Maum. She asked me to. You liked England, didn't you?"

"I liked the school and the country. It was a different world for a Negro who grew up in the Bahamas. I didn't like the cities, Liverpool and London. And they have their race problems, too. There are hundreds, maybe thousands, of Jamaican blacks fighting for small jobs. London doesn't know what to do with its Negro population."

"No one does." She glanced at his profile. It was a primitive mask. "I was in New York last spring. They talk about summer riots now as though they had become a part of the season. It's frightening."

He nodded. "I was in the Janis New York office for a while." His smile was brief, briefly bitter. "People I met, white people, always asked me: 'What does the Negro want?' When I told them he wanted the same thing a white man wants, they seemed to think that wasn't any answer or I was being unreasonable." He lit a cigarette and replaced the dash lighter.

They rode in silence for a few minutes. Here and there the highway skirted the shoreline, and there were bright flashes of beach and emerald water.

"How is it with you, Royal? You are educated and have a profession. It must make a difference. Can you identify Royal Keating with a Conchie Joe?" She used the expression for a Nassau Negro of the lowest class.

He shook his head. "No. I don't even try. Sometimes I walk down a village street in the Out Islands at dusk. For just a little while it is Africa. The sound. The feeling. The slap of bare feet on a dirt road. A fire with people squatting around it.

34

A girl balancing a load on her head. It isn't easy to remember they are my people."

"I wondered."

"But"—he half turned in the seat to look at her—"I don't think Jan Hertog identifies herself with a Mississippi share-cropper's illiterate, malaria-ridden daughter just because your skins are white. The truth is you don't give a damn what happens to her, do you?"

"No." The word was drawn with surprise. "To tell the truth, I don't even think about her. I don't remember she is there."

He drew reflectively on the cigarette. "I suspect," he said after a few moments, "that is the way it really is. Most persons say what is expected of them, but deep inside they really don't care. They have been jolted by the riots and scurry around with quack schemes to keep them from occurring again. The whites in the States are treating the results of the disease and not its cause."

She drove slowly. "What would you do? Just say you had unlimited authority to change things."

"I don't know. The black man wants now, today, what it is going to take a complete generation or more to achieve. That is what the whites don't have. Time. I walked through the slums of London and Liverpool. They will outmatch any black ghetto in Detroit or Newark. The escape there is possible. The one thing the white slum dweller doesn't have to fight is his color. The Cockney's speech may betray him, but"—he smiled again—"Bernard Shaw and a later musical comedy proved that can be corrected. At least the Cockney's color won't give him away. That is part of the Negro rebellion. He is trying to make black a color of which he can be proud. Listen when the Negro leaders in the States speak on television now. More and more they say 'the black man' or 'the black people' and not 'Negro.' The market for hair straighteners and skin bleaches has disappeared. The Negro wants an identity. The whites, particularly in the States, have put labels on everything. Chinese-American, Mexican-American, Italian-American, Japanese-American. They haven't decided what to do about the Negro. Certainly they don't refer to him as an Afro-American. I am a British subject. That should be the end of it. But to the whites I am a Negro who speaks with a funny British accent. No one thinks of me as anything else except when it comes time to fight a war or pay taxes. The black man has been given all the responsibilities of a first-class citizen but not the privileges."

They were approaching the downtown district of Nassau, and the traffic was heavy. Jan maneuvered her way in the line of small cars and horse-drawn vehicles.

"Drop me anyplace it is convenient, and thanks for the ride." Royal's smile of appreciation broadened. "It isn't every day a black gets a white, captive audience. I don't really think too much about the things I have just said. If I did, I guess I could get angry. Then I'd for sure be that 'smart nigger' your father said I was." As they slowed in the one-way traffic, he unlatched the door and stepped lightly to the curb, clicking the door behind him. "Thanks again."

She watched as he merged with the crowd on the narrow sidewalk. He walked, as always, with that junglelike, surefootedness. His body seemed to turn and sway with a lithe grace as it avoided contact with the morning shoppers.

> *Mama don' wan' no peas, no rice, no coconut oil.*
> *Mama jus' wan' her dandy handy all th' time.*

Nassau's Bay Street, running almost due east and west, paralleling the waterfront, is a pleasant thoroughfare despite its congestion. Two-story frame buildings, some of them tinted pink and yellow, with their shaded balconies, mellow in the sun. The shops offer liquors, French perfumes and British woolens at duty-free prices. There are bars, calypso joints, but no go-go girls and practically no commercialized sex for the casual tourist. He is supposed to bring that commodity with him.

This was once the way of the pirates. Along its sandy stretch, lapped by the sheltered harbor's waves, the buccaneers strode their boisterous paths. Three hundred years ago the colony adopted a motto: Expel the Pirates and Restore Commerce. Blackbeard, Morgan and Captain Kidd were eventually expelled. Commerce was restored. But now a new breed of pirate walks the shore. His step is precise. The bloodletting is less spectacular, and his yachts fly the burgee of an exclusive club instead of the Jolly Roger.

Within some dozen blocks on Bay Street there are thirty-five banks, innumerable insurance companies, land offices and investment corporations. Most of the last named are little more than postal drops offering a front of respectability to dubious enterprises. The banks, by their very nature, are more legitimate. That so many flourish in this limited community is due to a system of numbered accounts similar in operation to that of the Swiss banks. Here complete anonymity can be achieved. This is a state fondly desired by many who would conceal their assets and income. The mobs in the United States find them a safe depository for the millions drawn off the traffic in narcotics, gambling, extortion, prostitution and loan shark rackets. The cash is satchel-carried by the bagmen from Cleveland, Chicago, Detroit, New York and Miami and deposited in the numbered accounts. Later, in a process humorously known as dry cleaning, the money finally comes back to the United States in undetectable or seemingly legitimate channels.

Many of the insurance companies are out-and-out frauds. They are incorporated for a few pounds, sell their accident and old-age policies through the mails in the United States. When the beneficiaries try to collect, they discover they are dealing with a nonexistent fund.

Some of the land companies are also of shady background, but the booming tourist business in the Bahamas has made almost any coral head valuable. The land organizations can afford to be legitimate.

The fingers of Max Hertog held stock in several of the banks. He owned and operated a real estate development agency and an investment corporation. He contested with the Establishment for every profitable enterprise, from shipping to an exclusive fishing club in the Out Islands. Little moved in Nassau of which Maximilian Hertog was not aware. If a skull and crossbones did not flutter from a staff atop his offices, it was only because Max Hertog preferred not to advertise his activities.

He drew up to the curb now, halting his black Mercedes convertible in a no parking zone. At the corner the traffic officer, smartly uniformed in pith helmet, white blouse with its gold buttons, blue trousers with their stripe of red, saluted and pretended he didn't see the Mercedes. Max didn't flaunt his position to the point where even a traffic officer would be uncomfortable. In a moment a boy would appear to take the Mercedes to a parking lot. Standing in the bright sunshine, Max nodded pleasantly to several acquaintances as they passed. He looked over Bay Street with a proprietary attitude. The traffic here was constant. The sidewalks were crowded with tourists in their shorts, flowered shirts or brief halters. They shuttled in and out of the shops like hunting beetles. It seemed to Hertog there was always a cruiseship in the harbor these days. When he first came to Nassau, these were rare. There were no automobiles and few carriages. Only a limited number of persons in the United States knew of the islands firsthand. Havana drew the gambling and sporting crowd, offering gaudy sin and excitement. The Bahamas settled drowsily in the warm sun. Nassau was stodgy and insular.

Prohibition in the United States had shaken the Bahamas out of their lethargy. An opportunity for moneymaking such as this hadn't presented itself since the blockade-running days of the Civil War. Titled members of the Establishment waded enthusiastically into the roiling waters of rum-running. Nassau became a haven for as roistering a band of buccaneers as the islands had ever known. Liquor filled the warehouses, storerooms of private homes, dock space, and cases were sometimes stacked beneath tarpaulin sheeting on Bay Street. Fortunes were made in the traffic by the ultrarespectable old families. A little wistfully Max thought of this opportunity missed.

As he stood before the entrance of the Hertog Building, his ears were barely aware of the traffic sounds and the shifting pattern. Political and social change, he thought, occurred slowly here in the islands. But—and instinct told him this—change was on its way. There was a thing here, he felt, to be turned to Max Hertog's advantage. But its exact definition eluded him for the moment. Well. He turned from the curb. *When the time comes,* he told himself, *I will know it. This has always been the way with me.*

The various Hertog enterprises occupied the time and attention of a large staff. Early in his residence in Nassau, Hertog had purchased a two-story building on Bay Street. The soft pastel pink of its stucco, the balcony overlooking the street, a small park and the post office and government buildings, the high-ceilinged rooms—all pleased his eye and sense of proportion. The offices were beautifully furnished with a collection of colonial antiques which were all but priceless. The atmosphere was more a private club than a business establishment. Here there was no evidence of haste, no shrilling of telephones, no scurrying of secretaries or messengers. The lighting was subdued, falling from crystal chandeliers and reflecting on hand-rubbed and polished mahogany furniture. The carpeting was of a dark, deep and rich color and pile. Footsteps on it were soundless.

Hertog's office was the single large room running the width of the building. French doors opened on the balcony at the second floor. It was spacious and airy, flooded with sunlight most of the time. At the rear were the offices of his secretary and a stenographer. The suite was reached by a staircase off the reception room on the ground floor. A page boy, smartly uniformed, stood at attention there, ready to usher those who had an appointment with Maximilian Hertog into the presence.

Max took the steps lightly. He was vain about his physical condition and liked to display it by trotting up the flight.

It was a matter of secret delight to him that no matter how erratically he scheduled his arrival at the office, his secretary invariably anticipated his entrance. She stood, waiting beside his desk, in an attitude of smiling attention. He thought there must be some secret form of communication between her and the doorman, a signal telling her he was entering the building and on his way up. Without its ever being put into words, both understood this was a small game to be played in a polite and almost formal manner which denied its existence.

Carol Wainwright had been with Maximilian Hertog for five years. In her place of confidence she was familiar with the manifold details of his operations within and outside the Bahamas. Some of these were so delicately tuned that a careless word could easily destroy months of negotiations. There were men on Bay Street who would have paid handsomely for information on Hertog's intentions. For reasons which he did not completely understand, Max trusted her implicitly. Sometimes he thought, with a wry humor, this went back to the very first day of their association.

Carol was in her middle twenties now, a strikingly beautiful girl, poised, efficient and bearing the quiet assurance real beauty gives a woman. There was colored blood here. Of this Max was certain. It ran with that of one of the island's oldest families. How and when it had been introduced no one could say. No one inquired, for the subject was likely to be a touchy one in the Bahamas. The result of this alien strain in Carol Wainwright was a faint, dusky radiance. Her skin had the flush of darkest rose and with it a strange, luminescent quality. Sometimes Max would have sworn she actually glowed with an exotic incandescence.

From the first day their association had been marked by an unadmitted contest. Max Hertog was not a man to remain indifferent in the presence of a beautiful girl. She became, at once, an object of conquest to be assaulted in a frontal attack. Max had small talent for amoral fencing. A woman was never left in doubt about his immediate intentions. Max had discovered early this method of pursuit was extremely successful. He was in enthusiastic agreement with a comment said to have been made by Arnold Bennett: "If you try and make every woman you meet you will be surprised how much success you have."

Despite her youth, the world's Max Hertogs were no surprise to Carol Wainwright. The predatory instinct was latent in every male. She had been fending them off from the age of ten.

In response to Hertog's inquiry she had been sent to him by the colony's one employment agency.

Max took one look at her. "I'm hard to please. You're hired. Sit down."

Carol took the indicated chair with an unstudied dignity. She regarded him with a half-smile of what was close to interested amusement.

"Wouldn't you like to know if I can type, spell and take dictation?"

He admired her openly. "I have three or four girls in the office now who can do those things. I'd keep you around just to look at. How does it happen you're hunting a job?" He glanced at the information sheet supplied by the agency.

"As you can see"—she indicated the paper with a nod—"I was working for the Ministry of Tourism. I started as a stenographer. Little by little I was pushed into modeling for the brochures and tourist literature. Carol on a yacht. Carol on the beach in a bikini. Carol beside a swimming pool. It was dull, so I quit. I have"—the slow smile reappeared—"an idea it won't be at all dull here."

Max took this as a personal tribute. "How old are you?"

"Twenty."

"Married? Boyfriend? Are you involved with anyone so your time isn't your own?"

"No, sir."

"You can start now. Learn the job as you go along. It's personal and confidential. I have a secretary. Miss Simms. She's leaving. Getting married. She'll show you how the general routine goes. The salary is two hundred dollars a week."

Carol Wainwright displayed no surprise at the figure, which was far and away beyond any secretarial wage paid in the islands.

She stood up. "Thank you, Mr. Hertog. I'll do my best."

Max eyed her keenly. "Don't you want to know why I am paying you that much money?"

"Oh!" The smile was gone. The gaze level and direct. "But I do know, Mr. Hertog."

41

This was not an impertinence but a simple statement of fact. For just a moment it left Maximilian Hertog off-balance.

"The hell you do!" He was alert, interested.

The smile now was one of honest amusement and to be shared between them, but again, there was no shade of insolence in her attitude.

"You see"—she spoke slowly—"it has happened before. I'm getting used to it."

His gaze, frankly admiring, took in every detail of her appearance. She wore a dress of white nylon or silk, simply cut and flattering. It accented her long, slender legs, the small waist and high, full breasts. The only color was in her cheeks and a wisp of crimson scarf at the throat. Max Hertog was not a man to remain insensible to such things, and he was unabashed in his study.

"I suppose so." He nodded thoughtfully, and his eyes brightened. "How do you usually handle it?"

"Usually I just leave and don't go back. But this is different. I'd like to work for you." Again the laughter was behind the words. "But if I were going to bed with you, I wouldn't complicate it by pretending to be a secretary. Also"—fine teeth caught at her lip for a second—"it would cost you a great deal more than two hundred dollars a week."

"You're pretty damn smart for twenty." He eyed her morosely.

"I have had to be. There is something about the sunshine in these islands. Seductive."

"Are you related to Charlton Wainwright?" The name was old in Nassau.

"He's my grandfather. Do you know him?"

"No, but I know who he is." He caught the amusement she tried to conceal. "What's funny?"

"My grandfather said much the same thing. I told him I was applying for a position and asked if he knew you. He said no, as you did, but added: 'I know *what* he is.'"

Their association now was an easy one. Max admired her efficiency, her ability to deal with people on any level. She was aware of his moods and seemed to anticipate his wishes. He

42

was constantly aware of her beauty, and it pleased him. He discovered she could handle herself in almost any situation, had a mind for detail, and took great pride in what she was doing. She had traveled with him to New York, Canada, San Francisco and London, to the Out Islands, flying there in the private plane, wherever he had business interests. They were both aware that these trips raised the eyebrows and excited the tongues of their small world in Nassau.

Once, in Montreal, he had looked at her across the dinner table.

"Don't get the idea I have given up on you."

"Oh, I haven't."

"It's just taking a little longer than I expected."

Carol was at Windmere frequently. She and Jan had established an unaffected friendship. They were both devoted to water-skiing and played a sound game of tennis. When Hertog had guests, Carol frequently served as hostess in Jan's place. If Max had work to do and preferred to do it at home, Carol came with a packed bag and stayed for three or four days.

"You know," Jan once said, "you just might end up being my stepmother."

Carol had shaken her head. "I don't think so. I'm not sure I would want that."

"Are you still holding out?"

"So far." Carol was unembarrassed. "But he's a hard man to say no to even when he doesn't ask."

She was waiting now as Max entered the office.

"Good morning." She took the silky broad-brimmed Panama hat he liked to carry but rarely wore. "Mr. Harrington flew in from New York this morning. He called and wanted to know if he could see you. I said yes, at eleven."

"He wants me to take him off the hook." Max was pleased. "But he doesn't want it to cost him anything."

"I know. What are you going to do?"

"Oh, I'll see him but I'll let him hang a little longer until he's really ripe."

He walked over to one end of the room where, covering the wall, was a large map of the Bahama chain as it stretched from

43

a point at the Caicos Bank to the Grand Bahama. He tapped the latter island with one finger.

"I'm going to buy up Grand Bahama." He spoke half to himself, half to her. "Get hold of Chris Baildon. I need him for this."

He turned back to the map, whistling softly with a low, speculative note.

III

Two hundred years or so ago Phineas T. Hogg, having been blown out of his loosely constructed house on Andros Island by a seasonal hurricane, patched up his sloop and sailed to New Providence, some thirty-five miles away. Lying almost due east and west off the colony of Nassau was a long, heavily timbered earth and coral spit. Phineas Hogg built a shack there and settled down. In the course of time the place became known as Hogg's Island. Much later a careless cartographer set the name down as Hog Island, and so it remained for more than two centuries.

Aside from serving as a fine, natural weatherbreak for Nassau's anchorage, no one paid much attention to the island. During the wild days of Prohibition in the United States the place served as a storage depot for great piles of spirits. These were taken by the rum-runners and delivered to points along the Georgia, Florida and Carolina coasts. A few scraggly settlers squatted on the land, which seemed to have no real value or purpose. Few persons gave it a thought.

Willard Harrington, heir to one of the great fortunes in the United States, had a bent for investing in highly speculative projects. He came to the Bahamas each winter in his private yacht and spent his time cruising the islands and fishing their waters. He was, some reported, a lonely man who constantly sought an outlet for his money and imagination. He studied Hog Island from the deck of his yacht, and an idea began to form. Why not take this Hog Island and transform it into a magnificent tourist playground? It lay only a quarter of a mile, more or less, off Nassau proper. Landscaped, with a deepwater anchorage, a luxury hotel with every conceivable service, a golf course, tennis courts and swimming pools, the island would draw to it the wealthy who disliked the crowding they encountered in Nassau proper. What Harrington had in mind was the development of an exclusive, expensive winter resort for those who thought of money only as a secondary consideration.

Harrington examined his idea from many sides. He called on a firm of construction engineers to draw preliminary sketches and plans. Then he ventured into Bay Street and enlisted the services of a real estate agency to purchase Hog Island.

Although many of his ventures had been of a visionary nature, Harrington was realist enough to know what he had in mind would not be profitable without an added source of income. It was in his mind to have gambling rooms in the hotel or a separate casino. Here those who formerly went to Cuba or spent much of their time in Las Vegas would find their dice and roulette games within a few minutes' flying time of Miami.

Gambling in the Bahamas was prohibited, but oddly enough, the government, when pressure is expertly applied, grants what is known as a Certificate of Exemption. This is nothing more than official permission to do legally that which is illegal. It is a pretty example of the deviousness the British attribute to all Italians and a few Spaniards. Mr. Harrington, with a rare trust in human nature, queried the Bay Street real estate agents he had engaged. Hungry for the commission on the sale of Hog Island, they assured him the certificate was little more than a formality. The colonial government was eager to have Hog Island developed as planned and would do everything possible to assist in making the venture a success. When the time came a bill would be introduced into the House of Assembly. The Certificate of Exemption would be

46

granted, and the dice could roll, the wheel spin to the delight of all concerned.

Mr. Harrington then retained a Bay Street firm of solicitors at a handsome fee. They were to regard his interests as their own. Here, also, the head of the firm, with his eyes on Harrington's check, waved away the idea that any difficulty in the matter of a certificate would be encountered. The firm, long and honorably established in the Bahamas, had, it was portentously suggested, the right hand of the Premier, the Minister of Tourism and several members in the House of Assembly. It would all be too simple to warrant even a momentary concern on Mr. Harrington's part. Everything would be taken care of.

Having satisfied himself that he worked from a solid foundation, the millionaire entrepreneur began pouring several of his seemingly inexhaustible millions into this latest enthusiasm. As the extensive project took shape, Harrington pondered the name Hog Island. It did not exactly create in one's mind the beauty and luxury he strove for. He cast about for something better and came up with Paradise Island. Here, surely, was the ultimate. The Ministry of Tourism was enthusiastic. Hereafter all official correspondence, literature, brochures and promotional material would carry the name of Paradise Island. The head of the news bureau of the public relations firm in New York handling the Bahamas account was called in. Typewriters raced; mimeograph machines spewed their sheets. Paradise Island was an accomplished fact.

The Nassau newspapers hailed Mr. Harrington's entry into the cultural and economic life of the Bahamas with modest hosannas. Paradise Island would be a gem on the waters. Its creation would inject a large shot of adrenalin into Nassau's veins. Local merchants, contractors and laborers all would share in the bounty. Mr. Harrington was praised for his vision, and it was slyly mentioned along the way that an outsider had seen in Hog Island what local developers had long ignored. Here was the true spirit of a pioneer. All this so pleased Mr. Harrington that he became indifferent to cost. Luxury was piled on luxury. Here, in truth, was the hand of God engaged in the Creation.

Time and some thirty-five million dollars of the Harrington fortune produced Paradise Island, and it was opened to such a fanfare of press, television, radio and motion pictures as might have witnessed the Second Coming. Planeloads of celebrities, reporters, cameramen, announcers and press agents were flown from the United States to Paradise Island. Everything was on the house, and nothing was too good for the guests. Hundreds of thousands of words were filed or spoken. Thousands of feet of film were exposed as they captured the dimpled navels of bikini-clad starlets and upper-case call girls. Television stars were pictured on the startlingly beautiful golf course with Gary Player. The few Hollywood stars who were left in Hollywood were so busy trying to get into television for its residuals that only one showed up. The jet setters, who would go anyplace at any time if it were free and they could get their pictures and names in the papers, tumbled enthusiastically aboard the chartered planes. From a publicity standpoint the opening of Paradise Island was everything that could be desired and hoped for. The guests were photogenic; the setting was lush and tropical, the coverage in words and pictures complete. Harrington had created what was regarded as the ultimate in luxury resorts, and the response was immediate. Queries and requests for reservations occupied the time of two clerks. Paradise Island became smart, the place to be seen. Nothing that could contribute to the pleasure and comfort of the guests had been overlooked. The staff had been carefully selected and retrained. The chef was a man of international reputation. Rooms and guest cottages were triumphs of the interior decorator's art. Flowers in vivid colors set the gardens aflame. Each tree and shrub had been hand-selected and then planted according to a master plan. It was, indeed, Paradise Island, and Harrington had good reason to be proud of what he had built.

Within the hotel the gambling room had been designed for an air of gay elegance. Here one could lose his money in the most pleasant surroundings. The walls and ceilings were sound-absorbent; the carpeting was heavy and rich. The bar, with its complete service from champagne to vodka, was complementary. The walls were covered with exotic murals in which leering satyrs chased laughing nymphs through a tropical setting. It was a place where money was made to seem unimportant. "There is so much of it," the room seemed to say. The stick- and boxmen, the croupiers and blackjack dealers were Las Vegas-trained and expert. Following the opening the casino staff lounged around on the beach and wondered when they would be called to work. At the moment the tables were unattended and covered, for, despite the assurances of the solicitors, the Assembly had failed to act on a Certificate of Exemption. More than that, when pressed, the elected members displayed a determined reluctance to discuss the matter. Harrington was becoming more and more concerned now. He knew his way around Nassau, was well aware of how the tight hierarchy on Bay Street operated. A little uneasily he began to suspect he had blundered. His opening moves had been careless. The firm of solicitors he had engaged was respected but nothing more. It was without real authority or influence. The assurances he received now concerning the Certificate of Exemption were less and less positive. There was a coalition within the Assembly which fought down every attempt to introduce the bill. When Harrington demanded to know the individual names of those who were blocking the legislation, he was hastily advised against this sort of open action. The matter was delicate. Harrington pursued every possible avenue. He reached the Governor. The Premier. The Ministry of Tourism. All Nassau, he argued angrily now, had a stake in the success of Paradise Island. Nothing happened. The brief winter season passed without the turning of a roulette wheel or the chattering gallop of a pair of dice across a green felt field. Despite the fact that the guest accommodations operated at capacity this first season, Paradise Island faced a loss of one million dollars.

Confronted by the certainty of a continuing deficit, Harrington sought the investment of outside capital. There was no response. Legitimate hotel and resort operators were skeptical. Harrington moved into unfamiliar regions and made contact with the Cosa Nostra. Here again he was turned down. The mobs which operate most of the Las Vegas hotels and gambling casinos would be interested only when Paradise Island was issued the vital certificate. Harrington was tightly angry. He had invested in good faith and kept his promises. He took the first year's loss without whimpering.

Problems mounted. Earlier Paradise Island realized it must offer reliable and frequent transportation between the island and Nassau. Harrington had put into operation a fleet of mahogany-decked speedboats but found this method was not practical. Sudden showers and, sometimes, rough weather made the run uncomfortable. Harrington, still confident he would, somehow, get the gambling permit, proposed to the colonial government that a bridge be built from Nassau to Paradise Island. He would assume the cost of the span. Again he encountered the stubborn opposition. The suggestion was debated. The Assembly demurred. Finally Harrington was told the bridge would be a threat to normal navigation. This despite the fact that Harrington's engineers were prepared to demonstrate this was untrue.

Paradise Island went into its second year of operation, and Harrington continued to press for that which he must have. There was no longer any question in his mind. His moves were being deliberately blocked. There was, though, he discovered, a conspiracy of silence. Even those persons with whom he was on the friendliest of terms became oddly silent when he asked the obvious questions. Who? Why? There was a shaking of heads, a shrugging of shoulders.

Then, curiously enough, a small whisper began to move as the faintest ripple of a wind. Hearing it for the second or third time, seemingly innocently spoken, Harrington was convinced the murmur had been deliberately encouraged. He became certain of this one day at lunch. He was at a table on the Royal Victoria's pool terrace having lunch with the head of the Nassau News Bureau.

"Do you hear what I hear?" Harrington glanced up and across the table.

The young man smiled. He took a coffee spoon and with its end indented the word HERTOG into the tablecloth.

50

"Is that what you mean?"

"That's what I mean." Harrington nodded. "I keep hearing it. I'm meant to. It has to be deliberate. I mean the rumor had its start somewhere in Bay Street. Why? Hog Island has been lying there all these years. If he wanted it, why didn't he buy it when it was for sale? Why let me develop it and then try and choke it off?"

"I don't have the answers. I can only guess. He's a strange man with the conviction nothing should happen in the islands without his participation or, at least, his approval." The News Bureau man shook his head.

Willard Harrington was not a humble man. The very wealthy rarely are.

"Why the hell should I have to ask Maximilian Hertog if I can invest my money here?"

A shrug. The question. "Why don't you ask him?"

For a moment Harrington stared at his guest and then nodded. "By God! That's just what I'll do."

Hertog's office reported that he wasn't in or expected.

Harrington called Windmere. Max didn't surround himself with unnecessary services. When the telephone rang, he answered it.

"Hertog."

"This is Willard Harrington. I'd like to see and talk with you. Can we make an appointment?"

Hertog ignored the question. "Do you know? It is strange that in a place as small as Nassau we haven't met." He was pleasantly ruminative.

"It's not so strange if that's the way you wanted it." Harrington was crisply impatient.

"I?" Complete astonishment was in the pronoun. "Why should I have avoided meeting you?"

"I haven't any idea. That's the way it looks to me. I called to see if we couldn't get together. There is something going on I don't understand."

"What makes you think I have the answer, Mr. Harrington?"

"Because I'm damn well sure you're blocking me on Paradise Island. I want to know why."

"I do want to congratulate you, Mr. Harrington." The words rang with an enthusiastic sincerity. "You have made a really magnificent contribution to the Bahamas with Paradise Island."

Harrington was not devoid of humor and had a well-developed sense of the ridiculous. His half-smile was a tribute to the bland hypocrisy as it came across the wire.

"But"—and this came slowly, as an afterthought, and carried with it a mild tone of injury—"why should you imagine I have? What was the word you used? Blocked? Yes, blocked you."

"Because I have an idea I'm supposed to think just that. Somehow your name keeps coming up in almost every conversation I have in connection with Paradise Island."

"That is odd, isn't it?"

"I'm beginning to think so. That's why I'm calling. It might simplify things if I knew why your name was being dropped in front of me so often. I keep stumbling over it. I want to know why."

"I'm not sure I can be of any help, Mr. Harrington, but I do think we ought to meet." There was a pause, presumably thoughtful. "I hadn't intended going to the office. Why don't you run out here? Spend the weekend with us. We would be delighted to have you."

"A social call wasn't exactly what I had in mind."

Harrington regretted the reply even as it was spoken. It was cheap and boorish. Because of it, he was now on the defensive.

"Oh!" There was just a touch of the indulgent and paternal. "I don't know why we can't discuss what is bothering you here at Windmere, as well as in Bay Street."

You son of a bitch. Harrington was reluctantly impressed. *You are maneuvering me. You're leading me around the ring, and it's my own fault. I'll know better the next time.*

Aloud he said, "Thank you." There was a suggestion of an apology in the tone, and that wasn't at all what he intended. "I'd like to come out."

"Fine," the voice boomed heartily. "That's bully. Tomorrow. Make it for lunch. One o'clock. Arrange to spend the weekend. I'm looking forward to it."

Harrington hung up. He stared at the instrument and then shook his head bemusedly. He could be wrong. Maybe Max Hertog had nothing to do with the difficulties he was encountering with Paradise Island. No. He was suddenly angry again. The rumor was too persistent to be accidental. Well, he'd find out what Hertog wanted, get it out in the open over the weekend.

Beside the pool, where the water lay in a polished and unruffled slab of blue, the two deck chairs had been drawn up to face each other. On a low table, at the right side of each, a tall rum drink, with a sprig of mint protruding, chilled itself in a frosted glass.

With open admiration Willard Harrington mused on the vibrantly youthful figure of Jan Hertog as she lay back beneath the sun which had polished her to the dark color of rosewood. Two strips of bright fabric were all that separated her from complete nakedness.

Aware of his gaze, Jan half-smiled an acknowledgment and reached with a lazy hand for the package of cigarettes beside her drink.

"Max is trying to diddle you, isn't he?" She asked the question with amused interest.

Harrington was entertained by the phrasing of the question. He nodded.

"I think so. I'm not sure, but I think so."

"He has that smug look." The smoke drifted from a half-opened mouth. "I'd say yes."

Her voice had a throaty quality, and the words were lightly tripped by a small, elusive impediment which gave it an exciting character.

"He's tricky." Harrington offered a grudging tribute. "He's fast on his feet. I can't pin him down."

"I'd guess he's envious of what you did with Hog Island. He can't understand why he didn't think of it."

"So?"

"So," she continued, "I'd guess again he's trying to figure out a way of getting it from you at a bargain price."

"Then why doesn't he say so?" There was an edge of impatience in the question.

She shrugged and then laughed softly. "That isn't his way. He likes to be devious. To tell you what he is after would spoil it. But"—she half straightened up in the chair—"that isn't the reason he asked you down. He was really interested in meeting you."

"He took his time getting around to it." He was skeptical.

"That's the Hertog way. You have to take him as he is."

"I don't have to take him at all or any way." Again the suggestion of impatience.

She looked up quickly and then nodded. "No, you really don't, do you?" She crushed out the cigarette and then added irrelevantly, "I thought you'd be flabby."

"What?" He was astonished.

She grinned, pleased by the immediate reaction. "You know. The wealthy dilettante, sponsor of obscure art groups, archeological expeditions, patron of little theaters who gets his name in the papers and his picture on *Time*. A man who really doesn't know what to do with himself or his money. You're not at all what I imagined. When Max said you were coming for the weekend, I thought: Oh, God. Here comes Don Quixote with his interminable doing good. You see, I do read the papers and the newsmagazines. But you don't look soft or talk soft." She cocked her head to one side and studied him critically. "As the Victorian lady novelists wrote, you are a fine figure of a man—a little on the old side, perhaps, but well put together. You are not at all embarrassed or made uneasy by having a lot of money and spending it in all sorts of impossible ventures, are you?"

"No."

"You should be. That's what I tell Max. You ought to feel guilty as hell. That is my generation's philosophy: the rejection of all material things."

Harrington's gaze traveled around the pool, over the exten-

54

sive gardens and the marina with the two shining craft at their moorings. Then he looked at her with an expressive grin.

"You're not very successful at it, are you?"

"This I can't help. It is thrust upon me. But I try. I search constantly for the significant, the deeper meaning of things: man's conflict with himself; the why-are-we-here where-are-we-going enigma which must puzzle us all." The tongue was very definitely in the cheek. Her eyes were bright. "Like you, Max isn't troubled by those things either. It will be fun to watch the two of you have at each other. Max has absolutely no principles. That is where you may be vulnerable."

"Hello! Hello there!"

They both turned at the shout. Max Hertog was descending on them from the house. He wore bathing trunks with sandals on his feet and an enormous floppy-brimmed straw hat pushed down on his forehead. He moved with a heavy, purposeful stride, chewing vigorously on an unlit cigar.

"Sorry I missed you at breakfast, Harrington. Hello, Sis." He greeted them in turn. Feet wide apart and seemingly embedded in the pool's concrete apron, he smiled a benediction on them. "I had some work to do. Carol's typing the letters now. She'll be down later. We'll all go for a swim, maybe take the bugeye out, cruise down Exuma way." He had everyone's day planned.

"With that hat and more bosom you'd look like Gertrude Stein." Jan surveyed him with an impudent delight.

Max ignored her, addressing Harrington. "Comfortable? Anything we can do for you? Pretty informal around here. See for yourself. Like to have friends enjoy themselves just the same."

"He's trying to soften you up," Jan whispered loudly. "He's lulling you with incense, tempting you with a glimpse of the fleshpots."

"That's the idea I get." Harrington spoke directly to her as though Hertog weren't there. "It won't work."

"I was just telling Mr. Harrington you were completely without any principles." She looked up at her father.

"That's the trouble with today's kids." Max pulled up a

chair and dropped into it. "Insolence. No respect. Anyone over twenty-five is the enemy. There is what they call the generation gap. We can look across it but can't touch each other."

"Mr. Harrington and I have decided you are trying to diddle him out of something. Are you?" Jan half closed her eyes against the sun and watched her father.

For just a second there was a flash of harsh annoyance on Hertog's face. It cleared almost immediately, and his expression was benign.

"Well, you're wrong there." He examined the unlit tip of his cigar. "In the first place Mr. Harrington asked to see me. Isn't that right?"

Harrington nodded, listening carefully.

"In the second place, I know Mr. Harrington is having certain difficulties in connection with Paradise Island. If he hadn't come to me, I was going to call him and offer a suggestion or two, a helping hand, so to speak."

"Watch out," Jan cautioned Harrington. "I think there is a stiletto in it."

Hertog dismissed her with a wave of one hand. He reached over, took a tab of matches from one of the tables, and lit his cigar. He drew on it with stolid satisfaction.

"You didn't get off to a very good start here, in Nassau, Mr. Harrington." He was sympathetic. "You didn't learn your way around first."

"I'm beginning to believe that."

"There's a way of doing things." This was almost chiding.

"The wrong way and the Hertog way?" Harrington asked the question pleasantly enough, but his eyes were hard.

"You might say so." Hertog peered at his cigar as though it held a mystery. "You should have asked around a bit, made some inquiries. Things here move in channels. When you get outside them, you're almost always in trouble."

"The government was delighted with the plans I had for Hog Island. I was assured, unofficially, there would be no problems in connection with the operation of a casino. It was understood Paradise Island couldn't possibly succeed without the revenue from gambling tables."

"Unofficial promises don't mean a damn thing. You've got to have the paper in your hand." Max rubbed at his nose. "You might as well know the truth, Mr. Harrington. You are not going to be granted a Certificate of Exemption. The door has been slammed on that."

"By Maximilian Hertog?" There was cold anger in the question.

Max examined his cigar's ash with bland interest. Then he raised his eyes to meet Harrington's.

"Well, I guess." He spoke slowly. "You could probably say so. Yes. That's a pretty close approximation of the situation."

"But why?" Harrington was honestly confused. "Why now? I don't see any conflict of interests."

"Almost anything anyone else does here in the Bahamas conflicts with my interests, Mr. Harrington. I've built a couple of hotels, laid out the first airport, built a country club and with it an eighteen-hole golf course. I introduced a new breed of long-haired sheep in the islands. I established the interisland airline. I have a new fishing and yachting club on Cistern Cay, a development going on Andros, and I own a couple of banks here. So you see. Anything touching the Bahamas touches me."

"Well, by God, if you wanted Hog Island, why didn't you develop it?" Harrington was bitter.

"It just never occurred to me, Mr. Harrington. I hate to admit I overlooked something, but that's the truth. I never saw it. There it was. Right in front of my eyes and I never saw it." He shook his head and made a clucking sound of regret.

"Here comes the helping hand. I can feel it." Jan's aside to Harrington was pitched in a croak of warning.

Slowly Max turned and stared at her. In his eyes there was no glint of recognition. They were agate hard and cold. Jan was pinned uncomfortably beneath them.

"Why don't you"—the words were deliberately spaced—"go up to the house and see if Carol is ready?"

"Carol can find her way down here alone." It was an unsuccessful attempt to recapture a mood of banter. "She—" The word trailed off, and in that moment Jan Hertog was very young, a child being reprimanded before grown-ups.

"I still think it would be a good idea." Max did not raise his voice.

There was no mistaking the conflict. Slowly the bright façade of her youth was shadowed. A small, nervous smile betrayed her. Finally she rose, her gaze never leaving her father's face. Teeth caught at her lower lip for a second. As Harrington started to rise, she caught the movement and shook her head, still facing Hertog.

"Yes, Max." It was spoken simply in surrender.

Hertog watched as his daughter crossed from the pool to the marl path leading to the house. There was regret and unhappiness in his expression. Once he seemed to be on the point of calling after her but changed his mind. With a heavy sigh he faced Harrington.

"A thing like that sometimes has to be done. I don't like to do it. I have encouraged her independence of thought and speech. She's young, and it gets out of hand now and then." He seemed to slump in the chair, staring at his feet. "I feel as though I had slapped her. We only have each other, and maybe we both take advantage of that sometimes."

Harrington was uncomfortable. He understood Jan's small humiliation. It hadn't been pleasant to watch. A joke had abruptly ceased to be funny. He forced the conversation back to the subject which had brought him here for the weekend.

"I suppose you have a proposition to make me. Otherwise it would be difficult to understand your invitation."

Hertog nodded and raised his head. He seemed relieved.

"You're carrying a dead elephant in Paradise Island. I'll make you an offer of twenty million and take the entire project off your hands."

"You're pretty certain I can't swing it."

"I know you can't, Mr. Harrington." There was no triumph or conceit in the reply. "You're locked in."

"I have an investment of over thirty million tied up. I won't pretend it doesn't hurt. There's a bottom to every barrel."

58

"The situation being what it is, I don't see how you can get your money out. Mine is a pretty good offer. You might do better, but I doubt it. No one can operate Paradise Island without a gambling casino. That's the key to the whole thing, and I have it in my pocket. I think you know it."

"I'll sell you an interest in it. Forty-nine percent."

This was an offer born of defeat. Harrington knew it. Max Hertog knew it and shook his head. There was no need of words. As he made a final assessment of the situation, Harrington was astonished to discover he felt no outrage, no resentment of Max Hertog as a person. He was in a bind. The knots had been tied by a professional who had gone about the job with an impersonal skill. He had been clumsy and careless.

"You know"—he blew on the knuckles of a hand with a whistling sound—"I ought to feel like taking a poke at you but I don't. And," he added wryly, "I'm damned if I know why."

"It wouldn't do any good for one thing." Max seemed to give the idea serious thought. "And it would look pretty foolish for us to be out here swinging at each other. I'll tell you what I'll do. I'll come up with another two and a half million, and we'll make a deal." He waited.

"No." The word exploded. "I'm damned if we will. I just don't believe you can carry so much weight with the government. I'll blast this thing wide open with every publicity medium available. If Max Hertog really has control of the House of Assembly here in Nassau, I'm going to make the members admit it openly."

"I don't blame you for trying. I'd do it in your place." Max was amiable. "But I wouldn't hope for too much. This is a tight little island, and those who run it aren't used to making an accounting. Now"—his sudden smile was warm and almost sympathetic—"let's have a swim. When Carol and Jan come down, we'll plan something for the afternoon." He looked up at Willard Harrington with bright interest.

IV

In his office now, standing before the large wall map of the islands and waiting for Christopher Baildon, Max Hertog separated his mind into compartments. One section was assorting the details which had been assembling for a development on Grand Bahama. Another division speculated on the unexpected return to Nassau of Willard Harrington and what it might mean.

Paradise Island, its gambling rooms closed and their staffs dismissed, had operated through a second disastrous season. Capacity booking for the hotel and luxury guest cottages must be regarded as almost catastrophic. Every room occupied, each meal served meant a loss. Harrington had stubbornly refused to compromise on the service. Everything, as stated in the brochures, was here. The golf course was of emerald sheen; the pools and beach sparkled under constant maintenance; the kitchens offered gourmet menus. It was roughly estimated that Paradise Island had three employees for every guest. Max surmised it must have cost Harrington at least another million more to keep the resort open during the winter months. No one, not even Harrington, could continue to take this loss.

Hertog pinched thoughtfully at his nose. Actually, he bore a grudging admiration for Willard Harrington. The man was plagued by a flair for investing in grandiose projects which were doomed from the start, but he didn't whine and he didn't quit. Following his first meeting with Max, Harrington had hammered steadily on the doors of the Assembly, but no one answered. In an effort to enlist the community's support, he offered to turn over fifty percent of the casino's profits to the public. There was no response. Nassau's newspapers were guarded in their comments. Then, in a wildly foolish and thoughtless gesture, he made a large financial contribution to the rebellious Progressive Liberal Party. Later he said he had done this because a two-party system in the islands seemed desirable. The Establishment was so outraged by his political meddling that it lined up solidly against Harrington's efforts to secure a Certificate of Exemption. He had alienated himself completely. Continued pressure by Max Hertog against the application was all but unnecessary.

Max took no small, mean satisfaction in Harrington's difficulties. Actually he liked the man. Their occasional meetings were leavened with a certain wary respect. Harrington appeared to bear no resentment. He seemed to understand that Hertog drove with a single-mindedness toward whatever it was he wanted. Personalities were not permitted to intrude. If he didn't find Max Hertog exactly lovable, neither was he inflamed to hot anger in his presence. During the winter months he was in and out of Nassau several times. Although he was her senior by almost twenty years, a warm friendship was an effortless fact between him and Jan Hertog. They saw each other frequently. When he was at Paradise Island, she docked her speed craft there when she came down from Lyford Cay. They played the golf course together, and he sometimes drove the boat for her while she water-skied. Harrington was stimulated by her beauty and a healthy, young animal's delight in life. Only once had he mentioned the difference in their ages. He had called at Windmere to take her to a private party and dance. Returning home near daybreak, pleasantly tired and mellow with a last brandy warming them, she had moved against him as he drove. When he shifted his arm to put it around her, she took his hand and pressed it about her breast, sighing with a quiet pleasure at the contact.

61

"And," she murmured, "don't tell me you are old enough to be my father."

"No. I tell myself that."

"I'm twenty-five going on thirty-five, and when you grow up, I think I'll have you make love to me." She drew back to stare up into his face in the pale light. "Maybe even before. I don't know yet."

At her invitation he was at Windmere frequently. In his meetings with Max there was no constraint but no false heartiness either.

"I can't honestly say I number you among my most admirable or lovable acquaintances." He made the admission to Max over a drink on the terrace while he waited for Jan. "One thing, though, you do operate in the open. No one can mistake your intent. I wouldn't say that endears you to me, but I have to admire the honesty and that puts me at a disadvantage. I could handle a scavenger, skulking along behind, ready to snatch at the carcass. I still think we could operate Paradise Island with a partnership agreement. I don't give up easily, and you are costing me a lot of money."

Max had shaken his head. "All I have to do is wait, Willard." Max had come to a first-name basis quickly. "Sooner or later you'll have to let go. I'm the only out you have. No one else will touch it." He put a hand on Harrington's shoulder. "The offer I made still holds good. You ought to take it, get out, and cut your losses."

Harrington moved from beneath the hand. "You're a real bastard, Max. I'm something of an authority on them. They seem to gather around me. One of these days someone, without my tolerance, is going to put a bullet in you or beat your head with a rock. You ought to think about that."

Max had nodded a cheerful agreement. "I expect someone will but only if he can catch me when I'm not looking." His mood changed abruptly. "What in the name of God led you to make a big contribution to that nigger party and let it be a matter of public record? I thought you knew the islands better." He whistled a note of astonishment. "Even I would have advised you against such a stupid move."

62

"I made a contribution because I'm in favor of an opposition party. I didn't expect the PLP to make it public."

"Hell, man." Max snorted his disgust. "Those niggers were bound to use your name. Now"—he glanced about the empty terrace—"I don't mind telling you I've given them money, quite a bit, but I don't do it with a check that can be photostated. Those at the head know they'll never get another damn cent if they bleat about it. I do it for the sake of insurance. Besides"—his voice dropped to an unnecessary whisper—"I've got my eye on a nigger. I'm watching and keeping track of him. One of these days there just might be the goddamnedest upset in these islands, and I'll have me a made-to-order nigger Prime Minister. What do you think of that?"

"I think you're a couple of hundred years late. You would have been right at home with Blackbeard and Kidd."

Now Max speculated on Harrington's return to Nassau in the middle of the summer. It was just possible he was ready to give up on Paradise Island. The thought warmed him like a drink of good brandy. He turned at the sound of a knock on the door. It was opened by Carol.

"Mr. Baildon's here, Mr. Hertog."

She moved aside to allow Christopher Baildon to pass and then closed the door.

"Chris." Max acknowledged Baildon's presence. "I have something for you. Sit down."

Baildon, tall and, as Max often said, with that lean and hungry look about him, was in his early thirties and the end product of an old and decayed island family. The first Baildon had come to the Bahamas with the Eleutherian Adventurers, a group of colonists out of London who settled on Eleuthera around 1650 and later spread to New Providence with its capital of Nassau. At one time the Baildons had large holdings in the islands, but over the span of centuries the sturdy pioneer stock was diluted. Management of the estates became inept. The Baildon men grew indecisive, and their women were barren. All that remained to those who survived was the legend of past accomplishments, a dim glory, a raveled island aristocracy.

The Baildon home, a rambling frame relic of many rooms and dark hallways, of useless and unexpected small porches with bay windows and ornamental scrollwork surmounting slender pillars, stood on the hill ridge overlooking Nassau's harbor. It was a bastard product of a drunken architect's dream. Built in the early 1800's, it replaced the original Baildon residence destroyed by a fire which had consumed most of the settlement.

Chris shared the too-large house with his father, a rachitic and querulous man, and a wasp-tongued aunt, whose complaints and doleful predictions began with the morning's sun and ended only when she dropped off into a nervous sleep at night. Baildon senior fretted away his days in a clattering, nervous activity over nothing. He seemed to be forever on the move, making useless, cane-tapping journeys up and down the staircase and through uncarpeted hallways. He was out and on and off the porch in a perpetual scurry which was pointless and without destination. In the neglected gardens he would stand in knee-deep weeds, wave a threatening cane at one of the old trees, shriek his abuse and catalogue of misfortunes at the gnarled branches. He and his sister, Agatha, engaged in shrill-voiced arguments over nothing; what time the sun rose or set, the date when some unimportant incident occurred, what wine had been served at a dinner held fifty years ago. The continual exchanges further raddled their foolish wits and held off an unendurable loneliness. Each would have been miserable without the other. They held a common grievance against Chris, openly holding him to blame for their wretched existence. He should long ago have lifted them from the pig's wallow of poverty. They had sacrificed everything to send him to England and Oxford. In return he should have married well, an unidentified heiress, or become a merchant prince in Nassau. Chris agreed with them in everything, and this only served to excite them further and to greater demands.

Earlier Baildons had long ago disposed of valuable Out Island properties. Pressed by their creditors or desires, they had sold, for insignificant sums, land which now would have been worth a fortune. Brother and sister never ceased to remind each other of this depressing fact. They were loud in their indictment of grandfathers and uncles who had wasted their patrimony. This was their only point of agreement. In defense Chris had developed the faculty of not hearing anything they said. He spent as little time in the house as possible.

A few years earlier Agatha Baildon announced that she intended doing something about repairing the family's fortune. The many empty rooms could be rented to selected guests. She would establish not a boardinghouse but a home for gentlefolk and make a tidy profit. She threw herself into the venture with a noisy fury. Two Negro women were engaged to sweep and scrub. Old furniture was polished; rugs and carpets were beaten, floors waxed, long-stored mattresses, pillows and bed linen aired and sweetened in the sun. The huge kitchen was attacked. Copper pans were burnished, iron kettles scoured. The wood-burning stove was cleaned and blackened. Agatha, with a fine air of defiance, took the copy for a modest advertisement to the press. Two guests were lured by the promise of bountiful gourmet meals, a home atmosphere in a historic mansion, the company of gently reared ladies and gentlemen. The two, one a bank clerk and the other a maiden lady employed in a bookstore, arrived simultaneously. They were immediately set upon by Baildon senior, who questioned and cross-questioned them with the vigor of a prosecutor for the Crown. Breaking them loose from her brother, Agatha inquired about their religious beliefs. She abhorred Catholics. Satisfied that her guests were staunchly Protestant, she condescended to show them to their rooms and promptly forgot about them. There was no hot water. Dinnertime found Baildon and Agatha sharing half a cold chicken and a few boiled potatoes in the dining room's gloomy vastness.

Having installed the guests, Agatha ignored them. They came timidly to inquire about the dining hours and to point out there were no sheets on the beds, no water in the pitchers, no towels on their racks. Agatha eyed them with an icy hauteur. They were reminded that the Baildons were not tavernkeepers and then treated to a résumé of the family's past glories. The maiden lady from the bookstore conceded there was much in the Baildons' past of merit. However, this in no way put sheets on the bed or food in their stomachs. Bridling at this display of ill manners, Agatha told both her new lodgers they were free to leave if they were dissatisfied. As a matter of fact, she added, this was a most excellent idea. The bewildered roomers accepted it gratefully.

The venture provided a topic for argument. Baildon and his sister happily seized on it. For years thereafter it was heatedly discussed. Agatha accused her brother of first suggesting the Baildon mansion be reduced to a lodging house. She wept over the memory of her humiliation. Baildon, for his part, had jotted down all the details of the experience and read them off. A little notebook offered indisputable proof that Agatha alone was responsible. They shrilled and yawped over the incident and so filled many a dreary afternoon.

Chris, with a steady income now, sought to restore the house and its half-mad occupants. They would have nothing to do with any of his ideas, shutting themselves away in their rooms and refusing to discuss the matter. A plumber and his helper and, later, a carpenter were discouraged by the spectacle of Baildon patrolling the grounds with an old shotgun and loudly threatening to shoot anyone who trespassed. Finally Chris gave up, and the pair moldered away, flitting ghostlike through empty rooms and hallways and sometimes calling ribald obscenities to each other in cackling voices.

Christopher Baildon had never been quite sure why Max Hertog had suddenly lifted him out of a small job where he had been half clerk, half salesman and errand boy and brought him into the Hertog organization. A year or so earlier Max had wanted to purchase an extensive tract on Andros, and he had commissioned Baildon's employers to get it for him. Chris had done the spadework, clearing several conflicting claims and coming up with a secure title. Something in his manner caught Hertog's fancy. He bore himself with a sharp contempt for most persons, an attitude which extended to Maximilian Hertog. This both annoyed and amused Max, and he had hired Christopher Baildon with the intention of elevating him to a position of some prominence and then discharging him with-

66

out explanation. Later he abandoned the notion as being petty and spiteful and was secretly ashamed at having ever entertained it. Baildon had his value. He had a sharp and incisive mind. In the absence of a better definition, he became Hertog's confidential assistant. This meant that he performed tasks of a nature which Max preferred not to commit to paper. Both were aware of a mutual dislike. In Baildon's eyes Hertog was a loud and vulgar man who trampled over everything and everyone in his path. He, in Baildon's fancy, always swung a broadsword when a rapier would have served. Max was indifferent to his employee's disdain. Chris was useful, and Hertog was never one to discard a thing of value simply because its shape displeased him. He paid Baildon only just a little more than he might have made elsewhere. It was less than he was worth, but Max enjoyed holding his employee on a tight leash.

The secret of the continued association lay in the fact that the two complemented each other. Baildon could be charmingly diplomatic, adjusting himself to any situation and temperament. When it was desirable, he drew upon a cold, aloof contempt for everything about him. Max knew he could be depended on to carry out any assignment with complete detachment and an indifference to the personalities involved. Baildon also had the ability to talk charmingly and well and say nothing, and he was, Max suspected, completely unscrupulous. Handsome in the blond, almost gaunt structure of many Englishmen. His manners were impeccable. He played a good hand of bridge, a solid game of golf and tennis. Max used him for many things. They weren't supposed to like each other. Pressed for an explanation, Max would have been unable to say why he refused to reward Christopher Baildon according to his worth. He could have raised his salary two or three times over and passed valuable financial tips on to the younger man. These things he did not do for some obscure, sadistic reason. He liked to watch Baildon squirm at the end of a line. For his part, Chris was patient. Someday, somehow, he would catch Hertog at a vulnerable moment. It was worth waiting for.

Max now tapped a finger on the map, holding it on the northerly end of the Bahama chain.

"I'm going to buy up Grand Bahama."

"All of it?" Chris displayed no surprise. "The entire island?"

"Well." Max qualified his statement. "A lot of it. Say we draw a line at an angle west across from Settlement Point to take in the airstrip. Then we buy all we can in West End."

Baildon was too well trained to ask questions. Max would eventually tell him what he wanted done. He waited.

"If," Max continued, "Hertog goes in, you know what happens." He now and then used the third person in this manner. "The price of everything jumps. I want you to go to Miami. Round up half a dozen real estate brokers. I'm forming a dummy corporation. The Aunt Martha Candy Company. You have the real estate brokers buy up on Grand Bahama in Aunt Martha's name." He was boyishly pleased with the innocent-sounding designation. "Now." He moved to a window and stood looking down into the street. "After we have everything we want, we'll leak the information that Hertog is Aunt Martha. You know what will happen. There will be a scramble to get aboard. You might buy yourself a couple of lots in Freeport and hold them. They'll make you a profit."

"I'll go over on the afternoon plane."

Max nodded his approval. That was Christopher Baildon's value. He never asked unnecessary questions and could be depended on to keep his mouth shut.

"We'll open an account in Miami in Aunt Martha's name. Pay for everything through that." He spoke over his shoulder.

Baildon nodded and left. Max, whistling jauntily, gazed at Bay Street's traffic approvingly.

The sound of a church bell was lifted on a rippling breeze and carried to the high cliffs overlooking the bay. Naked to the waist, bare of feet, lying on his back on an old blanket, Royal Keating smiled to himself. Sunday and a church bell. Idly he wondered if special bells were cast for churches. He had heard them here, in the islands, in the United States and England. The tone never seemed to vary. It wouldn't be mis-

68

taken for a school bell, a fire bell or the tolling of a towered clock.

He half rolled over and propped himself on one elbow. Sunlight skittered along the tops of the waves below, filling Hatchet Bay with a dancing radiance. Hatchet Bay. The natives called it the Pond. Here, save for the palms back from the shore, the coastline seemed more Cornish than Bahamian. It was high and precipitous with the cliffs of weathered limestone. A short distance, four or five miles away, lay Gregory Town and beyond that the large resort development being laid out by the American firm. Working at his desk or in the field, Royal sometimes wondered at the American affluence which was transforming the Bahamas. Private clubs, luxury hotels, airfields, yacht basins and entire communities miraculously appeared where only scrub and sand had been. Practically every island of any size in the long chain was feeling the impact. Transit lines were run. Bulldozers ripped at the earth. Dredges tore and sucked at the ocean's bed to make deepwater anchorages. Airstrips were laid out while permanent fields were under construction. Masons. Carpenters. Laborers. They lived in well-organized camps or settled in the nearby communities, renting rooms where they could. There were jobs for everyone who wanted to work, and the end seemed nowhere in sight.

He lit a cigarette, sending the smoke out in a lazy cloud. He was happy to be back in the islands and with this job. He was the only Negro in the small group of architects, draftsmen and engineers for whom the company had built a large comfortable bunkhouse and mess hall on the site. They had tennis and badminton courts for recreation and laid out a one-hole pitch and putt golf course. He was working with men whose professions had taken them to far and scattered places in the world. They had laid pipelines in the Arabian desert, dredged harbors in the Far East, built roads in Alaska. Now the Bahamas were just another place on the map. They would do their jobs and leave. Royal, though, would stay. He knew that. He was bound to the islands by old ties not easily severed.

He had struck an easy companionship with his associates, but he often wondered if they were actually as indifferent to his color as their acceptance seemed to indicate. It had never intruded on their relationship. He sometimes thought that of them all he was the one most aware of black and white. Now and then, in the mess hall, he was kidded about his accent.

"Who dat mon mekkin' wid th' funny soun'?"

This was done with a broad, friendly grin or a wink. He was good at his job. That was all the others asked. They were professionals. Competence was their only standard.

He could have a lifetime job with the American firm. It was an attractive prospect, but he knew he would remain in the islands, even though it meant contesting with prejudices hundreds of years old. The established whites had locked the blacks out as effectively as though they were herded into a great barracoon. Because of his education, he would be regarded and watched with suspicion. A smart nigger. Maximilian Hertog had called him that. Always the whites would be doubtful. His own people were wary of him at first meeting. He smiled a little thinking he was walled in by distrust and a measure of hostility from both white and black.

He had come home after years in England and at first found little changed. Then—and he distrusted his own judgment at first—he became aware of a restlessness. Actually it was little more than a mood. Maybe, he thought, the movement for civil rights in the States had something to do with it. There were battery-operated radios on the smallest islands. The Florida stations came in strong. The Bahamian blacks who couldn't read were listening. What happened in Alabama, New Jersey, Ohio or California made an impression. The black man in the Bahamas was not thinking of burning and looting, but he was beginning to wonder if the white man's way was the best and only way.

Magnificent homes girdled the island of New Providence. Eighty-five percent of Nassau's inhabitants were black. This, it seemed, had never occurred to the whites. They continued to rule as though they were in the majority. Even the middle class in Nassau lived extremely well. But in a section known as Over the Hill the blacks existed in the meanest hovels without electricity or running water, with outdoor toilets, meager, if any, bathing facilities, with the water being drawn from a public tap in the street. The whites were well aware of conditions but did nothing to set them right. Royal found himself thinking of these things without anger. So it had always been. He snapped the half-finished cigarette into the air. A wheeling gull spun and dived, snapping at the stub with a sharp and angry cry.

Royal dropped again to his back and felt the sun's warmth wash over him as a wave. He glanced at a watch on his wrist. He was waiting for his girl. Alicia. She played the organ in the small church whose bell had sounded earlier. They met this way every Sunday. He thought of her with pleasure. She was a slender girl of dark beauty and walked with a fine pride, head up as though she carried a pitcher on it. Her people had been on Eleuthera for three hundred years, the first of them slaves to a family named Thatcher. That was her name. Alicia Thatcher. She had been no easy conquest, no island girl to be laid quickly on the beach or in the scrub. In her early resistance there had been an honesty. Once he had partially undressed her, taking from her a loose blouse and bra until she stood as some fanciful carving, black above the linen of her skirt, hard, outthrust breasts, her features composed, her eyes grave.

"Not now, Royal. I want to think about it."

She made no effort to put on the two small pieces of clothing but dropped to the blanket, sitting cross-legged, eyes upon her fingers as they played with a leaf, fallen from the tree shading them.

"You look like something Gauguin painted in Tahiti." He dropped beside her.

She smiled faintly. "I read a book about him once. *The Moon and Sixpence*. I've never seen a painting." She looked up. "About us. I want to. I've thought about it before. I really don't think it is a pearl of great price, my virginity. I don't believe you or any man thinks it's important any longer, so I don't really know why I preserve it."

Her fingers dropped the leaf and moved to the waistband of her skirt, unfastening the buttons. She pushed it down and away and with it the white rayon briefs. She waited for his touch, and when his hands moved upon her, she trembled as a nervous animal, making small, inarticulate, mewling sounds, and then gave herself with the full passion of her blood.

Later she lay within his arm, quiet now and passive. She took the cigarette from his mouth and drew on it. She raised herself on one elbow and stared down into his face with an expression of puzzled wonder.

"So that's how it is. I always wondered. It's not supposed to be that way for a girl the first time, is it?"

"Sometimes." His hand moved, following the shape of her breast. "I guess it depends on the girl or maybe more on the man if he is easy and takes his time until she's ready."

"Have you had a lot of girls?" She wanted to talk about it now.

"Uh-huh." He put his mouth in the soft curve of her belly. "Why do girls always ask that?"

"Have you ever wanted a white girl?"

He half turned, looking into her face. "Want is a strong word. If you mean have I ever looked at a white girl and wondered what she'd be like in bed, yes."

"Have you ever had a white girl?" She persisted.

"In England."

"Well?"

"Well, what?"

"Was—was it different?"

He laughed, reached up, and pulled her down upon him.

"How could it be?" His voice was muffled.

She strained, pushing him away. "Tell me." It was a demand.

Royal lit cigarettes for them both. The earth here was warm and fragrant. Within the small clearing the sun came through the trees as soft, golden rain. He wondered why girls liked to talk about it.

"It was different for her," he said finally. "She was white, real white the way a lot of English girls are. She got her kicks out of my black skin. The wall next to her bed was covered with a mirror. She used to watch us in that. She'd throw a leg up over me so she could see the white against black. I guess she liked to think she was being raped by a savage or a black

72

ape. She'd scream: 'Give it to me, you big black bastard. Fuck me, you black son of a bitch.' It was always the black that drove her crazy."

"Didn't you mind?"

"Mind what?"

"Mind being—being black for her?"

"But I am black."

"I know." She was a little confused. "But being black for her—the way she wanted it. That's different."

"No. I didn't mind. You see. I was using her too, only she didn't think about that."

Now, lying here atop the cliffs, he waited for her as on other Sundays. He usually borrowed one of the company's Jeeps, and they drove through the island countryside, which was rolling and dotted with lakes. The mess hall cook had put up a basket lunch of fried chicken, potato salad, fresh rolls, small cakes and a Thermos of iced tea. To this Royal had added a bottle of golden rum. They would find a place to spread a cloth, get mildly mellow on the rum, and probably make love beneath the hot sun. Later, ravenous, they would eat and smile at each other with complete understanding. Once she had said to him, "Now that I know what it's like, I may want to shop around. So if I don't show up some Sunday, you'll understand." He understood she didn't mean it. At some time a girl always tried to assert herself this way. It was a small declaration of independence.

"I'll beat you. I'll just beat the hell out of you."

That was the reassurance she sought. Her pride was reasserted.

Often, on these weekly excursions, they would draw into a village at sundown and pull to the side of the road. With the hush of evening on it, the settlement would grow strangely silent. The yellow, flickering light of oil lamps would appear, dotting the windows of small frame houses as amber cat's eyes. A woman would call to a tardy child. A man sat on the bare boards of his porch, leaning against a four-by-six upright, and pulled contentedly on an old pipe. A girl, in her best dress of printed cotton but bare of feet, walked with a boy. Her face

73

was a dark oval above the white of her dress, and her hair, freshly oiled, was bound in tight, pencil-sized curls which stuck straight out from her scalp. A woman, balancing a stem of bananas or a basket of pineapples and oranges on her head, spoke softly as she passed. The dust spouted in tiny geysers between her toes, and the spurts made a faint squeaking sound as of a little animal.

In the shadows a group of men would be hunkered down, smoking and talking quietly, and compelled, sometimes, by a strange atavism, they would kindle a small fire no bigger than a hand and take turns feeding twigs into it. When a woman or a girl passed, they would raise their eyes, following the rhythmic stride and the swing of buttocks. Sometimes one would call out, speaking a name or a word. The woman, with her back to them, would smile to herself and pretend she hadn't heard.

Although they had never attempted to put a name to it, these village scenes stirred something dark and primitive within them. Unconsciously Alicia's hand would seek Royal's. It was easy to imagine the beat of a drum, the muted cadence of a tribal chant, the pounding of bare feet on hard, sunbaked earth.

"It goes so far back, doesn't it?" She had whispered the question. "It's just a little scary to realize this mood, a reversion, I guess, has survived three hundred years or more. It makes me feel—" She paused. "I don't know."

"All black. Part of an Africa you've never seen. That's what it does. That's what they're reaching out for; only they don't know it."

"I guess so." She was doubtful.

On one of their trips they had halted in a little settlement called Benton. It was later than usual, and what activity was abroad centered on a church. It was small, square and badly in need of paint or whitewash. From an open door an oblong of light laid a path across a carpet of pine needles. The congregation came singly and in pairs, seeming to drift in from many directions and appearing suddenly out of the gathering dusk. At the door they halted for a moment to speak to the minister. He was a fairly young man in a suit of dark blue,

74

shiny and worn. His skin was the steely blue-black of his Congo ancestors. He stood on the top step, smiled at each arrival, and spoke a friendly word of welcome.

"Royal. Let's go in. We aren't in a hurry, are we?"

He shook his head, slid from the seat, and reached for her hand before she jumped lightly down.

The parson greeted them with a warm dignity. "Hello and welcome." He extended a hand to each. "We're glad to have you. We don't often get persons from outside the village."

Royal introduced himself and then Alicia. The minister's grip was strong and hard but without any false heartiness. He was taller than Royal by a good six inches, a great pillar of a man with heavily muscled shoulders and gentle eyes. He was obviously delighted by their presence.

"I'm the Reverend Whitman." His voice was deep and musical. His sudden smile illuminated them. "It always sounds so pretentious when I say Reverend. I'm not sure why. I am properly ordained. Where are you folks from?"

Royal told him.

"I preach, sometimes, in our church at Gregory Town." He glanced through the doorway to the filled benches, and his smile was a little rueful. "I always have a capacity congregation on Sunday evenings. The daytime service is sparsely attended. Sometimes I think they come in the evening for the entertainment rather than out of any religious zeal. Come. I'll find you seats." He ushered Alicia and Royal before him. "Usually we have organ music, but my wife, who is the organist, sprained her wrist badly. She isn't here tonight."

"I play a little." Alicia made the statement impulsively. "In our church."

"Well, that's just fine." He took her hand and led her to the lectern. There he turned to the congregation. "As you know, Sister Margaret hurt her hand. She isn't here this evening. But this young lady, a visitor, has kindly offered to play the opening and closing hymns. I want you to welcome her. Miss Alicia Thatcher from Gregory Town."

The response was immediate. They clapped and called, "Welcome, Sister Alicia." Their faces shone with pleasure.

75

A young boy ran forward and took his place at the long handle which pumped the bellows.

"I must tell you." The tone was confidential, and the minister almost seemed to be embarrassed. "We use the organ only for the opening and closing hymns. The congregation likes to sing unaccompanied. I usually give them the hymn number; they know them all and take it from there. I think you will understand why it is better without the organ."

Alicia nodded and took her seat before the small console. She flashed a smile at the boy, who waited expectantly.

"What's your name?" she whispered.

"Joe John." He was so overwhelmed by the novelty of her appearance he could hardly speak. "Joe John Arthur."

"Well, Joe John Arthur"—she winked—"hit it. Work us up a head of steam."

The music for the first hymn was on the rack, but she was familiar with it and didn't need the score. Glancing at the minister, she caught his pleased nod. Her fingers rested lightly on a chord. The organ was surprisingly good. Joe John pumped energetically. The sound went in a wave over the congregation, and voices filled the little church with a reverent ecstasy.

The sermon, Royal thought, was unique. Reverend Whitman didn't preach to his people. He talked to them. It was fundamental. Hell and the Devil. God and the angels. He didn't threaten them but said, simply, "This is the way it's going to be. If you sin, the Devil is going to catch up with you. He's right there, waiting all the time. If you lead a good life with love and charity in your heart, then you'll go to heaven. A man shouldn't have much trouble making up his mind how he wants it to be." The congregation shivered delightedly. He told stories and recited parables. In between, while he seemed to be deciding what he would talk about next, the congregation would sing. There seemed to be no leader. One voice would suddenly lift itself, and the rest followed without signal or hesitation. Alicia could understand why they liked to sing unaccompanied. What they did was to take a hymn, doleful and unimaginative in its composition, and turn it into something wild and exciting, punctuated by shouts and the steady beat of hands. An organist would have found it impossible to follow the sudden variations. The people took over the music and made it their own. It was primitive and stirring with wonderful, spine-tingling minor strains. Spontaneously they fashioned a barbaric paean to their God. When they finished, the minister calmly took up his rambling sermon.

After the services the congregation was reluctant to leave. Sunday evening church was, as the minister had said, a form of diversion and entertainment. Now there was no place to go, nothing to do but go home. Alicia and Royal stood with Reverend Whitman just outside the door. The people shuffled out. Some paused to thank Alicia. All inclined their heads and shyly murmured their good-nights. The yard emptied slowly. A moon was cradled in the treetops. An old man, inside the church, turned down the oil lamps and blew out the wick flame.

"We ought to start home." Alicia turned to Royal.

"It isn't late." Whitman spoke quickly. "Come to the house with me. My wife will be delighted. A sprained wrist won't keep her from making some coffee. We can talk. New faces are rare here. We don't have many opportunities to exchange ideas with persons outside Benton." He was obviously sincere.

Alicia made the decision. "We'd like that very much."

The Whitmans lived in a small cottage set within the white square of a picket fence. The yard was filled with the heavy fragrance of flowering vines, and the path leading from the gate was bordered by conch shells brought to a high polish by hand. The minister's wife was a handsome woman, tall and with a quiet charm and dignity. Her color was the smooth black of her husband. After the first small flutter of excitement at the unexpected appearance of guests she was completely at ease. Her accent was that of the islands. They had coffee with fresh gingerbread. Seated on the narrow porch, they could hear the evening wind as it hunted through the trees.

The Whitmans were both surprised and interested when Royal, in answer to a question, said he had gone to school in England.

"Not many island boys get such a chance." He accepted

77

one of Royal's cigarettes. "Matter of fact, few would be able to take advantage of it. It's not the policy of Her Majesty's government to encourage the Negro's education beyond the elementary stage. How was it arranged for you?"

For a moment Royal resented the question. It was a personal matter. Then he realized it was a sincere interest and not idle curiosity.

"My mother and father," he said. "She worked hard all her life and still does. She saved. I was the youngest. The others grew up and moved away, some to the Out Islands. My father owned some scrubland out where they built the airport. It brought a good price. My mother insisted I take the money and go to England. It was the thing she lived for, to have her son educated. Now"—he laughed—"she only half believes the things I tell her and refuses absolutely to believe white workmen, sometimes, take their orders from me."

"You were fortunate." The minister drew on one of Royal's cigarettes, and the glow momentarily illuminated his grave features. "I suppose you were," he amended. "Some young black men wouldn't know how to live with it. You seem to have learned."

"I only want to be allowed to do the job I trained for. So far it has worked out that way. Maybe I'm lucky. If so, I only want it to last."

"I often wonder if I am a fraud." The voice came from the shadows. "I tell my people to bear their afflictions. The reward is in the hereafter. I'm really not too sure about that. Maybe there isn't any reward; the whole thing, all of man, is just one huge accident. But"—he sighed—"I keep my doubts to myself. If I didn't, I wouldn't have a job. My church has been good to me. I went to the mission school. Later it was arranged for me to go to the missionary headquarters in North Carolina. I became a minister through a series of natural progressions. So the least I can do is keep my questions to myself. I try to give them faith, but I guess each man decides the shape of his God. I never really know what they believe or if they just come to church for the singing."

78

"I think we ought to be starting back." Alicia looked at Royal.

He nodded and rose. The Whitmans followed, and the four walked down the path to where the Jeep was parked.

"Next time come earlier and stay longer." The minister was sincerely reluctant to have them leave.

"I think I had better warn you." His wife smiled at Alicia and Royal. "Mark is reaching out for a couple of new converts in you. Political, not religious."

"It's true, I guess," Whitman admitted. "Although my church doesn't approve, I have interested myself in island politics. I am active in the Progressive Liberal Party. It needs people like you. The ignorant black man can't stand up in the House of Assembly. There are so few of the educated among us. The Establishment has seen to that."

Royal shrugged. "I would guess the Establishment looks after itself, as most of us do."

Whitman nodded. They had halted by the gate. "That's what the PLP is trying to do—look after ourselves. We are trying to educate the Bahamian Negro to use the ballot."

"That's a long road." Royal shook his head. "For three hundred years the black man here has been told government is the business of the whites."

"I wish you would come to one of the rallies. You'd change your mind. The black man is thinking." He turned to Alicia. "There's a rally at Rock Sound on the twenty-first. Why don't you come and bring him?"

"He isn't easily led." Alicia glanced at Royal. "But I'll try."

"I wish you would. We don't have any fanatics, no burn-baby-burn boys. Only people like you can help keep it that way."

Alicia could sense Royal's growing impatience. They said their good-nights quickly. The Whitmans stood by their gate looking after them until the Jeep was out of sight.

They rode the first few miles in silence. The moon was full, swinging high in a cloudless sky. It flooded the heavily wooded countryside with a ghostly play of light.

"Do you suppose it could really happen: a black majority voting in the islands? Why"—a note of astonishment crept into her voice—"that could mean a black Prime Minister."

His foot came up on the accelerator, and the Jeep slowed to an unsteady crawl. He turned and stared at her as he might at a stranger.

"It takes a little time to digest that, doesn't it? I'm sitting here waiting for the white lightning to strike you, and nothing happens. Jesus Christ. It could almost be that simple. A black majority. All of these jigs voting together. A black Prime Minister."

He dropped the Jeep out of gear and allowed it to coast to a halt. For a long time he sat there, staring into the shadowed night, until the cigarette in his fingers burned to the skin.

Now a shadow fell across his face, and he opened his eyes. Alicia stood above him, smiling. She was crisp and cool in a dress of blue and white checks, and she swept off a roughly plaited hat of straw; hair fell to her shoulders, framing her face.

Royal stretched a hand and closed his fingers about her ankle.

"You're too sexy-looking to be a schoolteacher and church organist. How was the Lord today?"

She dropped easily down beside him. "Up and about His work as usual."

"I was lying here thinking about the time we stopped off at Benton and met Mark Whitman for the first time. I didn't realize it was the beginning of my social conscience."

There was a small frown behind her eyes. "Is that what it is? Do you really care about the black people in the islands, or is this something for Royal Keating?"

"Royal Keating is black."

"So was Adam Clayton Powell, sitting it out over in Bimini. Do you think he really gives a damn about the people in Harlem? I have a feeling you're trying to make this Progressive Liberal Party something of your own—to your advantage. You are working at it too hard."

80

He sat up. "I've made a few speeches when I've been asked or made an appearance at the rallies. That's all."

"Is it?" She was appraisingly speculative. "Do you know? It never occurred to me that you might be something of a spellbinder."

He laughed, honestly amused. "I've just learned if you tell 'em what they want to hear, they'll eat it up no matter how impossible or ridiculous it is." He stood up, rising from the earth with a curious, winding grace of perfectly controlled muscles. "The other night, over at Governor's Harbour, I thought those niggers were going to carry me out on their shoulders."

With their arms about each other's waists, they walked down the winding path from the cliff's top to where the Jeep was parked.

"Doesn't that frighten you a little?"

"Why should it?"

"Because"—she felt her way with the words—"I have listened to you at several of these meetings and watched the people. They don't really touch you. Sometimes there is even a shade of contempt in your manner, but you have smelled something. I'm not sure just what it is you want."

"Maybe I only want to be a big man." He was amused. "The Emperor Jones or even King Christophe. Not in the twentieth-century Bahamas."

"Mmmm." She shrugged. "Maybe I've been imagining things. I hope so."

At the Jeep he swung her up in his arms and lowered her to the seat. She kissed him suddenly and hard and then drew back, staring into his face with an oddly baffled look.

V

Running freely under a steady east wind, the bugeye held on a southerly course out of West End, in the Grand Bahama, which would take her past Bimini, Cat and Gun Cays, between Andros and the Florida Keys.

Jan had christened her *The Witch,* and she sparkled now in her shimmering white, the polished brass and mahogany woodwork. Spray flew in opal-flecked lace as the bows took a beryl-tinted sea. Forward, on pallets laid beneath the sun, Carol Wainwright and Willard Harrington stretched in warm comfort. Aft, Jan had taken the wheel from the captain, a Bahamian Negro with the odd name of Spindle. She stood, lightly braced against the roll, and behind her *The Witch*'s wake ran true. She glanced at Spindle and winked. He smiled his approval and then lifted his eyes to study the shimmering canvas, taut wing against the sky. It was too bad, he thought, Miss Jan an' Mr. Max didn't use *The Witch* oftener. She made a man sing out here but most of the time lay unused at her mooring in the marina at Lyford Cay. Everyone was in such a hell of a hurry. Usually, when Mr. Max visited the Out Islands, he flew, but now, for the first time in months, *The Witch* was out and where she should be. Mr. Max said they might be away for ten days or two weeks, and they had provisioned for the cruise. Spindle had a proprietary feeling for *The Witch.* Sometimes he dreamed of owning her and set a course to cover all of the world's seas. He'd find one of those brownskin girls in a grass skirt, and they'd sail over the world and back.

Below, in a small cabin, Max Hertog, cradled by the lulling motion, slept with small, contented snores. He had taken two or three drinks before a fine lunch, smoked a couple of heavy cigars, told a few stories to an amused audience. Now he rested, and his mind was untroubled and free of dreams.

Shielding a lighter against the wind, Carol held the flame to a cigarette and then propped herself on both elbows. She half turned her head to glance at Harrington.

"For a man who has been done out of several million dollars you seem remarkably composed."

"Oh, I'm not really indifferent." He frowned slightly, and then his expression cleared. "A display of anger would be silly. I suckered myself into a bad investment. That's usually expensive."

"Just the same, I shouldn't think you would want to make a social occasion out of it. I bet Max you would refuse his invitation to come along. I said you'd tell him to go to hell or punch him in the nose. Why didn't you?"

He grinned a little sheepishly. "I thought about doing both. I'm still not sure why I didn't. I'm not happy with what Paradise Island cost. Also, it makes me feel something of an idiot. The strange part about it is I can't work up any strong, personal resentment where Hertog is concerned."

Finally, as he knew from the beginning he must, Willard Harrington had accepted the facts of Paradise Island. He was not going to get a Certificate of Exemption. This was obvious. Max Hertog had boxed him in. Without a gambling room the venture was doomed to a continued and mounting loss which would be ruinous to assume. He studied it from every angle and then made his deal with Maximilian Hertog. There were no other offers. Max assumed a foxy expression of regret over Harrington's untenable situation.

"It's too bad, Will." He had moved from calling Harrington Willard to the shortened and almost affectionate Will. "It's too damned bad things turned out for you the way they did."

"You are, Mr. Hertog"—Harrington spaced his words evenly,

but there was no bite in them—"a hypocritical son of a bitch if I have ever known one. Not only have you screwed me out of Paradise Island, but now you're ready to cry over it with me."

"Why, that's the least I can do, Will." He was smugly agreeable. "I took a liking to you. I truly did. You shouldn't go wading until you know how deep the water is, particularly in the Bahamas. You're taking a kick in the ass over this thing, but then I guess you can afford it. From some of your past ventures I'd say money doesn't mean too much."

"Thanks for the opinion. It makes me feel one hell of a lot better. I'd hate to have you worrying over whether I'd been hurt."

"What I meant"—Max was soothing—"was you aren't exactly reduced to selling pencils on a street corner."

"I could be if I spend much time around you."

"Now, Will, that isn't nice. I made a good offer. I could have waited and, maybe, picked up Paradise Island for twenty-five cents on the dollar. There are other people in Nassau who would have done just that."

"You don't have to tell me how lucky I am to be in your hands. Wherever you touch me, some skin comes off. It's like rubbing up against a shark."

Hertog made a small sound of regret, tongue to the roof of his mouth. He eyed Willard Harrington unhappily.

"I hate to think of you as being a bitter man, Will. I have a fine regard for you. I thought for a while you and my daughter were finding each other attractive. I was glad to see that."

"Jan is a child." Even as he spoke the words, he realized that they bore no conviction.

"She needs a man like you. Solid. Dependable. Stable. The islands don't generate a healthy moral climate for a young girl."

"You are a hell of a one to be talking about morals." Harrington was almost enjoying himself. "You're a sanctimonious bastard if there ever was one."

"You could do worse for a father-in-law, Willard."

"How? Name him."

Hertog cocked an eye ceilingward and whistled tunelessly,

84

giving the request reflective thought. Finally he dismissed it and turned to more familiar subjects.

"I don't want you to think I'm too happy about Paradise Island. Just to prove it, I'll let you go along with me on something."

"You sound like a dealer in a shell game."

"I hate to see you giving in to cynical notions, Will. They corrupt a man after a while. Now what I have in mind is a thing on Grand Bahama. I'll let you have some of it. It will make up a little bit for the polishing you took with Paradise Island."

"Do you know"—Harrington couldn't keep the astonishment from his voice—"I think you really believe this goddamned nonsense? Maximilian Hertog, the gentle, kindly philanthropist who goes about passing out shiny dimes to everyone. The truth is you're a bloody cutthroat."

"I guess I don't always make a favorable first impression." There was regret in the words. "You ought to get to know me better."

"To know you is to dislike you."

"You just say those things because you're sore about Paradise Island. You are going to have to get over it, Willard." There was a small reprimand here. "A thing like that will curdle the milk of human kindness in you."

"I'll be goddamned." Harrington almost whispered the words in awe. "I'll just be goddamned."

"Now"—Max ignored the exclamations—"I was going to fly up to Grand Bahama. Instead, suppose we take *The Witch*. You've never been out on her. Jan and Carol would like it. We'd make a congenial party, just the four of us. We'll sail up to Grand Bahama and have a look around. Then we can come back by way of Eleuthera. It will do you good. Do us all good." He was already experiencing the healthy benefits of the cruise.

Not very much to his surprise Harrington had accepted the invitation. Maximilian Hertog, he decided, was a man of many contradictions. He created an ambivalence. It was possible to be attracted and repelled by him at the same time.

Now, lying here in the sun beside Carol Wainwright, he knew the cruise had been a good idea. Much of the angry tension had drained from him. They made a good foursome. Both Carol and Jan played a solid hand of bridge. They were bright and attractive companions. He wondered, as a man will, how intimate the relationship between Carol and Max was. There was a fine, thoroughbred animal beauty about her to which a man immediately responded. He caught himself envying Max Hertog.

"You're scowling." Carol's voice brought him back to the moment. "Are you doing Max Hertog in in your mind?"

He was tempted to say he had been thinking what a great lay she must be. The notion tickled his fancy, and he smiled at her.

"How long have you been with Max?"

"Five—almost six years."

"Are you in love with him?"

If the impertinence of the question startled her, she didn't betray it. Her gaze was level and unembarrassed.

"I suppose so. In a way."

"I'm sorry." His apology was sincere. "That was rude."

"That's all right. I imagine a lot of people in Nassau have asked themselves that question. Not that it is any of their business."

"I wonder if he found what he wanted on Grand Bahama?" Harrington veered away to another subject.

"Oh, I think he already had what he wanted or was getting it. That's the way he operates."

Harrington was puzzled. Of all the Bahamas chain, Grand Bahama seemed the most unlikely for any large-scale improvement. It lay about fifty miles east of Palm Beach, was some sixty-five miles long and only seven or eight miles wide. The land, in many places, was low and swampy and heavily overgrown and timbered.

A small plane and helicopter service was operated out of West End. Hertog spent several hours on different mornings flying over the island, studying it with a critical eye. At his urging Harrington had gone along.

86

"Almost anything anyone buys here now"—Max's hand had swept out to cover all Grand Bahama—"has to go up in value. But that's small potatoes and not worth digging. I'm not interested in a real estate shuffle."

Harrington wasn't particularly impressed by what he had seen. He only wondered to what use Maximilian Hertog intended to put this unattractive strip of land. The Little Bahama Bank, of which Grand Bahama was one of several islands and innumerable small cays, offered superlative fishing grounds and cruising waters. But this was already known to yachtsmen and sportsmen and drew them annually. Beyond these moneyed transients who spent only a month or two here each season, there seemed no reason to anticipate a market for any large-scale development.

He put the question directly to Max. "Why should there be a land boom here? It doesn't make much sense."

Max put a knuckle to his nose and rubbed it. "The best reason for land prices rising is that I say they will. I have other plans. When the time comes, I'll offer you a piece of the whole operation."

Late that afternoon they were having a drink on *The Witch*'s afterdeck. The sun hovered above a low indigo streak of clouds, and the sea was flattened into a leaden plane.

"I think we'll pull out tomorrow." Max squinted through the amber of his scotch and water at the sun. "Unless anyone is in a hurry, let's go down and over to Exuma and then up to Eleuthera. It's been a long time since I've relaxed this way." He beamed on them as though they had conspired together to provide him with this tonic.

They went ashore that evening to have dinner at the Jolly Roger Club in West End. Jan and Carol burst out of their slacks and shorts, chrysalides to appear radiant in unexpected dinner gowns. They made an astonishingly beautiful pair with Carol's dusky loveliness against Jan's blond perfection.

The room was softly lighted and the service unobtrusive. On an elevated platform in one corner a calypso quartet softly beat out a compelling and darkly savage rhythm. It reached with a barbaric insistence at deep impulses. Harrington was aware of it and thought that the sound went right to a man's groin. He could feel it welling there. Looking across the table, he found Jan's gaze on him. It was sleepy-eyed, and the tip of her tongue rested speculatively on the full lower lip. Rising, he went over to stand behind her chair.

"Dance?"

She nodded without speaking, rose, and turned away from the table. At the edge of the dancing area she moved into his arms and there was a strange drowsy expression in her eyes as though she were half-asleep and awakening reluctantly. They followed the hollow sound of a metal drum which dominated the melody. Her body was pressed into him, molding itself to follow every movement. He had known her long enough to be familiar with her many moods, her moments of open sensuality which seemed to drug her. She was oblivious of anyone else in the room. He made an attempt to draw a little apart, but she flowed with him.

"Do you know what you're doing?" His whisper was harsh in her ear.

"Of course." The reply was sleepily voiced. "Don't you?"

"Well, stop it."

"Why?"

"Because, goddamn it"—he was an angry captive to a growing excitement—"I want to be able to walk off the floor."

She laughed, a small, rippling sound, and the tips of her fingers played over the back of his neck.

"You're so noble. Why don't you just give in? Usually I don't go to so much trouble with a man. I don't have to. I'm not sure why I do with you. Stop being so damned protective. All of a sudden, there at the table, I decided I wanted it."

"Well, not here on the dance floor."

"Where? Outside? On the sand? Standing on the porch?" She was teasing deliberately, and her leg slid between his. Her eyes widened with mock astonishment as she touched him. "Well! My goodness. *Mr.* Willard Spencer Harrington!" She drew back with an expression of startled modesty and shock. "What do you know about that?" The question was whispered.

He was angry now because she was making him appear fool-

88

ish in his own eyes. She was casting him in a role of stupidity or impotence. He was a vigorous man of considerable experience. His wealth had seen to that. Certainly he was no protector of maidenhood, no clumsy Galahad. Jan had never made a secret of the desires which frequently tormented her, and he couldn't explain to himself why he hadn't taken what was so freely offered. Suppose he was twenty or so years older? What difference did that make? He owed nothing to Maximilian Hertog or his daughter. No trust would be breached. No honor involved. Even as he told himself these things, he was disturbed because he knew the reasoning was specious. The truth was that she seemed to be so pitifully vulnerable. Her body's insistence stripped away her dignity, and against it she was defenseless. Once, years ago in college, he was in downtown New Haven. It was late afternoon and he drove slowly in a new blue convertible LaSalle. The girl—she worked in one of the clock factories—waited for a bus. He drew in to the curb, opened the door, and after the briefest hesitation she stepped in. They drove out of town, and he tried to make small conversation. She only smiled and had no reply. She was an exceptionally pretty girl and obviously nervous. Finally he understood her silence. She was a deaf-mute. They went to a roadhouse on the Boston Post Road, had a few drinks and dinner. Later, in a countryside lane, he made love to her on the cramped front seat of the car. In the act he could sense her desperation as though she realized her handicap would prevent her from ever having more than this with him. When it was over, he was a little ashamed, feeling he had taken advantage of her hopeless desire to be as other girls. This was the only way she could express it, and he understood it had never really worked for her. In much the same way Jan Hertog had no shield against herself. It was this nakedness which had disturbed him. Now he told himself he was being a fool. Jan Hertog was a hell of a long way from being defenseless.

Somehow—and this he had noted in her before—she was acutely sensitive to his change of mood. Drawing back just enough to be able to look into his face, she smiled out of some ancient wisdom, her hand tightening in his.

"Well, I finally got through to you, didn't I?"

"I had you confused with someone else. You're too damned smart to be only twenty-five."

"Twenty-five is the age of wisdom. Before that you are too opinionated to ask questions. At twenty-five you begin to wonder." She was relaxed and casual. For the moment her private demon was quiet. "Now that we are communicating, I'm not in such a hurry."

"It was getting a little critical out here in front of everyone."

"I'm sorry about that." She paused. "I guess I am. No-o-o. Not really." She drew the words out reflectively. "Sometime, somewhere I am going to find a man who will take me for what I am and not try to analyze me as a case out of Krafft-Ebing. I don't want to feel as if I am being laid on a couch for the advancement of psychology. I just want to rut around in the bush because it's good and exciting. From my point of view it is pretty simple. Why do you want to confuse it?"

"Does it occur to you this is a strange conversation or monologue for a dance floor?"

"Jesus. Don't be stuffy, Willard." She turned out of his arms but held his hand and walked toward their table.

As they took their places, he glanced across at Carol Wainwright. There was a veiled amusement in her eyes as though she were somehow aware of what had happened during the dance.

The Exuma Cays swing in a great series of broken links northwesterly from Little Exuma to Beacon Cay, and they lie as rough-cut gems in their seas of sapphire, blue, jade and purple. Here there are beaches which have never been marked by the footprints of a man and rolling hills and woods where a voice has never sounded. The few settlements are remote and scattered, small groupings of people left over from another time. These cays bear names which fall provocatively on the ear. Bitter Guana Cay. Big Farmers Cay. Little Farmers Cay. Pipe Cay and Shroud Cay. Who named them so and why?

Jan stood beside Spindle, who had the wheel now with *The Witch* under a light quartering wind. Here a man at the helm depends solely on his eyes, estimating the depths by the color of the water, for the sandbanks shift and what was here yesterday may not be here tomorrow. Spindle's features were in repose, but his gaze roved constantly with affectionate attention. These were home waters, and he had learned to handle a small boat on them almost at the time of walking. The Spindles had been long on Warderick Wells Cay. There he had been born and lived until young manhood. This cay is said to be haunted by the ghosts of black slaves, who, on moonlit nights, chant and call back and forth to one another from eternity. The story goes that a slave ship with a wretched cargo foundered and broke up on a reef. In their heavy chains none survived. Their spirits grow restless when the moon is high, and what they call and say at such a time no man can understand. Spindle believed this, although he had never heard the voices.

Watching him, Jan thought she could see alternate shades of melancholy, nostalgia and sudden pleasure as they played over his face.

"You were born around here, weren't you?"

"Yes, ma'am." He pointed to where a series of cliffs stood out against the sky resembling gray stone houses. The cay lay off the port bow. "Up neah theah I live till I was nineteen or somethin'. Den I go t' Nassau wid fishermon an' don' go back."

"Are you ever sorry?"

"Sometime, when I was lots younger, but I learn 'bout boads an' t' read an' t' navigate, den I gots job wid Mistuh Max. I say den, mon, ef yo' don' go Nassau, you never be captain en such a boad as *Th' Witch*."

She could feel his love, his yearning for the boat. His big hands on the wheel seemed to caress it, moving with a soft touch over the polished wood.

"What would you do with *The Witch* if you owned her?" The question came spontaneously, and she wondered why she had asked.

The enormity of this was too much for Spindle to translate into words. He shook his head, smiling helplessly and not knowing whether the query required an answer. He was embarrassed.

91

A believable fantasy began to take shape in her mind as Spindle shook his head again. She or Max could give Spindle *The Witch,* make him a present of her, say, "Here are the papers. She is yours." This act which would change Spindle's life and was completely beyond his comprehension wouldn't even touch them. Max could order a new bugeye laid down in one of the yards on Maryland's Eastern Shore, and it would really mean no more to him than the purchase of a box of cigars. The idea fascinated her. Never before had she thought about money, the kind of money represented by Maximilian Hertog or, for that matter, Willard Harrington. It was just something which had always been there and you wrote or cashed a check and it was put in your hand or paid a bill. She turned away and walked forward to where Max, Carol and Harrington were lazily comfortable in deck chairs.

"I want to give Spindle *The Witch.*"

"All right." Max was indifferent.

"Do you mean that?" She was incredulous.

He turned to look up at her. "Of course not." The tone was roughly impatient. "What would a nigger do with a boat like *The Witch?*"

"What he's doing now." She sat on the arm of his chair. "Sail her. Make a living with her."

"In six months she'd be so stunk up you couldn't tell her from some conch's Out Island sloop. What set you off to being Lady Bountiful with my boat this morning?"

"I don't know." She kicked out a foot and studied it critically. "It would be a magnificent gesture. Sort of like playing God."

Max snorted. "Let God play God. Or don't you think God knows what He's doing? You have to call these things to His attention? If God wanted Spindle to have a hundred-and-fifty-thousand-dollar boat, He would have given it long ago and not waited for you to nudge Him."

"I guess you're right," she conceded regretfully. "But it would be something, wouldn't it? Just to say: 'Spindle, take *The Witch*. Don't come back. She's yours.' I was thinking you or Willard could do that without a moment's inconvenience. It wouldn't make even the smallest nick in your bank balance. You'd never even know it or miss the cost of a new one. I think, when you die, I'll give all your money away."

He was unperturbed. "When I die and it's your money, you'll change your mind. It's easy to spread the bounty around when it's someone else's cash. When it's your own, you like to reach back and pat it now and then to be sure it's still there."

"Why?"

"How the hell do I know why? You just do. It's reassuring. Especially if you can remember a time in your life when you had nothing back there to pat but your bare ass. You wouldn't know about that; neither would Willard. I do. I didn't inherit mine the way Willard did and you will."

"And"—she asked the question sweetly—"that gives you a nobility of character Willard and I don't have?"

"Do you know"—he ignored the challenge in Jan's question —"the first time I realized I really had money? It was when I went out one day and bought four new tires at the same time for a Reo touring car I owned. No, by God." He corrected himself. "It was five. I had them put on a spare. All of a sudden that car rode better. I felt good all over. Solid. Secure. You and Willard can't ever know that feeling. You've missed something." He meditated on this with obvious satisfaction. "Another time" —he was enjoying himself—"I realized what a thing it was to have money. With it a man could make, what you said a moment ago, a gesture. There used to be a hard candy, Gibson's Fruit Drops. Most grocery and drugstores had them. They came in a tall, square glass container and were different flavors. Lime. Cherry. Orange. Lemon. Chocolate. Pineapple. Now if there was one thing I really hated, it was the lime flavor of candy. It used to fur up my tongue. But when you bought a dime's worth of Gibson's Fruit Drops, you were bound to get a certain number of lime in with the others. It was a mathematical certainty. I always ate every one of them because, having paid for them, I thought I had to. Well, after I made my first big strike up in Manitoba, I used to buy Gibson's Fruit Drops by

93

the jar. I'd pick out all the lime. I didn't have to eat a damned one. I threw them all away. I said to myself, 'This is what it is like to have money.' "

Impulsively Jan leaned over and kissed him on the forehead.

"When you tell something like that, it makes people forget what a bastard you are. I guess that's why you do it."

"Why else?" He winked at Harrington. "I think it's about time for a drink. Will you all join me?" He didn't wait for a reply but loosed a shout. "Major?"

The young steward's head popped up from the hatchway as if it had been propelled by a spring.

"Yes, sir, Mr. Max?"

"Fix us up some rum. You know what I like. Have we any fresh pineapple left?"

"Yes, sir, Mr. Max." Major disappeared as though someone had pushed him back in a box. "Yes, sir!" His voice echoed.

Hertog grinned. "That boy Major waits there. He thinks I don't know it. He waits there so he can do that jumping jack act when I call. It seems to give him the most fun. I forget where I got Major." He mused on this quite unconsciously as though he had actually bought the boy at some forgotten auction.

It was early afternoon when Spindle picked up the white silos and a pole beacon which serve as navigational aids to the entrance to Hatchet Bay. The passage is made through a cut between limestone cliffs.

Standing forward with Harrington, Jan watched the hills and the dense clumps of casuarina trees take shape. The Pond offers one of the finest protected anchorages in the islands.

"This isn't just one of Max's impulses. He doesn't indulge in whims."

"What?" Harrington was puzzled.

"Oh"—she smiled—"I was almost talking to myself. Sometimes I try to outguess Max just for fun. I was wondering why he wanted to come to Eleuthera. It is way off our normal course from Grand Bahama to Nassau. He has something on his mind. I wonder what." She glanced aft to where Hertog sat with Carol. "You'll see. Everything will be set up in advance. Ar-

94

rangements are not left to chance when Maximilian Hertog is abroad."

They waited for a few minutes at the Hatchet Bay yacht basin and clubhouse while Max left an order for fresh stores, a case of milk and cream and cut-up frying chickens. Save for the cream, they didn't really need any of these things, but the Hertog enterprises had extensive dairy, farming and poultry-raising interests in this section of the island.

"I always order eggs, milk, butter and chickens even if I only give them away later." He made the unnecessary explanation to Harrington. "I like to know the quality stands up. We might have Major fix some fried chicken for supper."

Outside in the driveway there was a small four-passenger Triumph roadster waiting. The top was down; paint and metalwork gleamed. A young man stood nearby with the keys. He stepped forward, touching his cap.

"Yes, sir, Mr. Hertog. Do you want me to drive?"

"No." Max took the keys. He made a critical inspection of the car and then nodded his approval. "You keep the cars well. Tell Harry Mason I said so. I'll leave the keys with the dockmaster."

That the Hertog interests included such a thing as a small u-drive-it agency on the island of Eleuthera didn't surprise anyone. It was a rare and certainly uninhabited coral head where the Hertog stamp was missing.

Max drove with a careless abandon, whipping the small car into and around the narrow road's turns as though he were quite certain the word had gone out that Maximilian Hertog was loose and all other traffic had been brought to a standstill. Perhaps it was, for they encountered only one car, and this was pulled hastily to the side of the highway. Here there was a rolling country of pleasant valleys and lakes. They toured in a southeasterly direction, and Max, quite obviously, felt any explanation of their destination was unnecessary. He handled the wheel with a ferocious scowl as though the little sports car were a wild and unpredictable animal which might turn on him at any time. An unlighted cigar was clamped beneath his teeth, and he made no effort at small talk. In the short back seat

95

Jan tucked her arm beneath Harrington's and thrust a tongue against her cheek as though to say: "See? I told you so. Max Hertog moves in a mysterious way his wonders to perform."

South of Governor's Harbour the road dipped. Fanning out at the bottom, an extensive development was taking shape. A yacht basin had been dredged, and breakwaters had been extended on two natural tongues of land to create a sheltered anchorage. Two power cruisers were at their buoys, and a light pontoon-equipped plane had been run up on a ramp. A recently completed golf course was already showing a fine, velvety green, and back from the fairways homes and cottages were rising beneath the hands of carpenters and masons. The main clubhouse was finished and in operation with swimming pools, tennis courts and guest accommodations.

Max drove slowly now, his eyes taking in every detail of the project. At the far end, where this driveway entered a turning circle, there was a large, many-windowed frame building which was of a temporary nature. At the front, above the doors, there was a sign: JANIS CORPORATION.

Harrington pretended astonishment. "Do you mean to tell me they are building something here without the Hertog label?"

Max grunted. He pulled the car to a shuddering halt in the driveway.

"I let this get away from me," he confessed. "Damned if I know how. What they first talked about didn't amount to much. They expanded the original plans." He added this with an inflection of injury. Something had gone on and he hadn't been advised. "Looks like a good job." This was a generous concession.

While the others waited, Max studied the frame building, whistling an off-key note, frowning a little. He was plainly trying to reach a decision. A couple of times he shifted in the seat as though to leave the car. Finally, and almost absently, he hit the horn button a couple of times. Nothing happened. No one came from the building or appeared at the windows in answer to the summons. Max lit a fresh cigar with the elaborate pretense of being only a casual visitor. Then he tapped the

96

horn again for two brief squawks and stared off into the distance.

"I don't think anyone is aware of the presence, Max." Jan suppressed a giggle. "Shouldn't there have been a sign in the sky or, at least, a roll of thunder?"

Max ignored her. His features were a mask of interested innocence. He was, it seemed to say, a simple tourist who had halted casually and briefly to inspect this interesting development. Carol turned in the front seat, faced backward, rested her arms, and lowered her chin to them. Her eyes were bright, and she bit on a knuckle to keep from laughing. Max had confidently expected someone to come, possibly even running, when he sounded the summons on the horn. This had not happened. Now he silently debated whether to blow it again and risk being ignored again. He was also determined not to make an undignified surrender by getting out of the car and going to the doors. So they would wait and pretend they were not waiting.

The impasse was broken by a Jeep which skidded to a halt beside the Triumph. A young man in dungarees, his skin darkened and hair bleached by the sun, moved from behind the wheel, and stood up. His eyes rested and held on Jan with a bright impudence.

"Hi! Can I help you?" He was earnestly eager, and the question was directed to Jan.

Max turned with an expression of mild surprise. His meditations had been interrupted. After a moment he took the cigar from his mouth.

"You have a nigger by the name of Keating working around here?" The question was asked in a tone which made this seem highly improbable.

Carol, her face still turned toward Jan and Harrington, winced at the calculated vulgarity, the deliberate coarseness. Her eyes closed for a second. Harrington was expressionless. Jan wondered, as she had so many times before, what strange and senseless anger drove her father to this grossness. When he spoke the word "nigger" the word was a lash, tipped and cruel, meant to cut deeply, to draw blood.

97

"Do you mean *Mr.* Keating?" The words were softly voiced, but the title had been unmistakably accented. "An engineer?"

"His name is Keating. Big black nigger. Royal. Something like that. Royal Keating." Max would concede only this much. "I want to see him."

"Well now." The smile was gone. The young man stared almost unbelievingly at Max. His glance, with a question in it, traveled over the others and then back to Hertog. "If I were you"—he spoke slowly, distinctly—"and wanted to see *Mr.* Keating, I'd get out of that car, go in the doors there, and ask for his office. That's what I'd do. I don't know what the hell you are going to do." He dropped from the Jeep's floor to the ground and walked away.

"You just say Maximilian Hertog wants to see him." The voice was not raised.

For a second and all but imperceptibly the man's stride was broken as the name registered. But he did not halt or turn, nor did he look back as he reached the screen doors. They closed behind him with a small slap.

"He'll tell him." Max addressed the statement to no one, and no one answered.

They waited in a silence heavily charged. When Carol lit a cigarette, her hands trembled slightly, and the abrasive sound of the match was harsh and, seemingly, unnecessarily loud.

When the doors did swing open, Royal stood for a moment on the small entryway porch and looked down at the car in the driveway. He was wearing white shorts, sandals and calf-length ribbed white hose, a white sleeveless shirt open at the throat. Against these things the black of his skin was in startling relief. He half lifted a hand in greeting and then came down the steps and toward them. He walked with that easy big-cat stride Jan had always noticed. It caught at her now as always. There was excitement in it, an assured and unconscious grace, and she felt a curious suffocation. It clotted in her throat, and for a moment she thought she couldn't swallow.

"Hello, Mr. Hertog." His smile and greeting were mechanical and without warmth. Then they changed. "Hello, Miss Jan." He halted at her side of the car.

"Royal." She put out her hand, and he took it without hesitation. His glanced shifted to Carol and Harrington with polite interest. "Miss Wainwright. Mr. Harrington." Jan made the introductions. "Mr. Keating. How have you been, Royal?"

"Fine, thanks."

"You have quite a development here, Mr. Keating." Harrington was interested.

"It's taking shape." He laughed. "I wish it were mine, Mr. Harrington."

Without being offensively obvious, Royal was actually ignoring the presence of Max Hertog. He did this, it seemed, not out of resentment but rather with a deliberate and mischievous pleasure. There was almost a wink of humor in his eyes as he turned again to Jan.

"What brings you down this way?" He rested his hands on the door's top.

"I wanted to see you, Royal," Hertog interrupted.

"Well, I am flattered."

There was here a tiny exaggeration of courtesy, but he did not add "Mr. Hertog" to the statement. This was salient and unmistakably intentional.

Max's eyes hardened. He was far from being a stupid man, and the nuance here did not escape him. Small knots of muscle gathered at the corners of his jaw, but he kept his temper.

"You come and see me in Nassau, Royal." This was spoken as a casual invitation, but the command was on the surface.

"I'm afraid I won't be up that way for quite a spell." Royal made Hertog's order seem unimportant. "We're busy down here, and there's nothing really to take me over to Nassau. Maybe, when the job is finished, I'll be coming up to see Big Maum."

Of the four in the car only Harrington, perhaps, was not fully aware of what was happening. Carol, born to the islands and with the Negro strain running in her blood, was acutely sensitive to the inflections in Royal's words and understood well what he was doing. They created a strange and unfamiliar excitement in her. A black man was intentionally goading Maximilian Hertog. He was doing this without fear. Jan also

99

knew what Royal Keating was doing. A twin splash of color fevered her cheeks for a second and then disappeared. Her mouth was suddenly dry. Max understood. Eyelids all but dropped over his eyes. A slitted gaze held on Royal Keating. For the first time a nigger in the Bahamas was quietly but unmistakably defying him. A smart one who had been away to school. A big black who returned his stare without insolence but with a half-smiling confidence which was almost worse.

"Oh"—Max was outwardly undisturbed—"I think you'll probably come. A man will do almost anything if he thinks it is to his advantage."

Royal was politely interested. "Why should it be to my advantage?"

"Goddamn you." This was a roar of anger, and Max's face was contorted into a twisted mask of fury. "You black son of a bitch. You say sir or Mr. Hertog when you speak to me."

This was the victory. They all recognized it. Max Hertog had surrendered to his temper. He was captive now to an unreasonable anger, had been maneuvered there, expertly prodded, deftly guided. He seemed to shrink and was suddenly an old man impotent and without stature or pride as he realized what he had done. Blood receded from his face. His hands on the steering wheel shook, and he strained with the effort to still their trembling.

"Of course, Mr. Hertog." Royal pretended not to see what was apparent to them all. He was gravely courteous now. In his manner there was no suggestion of triumph. "It's possible I may be in Nassau next week." He turned. "Miss Jan." He nodded to her. "Miss Wainwright. Mr. Harrington." His smile touched them all. Then he turned and walked away.

For perhaps sixty seconds there was complete silence. Max was staring straight ahead. Jan didn't dare look at him.

"I let him cut me up, didn't I?" The words came with a painful slowness. "I even put the knife in his hand." He took a glass tube from a leather case, broke it open, and slid out the cigar. "He's a smart son of a bitch, that one is." He was talking to himself. He lit the cigar and drew on it with somber reflection. "I'll have to remember. I don't know that I ever let a man see me naked before. It's not a good feeling." For a few moments he allowed the cigar's rich fragrance to cloud about him. Then he half turned to look back, facing Jan and Harrington. He had himself in hand now. His voice was steady.

"Anything more you'd like to see?"

"I don't think so." Harrington answered for them all.

"Well, then, suppose we go back and have a late afternoon drink on *The Witch*. Hatchet Bay at sunset is something to remember."

No one spoke on the way back, and the road seemed to turn and wind forever.

VI

Behind and above the darkly polished bar, three young girls twisted and writhed, jerking themselves into a series of awkward poses to the incessant beat of a long-haired rock trio. Breasts, bare save for small, glittering pasties over the nipples, bounced and trembled. Rhinestone-clustered G-strings covered shaved pelvic clefts. Faces were without animation, set in fixed smiles. The dance seemed interminable and without grace or rhythm. Certainly it offered no erotic stimulation to most of the patrons who drank, smoked, pondered over the *Racing Form,* talked, and occasionally glanced at the runway.

Sherry Melnick poked at an ice cube in his drink with a long, perfectly manicured finger. A plastic stirrer was handy, but Sherry's hands were tanned and graceful; he liked to use them, admiring their effortless dexterity. Across from him Christopher Baildon was slouched deep in his chair, pretending complete boredom, but his eyes strayed now and then to the go-go girls. He was mildly entertained by the way their buttocks snapped in and out as though impelled by the frenzy of an orgasm. He wondered idly what would happen if they displayed this gymnastic talent in bed. It could snap a man off as though it were a dead branch. He looked up and grinned at Melnick for no particular reason.

"Want some lunch before we go to the track?"

Chris shook his head. "Not unless you do." He looked at his watch.

Sherry Melnick had always insisted he could smell a thief. The odor was that of an electrical discharge. When he was with Baildon, the scent was strong. He wondered why and then came to the simple conclusion that despite the surface innocence, Christopher Baildon was a thief. This interested Sherry since he had his own share of larceny.

Melnick was indistinguishable from the dozens of young men who daily appeared on Miami's streets, in brokerage offices, at flag-studded real estate developments, on the beach, Flagler Street or in a convertible with vivid brunettes or blondes. He was deeply tanned, brisk, affable with a ready smile, handsome, gracious and as acquisitive and unmoral as a raccoon. He was the energetic and acting head of the Melnick Realty Enterprises with offices in a Flagler Street building and desk space in several of the best hotels, both in Miami proper and on the beach.

Sherry was New York born, the family having progressed in three generations from Clinton Street to the Grand Concourse, to Riverside Drive and then Great Neck. He had been educated in the public schools, matriculated at Columbia, was taken by Sigma Nu with its house on 114th Street. He was swarthily handsome, an outstanding swimmer and tennis player on the university's teams. His manners were unobtrusive and, therefore, good. He was shrewd and ambitious and successfully escaped the entanglement of marriage. He had been tempted a couple of times, not because he was overwhelmed by sentiment but because the girls' fathers were well established. He thought better of it, however, and decided there were easier paths to success.

An uncle had guided the Melnick Realty Enterprises through the dizzy ascent of the boom, held it together while Depression years wore less determined men down, rode with it during the second and really substantial activity in Florida land. When the years suggested his retirement, he sent for Sherry, who had always been a favorite nephew. He offered the young man a job with a drawing account and commission.

Sherry refused. The uncle then suggested a regular salary and a higher commission, plus the use of an apartment, in a Melnick-owned building, and a company car. Again Sherry refused, and this pleased the old man. His nephew was not hungry or too eager or willing to try any position with the hope of bettering himself. He then made the offer of a partnership. They had a drink on this, and the papers were drawn by Sherry's lawyer.

The old man never had an occasion to regret the move. Sherry doubled and tripled the business. He trained a small corps of hard-hitting, fast-talking and -acting salesmen. He branched out to take in property on the Florida Keys, the state's great farmland and grazing acres in the interior. He developed moderately priced housing projects all along the east and west coasts of the peninsula. He was once voted Miami's Young Man of the Year and was known to every hotel doorman, restaurant and nightclub maître d'hôtel, taxicab driver and topflight call girl in Miami and the beach as an easy spender who never became drunk and troublesome. Miami had been created for the Sherry Melnicks, and they returned the compliment.

Sherry had taken an immediate interest in Christopher Baildon and the Aunt Martha Candy Company. The odd combination set up an extrasensory vibration. Baildon had expressed an interest in a certain tract on Grand Bahama and wanted Melnick Enterprises to act for him. Ordinarily this would have been a simple matter of closing a deal for a client and collecting a commission, but Sherry smelled thief.

He began a systematic cultivation of Christopher Baildon. This wasn't difficult, for they had many things in common. They shared the natural exuberance of youth; both were personable; both, apparently, were without an immediate need of money and so met each other evenly balanced. Chris played a well above the average game of tennis, and Sherry had an extended guest card arranged for him at the beach and tennis club where he was a member. Both were familiar with and enjoyed small boats and deep-sea fishing. Baildon was immediately attractive to the many girls Sherry brought around.

Chris asked no favors. He picked up his share of bar, restaurant and nightclub tabs, but no more. He occupied a large two-bedroom suite in one of Miami's most glittering beachfront hotels. Sherry never asked him why the extra bedroom, but he was curious. At the desk and with an assistant manager with whom he had a passing acquaintance he asked about the suite with its sun deck, bar, living room and bedrooms. The inquiry was met with a flat answer. It was maintained the year around by the Atlas Company, whatever that was.

Sherry had a Levantine flair for and a delight in intrigue. There was a mystery here. He could find no listing for an Atlas Company, so it must be linked with the equally unobtrusive Aunt Martha Candy Company. Information was easily passed back and forth between Miami's real estate brokers. He knew two other firms had been commissioned by Baildon to negotiate for tracts on Grand Bahama. He set about separating them and diverting the entire operation to Melnick Enterprises. Without effort he and Chris had reached a first-name basis, and a day rarely passed when they were not in each other's company. They found each other congenial. It was no more complicated than that. Despite the fact he sometimes appeared an ingenious man, Chris actually didn't open up much. When asked where he lived, he simply said, "The Bahamas." Christopher Baildon, Sherry quickly learned, was no simple character. There was a cold and inflexible streak in him. He didn't parry or evade questions he preferred not to answer. He simply ignored them and kept silent while the questioner's embarrassment grew.

The purchase of Grand Bahama was involved and in many cases maddeningly slow. Over the hundreds of years there had been conflicting grants made by various governors. In some cases the same parcel of land had been given to half a dozen different persons. Records were incomplete or nonexistent. Some property was claimed by squatters. Some was in clear title. Most of it was Crown land. These things Baildon had reported to Max Hertog. Such small acreage of clean title as they could find they bought in the name of the Aunt Martha Candy Company. The checks carried the signature of Christopher

Baildon and a Miami attorney. From this Sherry concluded Baildon was not Aunt Martha. If he had been, a co-signer would have been unnecessary. Sherry puzzled over these things and found the activities of Melnick-Baildon-Aunt Martha increasingly entertaining. The commissions were small and of little consequence to Melnick Enterprises. They meant nothing. Baildon and Aunt Martha did. Sherry smelled a thief somewhere. He knew he could get all the information on Christopher Baildon. A few, quietly voiced inquiries in Nassau would yield everything he wanted to know. Sherry decided to allow the skein of tangled identities to unwind itself.

They were on their way to the races at Tropical Park. Sherry had picked Chris up at his hotel. They drove across the causeway to Miami proper, and the go-go bar had been a sudden impulse on Chris' part.

"I've never been in one of these damn things. This time of day should make it particularly gruesome."

So they had gone in, found a table, and ordered drinks neither wanted at this hour. Now there was an abrupt cessation to the ear-numbing beat of the music. The girls disappeared. No one missed them. The flow and ebb of conversations were again audible.

"There must be some other reward for what they do." Chris nodded in the direction of a girl as she disappeared from the runway. "Or"—he grinned—"is it as they say, money is everything?"

"I think they're waiting to be discovered by a wealthy Cuban refugee. Blond whores and mistresses occupied special places in pre-Castro Cuba." Sherry indicated a large round table. The chairs were occupied by neatly dressed men who were obviously Latin. Their blue serge was a sort of uniform, as were their small mustaches and pointed beards. "Cubans in Miami always seem to be engaged in a dark conspiracy. They're probably talking about last Sunday's soccer game but give the appearance of putting together a revolutionary junta. Some of them honestly think they can overthrow Castro from a bar or coffeehouse in Miami, but most want someone else to do it for them."

106

The lank-haired musicians and a different trio of girls appeared on the runway. They were greeted with complete indifference and, in their turn, accorded the same contempt for the patrons.

"Some of these places," Sherry continued, "advertise the Happy Cocktail Hour. It begins at eleven o'clock in the morning, complete with go-go girls, topless, bottomless, sexless. Imagine what sort of hangover you'd have to have to want go-go girls at eleven in the morning?"

"Let's get out of here." Chris pushed back his chair. They left their drinks untasted.

Sherry drove out Okeechobee Road to Le Jeune on the way to Hialeah. Melnick Enterprises kept a box at the track for the winter meet. He and Chris used it almost daily, making modest bets, winning or losing a few dollars. Neither was a compulsive gambler. They liked the stimulation of the crowd and the running grace of the animals.

They were well out on the highway before Chris spoke again. "Is Sherry short for something?"

"No. My mother just liked the sound of the word."

"The hell you say? It's really Sherry?"

"Uh-huh."

"Well, I'll be damned."

The car's top was down; the air, as it flowed past, was soft and richly fragrant, sun on newly turned earth, still water in the drainage canal. Chris leaned back, tilting his face to the warm sky.

"Do you know." It wasn't a question but a rambling introduction to his thoughts. "I'm working around the edge of something, but I'm damned if I know what it is. There's a lot of money involved and some to be made if we're smart enough. But we have to know what to be smart about."

This was what Sherry Melnick had been waiting, hoping, for. Chris was opening up voluntarily. He wasn't to be hurried or, Sherry sensed, even replied to at this moment. He remained silent.

"Between us," Chris reflected, "we ought to be able to cut ourselves in on something big. I'm not giving anything away.

I'm including you because I'm sure we will need each other."
He stopped talking abruptly and was silent for the next couple of miles. "You see, I don't exactly know what is going on.
Something is shaping up for Grand Bahama, but I'm not sure
what or even where. That's how we could get the hair burned
off of us, by trying to play when we don't know what the game
is."

"Who or what is Aunt Martha?"

For a long moment Sherry thought he had moved in too
quickly. He had a feeling Baildon could be scared off by a
too-eager curiosity on his part.

"I suppose so." Chris made the statement doubtfully.

"What?"

"I mean—" Baildon nodded agreement—"I suppose you
have to know that. Otherwise, none of it makes much sense.
Maximilian Hertog is Aunt Martha."

Sherry whistled and held the note for a long time. He experienced a growing charge of excitement. Wherever Max
Hertog moved there was action.

"What does Hertog want with Grand Bahama?"

"That's what I don't know." He turned to meet Sherry's
skeptical glance. "I really don't. If I did, it would be simple."

"Well, we ought to find out, don't you think?"

"He's sure not going to tell you or me." Baildon smiled at
the preposterous fancy. "I work for him, usually doing this
sort of thing. The front man. He never opens up all the way.
Most of the time I have to do things in a half-light, like now.
Max doesn't like me, but he trusts me. I don't talk. Or," he
amended, "I never have before."

"How did this start? His interest in Grand Bahama?
Maybe," Sherry prodded gently, "if you go back over it,
something will occur to you."

"No." Chris shook his head. "There was no lead-in. No preliminary work I know of. He just said one morning he was
going to buy up Grand Bahama and for me to come to Miami and get things moving. He set up the Aunt Martha Candy
Company so he wouldn't appear. He often operates this way.
God knows how many corporate setups he has."

They were in the heavy track-bound traffic on Bougainvillea now. Occupied with it, Melnick didn't press additional questions. There was no reason for Baildon to hold back anything. He had opened the subject voluntarily.

They had lunch and a few drinks in the Turf Club, made their calculations on the *Racing Form,* placed their bets, and won or lost without any real interest. Both were absorbed now by the possibilities on Grand Bahama.

"A real estate boom on Grand Bahama just wouldn't make any sense." Melnick made the observation without any preliminary discussion. They were waiting for the fifth race. "I could see it on almost any other Out Island but not there."

"When Max Hertog moves, the impossible happens."

Sherry nodded. He was certain Bay Street would erupt once Max Hertog's interest in Grand Bahama became known. No one would stop to consider his motives. It would be agreed that where Max Hertog rooted, there were bound to be financial truffles. Bay Street would be snout-deep in the island. It might not be Hertog's intention, but a boom would be created. Then it would be a question of getting in and then out with a profit. Still a question nagged at Sherry Melnick. Was that Hertog's only purpose: to create an artificial flurry? Somehow he didn't think so. He turned to Baildon.

"Is Hertog a hard man to meet socially?"

"He would be for you."

"Why?"

"You're Jewish." It was a simple statement of fact. "Niggers and Jews with"—he grinned with a disarming good nature—"maybe a few white Protestants and Catholics thrown in."

"It's really just like that?" Sherry wasn't offended.

"Just like that. Blacks and Jews. No reason I know of."

"It's common enough. It used to bother me, but it doesn't anymore."

"I didn't like to say it."

"Forget it. I had an idea that meeting him socially and with the Melnick real estate operations in Florida, he just might say something about this Grand Bahama thing. It was a half-cocked idea at best. If you don't know, it isn't likely he would open up to a stranger."

They left after the sixth race to avoid the traffic jam which would develop later. Sherry drove at a leisurely pace, absorbed in his thoughts. He had been right about Baildon. The thief was there, waiting for the opportunity. Together they might hurry it along. He was just a little dubious of the value of Chris' information, but he couldn't ignore the fact Aunt Martha was buying on Grand Bahama and Maximilian Hertog was Aunt Martha.

"I may go over to Nassau for the weekend. Want to come along?" Chris made the suggestion.

"I might. What's the action?"

Chris grinned. "A few native girls with hibiscus blossoms in their hair. Bongo drums. Maybe they'll think you're a Great White God come in big ship with wings."

"It sounds pretty good. You have a family?"

"My father and a half-cracked aunt. Come to think about it, the old gentleman is a little dotty also. They rattle around together in a hell of a big house on the hill." This was the first time he had revealed any of his private life. "I keep an apartment of my own where the native girls can come and lie down when they want to get out of the sun."

"You are, indeed, a benefactor. We'll have a go at the natives."

Jan was stretched out on a deck chair within a shaded section of the suite's lanai. Below, the sugar-white sand of the beach was dotted with brightly colored umbrellas. Beneath them the tanned vacationists sprawled, drinking gin and tonic or assorted mineral waters. They played gin rummy, talked, stared at the purple ocean, and critically assayed the various shapes of the men and girls who were strewn about. Almost everyone was a little on the make, and the results were generally surprisingly good. Jan had thought about joining them and then decided against it. She reached for the rum collins on a taboret, took a long swallow, and lit a cigarette. Actually, she didn't particularly want to be in Miami. It had been an impulse of the morning. She had packed a bag, called the Hertog offices, and told Carol she wanted Max's plane to fly her to Miami. Then she had called some friends there and accepted an invitation to a party that night. Max kept the suite on a yearly lease, and it never occurred to her to go any other place. She knew Chris Baildon was occupying the rooms, but one of the bedrooms was free. Checking in, she was warmly greeted by the hotel's first assistant manager who discreetly made no mention of the fact that Christopher Baildon would be sharing the accommodations with her. Now she wasn't at all sure she wanted to be in Miami. Max's plane was on call for her at the airport. She decided to wait for Chris.

There had been a time, shortly after Chris had gone to work for Max, when she had indulged herself in a brief unromantic interlude. It had always struck her as a little odd that there was no real heart in the affair. She never really gave much of herself, but the men who had been her lovers were usually captive. Chris seemed totally unimpressed by the fact that he was making love to the beautiful Jan Hertog. They mated with the intensity of alley cats and with as much affection, and the affair tapered off into a state of pleasant indifference. If Chris were free, he could take her to the Markoes' party tonight. If not, she'd go alone. Enid Markoe always provided a few extra men.

There was a sound of voices in the foyer, and she half turned as Chris and Melnick came into the living room.

"Hi!" she called.

At the unexpected sound of a voice both men turned with quick surprise. Baildon moved toward the lanai with Melnick following.

"Oh!" Chris halted within the sliding doors' frame. There was an unmistakable shade of annoyance on his face. "I didn't know you were coming over, Jan."

"Neither did I until this morning." She spoke to Baildon, but her gaze went past him to Melnick.

Baildon covered a half-smile. "Miss Hertog. Sherry Melnick."

"Hello." She continued her lazy inspection.

111

"Miss Hertog."

The exchange was brief, but it held a frank appraisal. Both knew exactly what they were doing. Melnick deliberately allowed his gaze to travel over her near nakedness, pausing momentarily at her navel, resting again at her breasts, and then holding on her face. In his smile there was open approval. He was undisturbed by her mocking expression as she coolly surveyed him. She concluded her estimate and half nodded. The preliminaries were concluded. They observed them as do two fighters who touch gloves briefly in the ring's center before the contest.

"I'll get another room, of course." Chris made no effort to hide his displeasure.

"Why?" Jan answered mechanically. Her attention was still on Melnick. "I'm not afraid of you. The doors have locks."

"Didn't your father tell you I was here?"

"I didn't tell Max I was coming over." She turned to him now. "For God's sake don't be so prissy. Make yourselves a drink." She indicated the portable bar drawn to one side of the sun deck. "Sit down. Are you tourist or native, Mr. Melnick? Is your name really Sherry?"

"I'm native by adoption." He crossed to the bar and mixed a short scotch and soda. "My name's really Sherry." He came back, halted above her. She waited a moment and then moved to give him room on the chaise. He sat and felt her toes dig into his side. "Am I crowding you?"

She laughed. A healthy, amused burst of sound. Then she turned to Chris, laughter still bubbling within her.

"What are you doing tonight?"

Chris shrugged. "Nothing in particular. Why?"

"I want someone to take me to Enid Markoe's party."

"I'll take you." Sherry made the statement without emphasis.

Her head swiveled, and she stared at him with mild astonishment. Their eyes met, and in Melnick's there was a challenging insolence.

"Yes," she finally said. "I guess you will. Do you know Enid?"

"No. You do."

Jan reached for a cigarette. Sherry leaned toward her with a lighter. His fingers deliberately touched and held hers. Watching, Chris permitted himself a smile of wry amusement. Once he had followed the antics of a pair of cranes as they thrust and pecked at each other with their long beaks. They circled warily and flew upward in a sudden flurry of wings and feet. It was all part of a mating dance, the ritual before the hen submitted to the cock's mastery. That, he thought, was what went on here now. Both Jan and Sherry were aware of what was happening. They were certain of the outcome and were moved by instinct. Baildon was always amazed by Jan's ability to play the demure wanton with such consummate skill.

"What do you do in Miami?" Jan leaned back against the cushions.

"Real estate. Development. Right now I'm working with Chris on something for your father."

"Really?" She wasn't particularly interested. "Do you know my father?"

"No."

"Max will despise you almost on sight."

"Because I'm a Jew?"

"No." She was surprised by the question and half sat up. "I hadn't thought about that. You don't look Jewish."

"I suppose that's meant as a compliment."

"You can suppose any damn thing you like." The quick impatience had a honed edge. "I meant there is a brassy cocksureness about you Max will find offensive. He likes to think he has a patent on it and reserves it for himself. You will probably infuriate Max. Won't he, Chris?"

"Probably." Baildon was uninterested.

"Then," Sherry mused. "I ought to stay out of his way."

"You ought to, but you won't. I'll see to that." She grinned at him. "I can't wait to bring you home to Father. He needs to be shaken now and then. It's good for his liver." She swung her legs over the side of the chaise and sat up, turning to Chris. "Why don't you come along? Enid can always use extra men at her parties. She needs replacements for those who pass out."

"No, thanks." Chris shook his head. "You're sure you don't want me to move out of here until you go back?"

"Why? It's always nice to have a man around the house. Stay where you are." She turned to Sherry. "Pick me up about eight."

They both watched her as she crossed the living room and closed a door behind her.

"So that's Jan Hertog," Sherry speculated thoughtfully.

"Wearing one of her many faces." Chris wasn't particularly interested in Melnick's reaction. "Don't try to fit her into a mold. She's one thing now and something else an hour later." His brief smile was one of anticipation. "It ought to be an interesting contest."

"I'm going to marry her." Sherry dropped the statement casually.

"Never." Chris was emphatic. "You'll only make a fool of yourself. Romp and have fun together. Let it go at that. I know her pretty well."

"How well?" Sherry was deliberately crude.

"Max would kill you." Chris refused the question. "I really believe he would."

"Well, I'll give him a chance."

"Never." Chris repeated the statement, but this time it carried less assurance. He studied Melnick intently. "At least," he temporized, "I think never. Jesus," he whispered, "I can hear Max Hertog all the way over here."

Sliding far down on her spine in the convertible, Jan leaned her head back against the cushions and watched the moon as it sliced through scattered clouds. Sherry drove with an assured familiarity of the road, glancing down as her cheek pressed lightly against his arm. It was almost four o'clock in the morning. The party had run to a pattern: overly long, noisy and generally dull with everyone drinking too much with the idea that something wonderful and exciting would happen any minute.

"Where are we going?" Jan asked sleepily.

"Over the causeway to the beach and your hotel."

"It will be crowded, won't it? You and I and Chris? Don't you have a place?"

"Yes. But I'm not taking you there."

"Why not?" For the first time she displayed a mild interest in what was being said. "Won't your wife understand?"

"If I had a wife, I would have told you."

"Yes," she admitted. "Yes. I think you would but only because I'm sure you know it wouldn't make any difference to me."

"You work pretty hard at being a character, don't you?"

"No. It comes easily enough." There was a faint trace of regret.

She settled against him more firmly, one hand resting on his leg. This was a new experience. She didn't question for a moment his intention to take her home and this wasn't the way the game was played. He was making up new rules and she had to wonder why. It wasn't simply to nudge her curiosity. Already they understood each other pretty well. Jan was puzzled, not by Sherry Melnick, but by her reaction to him. Half a dozen times during the evening, when they had stood talking, eating and drinking with a group, her hand had sought his. For some reason she wanted the reassurance of his presence. It was a small, conscious gesture of dependency on her part. She wondered why. It was not in her nature. Certainly she wasn't being swept away, lost to all reason, by a man she barely knew. She wasn't even sure she liked him. That was the strange part of it all: to know the attraction was there and at the same time question its quality. She dismissed as shoddy the notion that Sherry's appeal to her was entirely physical. There had been several men at the Markoes' party who were equally handsome in the same tanned and burnished fitness. Two or three of them she had known for a long time. One had briefly been her lover in Nassau. Neither he nor the others stimulated her now. She was pleasantly amused by their attention, but she had no illusions. The word, once having been spoken, came easily with its repetition. Jan Hertog the nymph. The easy, uncomplicated lay in the back seat of a car or even standing in the shadows of an unlighted terrace. She was not really disturbed by the knowledge. Those things she had done and might well do again. She had indulged her body in its demands. If it sometimes defiled the spirit, there was no visible mark. The spirit was a thing of great resilience and meant to survive the outrageous commands of the flesh. No. What she felt for Sherry Melnick, this stranger, was outside all previous knowledge. He had, she sensed, the alert predatory instincts of a hawk. He was, she thought, an opportunist and ruthless, but, she felt certain, there was no cheapness in him. He would not debase himself for an end. In these things he was much like Max. He could be relentless in the pursuit of what he wanted, but every move would be plotted and calculated in advance. That he had no intention of taking her to bed this night piqued her vanity and perversely aroused a desire. *Damn it,* she told herself angrily, *I'm letting him confuse me deliberately.*

"Why aren't we going to your place?" Genuine curiosity forced the words. "Are you playing hard to get?"

"No. I'm saving you for another time."

"You're taking a hell of a lot for granted."

"Am I?"

There was only the steamy sound of the tires on pavement, wet at this hour with a heavy dew. Jan stared through the windshield as the wipers clicked back and forth.

"No. No. I guess not."

She took a package of cigarettes from the dashboard shelf, lit one, and inhaled deeply. Oddly enough she discovered she was trembling inside, although the tremors did not show on her hands.

"What is it you want? What are you after?" She waited.

"You."

She expected him to amplify the statement, but he seemed to feel everything had been said.

"Aside from the obvious," she spoke slowly, "why?"

"Until you made the obvious obvious, I had almost forgotten you were Jan Hertog."

"You mean Max Hertog's daughter, don't you?"

"Yes. I suppose so."

116

Crinkles of amusement gathered about her eyes. "Have you any idea what Max Hertog would say?"

"But I haven't any intention of asking Max Hertog to marry me."

She was incredulous. "You're asking me to marry you?"

"Uh-huh." He reached for her cigarette, drew on it a couple of times, then handed it back. "That's what I have in mind."

"Aside from how I feel, and that doesn't seem to be important right now, Max wouldn't stand for it."

"That's what Chris said."

She sat upright, complete astonishment stamped on her features. "You told Chris Baildon you were going to marry me?"

He merely nodded while she stared at him.

"Well, I'll be damned." She sank back into the seat. "What did Chris say?"

"He said Max Hertog would kill me or have it done. I don't believe it. He may yell a little. That's all."

"Yell a little? Would you like to hear what he'd say?"

"I can guess. The names have been popular for a couple of thousand years. Jew. Kike. Yid. Sheeny."

She stared at him, shocked by the vehemence. The words as he spoke them were obscene, foul, coated with hatred, slimy with unreasoning prejudice.

"This is ridiculous." She sought to make the statement convincing.

"I can't argue with that. I'm a little surprised myself."

"I just bowled you over? Swept you off your feet? One look at me and you were reduced to an emotional jelly? You touched me and your heart stood still?"

"You're getting the idea." He was approving.

She shook her head bemusedly. "When is this happy event to take place? When are we to be one?" She made herself appear wide-eyed and breathless.

"I'll give you time to get used to me and your old man accustomed to seeing me around."

The car swept into the wide driveway of the hotel's entrance. A porter, mop in hand, paused to watch as Sherry came around, opened the door, and held it for her. His eyes followed them as they moved up the canopied walk. He thought they were a fine-looking pair and wondered, as he had many times before, how it must be to be young, white and with plenty of money and never a worry in the world.

VII

From the eminence of her marble throne the sculptured likeness of Her Majesty Queen Victoria turns an admonishing eye on Bay Street, reminding those who glance her way that life should be more than a frivolous pursuit of happiness. Few of those who pass give her much attention. Tourists, with their flowered shirts and bony knees below plaid shorts, frequently have their pictures taken at her side. Birds sometimes perch on the serene and regal brow and leave their droppings there.

For many years Victoria has stared disapprovingly at a two-story building of pink stucco. It is an unpretentious structure, and its second floor with a balcony is a refreshingly dim retreat. Street noises come faintly here. Overhead fans, with their broad mahogany blades, turn and sweep the air to keep it fresh. Jalousies are drawn over open windows to hold back the sun's glare. The rooms are pleasantly furnished; the small bar is deftly tended by a smiling white-coated Negro. The servants move with quiet efficiency and are unfailingly attentive without being obtrusive. Here all voices are muted, and the gentlemen of Nassau, with now and then their American guests, gather regularly in the afternoons to gamble. Tradition and gentility rule the Eleutheran Club. In the central room with its walls of an eye-soothing pastel green, there is a roulette table and one for baccarat. The smaller rooms are for bridge and poker with the club taking a percentage of the pots and play. The intrusion of such vulgarities as dice and black-jack have been staunchly resisted by the club's operator and owner, Mr. Stanley Makepiece.

The club is an institution, venerable and respectable. For many years it has operated discreetly under the special dispensation of a Certificate of Exemption quietly granted to Mr. Makepiece's father. At that time a liberal-minded government recognized and approved of the sporting instincts of gentle-men who were willing to wager considerable sums of money on the turn of a card or the dropping of a small pellet into a numbered slot. It was desirable that they have a place where such enthusiasms could be quietly vented, and the Eleutheran Club was constituted for their pleasure. So well established is the place that those who play there regularly think of it as their private club, a personal institution. Mr. Makepiece was regarded as its chief steward, rather than the actual owner at whose pleasure or whim any one of them could be blacklisted and barred. As for Mr. Makepiece, he was tolerant of this pro-prietary attitude as long as it did not get out of hand. Elegantly tailored, he frequently strolled about the rooms nodding or speaking a pleasant word to the members at their tables. Now and then he condescended to take a small glass of sherry at the bar, but he never sat in on the games. His lean, aristocratic frame, the long, almost equine face, the neatly brushed and parted silvered hair, the grave but friendly features lent a proper dignity to the establishment. He didn't mind in the least that some of the members spoke of him among themselves as "good old Makepiece," the faithful retainer. He was an ad-mirer of the Dickensian mood himself. He lived with quiet distinction in a fine house on the Hill, was acknowledged to have a place among the island's first families, contributed generously to all worthy charities, and had a proper respect for the theory of empire. He thought affectionately of the Eleu-theran Club as a personal monument, which, gratifyingly enough, annually contributed a substantial sum to his already comfortable fortune.

He sat now in one of the large, soft leather chairs in Maximilian Hertog's office and turned a bland expression of polite interest on Max, who was roving up and down over the rare Oriental carpeting with an attitude of hunched belligerency. He whirled suddenly and stabbed a finger in Mr. Makepiece's direction.

"I'll go to seven hundred and fifty thousand, Stanley." He dared his visitor not to accept.

"But, my dear fellow, I have already said a million."

Although he was island-born and the native speech was ready upon his tongue, Mr. Makepiece frequently resorted to such locutions as "my dear boy" or "dear chap." He had discovered the expressions in second-rate British novels, and they delighted his sense of humor. They never failed to infuriate Max Hertog, as they were meant to do.

"I am not your dear fellow," Max all but shouted. He lowered his head with a bull-like gesture and glared at Mr. Makepiece, who was undisturbed. "I am not your dear fellow at all, and you damn well know it." He took a cigar from its tube, bit off the end, and spat it onto the beautifully faded carpet.

Mr. Makepiece winced and made a reproving steeple with his fingers. Over it he regarded Maximilian Hertog sadly.

"And you know, Stanley," Max continued, "if I want to bring the pressure, I can, probably, run your ass right out of the Bahamas. I could make it so uncomfortable you'd want to leave. What do you say to that?"

"I say," Mr. Makepiece replied in a soft voice, "even if you could do such a thing, and there is a small question in my mind, dear boy, it still would not solve your problem." He clicked his tongue against the surface of his upper denture to make a sound of commiseration. "I have you, as the saying more or less goes, on the hip. Haven't I? Not many persons can claim that distinction over Maximilian Hertog."

Max brooded on this for almost a full minute. He could, he believed, make things so unpleasant for Stanley Makepiece the man might actually be forced to leave Nassau. But, as Stanley had just pointed out, this would solve nothing. At issue was the Certificate of Exemption held by Stanley Makepiece in the Eleutheran Club's name.

"Now, Stanley"—Max adopted his most conciliatory tone—"why do you insist on a million dollars? You are already a wealthy man."

"But so are you, Max. Why do you object to paying the sum? One million. It has a nice round sound, like that of a ripe melon. One million. It has a fine, solid ring to it. Substantial. Very substantial, dear chap."

Max growled, scratched at his ear, dug a finger into the hairy cavity. He glared at Stanley Makepiece as though this would somehow wither him. Mr. Makepiece, though, seemed to flower beneath the heat. He smiled affably back.

"Now you just suppose I have a Certificate of Exemption rammed through. It might be difficult, but I have enough influence to do it. You know damn well I have." His hand slammed down on the desk's surface.

"But, my dear boy"—Mr. Makepiece's expression was one of complete bewilderment—"why don't you do just that instead of having at me with those unpleasant threats? It would solve everything. This heated talk of money is really vulgar."

"Because"—Max bellowed the word—"you know god-damned well it would make too much of a stink right now. It's just the thing the Progressive Liberal Party would grab on to. Those smart niggers would make a banner of it to wave in everyone's face as an example of more and more white privilege. I'm not going to give them another issue. There may come a time—" He halted abruptly, leaving the thought unfinished. Anger almost brought him to the point of being indiscreet. "Now, Stanley"—he spoke with a soothing guile—"seven hundred and fifty thousand." He spoke the words as though they were diamonds and dangled them enticingly before Makepiece's eyes. "Seven hundred and fifty thousand. Is it a deal?" He paused expectantly.

"It just doesn't have the right sound, Max." Makepiece shook his head regretfully. "It's not rounded out. I'm sorry."

Max took a deep, shuddering breath. Pain clouded his eyes. He made a gesture with one hand as though to clutch his agonized heart and appeared to sink weakly against the desk. It propped him up. He waited.

Stanley Makepiece took a cigarette from a brightly decorated cardboard box. He clung to an old habit, a taste for the heavy, rich flavor of Egyptian tobacco. He imported these from London, where a few smokers still made a small market for Egyptian and Turkish tobacco. He lit the cigarette now and inhaled with pleasure.

Max watched him and then yelled, "Carol. Carol, come in here." He straightened up, no longer stricken.

The sound must have carried into Bay Street. Recounting the story later, Makepiece insisted all traffic halted and the waves froze for a moment before breaking on the beach.

Carol came to the office and closed the door behind her. Makepiece regarded her with open approval. She smiled at him.

"Carol. Make out a check to—" He pointed, unable to speak the name. His finger trembled. "For one million dollars. Draw it on the Inter Island Bank."

"I would prefer it be made to the Eleutheran Club," Makepiece interposed, and winked at Carol.

"Very well," Max agreed weakly. He was enjoying the scene now. This was the dying gladiator speaking. "Make it payable to the Eleutheran Club. Then dictate a short memo. We'll have Sutter, Tracy and Longworth draw a formal agreement later. We're buying the Eleutheran Club and with it the Certificate of Exemption it holds. Have Sutter prepare an official notification of a transfer of the Eleutheran Club to Paradise Island."

Carol nodded and left. Makepiece's eyes followed her, resting with pleasure on the curve of her hip.

"Damned fine-looking girl, that one." He shook his head enviously. "Pleasure to have her around. Gets your pecker up, doesn't it?"

Max ignored the gambit for a discussion of Carol's physical assets.

"Isn't it fortunate for you, dear boy, Mr. Harrington doesn't have your mind of devious cunning? He might have thought of this himself. With all he had invested, another million or two for the certificate would have been nothing. As a matter of fact, at one time I thought of approaching him with the idea. I could have really whipsawed the two of you then."

"I'm surprised you didn't." Max was again pleasantly relaxed. The deal had been made. He nursed no resentment. "I would have hated to bid against him."

"I didn't go to him, dear boy, because we of the Establishment must hang together. Mr. Harrington is an outsider. Whatever pie is cut in the islands we should share among ourselves. Isn't that so?"

Max nodded. Those within the Establishment might knife one another and take delight in the bloodletting. But they drew into solid ranks against the intrusion of an outsider.

"You know"—Makepiece rose and strolled to the windows—"I shall miss going to the club." He stood, looking down on Bay Street. "I hadn't realized until now how much a part of me the old place is. I will look back on it with affection."

"You can come and manage the casino for me." Max was sincere. "I'll have to have someone."

Makepiece turned to regard him with surprise. "My dear boy, you can't be thinking of operating it yourself."

"Why not?" Max was astonished.

"My dear, dear boy. Do sit down." He was honestly concerned and motioned Hertog to a chair. "Now listen carefully. I know it is not in your nature to take advice. A casino, such as you plan on Paradise Island, is not a simple thing. You will have dice, roulette, blackjack, slot machines, cashiers, security guards. My dear boy, you would be a lamb. Your dealers, pit bosses, bookkeepers and boxmen would steal you naked. You wouldn't have the slightest idea what to expect, and your employees would discover this the first day. You simply can't hire someone to look after your interests. He wouldn't do it. The temptation would be too great. You are naïve, dear Max."

Hertog rubbed at his chin. Actually, he confessed to himself, he had not thought far beyond securing the Eleutheran Club's certificate. Then, as with his many other enterprises, he planned to hire the right man or men to do the job. He realized now this wouldn't do. He had no notion at all of how a

124

casino should be run or what the return to the house from the play should be. Stanley was right. He would be a fat goose for the plucking.

"What do you suggest, Stanley?" He was almost meek.

"Were I you"—Makepiece was thoughtful—"I would put the operation of the casino into familiar hands. Say to them, 'You come in. Select your own trained staff. Bankroll the tables. I will take a percentage of the gross. The rest is up to you.'"

Max plainly didn't like the idea. "I have never taken in partners when I could help it," he objected.

"Believe me, you can't help it this time. I don't say those you will do business with are the most savory characters or the organizations behind them spotless, but they do control all the big gambling. Las Vegas. Reno. Miami. Call it the Syndicate if you like. Cosa Nostra. The Mafia. It doesn't really matter. You will be honestly dealt with because it will be to their advantage to see that you are. They have wanted to get into the Bahamas ever since Cuba was closed. I can give you certain names. I have been approached several times for the Eleutheran Club. I refused. My operation was small and intimate. I really didn't need the money. I sold to you because it pleased me to do so."

Max nodded. Everything Makepiece had said made good sense. "Is there someone to contact in Miami? I have Baildon over there now on something else. He could make the initial meeting."

"I will make a couple of telephone calls for you tonight. One to New Orleans. One to Las Vegas, possibly." He smiled with an almost childish delight. "That does sound sinister, doesn't it, my dear boy? Right out of the gangster movies. Bang! Bang!" He laughed. "There is a fraternity among gamblers. Small as the Eleutheran Club was, its certificate was highly prized. I have been much sought after. You hear things. How vice, narcotics, gambling and a hundred smaller enterprises are controlled by a syndicate. This is probably true, but the men at the top no longer talk from the sides of their mouths or spit on the floor. This is a third generation from the immigrant stock. They are college-educated, well mannered. They can,

125

of course, be ruthless." Makepiece beamed. "But in that field, my dear boy, you have no peer. I would pit you against them any time." He rose as Carol entered the room, signed the memorandum, accepted the check without bothering to look at it. He took Carol's hand, gazing earnestly at her. "My dear child, if you should ever take it into your head to run away with an old man, do remember me. I shall keep this check." He tapped his breast pocket. "I shall hold it for you against that most unlikely day." He bowed to Max, made a semisalute with his stick, and marched erectly out of the office.

Carol looked after him. "That's the best offer I've had today." She sat on the corner of the desk.

Max leaned back in his chair, smiling. It had been a good morning. The Paradise Island venture was secure. Carol, familiar with his moods, studied him.

"How long have you had the Eleutheran Club's certificate in the back of your mind?"

"From the beginning. I could have, I suppose, had Sir Stephen force another one through the Assembly. He would have done it and for less than a million. But I'm saving one for the Grand Bahama. When that's wrapped up, let's you and I take a trip. Europe. The South Seas. What's left of the Orient. Would you like to be married first? I've been thinking about it."

"I'm not sure." She was sincere. "Oh, you're a fine catch for a working girl. No doubt about it." She bent over and put her hand against his cheek with affection. "It's a little ridiculous, my holding out this way when everything could be arranged so much more comfortably. Everyone in Nassau thinks I go to bed with you as it is. Might as well have the cake along with the candle. I'll think about it." She slid from the desk. "Chris Baildon called while you were with Mr. Makepiece. He's coming over for the weekend unless you want him to stay."

"Call him back. I'll talk with him." Max leaned back in his chair and whistled contentedly at the ceiling.

The Lockheed, on Jan's instructions, had taken a southeasterly course out of Miami's International Airport. It swung

126

now over Crooked Island and Rum Cay on a heading which would bring it to Oakes Field, in Nassau.

Facing each other in the deep, comfortable chairs, Sherry Melnick and Jan leaned back comfortably, iced drinks of lime and rum at their hands. The boy, Major, who was always delighted by these unexpected excursions aboard Hertog's private plane, stood at the rear in case he was needed. Sometimes Miss Jan or Mr. Max told him to go forward, where the pilot would let him take the right-hand seat and pretend he was flying the ship. He thought of himself as more of an air steward than a member of *The Witch*'s crew.

At the last moment Chris Baildon had told Jan and Sherry that Max wanted him to remain in Miami. He offered his apartment key to Sherry.

"I'm taking Sherry home to Papa." Jan's eyes held amusement at the idea. "I think they ought to meet."

Chris had shrugged. He had been looking forward to the weekend in Nassau; then a call from Max had changed everything. He was to keep himself available in Miami. Max would talk with him again later.

"He was being very mysterious about the whole thing." Chris was unimpressed by his employer's eccentricities. "Someone would get in touch with me. If I went out, leave word where I could be reached. Hush! Hush!"

Now Sherry's gaze roved over the Hertog plane's fittings. The seats and cabin walls were finished in a beige leather. The appointments, down to the ashtrays, looked to be and probably were sterling. There were places for eight persons. The chairs were deep and comfortable, placed on swivels which might be locked in any position. There was a bar and a compact galley. It all had the fascinating smell of big money, so big no one bothered to count it any longer, so big it had really lost meaning save as it was used as counters in a game. It wasn't for spending. There was too much of it. It was for manipulation.

"The king was in the countinghouse counting out his money." He hummed the bit of doggerel.

"It impresses a lot of people." Jan studied him. "Somehow I didn't think it would you."

"It doesn't. Not the way you mean. It's the power it represents." He changed the subject. It would be difficult to explain what he meant. "Do you really want me to stay at your place?"

"Are you afraid of the old man?"

"No. Curious."

"We may not even see him. It's that sort of household. We sometimes go days at a time without running into each other. Lately, though, he has been softening up a little, getting paternal, worrying about my future. Do you know?" The notion interested her. "The two of you might like each other." She broke off.

"Until he finds out I'm a Jew?"

"You don't have to be so damned offensive, so ready to be challenged. Are you always this way, looking for trouble?"

"No." He was apologetic. "I don't think it would have occurred to me if Baildon hadn't emphasized his prejudices, I guess." He grinned good-naturedly. "I'm trying to do a little Christian baiting. Don't worry. I'm not going to stand in front of him and yell, 'I'm a Jew, Hertog. What are you going to do about it?' "

The pilot's voice came over the intercom. "Seat belts, Miss Hertog."

They could feel him letting down for his approach. Sherry leaned forward to fasten the buckle on her belt. He remained in that position to hold both her hands.

"When I go to Nassau, I usually take the overnight boat. Everyone thinks I'm afraid to fly. They can't understand anyone not being in a hurry. I just happen to like boats."

"I'll have to show you *The Witch*." She looked at him for a moment with a disturbing intensity. "Do you honestly think we can make it? I mean for real? For good?" She seemed to be so young asking the questions. "Everything tells me there is something phony about this. It's too fast. Too pat. I've been around enough to know better. I should be hard to fool."

"No one is hurrying you. You're not being rushed. No one is trying to sneak you off to a quick marriage. I think it will work out if that's the way you want it."

"I honestly think I do. I have to admit to some reservations.

128

The way it happened. I thought we were both having our private joke. All of a sudden it stopped being funny. How serious should you get over a jump in the hay? Marriage. It wasn't at all what the lady had in mind. I'm still not sure about it."

"Let's just let it bump along in its own ruts and see what happens. It could be that by the time the weekend is over we won't be able to stand the sight of each other."

"That's a pretty smart approach." She approved. "It's disarming. See, it says, 'I have nothing up my sleeve, and the hand is still quicker than the eye.'"

There was a small jolt as the wheels touched the runway.

"You're too young and pretty not to be cynical." He glanced out the window. "Well, here we are in the land of the fabled Hertog who snorts fire at all intruders."

They walked through customs and immigration without any delay. The inspectors made an informal salute and smiled their recognition of Jan, checked Sherry's name against a list, and then nodded them on. Major had taken their two bags and was waiting at Jan's small car, which had been sent out from Windmere.

"Want to drive?" She indicated the wheel.

"No. Driving on the left-hand side of the road scares the hell out of me. I always expect to see someone coming head on around a curve."

The narrow, thickly wooded road from the field to Lyford Cay winds through heavy underbrush and skirts the shoreline. In many places it is barely wide enough for two cars abreast, and there is little room for passing. Here and there are small signs which warn the drivers: NO OVERTAKING.

Sherry pointed to one. "I've always thought those signs were a deliberate effort to be quaint. No overtaking instead of no passing."

"Workin' for th' Yankee dollar. You're all alike, wanting to change everything to your own image. You know the story of the American tourist who said: 'Rome? Rome? Oh, that's the place where I found that good tobacco.'"

The dining room of the Buccaneers' Club fronts on the harbor, and its broad windows offer the effect of a wide-angle camera lens held on Nassau's waterfront and the protected basin where yachts, power cruisers, needlelike speedboats and trim sloops rock sedately at their moorings.

The room is high-ceilinged, airy and sunshine-bright with color. The air conditioning is completely soundproof, and in everything there is a feeling of crisp freshness. There is one long table in the room's center for those of a communal spirit who enjoy the boisterous exchanges over a two- or three-hour luncheon. Smaller tables for two or four persons are spaced widely, and at these the members may talk with a quiet confidence that their conversations will go unheard and unrecorded. The atmosphere of well-being, of wealth and the assurance which goes with it, is unmistakable. It is reflected in the club's appointments and the dignity of its employees, the pride they seem to take in the routine tasks assigned them. On the walls are vivid murals depicting much of the Bahamas' history from the early pirate days through the tempestuous era of blockade-running during the Civil War down to the golden time of rum-running during the American experiment with Prohibition. The times were gaudy, and the artist caught the spirit in vivid reds, blues and stark black seascapes and portraits. Voices seem to call from the walls and echo in marching history and a taut sail against a crimson sky.

Founded a hundred or more years ago by a half dozen of Nassau's first citizens, it was originally called simply the Club. This confused no one. As time passed and the membership grew to include, eventually, everyone of importance on the island, someone with a ribald sense of humor spoke of it as the Buccaneers' Club. This was frowned on by a few who were sensitive of their family history and the source of its wealth. Others, their positions so well established they could afford to join in the laughter, agreed the designation was not without merit and truth. As a matter of fact, they liked the swaggering implication. In truth they had taken Nassau and the island of New Providence with the same confident insolence earlier pirates had displayed in their sacking of the town. To their ears the Club had a musty, fusty sound. A meeting was called, and after some small argument the name was officially changed to the Buccaneers' Club. So it has stood and will remain.

At a corner window table Max Hertog sat with Sir Stephen Simon, a large, heavy-girthed, florid man who was given to frequent laughter in which there was no mirth. Although he frequently insisted he no longer concerned himself with the affairs of public life, he managed to exercise a remarkable influence. The Bahamas are self-governing through the House of Assembly, which is elective, and the Senate, which is appointive. The office of Governor is usually filled by a well-meaning and ineffectual appointee of the Crown. It is an empty honor. The Premier wields the power with the consent of his cronies. Sir Stephen, having left the government, made capital of his connections. Little occurred in the islands now without Sir Stephen's permission and approval. From a Bay Street office, which also served as a mail drop for half a dozen outright fraudulent insurance and securities companies, Sir Stephen acted as "a consultant." No development, no merger, no transaction of importance occurred in the Bahamas in which Sir Stephen did not have an "advisory" role and from which he extracted a large fee. He held stock in several banks and hotel corporations and had interests in the Out Island developments. A widower of some twenty years, Sir Stephen lived in a magnificent establishment on a high ridge overlooking the sea. He entertained lavishly and had as frequent guests some of the loveliest young ladies to visit the islands. They stayed for weeks and months and were introduced by Sir Stephen as his wards. Sir Stephen put his fortune to what he considered its best possible use: the furthering of the pleasures, diversions and appetites of Sir Stephen Simon. In this he was most expert.

If the fount of power in the Bahamas had to be indicated, it would seem to lie somewhere between Sir Stephen and Maximilian Hertog. Since neither had ever been forced to make contest with the other, they remained as friendly as it was in their natures to be.

Max tasted the dry, pale, lime-colored daiquiri for which the club's bartender was famous. Sir Stephen had the straw-tinted sherry of manzanilla.

"When I make a mistake, I like to say so right away and get it off my mind." Max offered no preliminary explanation to this statement.

Sir Stephen nodded and smiled without warmth.

"I went into this Grand Bahama thing without thinking it through first," Max continued. "It's been on my mind for a long time. Because I've been playing with it for years, I just assumed all the details were taken care of. Well, they weren't. Now I figure it's nonsense trying to pick up Grand Bahama a little piece at a time. There must be a better way."

Sir Stephen smiled again and absently turned the slender glass between his fingers. He did not lift his hooded eyes.

"There ought to be some way of wrapping it all in one piece." Max finished the daiquiri.

"Are we"—Sir Stephen spoke softly—"are we just chatting, my dear Max, or are you asking my opinion and advice?" He looked at Hertog now, and his eyes were the color of milky jade.

"Naturally." Max enjoyed the game. "I should be most happy to have the value of your advice at whatever fee you care to name."

Sir Stephen inclined his head in agreement. "When I heard of your interest in Grand Bahama, I wondered why you were permitting the operation to become so unnecessarily involved. Simple things are best done simply."

Discovering Sir Stephen knew of his participation in the Grand Bahama activity didn't surprise Max as much as it should have. A secret was difficult to maintain on Bay Street. He wondered, though, if Chris Baildon had been careless. An imprudent word could be expensive.

"By the way"—a frosty smile accompanied the words—"let me congratulate you on the Paradise Island-Eleutheran Club merger. It was clever. I have always admired your dexterity. Now. Have you ever heard of the Out Island Development Act?" He seemed to ask the question idly.

Puzzled, Max shook his head. He understood Sir Stephen was not really expecting a reply.

"It is not surprising." Sir Stephen smiled again, this time with pallid amusement. "No one else has. I just thought of it."

He emitted a soft belch and touched a napkin to his lips. "The Out Island Development Act," he repeated, savoring the words. They had a flavor. "Properly introduced," he continued, "and steered through the House of Assembly, properly signed by the Governor at my suggestion, the legislation should open Grand Bahama to whatever piratical raids you have in mind. My fee is five hundred thousand dollars." He mentioned the amount casually.

There was no change of expression on Max Hertog's face. He had no inclination to press Sir Stephen for details. There was between them an understanding of what needed to be done. Max did not consider the fee excessive. He was preparing to deal in millions, and Sir Stephen was aware of this.

"My office will have a check to you this afternoon." Max concluded the oral agreement.

Sir Stephen folded his hands across his ample paunch and patted fingertips upon the mound. He smiled with a gracious benelovence and nodded something close to a benediction to several acquaintances. Although he was a careless Presbyterian in matters of the church, he had always fancied himself as of the breed of men from which Popes are drawn. He saw himself with the Medici. Stephen the Magnificent, making a sign to the multitude in a hush of reverence. To be absolute. That was the goal. Even in such a limited sphere as the Bahamas. The idea quickened his appetite, and he reached for the menu with a greedy hand.

Sherry Melnick lit a cigarette and refilled his cup from the silver pot, kept warm by a candle's low flame. The morning sunlight falling through the leaves and branches of a giant banyan tree drew a curious pattern on the tablecloth of circles and ovals twisted together. Half-turned, he watched a parrot as it came from the rear of the house. The bird, aflame with its vivid colors of red, orange, yellow and green, made its way toward where he sat in short bursts of flight which carried it from shrub to shrub. Every couple of yards it halted and screamed hoarsely. Then, with its head cocked, it waited expectantly for a reply. When there was no answer, it waddled across the lawn with an uncertain dignity, making a few steps before becoming airborne again to the nearest branch. From this perch it examined Sherry with bright-eyed curiosity.

Except for a couple of men at work clearing the beach and raking through the white sand and a third cleaning the pool with a vacuum hose, Sherry had seen no one save the maid who brought his first coffee. Awakening early, he had lain in bed listening to the brushing murmuring sound of a light surf on the beach. On the bedside table was a telephone with several buttons in the base. One was marked KITCHEN.

Before she said good-night at the door of her room down the long corridor, Jan had told him not to wait for her in the morning.

"Tell the kitchen what you want when you wake up and want it. I'll join you later."

It had seemed to him then, and he thought about it again now, that in her own home Jan Hertog was a different person. Much of the brittle, almost compulsive brashness, the inclination to add a topper to everything said, disappeared. By contrast with her mood in Miami, she seemed only a little short of being prim as she turned to take his kiss on her cheek.

Anyhow, he had telephoned downstairs for coffee. When the young maid who brought it inquired about breakfast, he suddenly realized he was hungry and ordered an omelet, bacon, toast and more coffee. The sun was brightly warm outside.

"Let's have it in the garden somewhere."

"Yes, sah." She ducked her head with a shy smile. "It a faiah day."

Max Hertog hadn't been at home when they came from the airport. Or if he was at home, he didn't make an appearance. In the early evening they had drinks on the terrace.

"We can go to the club for dinner"—Jan had stretched back comfortably in a deep wicker chair—"or have it here." She smiled warmly at him. "You name it."

"Your father?" He left the question unfinished.

"If Max wanted to join us, he would. We never intrude on each other. If he is at all curious about you, he'll show up in his own time."

134

They had gone to the club, a low, rambling building of white-washed stone on a point at the west end of the island. Jan apparently knew everyone, and Sherry watched with a growing amusement the guarded reactions of the women to her presence. The men were openly admiring, frank in their interest, responding immediately to her attraction and unconsciously forming a ring about her in which she became the center of attention. The women were almost too cordial. Sherry thought that if they could have afforded to ignore her, they would. As it was, they became overly animated, brightly attentive to their escorts and deliberately linking their arms with those of their men in a protective gesture. They joined a small party finally on the broad deck overlooking the water. The evening had passed pleasantly enough with dinner, inconsequential chatter, some dancing and considerable drinking. They left early and drove back to Windmere through a velvet-textured night.

In a narrow lane of bright sunlight the parrot now halted only a few feet away from the table. The head was tilted again with an almost human expression of curiosity as it peered intently at this stranger. Then it executed a small dance, lifting its feet as though they were heavily weighted and loosing an earsplitting screech. Sherry broke off a piece of toast and tossed it. The bird seemed to consider the offering for a moment. Then, picking it up in the sharp beak and with a snapping motion of neck and head, it sent it flying back with an unmistakable gesture of rejection.

"You're supposed to feed Sir Rupert by hand. Then the son of a bitch nips your fingers. He won't eat anything thrown to him."

Sherry looked up in startled surprise. He had been so intent on the parrot he had heard no sound as Maximilian Hertog came toward the table. A maid, carrying a heavily laden tray, was following. Max dropped a handful of unopened letters on the table and pulled out a chair.

"I'm Max Hertog."

Sherry stood up, but he did not offer his hand. "My name is Melnick. Sherry Melnick."

Max waited until the maid had placed the coffee, cups, plates and covered dishes on the table.

"Friend of Jan's." It wasn't a question. He was stating an obvious fact.

"No." Sherry couldn't resist the temptation. "I was just driving past, liked the looks of the house, and dropped in to spend the night."

There was the faintest glint of acknowledging amusement in Max's eyes as he took a swallow of the coffee. His lips pursed with thoughtful approval, and he half nodded.

"One thing about the place. You won't find a better cup of coffee."

"Howard Johnson's maybe." Sherry offered the suggestion gravely.

Max seemed to consider this, chewing thoughtfully at his lower lip. Then he looked up, and his eyes held Sherry's. He appeared to be seeing him for the first time.

"Melnick." He tested the name. "What do you do?" It was rude and meant to be.

"Right now I'm thinking about marrying your daughter."

"Is that so?" Max dipped a spoon into the small bowl of stewed guavas. The meat was a soft pink, the syrup clear and thick. He chewed with evident pleasure. "I wonder why no one ever tried to develop a seedless guava?"

"I never cared much for them. The jelly, maybe, but not the fruit."

Carefully, as though he were making an incision at a vital point, Max cut through a thick slice of ham.

"I don't remember Jan ever mentioning you."

"We've only known each other for a couple of days."

"Love at first sight, eh?" Methodically he divided the ham into squares. "I suppose it could happen when the girl's name is Hertog."

"I imagined something of the sort would occur to you."

Max broke open a muffin and spread the steaming surface with butter.

"I don't think I am going to like you worth a damn."

136

"We start even there at least."

"Aside from trying to marry Jan, what do you do?"

"I'm in the real estate business in Miami. We are an old firm. I'm solvent if that's what you mean. We laid out and completed two developments on the west coast. Fairhaven and Tides End. Lately I've been trying to buy up some of Grand Bahama for you through Chris Baildon. That's how I met Jan."

Max displayed no surprise. He finished the ham and muffin and refilled his cup.

"How did you know I was interested in Grand Bahama?"

"I made it my business to find out."

Max shook his head impatiently. "Don't try to impress me by being mysterious. You couldn't have just found out. Someone had to tell you. And that someone had to be Christopher Baildon. Funny." He ruminated on the thought. "He never talked before. It was one of his few virtues. Now I'll have to fire the son of a bitch."

"That's what I would do if I were you."

Max looked up, surprised. He studied Sherry with a cold sharpness. Then he grunted.

"I just might be wrong about you."

Sherry smiled. "I don't think so. What are you going to do with Grand Bahama?"

Max ignored the question. "Melnick? That's a Jew's name, isn't it?"

"Yes."

"I don't want a Jew in my family."

"Do you know? My father would say the same thing about a Gentile. Both of you will have to make an adjustment. Then, maybe, you will be able to say, 'Some of my best friends are Jews.'"

"Why do you want to marry Jan?"

"Because you're so goddamned rich."

Max slid one of his cigars out from its tube and turned it slowly between his fingers. He bit the end off and spat it into the palm of his hand. Sherry snapped a lighter and half leaned across the table to hold the flame. Max eyed him over it and then took the light. He drew on the cigar and allowed the smoke to drift from his mouth. Finally he grunted.

"That," he spoke slowly, "is the first thing you've said to me I haven't believed."

VIII

The effect had been contrived deliberately, and Royal studied, planned, and expanded it as an experienced actor would prepare himself for a new role. Standing now at one side of the floor-to-ceiling window in the reception room adjoining Max Hertog's office, he kept a smile hidden, knowing how well he had succeeded.

A cab had brought him from the airport to Bay Street and the Hertog Building. As he stepped from it to the curb and then half leaned in the door's open window to pay his fare, he winked with a broad humor at the Negro driver. The man's face slowly creased into an appreciative grin. He pinched his lips in a soundless whistle of admiration. He was saying, without words: "I don't know who you are or what you're doing on Bay Street, but, mon, you do look like a biggety somethin'." Turning away from the cab, Royal could feel the impact of startled curiosity as those persons passing him on the sidewalk broke their stride or turned after they had passed to look back at him with frank interest. For an interval of a few seconds his presence commanded this section of a busy street.

Crossing to the Hertog entrance, Royal had no need to glance at his reflection in a shopwindow. He had studied himself well and critically in a mirror before taking an interisland plane from Eleuthera. There was a purpose in it all. The burnished tan shoes were London bench-made by a craftsman. The suit of heavy sheer white silk was Nassau-tailored. The shirt with button-down collar and a tie of dark marine blue with a tiny fleur-de-lis embroidered blended as they should. The Panama hat had been so carefully and expertly woven that it had the smooth texture of linen. All these things brought his size and the black polish of his skin into startling relief, making sculptured lines of the broad shoulders and lean flanks. His movements were as indifferently graceful as those of a stretching cat, and he carried himself with a proud and certain instinct.

The uniformed page boy who stood at stiff attention at the foot of the stairs leading to Max Hertog's office made no effort to conceal his admiration for this handsome black man who walked with such assurance. He, as a formality, checked Royal's name against a short list carried in the pocket of his blouse.

"Yes, sir, Mr. Keating." He indicated the flight of steps. "This way if you please." He allowed himself a shy smile.

At the door of the reception room the page announced the name with a flair which gave to the words the sound of trumpets. The young woman behind the desk rose. She had trained herself to be impersonally polite, but at the moment she was shaken out of her professional equanimity. Royal thought if he had appeared in the full barbaric regalia, wearing the feathered headdress of a Masai warrior and carrying a spear, she would not have shown more fluttering uncertainty. Black men simply did not call on Maximilian Hertog. Black men did not smile at a white girl as this one did, a smile that was warm and tingling. Black men were not handsome—beautiful was a better word. The words "Royal Keating" on the appointment sheet had not prepared her for this.

"Yes. Of course. Mr. Keating. Mr. Hertog expects you. Please take a seat."

Royal had nodded but walked to stand at the window. From it he could see the piers where the Out Island sloops were moored. He watched the young boys as they dived and frolicked in the clear water. He heard the receptionist pass his name on to someone through an intercommunication system. A moment later he turned at the sound of his name.

140

"Mr. Keating."

Carol Wainwright came from an adjoining room and crossed toward him. She offered her hand with spontaneous friendliness.

"Miss Wainwright." Royal took her hand, thinking what a remarkably pretty girl she was.

"How nice to see you again." She smiled up at him. "This way, please."

They walked toward the door opening on Max's office. Carol glanced at Royal, and there was a touch of dancing mischief in her eyes.

"My," she whispered, her hand on the knob, "you do look ever so impressive." She opened the door. "Mr. Keating, Mr. Hertog."

Max was standing behind his desk. His sharp glance covered every detail of Royal's appearance. *This,* he told himself quickly, *is a big, smart nigger who already knows I want something.* He waved a hand toward a chair.

"Sit down, Royal."

Carol closed the door. Royal remained standing.

"Sit down. Sit down." Max spoke impatiently.

"After you, Mr. Hertog."

They were joined now in this immediate conflict of wills. Royal understood exactly what was going through Maximilian Hertog's mind. Never before had he sat with a black man and talked. The act, he felt, would be an admission of equality. One sitting and the other standing. That was the proper order of things. But he sensed Royal had already come to the same conclusion and would remain standing only as long as he did. When he sat, Royal would sit. When he stood, Royal would stand.

"You're trying to outsmart me, Royal." There was no bite in the statement.

"I think, maybe, I already have." The accompanying smile was understanding. "Why don't you sit down and then we can talk?"

Max sucked at a small space between his teeth. He could fall back on no precedent for this situation. As a matter of fact, he had the feeling he was being pressured into unfamiliar corners. He didn't like it. There was Jan and her Jew. How did a man handle a thing like that? Lock her away in a convent? Now he was confronted by this big black bastard who stood, regarding him as an equal. And this wasn't a pose. He was certain of it. The hell of it was both the Jew and the nigger had strong qualities which appealed to him. They refused to be pushed off-balance. Underneath the surface calm the strength was unmistakable. Over the past week he had felt the impact of personalities as strong as his own. It was a little unnerving to a man who had always walked in heavy boots. He had tried to dislike this Melnick and failed. There was a raffish humor in the man which appealed to him. Why the hell did he have to be a Jew? Now he was confronted by this nigger, Royal. By turning, Max could look out of the window and see the old Vendue House where, during the early days of the colony, slaves had been bought and sold. It took but a little imagination to see Royal stripped and standing on the block with his muscles in heavy cords. There was fury and hatred in his eyes as the gentlemen walked around, poking him with their sticks and hefting his balls as an indication of his breeding potential. That's where the black son of a bitch belonged. Instead, he stood there, impeccably tailored, confident and asking a favor of no man.

"Oh, hell." He surrendered almost wearily. "Let's sit down." He dropped heavily into a chair.

Royal took a seat at the desk's end, where they could talk without having it between them. He watched as Max flipped up the lid of a mahogany humidor, reached for a cigar, and then, abruptly, drew his hand away empty. He understood why. Max Hertog was not as insensitive as he seemed to be. If he took a cigar now, ordinary good manners would demand he offer one to his visitor. To smoke with a nigger. This he could not bring himself to do.

"I don't care much for cigars anyhow, Mr. Hertog."

The anger was silent but visible. The neck muscles leaped up in tight strings beneath the skin. Royal was a little ashamed now for having goaded him to this point.

"You're too goddamned smart for a nigger, Royal." The

142

words were quietly pitched, but the tone was hoarse. "It could get you killed one of these days if you're not too careful."

"I'm pretty sure you didn't ask me to come in today just so you could tell me I'm a smart nigger. By the way, that word doesn't really bother me much anymore."

"No, I didn't send for you to say that." Max shook his head, his eyes never flicking away from Royal's. "I wanted to find out what you're really up to in the Out Islands with all those speeches you have been making."

"Exactly what is it you want to know?" Royal refused to ease the pressure. Max Hertog would have to spell out every word. "Why are you interested?"

"I want to know what you're after. Information comes to me. I put it together. I want to know what it means. You're getting to be a big nigger in the Progressive Liberal Party or whatever the hell they call it."

"Oh, you know well enough what it is called, Mr. Hertog." The smile carried with it a shade of tolerance. "Like the other whites, you think if you don't speak the name it will go away. It won't."

"You're supposed to be a goddamned engineer. Why don't you stick to it?"

"Why do I make you so angry, Mr. Hertog?" The question was softly, innocently asked. "It can't just be because I'm black. You've had black men around you for years."

"And by God," he shouted now, "they acted black. They didn't pretend they were white."

"You know I'm not pretending to be white. It's because I'm all black—all nigger. That's what you can't get over. You'd like to have me say: 'Yaas, Marstah. No, Marstah. Ah'll fotch hit raight away, Marstah.' That's the nigger you want. This one you can't touch and you know it because I'm all black and don't want any part of you." The words had the impact of solid blows.

Rarely had Maximilian Hertog felt the uncertainty he experienced now. The nigger refused to lose his temper. He was being crowded into making a fool of himself. *Maybe,* he thought, *a little honesty would serve.*

"I don't know, Royal." He took a cigar now and pushed the humidor in Royal's direction but without a word of invitation. "There may be something in what you say." This was close to an apology.

"What is it you really wanted to see me about? To find out if I can be managed?"

There was a shade of admiration in the way Maximilian Hertog shook his head. He lit his cigar and stared at the ceiling. Then he grunted. The sound had grudging laughter in it.

"I guess so. That's pretty close anyhow. Do you really think you can hold all those niggers together for an election, a nigger bloc? It's never been done before."

"It's never been tried before. No one took the time to explain to them what being eighty-five percent of the population in the Bahamas meant in terms of power. They're beginning to understand now, and it excites them." Royal ignored the cigars and lit a cigarette.

Max watched as a tendril of smoke unwound itself from his cigar and climbed toward the ceiling. He shook his head, a little baffled by his own thoughts.

"A nigger government." He lifted his eyes to stare at Royal.

"Go ahead." Royal smiled encouragement. "It comes hard the first time but gets easier."

"A nigger Prime Minister." Max barely whispered the words. "I guess that's you, isn't it?"

"Yes."

Max whistled an audible note, sharp and incredulous. "After three hundred years. Bam!"

"It doesn't have to be Bam! We're in a different time. This is no senseless revolt of the slaves. The niggers aren't going to burn the manse, rape the white women, string up ol' massa and the overseers. That isn't what the PLP has in mind. I know that is what the Establishment would like everyone to believe, but it just isn't so."

"Do you think you can do this alone? It will take money."

"That's really why you asked me to come and see you, isn't it?"

144

"I'd be a damn fool if I didn't protect myself and my investments in the islands."

"So you want to buy a piece of the nigger party? What makes you think it is for sale, because it's black and ought to come cheap?"

"No." Max carefully placed his cigar on a tray. "I'll tell you what makes me think it is for sale. You. I don't think you give a damn about those Out Island niggers. You'll exploit them for your own purpose. They tell me you're a real spellbinder when you get up to talk. Looking at you, listening to you, I can believe it. I hear you have those niggers on their feet, yelling, clapping, stamping every time you speak at a meeting. You're the power and the glory."

"It's not a bad feeling. You ought to know, Mr. Hertog."

"All right." Max picked up his cigar. He was on familiar ground now. This was a simple matter simply stated. "I'll buy a piece of your black revolution. You name it."

"At the same time you'll make your usual large contribution to the United Bahamian Party?"

"Of course." Max was impatient. "You don't think I'd go out on Bay Street naked? I'm not sure what I'm buying from you or whether it will stay bought. When I back both sides, I can't lose."

Royal nodded. He stood up. Max didn't rise but simply tilted back in his chair, from which angle he could look into Royal's face without effort.

"I'll say one thing, Royal. You're about as imposing a nigger as I ever saw. It's no wonder you get those conchs screaming out there in the islands."

"Thank you." Royal was amused. "As the party's financial sponsor you ought to come to a meeting sometime. The black man is learning fast. He's not yet quite as devious as the white man, but this will come in time. Monkey see. Monkey do. It's been an interesting morning. I'll be in touch with you."

"The hell you will." The response was fast. "I'll make my contribution as I have before, in cash. This time it will be more substantial. I'll see that it is delivered to you and only you." He paused thoughtfully. "Big Maum will do. You let me know when you want it."

"I'll do that, Mr. Hertog." Royal moved toward the door. On the point of opening it he turned. "By the way"—the tone was courteous, respectful—"when I'm Prime Minister and the government is all black, you'll have to find another word for nigger. It isn't that I mind, but some of my friends are sensitive. They just might think you mean it the way it sounds."

Max stared at the door after it was closed. His lips puckered thoughtfully. If, he thought, there was ever a man for the job of leading a black revolution at the polls, then this Royal was he. There were those of the Establishment who were convinced the island blacks could never be welded into a political bloc. They, he knew now, had never taken the trouble to learn what manner of man led them.

The table had been cleared. There was coffee now and brandy within reach on the portable bar wheeled to this corner of the garden where luncheon had been served. Earlier both men had made a quick estimate of one another, found something to their liking, and reached an almost immediate accord.

Max moved the cigars toward his guest, who shook his head in refusal and smiled what seemed to be a good-natured apology.

"I've never been comfortable with a cigar." He shook a cigarette from a pack and chuckled with a quiet, good humor. "I remember my father's contempt for these." He lit the cigarette. "A man smoked a pipe or a cigar. Cigarettes were for whores, who were supposed to die from them at an early age if they didn't succumb to syphilis or any of the other natural hazards of their occupation."

Nothing in his experience had prepared Max Hertog for Charles Rich. He wasn't certain what he had expected but certainly not this. Slender, faultlessly tailored, easy of manner, quiet and exact of speech, he refused to conform to Max's vague idea of what a member of the Mafia or Cosa Nostra hierarchy should be. The complexion, dark eyes, unconscious gestures indicated a Latin heritage, and, Max thought, the immigrant

146

Charles Rich had probably been Carlo Ricco. This third or fourth generation was polished and assured without being arrogant. Relating him to the word "gangster" was ridiculous. Yet, Max knew from what Stanley Makepiece had said, this Rich was a member of the gambling syndicate's inner council.

Christopher Baildon had made the introduction over the telephone from Miami. Since both knew what they wanted, the conversation was guarded, brief and polite.

"I'll send a plane for you, Mr. Rich," Max suggested.

"Thank you, Mr. Hertog. I have my own."

Max had grinned over this. It was said as he might have phrased it. Simple. Direct. The implication unmistakable.

"That's fine then. Baildon will bring you to the house. I'll be looking forward to seeing you. If you can spare the time, arrange to stay with us for a few days."

Now, without seeming to do so, they studied each other at their leisure. They had yet to talk about that which had brought them together. Max, usually direct, waited for Rich to open the subject. He had something the other man wanted, and this was a position from which he liked to deal. He could afford to keep quiet, wait and listen.

Rich's eyes swept over the sun-scattered garden, the high palms and gentle sea and then returned to Max.

"It's hard to imagine a more pleasant setting."

"For a conspiracy?" Max suggested.

"I imagine you must think of it that way." The shoulders lifted and dropped with an exaggerated gesture of humor. "Most persons link professional gambling with a sinister underworld."

"There's no connection?" The question was innocent.

"Oh, at certain levels."

"But not at this altitude?" Max was amused.

"Well, let's put it this way. I represent a branch of a large investment syndicate. We have interests in many places. Resort hotels. Airlines. Real estate. We have watched what has been done with Paradise Island. We are prepared to take over the casino operation there. We will finance and staff it in the same manner as we now operate three casinos in three Las Vegas ho-

147

tels. Our management will be efficient and honest. There is no reason for us to be dishonest. The odds are in our favor. We'll work out a percentage fair to you and to us. I don't imagine you really have any idea what the return can be. Let's just say it is geared to the millions. There will be plenty for everyone. As you must know, we have tried to establish ourselves in the Bahamas without success. We are prepared to make a generous concession to you for this opportunity. Frankly, we're a little curious why you went into the Paradise Island venture after Mr. Harrington failed."

Max was surprised by the question. "Why"—he spoke half to himself—"I suppose it was just to prove I could do it. Ego is involved, I guess. Why does your syndicate go on making money when it has no need for more? It's fun. It's a game. Some men collect stamps. I like to make money. When I was a kid, I used to shoot marbles. When I won all the marbles from the other kids, it made me feel good. I'm damned if I really know why. It's the satisfaction you get from being a winner."

They both looked up at the sound of voices. Crossing toward them from the house, Jan, Melnick and Chris Baildon were in animated, laughing conversation. As they came to the table, Rich stood up. Max frowned from his chair, annoyed by the intrusion.

"I'm busy, Jan."

"Sorry." She looked at Charles Rich with interest.

Max accepted the interruption but refused to rise. "My daughter, Jan. Mr. Rich."

"Hello." Jan offered her hand.

"How do you do, Miss Hertog?" Rich's gaze went past her to Melnick. "Oh, hello, Sherry."

"Hello, Mr. Rich."

The distinction Charles Rich and Sherry Melnick had made in the use of first and last names was not lost on either Jan or Max. She turned questioningly to Melnick.

"I sold Mr. Rich a home in Miami, and we sometimes run into each other at Hialeah tearing up losing tickets."

"Oh, well." She smiled her brightest. "I'm taking Sherry out in the boat." She turned to Baildon. "Come along, Chris?"

148

"No, thanks. I have to get on into town." He started to turn away.

"There's no hurry, Chris." Max was at his most casual best. "You might as well take a boat ride. I meant to tell you. You're fired!" The brutality of the statement, made before others, was deliberate and calculated.

All color drained from Chris Baildon's face. He stared at Max Hertog incredulously and then half turned to look questioningly at Sherry Melnick.

"I see." The words came with difficulty. Teeth clamped for a second on lower lip. "You are a real bastard, aren't you? I don't know why it always surprises me." He turned and walked across the garden.

"Max." Jan was honestly distressed. She shook her head. "Come on, Sherry. It's nice to have met you, Mr. Rich." She looked again at her father. "Did you really have to do it that way, Max?"

"That's the way I wanted to do it. He talked too much. Ask Melnick. He'll tell you. It might have cost me the whole deal." He was just a little ashamed now of what he had done and sought to hide it by being unnecessarily harsh. "I said we were busy, Jan."

Rich waited until Jan and Sherry were well down the path before he reseated himself. He was surprised by Max Hertog's behavior. It had been the action of a small man consumed by pettishness. It was, he felt, a weakness where none might have been expected. Certainly it was out of character for a man of Maximilian Hertog's stature. Rich tucked the revealing moment away as something to remember.

"What"—Max spoke as though there had been no interruption—"what is your idea of a reasonable offer for the operation on Paradise Island?" He waved with impatient rudeness to forestall Rich's answer. "I'll tell you now I don't like a deal where the other side knows more than I do. So before we agree on anything, I'll make it my business to find out what I should expect."

"That's reasonable. As a matter of fact, I'll help you get some comparative figures. You'll discover our offer is more than fair."

"Why the hell should it be more than fair?" Max was suspicious.

"Because"—Rich smiled—"we've been trying to get into the Bahamas ever since Cuba shut down. This is the first real opening. We'll take over the entire casino, assume the expenses of the staff and maintenance. Our end will be thirty-five percent of the gross or twenty percent of the net."

"It sounds all right. I'll let you know."

"You won't get any other offers, Mr. Hertog."

The statement was quietly voiced, but the meaning was unmistakable. Max looked up with a quick challenge.

"That sounds almost like a threat. Do business with me or else." He waited.

"I don't like the word 'threat.' Let's just call it a piece of information. My associates and I don't permit competition in areas where we have interests. If you don't do business with us, no one else, certainly no one in the States, would presume to touch it."

"Well, I'll be damned." Max's admiration was generous. "I've heard about this control but never really believed it."

"Tell me"—Rich moved easily away and to another subject —"how strong is this black movement in the islands? If what everyone in Nassau seems to think impossible should become a reality, how would it affect Paradise Island?"

"Niggers like to make a lot of noise, so you never really know whether they mean anything or are just beating on the drums. This could be for real, though. I'm not taking any chances. I have bets at both ends."

"Well"—Rich glanced at his watch and stood up—"I have to be back in Miami this evening. We'll be in touch."

Waiting while a dock boy brought out the speedboat, Jan was strangely silent. Standing beside her, Sherry sensed her resentment.

"Who," she asked after a few moments, "is this Rich?"

"Oh"—Sherry was indifferent—"I don't know too much.

150

Only what I hear. He's supposed to be a top man in the Syndicate."

"What syndicate?" She was impatient.

"Gambling. You name it."

"What business can he have with Max? Besides"—she looked squarely at him—"why should he call you Sherry while you say Mr. Rich to him?"

"What difference does it make?"

"I think it makes a great deal of difference." She was angry.

"It doesn't mean anything. Most people call me Sherry." He refused to take her objection seriously. "Maybe they just sense the eternal Peter Pan in me. It has never offended my dignity."

"I don't think it's funny. There isn't enough difference in your ages. He made it sound almost patronizing."

"I don't think so. It was friendly. Casual." He was becoming a little annoyed.

"What's his first name?"

"Charles."

"All right." She was determined. "The next time he calls you Sherry you call him Charlie."

He stepped back in simulated horror. "And get rubbed out by the mob? Not bloody likely."

"It isn't a joke. Max noticed it also. It was a deliberate distinction. I wouldn't let him get away with it."

The boat was alongside now, twenty-eight feet of slim, dark, gleaming beauty. The boy held her against the padded pilings. Jan dropped lightly down, and Sherry followed. He touched a finger to one corner of her mouth, forcing it up.

"You look better when you smile."

Her eyes softened. "I just didn't like it."

He moved past her to take the seat behind the wheel. After a moment's hesitation she took a place beside him. The big motor was barely ticking over. He checked the dials, touched the throttle, and nodded to the boy.

"You know what you're doing?"

"Yes, Miss Hertog. I have been exposed to the idle rich before, and they sometimes let me drive their boats. As a matter of fact, I once owned one—nothing as expensive as this, of course."

151

"You're being nasty."

"Uh-huh." He agreed.

"Why?"

"Because you were being just a little supercilious and condescending."

He took the boat past the buoys and out through the marina's breakwater entrance. Once in the open he touched the throttles lightly, looked around, and then gave the engines full power. The craft reared as an enraged sailfish and nearly stood on her stern as she ripped a trail through the green water. Spray created two great lacy fans at the bows, and a furious wake boiled aft. Sherry held the speed for five minutes or so and then reduced it. He bent to light a cigarette and glanced at her.

"I've never seen you angry before." She was almost laughing.

He passed her the cigarette and lit another for himself. There was little sea and a cloudless sky. Ahead, some twenty miles and barely a low shadow on the sea, was Andros Island.

"Today you were lucky. I had a boat to take it out on. Usually I punch girls in the nose when they make me mad."

"Really?" She moved closer, linking her arm with his. "That's Andros Island there. It's inhabited by Chickcharneys. Tiny people who hang from the trees. It doesn't pay to fool around with a Chickcharney. I have Chickcharney blood in me." She paused. "It isn't very smart to go out that far in this kind of boat, but let's go over to Andros. We can get in around Fresh Creek."

"Will you tell me more about the Chickcharneys?"

"Yes." It was murmured. "They take their clothes off, lie on the sand in the hot sun, and make love. That's what I want to do now. I'm tired of being saved for a wedding night or whatever the hell it was you had in mind. I want you to make love to me now. Today." She reached past him and nudged the throttles with the heel of her hand.

The twin screws bit heavily, and the boat seemed to strain upward as a harnessed projectile. Sherry checked it slightly, and they settled back, the motors beating a steady, muffled roar. Jan half turned on the seat, leaning against him and lifting her face to the spreading warmth of the sun.

152

IX

In the spectators' gallery in the House of Assembly Sir Stephen Simon bulked over the inadequate seat, the flesh seeming to lose substance and become an amorphous spread. Occupying places to his immediate right and left were two exceptionally beautiful girls, who looked about them with the bright interest of inquisitive sparrows. Sir Stephen's pink, fleshy hands rested on their yielding thighs which were glowingly warm beneath the sheer covering of the shortest of skirts. He worked the youthfully elastic areas of flesh with a gentle but persistent motion of his fingers, beaming and nodding to acquaintances and colleagues within the hall. The young ladies seemed completely unaware of or indifferent to what he was doing. As a matter of fact, Sir Stephen appeared to be quite detached from any interest in his exercises.

The proceedings of government were carried on in a routine fashion and with what the members felt to be the traditional British reserve. Three or four bills of minor importance were passed. There were no objections or debate. One authorized the construction of a bridge between Nassau and Paradise Island. It had been discovered, through the efforts of Sutter, Longworth and Tracy, that such a span would not interfere or be a menace to navigation. The danger, it seemed, had been imaginary after all. The truth was that such a span would be a tremendous asset

153

to tourism, and Mr. Maximilian Hertog was to be congratulated for his wisdom in sponsoring the idea.

With the calling up of the Out Island Development Act, Sir Stephen inclined himself slightly forward. His hands, now motionless, rested near the pelvic areas of his attractive wards. This piece of legislation was, Sir Stephen felt, one of the finest achievements of his career. It had scope, vision. It was worth a great deal more than the half million dollars he had collected as a fee from Max Hertog. However, in such matters Sir Stephen felt himself to be the true artist. There were, he realized, certain things which were beyond price. The sheer artistry of their creation was recompense enough. The Out Island Development Act was such a masterpiece.

The bill was routinely passed. There was no dissenting voice. It was offered as another evidence of the government's unflagging enthusiasm for the continual development of the islands and the prosperity of their inhabitants. With the passage by the Assembly the signature of the Governor was taken as a matter of course. There would be no quibbling, no questions asked. Sir Stephen had already seen to that.

The act, but vaguely understood by anyone except Sir Stephen, was, in truth, little less than a charter, a royal patent, issued to Maximilian Hertog for the development of Grand Bahama. Only in scope did it differ much from some of the great land grabs made by the railroads when their tracks were being laid over the virgin territory of the United States. Reduced to its essentials, the act permitted Maximilian Hertog to buy the two hundred and eleven square miles of Crown property at a figure just short of three dollars an acre. To any critics who might raise a question, it was pointed out that this was a small inducement offered Mr. Hertog to invest heavily in the commercial development and promotion of the island. Mr. Hertog had plans for a town of Freeport, fine hotels, clubs and yacht basins. Certainly his dreams must be encouraged. It was also proposed in the act that Maximilian Hertog, his heirs and associates be relieved of taxes in connection with the project for the next ninety-nine years. To this there were cries of "Hear! Hear!" from the members of the Assembly.

With the calling of a recess Sir Stephen heaved himself from his seat with a ponderous dignity. He nodded, smiled, and made small, finger-twiddling motions to those who were graced by his recognition. The pair of young ladies—one a blonde who, despite the fact she was adequately clothed, seemed as astonishingly naked and pale as a peeled willow switch; the other a chocolate-eyed brunette who moved with a dreamlike indifference to her surroundings—had no idea what the Assembly's session had been about. They tucked their hands beneath Sir Stephen's flabby arms, shivering a little as though from the cold, while their pouting lips made cooing sounds of pleasure.

"My dears"—Sir Stephen gazed down at them fondly—"you have just witnessed the parliamentary system at its best. Free men engaged in free debate coming up with the right answers. There will always be an England!"

"Can we go home now, Stevie-weevie?" the blonde piped.

Sir Stephen glanced quickly around. "My dear child," he whispered, "you simply must not call me Stevie-weevie in public." He straightened with frowning authority and then inclined his head benignly in the direction of a slender, dark and intense-appearing young man who was regarding him and the girls with sardonic interest.

"Ah! Sir Stephen."

"DuPres." Sir Stephen returned the greeting without warmth.

DuPres studied the girls with open admiration and pleasure. He winked broadly, and they smiled before dropping their eyes with maidenly shyness.

Sir Stephen coughed. It was a signal for attention. "My dear DuPres," he rumbled, "I trust you, as I do, count this a most memorable and progressive day in the history of the Bahamas."

DuPres, the editor of one of Nassau's newspapers, thought this over. Finally he nodded an agreement.

"I intend to congratulate you editorially tomorrow, Sir Stephen. I think nothing quite so spectacular has occurred since Nassau was sacked by Captain Kidd."

"You will have your little joke, will you not, my dear Du-Pres?"

"Did your wards enjoy the proceedings?" He deliberately leered at them.

"I believe they found them most instructive. Is it not so, my dears?"

"Oh, yes, Sir Stephen." The reply was a twittering chorus. Their expression was hopeful that they had said the right thing. "Oh, my, yes." The brunette stuck the tip of a moist tongue out at DuPres with an unmistakable invitation.

"It would be most unfortunate"—Sir Stephen drew his eyes into slits—"if faulty conclusions should be drawn in connection with Grand Bahama. I trust your editorial will mention the great economic benefits bound to accrue to the islands through Mr. Hertog's development."

"I intend to mention this, Sir Stephen." DuPres' smile was not without admiration. "I shall also point out the undeniable benefits to Maximilian Hertog. I trust you have not been forgotten in this distribution of largess."

A glowering thunderhead darkened the normally serene expanse of Sir Stephen's features.

"You are more than ordinarily offensive this morning, DuPres."

The younger man grinned, touched his brow with a finger in a mock salute to Sir Stephen, bowed to the girls, and walked away. They looked after him with a wistful longing.

"Insolent pup." Sir Stephen gathered his charges about him.

"Sir Stephen," Carol Wainwright called.

"Miss Wainwright." Sir Stephen extended his hand with a gesture which implied he would not be surprised if she genuflected and kissed his ring. "How very nice to see you." He hesitated. "May I present my wards? Miss Yvonne Longwood. Miss Evelyn Scott. Miss Carol Wainwright."

"How do you do?" Carol nodded pleasantly and then turned to the man. "You are lucky to be entrusted with so many attractive wards, all girls, too. It must take a great deal of your time and energy."

"Oh, but well worth it, I assure you." Sir Stephen was pleased. "I take a great interest in young people. Their presence is constantly refreshing." He looked about the yard. "Is Max here? I didn't see him."

"No." Carol shook her head. "Sponsored as it was by you, I don't think Mr. Hertog had any doubts about the act's passage. I'll be telephoning him later."

"When you do, give him my best regards and congratulations. Men such as Max Hertog are the builders of empires. Now"— he took his wards by their arms—"we must be going. Indeed we must."

Carol watched as the trio entered the dark-blue Rolls. It was far too large a car to be practical on the island, but Sir Stephen's size demanded it. He waved cheerily to her from deep within the back seat, and she replied with a brief lifting of her hand.

She walked slowly, enjoying the freshness of the day, the leisurely progress of a fringed-top surrey drawn by an ancient nag and driven by an equally ancient Negro, the tourists straggling down the incline from the Royal Victoria Hotel, the sparkling sheen of the harbor's waters. As she crossed Bay Street, DuPres fell in beside her.

"Hello, Pete." She liked and admired Pierre DuPres. They had known each other from childhood.

"Hi, Carol." He smiled at her. "I'm surprised the great man didn't come down to receive the plaudits of the natives, particularly the black ones. After all, the Out Island Development Act is for their benefit. I heard the man say so."

"You know better than to talk to me that way, Pete." Carol wasn't annoyed.

"Could you set up an interview for me?"

She shook her head. "Mr. Maximilian Hertog," she recited in a monotone, "was unavailable for comment."

"But his beautiful secretary, Miss Carol Wainwright," Du-Pres continued in the same register, "said."

"His beautiful secretary said nothing." She finished the sentence for him.

"Well"—DuPres glanced about him at the crowded street— "like all great days, the beginning of this one does not seem at all unusual. I'll be seeing you."

He dropped away from her side at the entrance of the Hertog Building and continued on toward the British Colonial Hotel. Carol shrugged. Pete would be at his sarcastic best in tomorrow's paper. He never missed an opportunity to needle Maximilian Hertog.

Max, in bleached dungarees, old sandals and a white shirt, stood on the balcony of Jan's suite. Resting his hands on the railing, he stared down at the dappled stretch of garden with a frown of displeasure. At the edge of a gravel path Sherry Melnick stood talking with one of the yard boys. Max grunted. His open disapproval of the man was met by an almost bored indifference. Sherry actually ignored him. For the past two months he had been a regular weekend guest at Windmere, and sometimes, when they encountered each other on the terrace or in the house, Melnick simply looked past him as though they were strangers passing each other in a hotel lobby. God knows, Max thought, he had made his disapproval of the fellow plain enough. That Sherry was unaffected only strengthened Max's contention that you couldn't insult a Jew when he wanted something you had. Actually, though, they saw little of each other from Friday afternoon to Monday. Lately Sherry and Jan had been taking *The Witch* out, running down the Exuma Cays and sometimes over to the Florida Keys or into Miami. When he remembered he had her, Max enjoyed *The Witch*. Now he felt abused because Jan never asked whether he wanted the bugeye. She and her friend simply appropriated the boat.

He turned from the railing and crossed to the open French doors leading to Jan's rooms. She was in shorts with a band of metallic blue across her breasts.

Max stared down at his bare toes for a minute. "Are you"—he looked at her—"really going to marry this Jew fellow?"

Anger made flinty points of her eyes. Then in a bemused manner she shook her head, unwilling to credit him with the words.

"Well? Are you?"

"*Ja, mein Führer.*" She executed a stiff-arm open-palm salute. "Is ready der gas chamber?"

"I don't think you're funny."

"Funny?" She exploded. "God Almighty. Who is trying to be funny? A man with your intelligence talking the way you do, feeling the way you do. There is something foul inside, dark and abscessed. It stinks. If there were no other reason, I'd marry Sherry now because you dislike him."

"You ought to have a better reason."

"I have. I need him. He's good for me. He makes me feel that I'm something of value."

"You're getting close." He was grimly sarcastic.

"With him I'm alive. I'm wanted. It's fun just being with him, and I don't think he gives a damn about your money."

"There have been boys and men around you since you were twelve years old. Did it have to be this Jew?"

"Why don't you stop chewing on that word? Frightened, insecure people use it. What is Max Hertog afraid of? No." She snapped the reply. "It didn't have to be a Jew. I might have gone off with a black man. You're damned right. It could have been Royal. If he had so much as put his hand on me I would have laid for him. Nigger. You like the word. It makes you feel good. Well, think about this. He could have had me at any time. All he had to do was say the word. Just looking at him made me feel all empty inside wondering what it would be like. Do you understand what I'm saying?" She was lashing him savagely with words.

Max raised his hand, on the point of striking her across the mouth. She did not flinch or back away. His arm dropped to his side. Suddenly he seemed old and without spirit. His eyes were dull. Not for a moment did he question what she had said. She meant it.

"I don't know." He fumbled for words. "I always thought we understood each other. There was a bond no one else understood between us. I've tried to be a friend and a father."

"Oh, for Christ's sake." She all but shouted her impatience. "Don't make me puke. I'm not accusing you. I've never felt neglected. You had your way to go, the mountain to climb. When you had done that, you sent for me. I always thought that was reasonable. What would you have done with a pig-tailed daughter tagging along? There is no bitterness, no resentment in me. Actually, I like most of what you are. There is or has been an affection between us. It is as much as I have ever asked, ever wanted. I've been satisfied with it. But don't give me that sanctimonious crap about being a father."

She pushed past him, striding out onto the balcony. For a moment she stood there, resolving her mind. Then she called.

"Sherry."

He turned, looked up, shading his eyes against the sun with one hand.

"Yes?"

"When are you going to marry me?"

He was casual. "How about today?"

"There will never be a better day for it."

"That's fine." He walked until he was almost directly beneath the balcony. There was a question in his gaze. Then he nodded as though satisfied to allow it to stand. "Where will it be? Here, at the old manse with the slaves and pickaninnies running through the magnolias? Miami? Paris? Madrid? I have a few bucks put away for just this sort of thing."

She hesitated, half turning to where Max stood. Their eyes met. She swung about, leaning over the railing.

"I promised Big Maum we'd take her over to Eleuthera. She's scared to death of flying. I thought we'd go in *The Witch*. How would you like to be married by a missionary there with the natives looking on, drums beating, bare feet stamping on the earth?"

"Sounds like an old Gable picture. Let's have a go at it. I'll get my pith helmet and elephant gun."

"I'll be down in five—ten minutes."

Max watched her pack a small bag in gloomy silence. He would have liked to talk, talk the way they usually did when there was a difference of opinion. He was shut out now. She ignored him, and he couldn't help feeling that what was happening was his fault. If he hadn't attached so much importance to the affair with Melnick, it would probably have worn itself out as most affairs do. One or the other would have become

160

bored, and the great rapture would have tapered off. His objections had given it substance.

"What's this about Big Maum going to Eleuthera?" He growled the question, almost muttering to himself.

Jan looked up and laughed. "It's hard to stay mad at you. I swear it is. You're standing there, shoving out your lower lip, pouting and being abused, a little boy who wonders who is going to fix his supper. You know damn well Big Maum goes to Eleuthera for a week every year around this time. She visits her relatives. Maybe she gets herself a man there."

"No one asked me."

"Big Maum never asks anyone. She just says she's going." Jan closed the overnight bag. "One of the girls will bring your breakfast as she always has. You're never here for lunch and dinner." She looked about the room and then back at Max. "If you weren't such an evil-tempered old bastard, I'd ask you to come along. I'm damned if I will, though."

Later Max stood on his own balcony watching as Spindle brought *The Witch* alongside the pier. Then he moved back within the shadow of his room. Here he could watch without being seen.

Big Maum, bare of feet, in a skirt of bright yellow, plum-colored blouse and with a blue bandanna wound about her head, was waiting. Beside her was a large wicker hamper. Max was certain the basket had been packed with hams, flitches of bacon, cartons of cigarettes, two or three bottles of whiskey, which Big Maum was taking as presents to her friends. It really didn't occur to him to question her right to take these things from Windmere's pantry. No one, he thought with sudden humor, would question Big Maum's right to do anything. She ran the house, and everyone knew it.

A dock boy took stern and bow lines, and Major leaped from *The Witch* to the pier with the idea of assisting Big Maum in boarding. She gave him a good-natured shove which all but sent him careening off the dock. Big Maum, shouldering her hamper, went aboard with certain-footed agility. Max smiled. Big Maum was island-born. A boat had been her cradle most likely. She was probably capable of taking *The Witch* to Eleuthera by herself. Major brought her a chair, and she settled herself aft on the starboard side and lit one of her long, thin cigars.

As Max watched, Jan and Sherry came from below. He could see they were laughing over something, and for a moment Jan's face was turned in his direction. He pulled back deeper in the shadow. Damned if he wanted her to think he was spying. Under auxiliary power *The Witch* moved out and away toward the breakwater opening. Max kept her in sight long after she had cleared the point of Lyford Cay. An unfamiliar sensation of loneliness enveloped him. Something now was irrevocably lost, and things between them would never again be quite the same. He had never before made an attempt to intrude into her private life. He had known about or, at least, suspected some of her affairs. These he had never actually framed into words. How did a man question his daughter about such things? Is it true Edith Montgomery is leaving Walter because you and he have been going to bed together? Jan would have told him it was none of his damn business, and that would have been true. A lover was something of passing fancy. A husband was quite another thing. Pulling a chair to a shaded corner of the balcony, he lit a cigar, drawing on it with a brooding satisfaction. In the end she'd have to admit he was right. This was no marriage for her. It occurred to him Jan would no longer live at Windmere. Melnick's business was in Miami. That is where she would have to make her home. This would make Windmere a lonely place. Even though they frequently did not see each other for days, he had always been aware of her presence: her laughter coming from some corner of the house, a sudden snatch of song. He would miss her. It would be a hell of a thing to grow old and die in this place all alone. He found himself thinking about Carol Wainwright. A hell of a fine girl. He wasn't too old for her. She'd fit in well here, the mistress of Windmere. He began to feel better. Damned if he'd sit here alone. He'd dress and go to the club for lunch. Call Carol first and have her join him.

We're goin' to tell it like it is. We're goin' to nail the truth to the door so everyone can see it. We're goin' to rise up in black majesty and shout: "You're not goin' to have it the way it's been. We're goin' to do it our way for a change."

Yes! Yes!

For three hundred years the white man in the islands has put his burden on the black man's back and said: "Carry it, nigger." For three hundred years black hands have built white mansions on the hills. Black hands broke the soil and harvested the crops. For three hundred years the whites have told the black man where he can walk, where he can sit, where he can live. Majority. Minority. If you don't understand those words, I'm goin' to say them so you will. You, we, the black men, are the majority. That means the most. The white people, the minority. That means the littlest. The littlest tells the most how it is to be done. Pick it up. Put it there. Move over, nigger. Get off the sidewalk. Don't come to town after sunset.

Yes! Yes! Yes!

For every hundred persons in the islands eighty of them are black. The twenty whites tell the eighty blacks what to do. They don't put the lash to you anymore, but they beat you with words. "Come here, nigger. Go there, Conchie Joe. Say, yes, sir. No, sir. Thank you. Please." The whip is in the wrong hands. So I tell you to take it. It's there on the wall. That banner. It says the Progressive Liberal Party. That's us. So you use it when the next general election comes. Go an' vote an' you raise such a black storm that the big wave roll right over the whites. You can have it all. A black Assembly. A black Prime Minister. Then we make the laws, an' we tell the white men when they can come to town, where they can sit, where they can eat or have a drink. You hold your heads high for bein' black, an' let the whites move over for a change.

Yes! Yes! Yes!

The fervor of the chanted responses to the words seemed to sway and rock the small frame church as though it were caught in a violent wind. There was a steady beat of hands and the rhythm of feet on the floor as they sounded the measure of excitement. Faces were sweaty, glistening now as though oiled.

163

Eyes cut about to hold those of a neighbor, and heads nodded with approval. The man said things as they were. He told it to them, and they understood. When he bent and moved up there on the little altar, they bent and shifted with him. This was the black man speaking, and the voice was deep, thickly rich. Sometimes it throbbed with an emotion which gave it the sound of a drum. "Yes! Yes!" The words boomed like a heavy surf breaking on a reef.

Royal stood looking down at his audience. His expression held no smile. He was grave, almost forbidding. He put a handkerchief to his face and dried it slowly, listening to the sound he had evoked. It was there as always, complete capitulation. He covered a smile of satisfaction behind the ball of white linen. It was almost too easy. If he told them to burn the church down, they would do it now without question. In all the island settlements it had been the same. He talked. They listened, interestedly at first and then raptly. Little by little the passion of his words reached them. He drew vivid oral pictures they could recognize. Deep within them all was a longing for dignity and a better way of life. They were not yet really angry with the whites, but an emotion was growing. It flamed here and there and must be controlled. He told them there was a better way of life and showed them how it could be reached. They raised their faces to him with shining expressions of hope and gratitude.

Seated on either side of Royal, the Reverends Whitman and Jacob Michaels were stiffly uncomfortable in the dark serge. They were also uneasy. This man Keating. Was he a mountebank? Could he be trusted? They were no longer sure. With an effortless charm Royal Keating had taken the direction of the movement from their hands. In the minds of so many, he was this thing called the Progressive Liberal Party. The Out Island people were beginning to look to him for guidance. He had their trust, their faith, their hope. What would he do with it? Was he a false prophet? Unhappiness shadowed their eyes, for they were sincere men devoted to a cause. If Royal Keating turned charlatan, he would destroy what they had worked patiently for: to arouse pride and a sense of unity among the black people. Would he keep the faith? They were unhappy but helpless.

Royal created an effect. Where his sponsors were clothed in the dingy black of their calling, he was a startling contrast. His feet were in sandals; he wore unpressed slacks of a white tropical weave. A white shirt, unbuttoned almost to the navel, was knotted at the waist by its tails. He seemed to walk among them like some raffish beachcomber, and the people, with their delight in the theatrical, responded. Royal was careful with his words and accent. He was a more than fair mimic, and when he spoke to the people, his accent was theirs. He did not come among them as an alien. He was in the image of all black men.

Royal turned now and with a gesture of a hand seemed to bring the two ministers from their seats. He was presenting his sponsors to his audience, and the people shouted their applause. Royal was not unaware of the ironic humor of the situation, but his manner was courteous and deferential. He raised his arms, hands high above his head, and the cries were abruptly halted. Then, with a slight inclination of his head to the ministers, he walked from the altar down the center aisle. Hands reached out to touch him. He took them when he could but did not break his stride. Behind him the people began to rise. It was as though his passage had lifted them from their seats, and they fell in behind him, following him from the church.

Jan and Sherry had been wedged uncomfortably into a narrow space against the rear wall of the church. They were pressed in on both sides by the swaying ranks of black men and women who seemed indifferent to or oblivious of their presence. Earlier in the week the church had held a fruit sale, and the perfume of oranges, pineapples and bananas was churned with the musk of perspiring bodies. The odor was sharp and unfamiliar. Jan glanced at Sherry and pinched her nose. He shrugged with a gesture of helplessness, blocked in as they were.

They had walked up from the mooring slip in search of the church and a minister who would perform a marriage ceremony. Attracted by the crowd and the air of excitement, they had remained. They managed to get just inside the door, and Jan caught sight of the speaker for the first time.

"That's Royal." She whispered her surprise. "Big Maum's son. Well, what do you know?"

The sound of the deep voice rolled over the audience like a wave. Every face was turned toward the speaker. As he talked, Royal shifted with a graceful movement of his body. He caught the cadence of his words, the response from the crowd, and made of it a beat to time the almost hypnotic measure of a slow dance. The audience moved with him, back and forth like a giant metronome. Over all there was a constant, uneasy murmur.

"Your friend is talking about a black revolution." Sherry put his lips to her ear. "I can think of a better place for a couple of white chillun."

There was no way to leave the building without attracting attention. The rows of those standing blocked the entrance and exit. They would have had to push and force their way through. Jan shook her head and took his arm.

They watched now as Royal moved down through the crowd's center. Those who blocked the narrow aisle shifted to clear a path for him. He smiled and nodded, reaching out to take a hand here and there. He was smiling, friendly and no longer the thunderous teacher of revolt. His gaze roved over the crowd, and as it caught and held on the two white faces, he betrayed his surprise for just a second. Then, as he was about to pass on, he dropped an eyelid in a deliberate wink at Jan, and a small lump formed where tongue was thrust against cheek.

Trailing the audience whose members now, seeing them for the first time, accepted their presence with no more than a friendly curiosity, they left the church. Outside, the sun was brilliant. Purple, red and pink phlox grew abundantly in the grainy soil. Orange trees and oleanders had been planted indiscriminately. There was the hum of many eager voices, and as the people stood about in small groups talking, there was an unmistakable aura of exhilaration hovering over the church's yard.

Royal was surrounded by men and women who clamored

166

and stretched to touch him or receive a word. The two ministers were effectively blocked, and they waited uncertainly on the fringe. After a few moments Royal good-naturedly cleared a way out, thrusting with his hands but making the movements seem an embrace. He laughed and joked with those who were pushed aside. As he came toward where Jan and Sherry waited, his fingers were locked with those of the girl at his side.

"Hello," he called. Reaching them, he spoke to Jan. "I certainly didn't expect to see you here."

"I'm a spy for the Establishment. Hello, Royal."

"Miss Hertog, Miss Thatcher."

Jan offered her hand to the girl of striking black and, somehow, radiant beauty. Alicia Thatcher smiled back. Jan introduced Sherry.

"I had no idea you were such an exorciser." Jan surveyed Royal with a quizzical interest. "I thought you were an engineer."

"Oh"—he shrugged—"I make a small pitch now and then for liberty, equality and fraternity." With an almost protective gesture he placed an arm about Alicia's shoulders. "What are you doing down this way?"

"We brought Big Maum in *The Witch*. Also, as a sort of afterthought, we want to get married."

"Congratulations, Mr. Melnick." He looked over the yard, which was emptying slowly, and then called, "Reverend Whitman." When the minister turned their way, Royal beckoned to him. He joined the group, and Royal made the introductions. "Miss Hertog and Mr. Melnick are interested in the marriage ceremony if you have one handy."

Whitman's surprise was apparent. He glanced from Royal to Jan to Melnick and almost seemed embarrassed.

"I would be happy." He was satisfied now it wasn't some sort of an obscure joke. "If you really—" He was confused. The idea of a black minister performing a marriage ceremony for Maximilian Hertog's daughter, here on one of the Out Islands, was something not easily accepted.

Jan understood his confusion. "We came over in our boat." She smiled at him. "I'm fond of her. I think I'd like to be married on deck. We'll put some champagne on ice and have a wedding party."

In a group they walked slowly down the short incline to the docking area. The wind had dropped, and the small protected harbor was a plate of lightly hammered pewter. A boy lay on his belly at a dock's end fishing with a handline for snapper. Gulls dived like shining white bolts into the water for their meal and screamed a challenge at the intruders.

"I heard Big Maum was coming down." He turned to the Reverend Whitman with an explanation. "My mother." He was puzzled, speaking now to them all. "I've never been able to understand how she does it, but she has some mysterious method of communication. Maybe she has a drum in the hills." He grinned. "I don't know. A man I never saw before came up to me yesterday and said, 'Big Maum be here tomorrow.'" He saw the doubt in their expressions. "Really. That's exactly what happened."

"But she couldn't have known. I didn't know myself until this morning. I told her a week or so ago we would take her to Eleuthera, but I didn't say when."

"Well"—Royal was still mystified—"she knew she was coming."

"Juju," Alicia suggested.

"You may be right." Royal didn't laugh. "I've often wondered."

As they boarded *The Witch,* Sherry laughed quietly and drew Jan a little to one side.

"There's nothing like a happy bridegroom." She smiled with him.

"I was just thinking this is a day of days for Maximilian Hertog. His daughter being married to a Jew by a Negro preacher on the deck of a boat with colored witnesses."

168

X

There was a subdued elegance, an undeniable air of quiet opulence, about the Eleutheran Club following its transfer from Nassau to Paradise Island. It seemed to Max Hertog to be a most unlikely place for what he had always thought of as a lowly game: a pastime for stableboys. Dice. Yet, he discovered to his surprise, it was the principal activity of the casino's central room. There eight tables, with stick- and boxmen, were devoted to a form of diversion which, with minor variations, had been indulged in by the rude soldiers of Caesar's legions along the roads of conquest.

There is something about dice that excites a man's vocal qualities. At most games of chance he can be counted on to be reasonably quiet. Players will stand or sit for hours at a roulette table and watch with silent concentration while a ball, with chattering sound, leaps within a colored and numbered wheel. He will take a place in a blackjack game and remain there throughout an entire evening without saying more than "Hit me" or "That's good." Give a man a pair of dice, though, and he immediately fills the air with a series of frantic and weird incantations. "Gimme an eighter from Decatur." "Little Joe from Kokomo." "Phoebe with the fever." "Big Dick from Boston." "A six in the sticks." "Up jumped the Devil." Few persons, it seems, have willpower enough to pick up the dice and send them rolling the length of a green baize strip without uttering a sound. As a matter of fact, such unusual behavior would excite the suspicions of the house functionaries who make certain no one tries to take a dishonest advantage of the management.

The architects of what was to have been Willard Harrington's isle of happy hours had planned discreetly for the casino. The original drawings had shown only a large, rectangular area designated, innocently enough, as Handball Court. This had been to avoid a suggestion of brashness before a Certificate of Exemption had been granted. Now, though, through the ingenuity of Maximilian Hertog, the space was being put to its proper use. Day and night the tables were crowded with avid gamblers. They came from the Florida mainland, New Orleans, New York, Chicago, San Francisco, Los Angeles and Las Vegas. The men, for the most part, wore white dinner jackets. The women were vividly colorful in bright short evening gowns. Everyone appeared to be healthy, tanned, carefree and, above all, solvent. Mini-mini-skirted waitresses, most of them runners-up in Miami beauty contests, moved with a leggy grace, weaving in and out with their trays of champagne, highballs and brandies, which were in constant and unlimited supply. Courtesy of the management.

Almost any scheme or device for the making of money captured Max Hertog's immediate consideration. Oddly enough he had paid little attention to the opening of Paradise Island. Once he had acquired it from Willard Harrington and assured its successful operation through the acquisition of the Eleutheran Club's certificate, he simply added it to his long list of properties and all but forgot about it. This may have been due to the fact he had never thought of himself as a gambler. He had invested hundreds of thousands of dollars, millions, in varied projects, but he didn't consider this gambling. These were ventures backed by his judgment or hunches. Gambling was sitting at a table over cards, betting on a horse race, rolling dice, or wagering a certain number or color would come up on a wheel. These things bored him. He had no real idea of the range of gambling fever or that it could become a compulsive thing and was not prepared for the immediate success of the casino.

170

The first monthly statement from the associates of Charles Rich startled him. Carol had placed it on his desk with some other papers but gave it top priority. Max read it through with an almost incredulous interest. Then he did a little quick mental calculation. If the month in hand could be considered average, then the Paradise Island Eleutheran Club might be expected to gross something close to eight million dollars a year. He rang for Carol.

"Did you read this?" He looked up as she entered.

"Yes. It's astonishing, isn't it?"

"I would never have believed there were so many persons with money and so little to do. Oh, I expected it to be profitable but not on this scale. I think I ought to drop in some night."

"Do you mean to say you've never been inside the casino? You don't know what's going on over there."

Max leaned back in the chair. "I have you to tell me. By the way, who did you go with?"

"There are still a few courageous males who haven't been scared off by you. I get invited and propositioned frequently. Any number of men, resident and tourist, would like to have carnal knowledge of me. As a matter of fact, I went with Chris Baildon."

"The hell you did." This was accusing. "You know I fired him and why."

"Of course I know, but that doesn't make a social leper out of him. I've always liked Chris. He's doing very well."

Max grunted indifferently and pretended interest in a letter on the desk.

"He is much sought after," she continued, aware of Max's growing impatience. "Everyone on Bay Street is certain he has firsthand knowledge of your innermost thoughts and plans. Such information could be put to profitable use. At the moment he is with Charles Stanford. Confidential assistant. Chris figures the job is good for a year at least. It will take that long for Stanford to discover he doesn't really know anything of value. He has had other offers."

"He talks too much." He looked up irritably. "So do you."

Carol was undisturbed. "By the way, he hasn't forgiven or forgotten. So if you should feel a sharp pain between your shoulder blades some night, it just might be Christopher Baildon sticking a knife in you." She dropped the air of banter. "Why do you go out of your way to have people dislike you? Hate is a better word."

Max was only half listening; part of his mind was occupied with a revision of plans for Grand Bahama. Part also played with the idea that he had made a mistake in becoming attached to Carol Wainwright. The intimacy too frequently intruded on their business association. He was thinking: *I ought to take her out of here and marry her. Either that or reassert the distinction between employer and employee. Maybe I ought to fire her and have done with the whole thing. Sometimes she gets too damn chatty.* He knew, though, he would be unable to replace her. For all her freedom of expression, which, he had to admit, he encouraged, she was too valuable to him in the office.

He looked up to see her, head slightly tilted, regarding him with an expression of amused interest as though she were aware of what he was thinking.

"You know you wouldn't do it," she said calmly.

"What?" He regarded her with astonishment. She had this disturbing faculty of seeming to know what he was thinking. "What are you talking about?"

"You. Me. The way things are between us. Sometimes I've thought it might be better if I quit. Then we could start all over again in a different way."

"Don't talk nonsense." He was unnecessarily rough. "Suppose"—his manner and tone changed—"you have dinner with me tonight and we'll take a look at the action on Paradise Island. You are right. It's time I understood a little more of what is going on." He turned back to the documents on the desk. "I'll pick you up about eight."

"No." The rejection came softly.

For a moment what Carol said didn't register. When it did, he looked up with quick surprise.

"What did you say?"

172

"I said no. I'm sorry. I have a date for this evening."

"Well"—he was unimpressed—"break it."

"I'm sorry. I can't."

His eyes held hers. He was puzzled and a little annoyed. "Of course you can." The subject had been exhausted.

"All right." She was politely obliging. "I can, but I won't."

"Well, I'll be damned." He was astonished by the rebellion. "Why not? I want you to go with me."

"It didn't sound that way." She relented a little. "It sounded more like: 'Get your book and come with me, Miss Wainwright.' It was your Bay Street nine-to-five voice."

By God, he thought with exasperation, *they're all alike.* Even the best of them—and Carol was certainly out of the top drawer—wanted to be courted, soothed, placated. God help a man who took them for granted.

"All right." His smile embraced her. The Hertog charm was being exercised. "It would make me happy if you would change your plans and have dinner with me. I need your help."

"Of course, Mr. Hertog." She managed to convey a sweeping curtsy with the words. "I shall be delighted." At the door she turned. "I didn't really have a date. You know that."

After the door had closed, Max picked up the Paradise Island casino statement again and scanned the figures. They opened up an entirely new avenue of thought in reference to what he had been planning for Grand Bahama.

There had been a mild flurry of public indignation when the full nature of the Out Island Development Act was realized. The Nassau papers commented editorially, but the criticism was tempered by references to Maximilian Hertog's unflagging interest in the development of the Bahamas. The indisputable fact that Grand Bahama was one of the least attractive of the group was pointed up. And, it had been added, there were few men of Maximilian Hertog's caliber who were willing to risk a fortune on such a bleak prospect. True, the government had made a sweeping concession, but without it Grand Bahama would remain what it had always been: an unlovely spit of sand, coral, swamp and scrub. The Progressive Liberal Party had tried to coin political capital from the grant but had

had small success. In Nassau it had provided a topic for conversation but there had been no real protest, as Max had been certain there would not be.

Leaning back in his chair now, he made an attempt to assess Grand Bahama in relation to the casino on Paradise Island. His imagination took flight. Nothing was impossible. He would create a town—not just a façade of one but a complete municipality, starting from the ground itself. The idea was stimulating. He had never owned a town before. This one would be complete. Call it Freeport. It had a fine wide-open sound. Freeport with paved streets, a shopping center, specialty shops with duty-free merchandise, restaurants, nightclubs, bars, hotels. He would import domestic help from Jamaica, where the niggers were more tractable. He would have a police force made up of those Jamaican boys who wore a uniform with such dignity and pride. At the moment there was little on Grand Bahama but the settlement of West End. Freeport would change everything. He'd bring in outside capital for the development of the community, but he'd never allow the control to get out of hand. He was whistling now, the tuneless dirge which always indicated a pleased and thoughtful mood. Freeport would have a casino, and he would build it in the exaggerated Oriental style of a motion-picture set with its domes, spires and minarets. He would leave the exterior unlandscaped so the sandy stretch would give the impression of a desert and import some camel drivers with their animals for atmosphere. The waitresses and bar girls would wear the diaphanous pantaloons and jeweled breast cups of the harem girls of fiction. The whole damn thing would be so preposterously gaudy it would have to succeed. It would be a super-Hollywood epic.

Although he had no real knowledge, it did seem as though Paradise Island might have a limited appeal with its clientele drawn from the upper financial and social brackets. That was all right with Max Hertog. The rich had to have a place to go. He understood this. A casino on Grand Bahama, bolstered by the novelty of Freeport, would be an attraction for everyone from the professional gambler to the man who would buy ten

174

or fifteen dollars' worth of chips at a time. The poor man's Monte Carlo. It was only minutes away from the Florida shore and could draw upon a vast reservoir of the middle and upper middle class. Let Paradise Island cater to the nobs. He had never been in Las Vegas, but he had read enough to know it had not been built on the theory of exclusiveness. In a little over twenty years, he had been told, what was now the famed Strip with one garish hotel after another had grown from a single establishment on the town's edge. This was the mass appeal he wanted for Grand Bahama. Its success would depend, not on the big no-limit professional gamblers and high rollers, but on those who would drop fifty or one hundred dollars at the tables. It was the same old story. A man could make millions if he could sell enough five-cent packages of gum.

He lit a cigar and drew on it thoughtfully. He would like to have someone with experience to talk with. It seemed probable that a casino on Grand Bahama would cut seriously into the play of Paradise Island. It would also divert a large segment of the tourist traffic. There was little in Nassau to attract the young. Night life was practically nonexistent, and what there was soon became an insufferable bore, limited to calypso. Grand Bahama would be different. Name bands and entertainers could be brought over before or after their engagements in Miami. The yachting crowd, the old money would still put in at Nassau. Paradise Island would be for them. The young money—the five-cent packages of gum—would be attracted to Grand Bahama. Now he was on uncertain ground, and he paused to consider the sequence of things. Although Charles Rich and his associates were still shadowy figures, they did exist. The contact was real. The Paradise Island statement was proof of that. So how could he divest himself of them? Or, and this was also a problem, did he want to cut them loose?

Ordinarily he was insensitive to criticism, but some of the national publicity the operation of the Eleutheran Club had drawn was disturbing. In his mind the word "Mafia" had overly melodramatic connotations. The Mafia. Sicilians with gold rings in their ears, knives between their teeth, and bombs in each hand. The Black Hand. Little men in greasy blue serge suits skulking in alleys or basement rooms. They were the products of fiction. But it seemed this was not the case at all. There was a Mafia, a Cosa Nostra, and its sinister activities were worldwide. The articles which had appeared linking the Cosa Nostra, through Charles Rich, to the Eleutheran Club and, incidentally, Maximilian Hertog had been too thoroughly documented to be ignored. With grim humor Max thought he was one of the brotherhood and, sooner or later, would be asked to exchange blood vows, tapping a vein and inscribing his name on parchment. He wondered a little idly how the press had winnowed out the fact that Charles Rich and associates had entered into a business arrangement with Max Hertog. Many of the stories had an unpleasant ring. Max was accustomed to ignoring charges of unprincipled conduct. But to be linked with a stranger's knavery and forced to share it was damned annoying. The Miami *Herald* had dug into the story with its usual thoroughness. *Life* published a detailed article pinning him to Rich, Meyer Lansky and other characters who had achieved a dubious reputation. It seemed highly improbable that Rich and associates would regard the opening of a rival casino in the Bahamas lightly. This, to Max's mind, now was the bind, the rub. He would have liked to have drawn Rich into the development of Grand Bahama, which might well run into a hundred million dollars. If the Mafia or Cosa Nostra were looking for a legitimate investment, this could be it. But he only wanted to give them this and keep the casino for himself. It was the sort of deal he liked, seasoned with a touch of larceny on his part. It gave flavor to the manipulation. The question was: Could he get away with it? He considered this briefly and decided it was worth trying. He would offer Rich the opportunity of making a substantial investment in the creation of Freeport. He could easily afford to make the Syndicate a large grant of land and let it build the town for him. The general increase in property values would more than compensate for what he had given away. From this point on he would have to be careful. Rich would want to have an understanding in the matter of a casino on Grand Bahama. He would have

176

to be reassuringly vague but nothing more. He would make no flat promise. All conversation would have to be speculative, based on securing a Certificate of Exemption. It would have to be "iffy" talk. If we get this or that. If a certificate can be arranged. If we agree on terms. He didn't believe for a moment this would satisfy Charles Rich, but he might be persuaded to go along.

A small light winked on his desk, and he flipped a switch on the intercom box.

"Yes."

"Miss Hertog." The receptionist corrected herself. "I mean, Mrs. Melnick is here, Mr. Hertog."

Several seconds ticked away before he replied. He hadn't seen Jan since her runaway marriage some six months ago. She had sent *The Witch* back from Eleuthera and flown from there to Miami. She had called him at Windmere, but he had been stubbornly resentful.

"Sherry and I were married today." He could recall now the small catch of excitement in her voice.

"I hope you know what you're doing." He had been blunt.

"Is that all you have to say to me, Max?" There was a plea here, and he had ignored it.

"What am I supposed to say?"

"Nothing, Max." The little-girl tone in her voice was gone. "Not a damned thing."

He had read later in one of the Miami papers that she and Melnick had gone to Spain on a wedding trip. She made no effort at further communication. Max sulked. He grew bitter and then resentful. Now, knowing she was outside, he experienced a conflict of emotions.

"Mr. Hertog?" The question was in the receptionist's tone.

"Damn it," he shouted to relieve his uncertainty. "She knows she doesn't have to be announced. Jan! Come on in here and stop this nonsense." He boomed the order into the transmitter and cut off any reply with the switch. Leaning forward on the desk, arms half-outspread, he waited.

"Hello, Pop." She smiled at him from the doorway. Her manner was confident and assured. She hadn't come to be forgiven. "How are you?" She rarely called him anything but Max. The "Pop" was her concession to an understanding.

"You look fine, Sis." He studied her briefly and then rose.

They stood, facing each other. Both were embarrassed by the situation and their emotion. Each waited for the other to indicate the tenor of this meeting. There was a deep affection here, affection, pride and, in some measure, understanding. They knew each other well. It was Max who made the move. He took the few steps necessary to cross the distance between them. His hands closed on her shoulders, and he discovered she was trembling lightly. He bent then to kiss her cheek and held her to him.

"Are you all right?" The question was muffled. He released her.

"I'm great." Her eyes were shining, and she was unembarrassed by the tears. "This is silly talk, isn't it?" She linked both her arms with one of his. After leading him back to his chair, she perched herself at his side. "I've missed you."

"It has been a big house without you." He hesitated, knowing it was up to him. She expected it. "How is, you know, what's his name?"

She loosed a hoot of laughter. "Well, I'll tell you, Max. What's his name sure isn't outside waiting for you to tell him he can come in." She shook her head. "No one will ever accuse you of not being firm in your convictions."

"Are you happy?" The question was trite, and he knew it. He was being the conventional father asking the conventional questions.

"Yes, Max. Happier than I can ever remember being. It's been good for me in ways you wouldn't understand. Do you know"—she seemed honestly surprised—"going to bed with your husband is different from going to bed with a lover?"

"You're not supposed to know the difference. Or at least don't talk about it. All right." He managed a gusty sigh. "It's done. If you're happy, I suppose nothing else matters. I'll be civil, at least. But I still don't think I like him."

She lit a cigarette. "Do you know something? Weeks go by

178

and Sherry never even mentions your name. He's learned to live with his sorrow."

"What brought you to Nassau?"

"Jane and Larry Hendricks asked us for the weekend on their boat. We're at the Harbour Club."

"There's plenty of room at Windmere." This was as close to an invitation as he could bring himself. "Everything is just the way you left it."

She all but shouted her amusement. "You old ham you. There ought to be concealed violins playing 'Hearts and Flowers.' Everything is just the way you left it. 'The little toy soldiers are covered with dust.' Max, you ought to be ashamed of yourself."

He was forced to grin. "I just meant. Well, you know. I mean, why don't you bring everyone up to the house? You'll be a lot more comfortable. We'll have dinner. Carol will be along. I want to show you the moneymaking machine I have on Paradise Island."

"I read about it. You're in strange company, aren't you?"

"Different, maybe, but not strange." He stood up. "Now do we have a date?"

"Yes." She eyed him gravely. "I'll bring what's his name and the Hendricks. And"—she was severe—"you behave yourself with Sherry. Do you hear?"

Max lingered in the corridor leading to the casino's central game room. It was a pleasant area, deeply carpeted, softly lighted and with walls paneled in cypress. There were a few small tables and chairs evenly spaced, served by an exceptionally pretty girl in a short, ruffled skirt with a handkerchief-sized lace apron above long legs in sheer black stockings. Max eyed her with approval and gave his order.

The casino's floor plan was such that this corridor was connected to the entrance. Those who came to play must walk through it to get to the games. It also was the only passage from the tables to the rooms marked LADIES and GENTLEMEN. Against the walls were ranged a dozen or more slot machines. They glowed and sparkled in their chrome and color. These

179

had been a surprise to Max. Slot machines, he thought, would have little appeal for Paradise Island's clientele. They would, it seemed, be more appropriate to a bar or pool hall. Now, though, as he idled over a brandy and small coffee, his admiration for whoever had planned the casino increased. There was an almost constant movement here of those entering or leaving, of others on their way to or from the washrooms. It was, he noted with pleasure, a rare individual who passed through without dropping a quarter or half-dollar into one of the machines. They did this without seeming to halt, and the action was one continuous movement. A coin was placed in the slot, and the same hand moved smoothly to pull down a lever. Then the man or woman appeared to glide on without a break in stride. But—and Max smiled at this—a head was always alertly tilted for the sound of rushing coins should the machine pay off. Once in a while a man or woman would stand before a machine and feed into it all the loose quarters and half-dollars in purse or pocket. No one ever walked away with winnings. If the machines did hit for them, the players invariably stayed to replay the coins.

Because almost everything Max knew was measured in dollars, in profit or loss, he wondered what the nightly take was for these mechanical con men. There were no dime or nickel machines. The quarters and halves fed into them must make an impressive total. Here, if any place, he thought, was the perfect example of the five-cent package of gum.

Having finished his coffee, he strolled into the central room. It was brightly lighted and crowded. He had left Carol with Jan and her party at one of the dice tables, excusing himself with the explanation he wanted to look around. Everything here fascinated him. He studied the faces. Some appeared bored. Others betrayed excitement or, occasionally, the strain of losing. A few mirrored an impassive indifference. Win or lose, the expressions did not change. These, Max noted, were the ones who played the house limit of five hundred dollars. They made their bets, backed them up for the house odds on a point, and paid no attention to those around them. They gambled with a professional dexterity, a minimum of effort and no conversation. Save for a few young women who squealed their delight over a small win, no one seemed to be enjoying himself. There was little in the nature of a social exchange. The players rarely spoke to each other. No one smiled or appeared happy or entertained. An air of grim concentration hovered about the tables. It was, he thought, a most unrewarding way to spend an evening. Even the few winners who racked up their chips in neat stacks didn't seem to be having much fun.

Having absorbed the mechanics of the play, he began a study of the room. Everything had been planned for an efficient operation in which the house must win. This, in turn, required security measures in order that the house could keep what it had won. At an end wall, high above the floor, there were two windowlike slits. Now and then it was possible to detect a movement behind them. Max surmised there must be men posted there whose sharp eyes constantly roved over the room and the tables in search of any irregularity. One side of the long room held the cashiers' cages with their grilled windows. Joining this section were office space and the accounting room. A single door marked PRIVATE led to this. Men in dark dinner jackets seemed to be posted about the room. Others strolled with a seeming lack of purpose. Despite this studied attitude of aimlessness, they maintained a constant vigilance. Having identified them as security guards, Max was pleased by the professional manner in which they went about their duties. They were looking after his money. He had an almost juvenile desire to identify himself. After all, the place was his. They worked for him whether or not they knew it. He wanted to say: "I'm Max Hertog. I own the island and everything on it." He was unhappy with his anonymity. The casino was a new possession. It was successful, and Maximilian Hertog liked to be associated with success.

As he wandered about, unmistakably studying every detail of the room, he attracted an immediate but unobtrusive attention from the men in conventional dinner jackets. Without seeming to do so, they moved into positions which created a wide circle. Within this Max Hertog was permitted to walk, but by now he had become an object of attention for many eyes. To those who watched he appeared to be a man of erratic behavior. A signal had already gone from the pit boss to those who were posted at the lookout slots. The chief security officer checked the positions of his men. This, his manner told them, may just be a harmless tourist paying his first visit to a casino and interested in every phase of its operation. Again, he could be a diversionary tactic created to draw attention away from a well-synchronized effort at a mass holdup. Now there was a shift in positions of the guards, and the circle about Max tightened and grew smaller. For his part, Max was happily unaware of the tension he was creating. When he walked past the cashiers' cages for the second time, slowing his step while he peered with an almost paternal curiosity between the narrow bars at the men seated on their high stools behind stacked bills and silver dollars, there was an all but breathless moment for those who followed his movements. The hands of the cashiers slid beneath counters, and fingers rested on buttons which would release steel shutters covering the windows. Max paused at the door of the accounting room. Later he would admit to himself that his actions had been stupid. He was accustomed to having complete authority in any of his ventures. It simply did not occur to him that he was a complete stranger to the casino's employees.

As his hand reached for the knob and before he could turn it and find the door locked, two men had stepped forward to flank him, pressing tightly against his sides. Startled, he attempted to shoulder them away and felt the unmistakable pressure of a gun at a point just below his ribs.

"Yes, sir?" The question was polite and whispered.

"What the hell's the matter with you?" He was startled and angry. "Take that damned gun away."

"Now we don't want any trouble, do we?" The voice was soothing. The tone which might be used to reassure a harmless nut.

Three additional men had moved in, and Max realized he was effectively boxed and screened from sight.

"I'm Max Hertog." This was a furious growl. "And if you

don't know who that is, I own this damned place. Now get away from me."

"Yes. Of course." This was a polite agreement, but no one moved away to release him.

So rapidly and lightly did the hands travel over him that it was a second or two before he realized he was being searched for a weapon. For a moment he was the victim of a consuming and unreasoning fury. He was a big man who could not be subdued without a threshing scuffle. He was on the point of striking out when reason took the place of anger. It would make a fine spectacle. Max Hertog in a free-for-all brawl, creating an outrageous public scene from which he could only emerge as an overbearing idiot.

"I know the gentleman. I'm sure it is all right, Martin." Sherry Melnick spoke from just outside the group.

The man called Martin turned. "Oh, hello, Mr. Melnick." He seemed relieved. "You know the gentleman?"

Sherry nodded, and the pressure on Max was released. He thrust out with both arms, clearing a space. Shaking himself with the ponderous dignity of a rumpled bear, he glared at Melnick.

"If you know him, Mr. Melnick"—the security man spoke wearily—"then tell the damned fool to stop behaving as though he was going to try and hold the place up. And"—the voice was heavy with sarcasm, and he glared at Maximilian Hertog —"the word on the door is 'Private.' It means keep out." He shook his head with disgust. "It sure takes all kinds, and I usually get them." He nodded to his men, and they drifted away, losing themselves in the crowded room.

Max shrugged, settling his shoulders in his coat. He grunted and made a determined effort to avoid looking at Melnick. He was uncomfortable and embarrassed.

"All right," he rumbled finally. "Don't act as though you saved my life. I would have straightened it out."

"Not the way you were going about it." Melnick eyed him with amused pleasure. "After all," he continued, "I didn't want everyone to see you in a tangle. I have the family to think of.

183

How would it look in the newspapers? Sherry Melnick's father-in-law in casino brawl."

"Goons!" Max snorted his disgust. He refused to admit he was aware of Melnick's sly needling. "Gorillas."

"They are top men at their jobs. Martin Quinn was on the Miami police force. That's how I happen to know him. Since you have a piece of the action here, you ought to be satisfied it is so well protected."

Max rubbed a hand over his mouth. A hidden smile was reflected in his eyes. The more he thought about the incident, the more embarrassing it became.

"I suppose"—he spoke slowly—"you'll have to tell Jan about this?"

"I don't know why I should. You aren't exactly my favorite topic of conversation. Days go by and I never even mention your name in our house."

Normally Max would have risen to this. Now, though, he was satisfied to let it pass. Sooner or later he knew he would have to make an adjustment to Jan's marriage. It was either that or alienate her completely.

"How about a drink?" There was little enthusiasm in the question.

Sherry nodded. "That seems a reasonable enough suggestion. As long as we don't get mired down in sentiment for each other."

"You understand this doesn't commit me to anything?"

"Naturally not." Sherry was satisfied.

"If I think of you at all, it is as an unfortunate occurrence."

"An unavoidable one."

"I tolerate you because of Jan."

Sherry was amiable. "I think of the whole thing as a step up for me. I have become a gentleman through marriage."

On their way to the bar they passed a table where Jan was earnestly and vocally trying to make a point of ten. She glanced up, caught sight of Sherry and her father seemingly in amicable conversation. Her expression was one of pleased astonishment. Sherry winked in return, and Max, unwilling to unbend further at the moment, pretended he hadn't seen her.

184

XI

The philosophy of laissez-faire has been refined and perfected to such a point in the Bahamas that one person will hesitate to inquire after another's health for fear of being thought intrusive.

The code of behavior among the old families is simply stated: "I'll pretend I don't know what you're doing if you'll act as though you don't see me." As a result of this see-no-evil, speak-no-evil arrangement, a variety of peccadilloes from bed to countinghouse flourishes. The participants are comfortable in the knowledge no one will want to be the first to disturb the balance of things as they are.

Normally, Maximilian Hertog's outrageous grab of Grand Bahama would not have aroused more than some professional envy on Bay Street and provided a topic for dinner-table conversation in the fine homes on their high ground above the sea. Time would dull this interest, and a few members of the Establishment would maneuver themselves into positions where they might share in the spoils. The first indication that these were not normal times came in a shower of leaflets, heavily distributed in Nassau and throughout the black districts of the island. They appeared mysteriously on the seats of taxicabs, on the tables of restaurants and bars. They were folded into the newspapers and magazines on sale, discovered on porch and steps. In the black slums Over the Hill they were read aloud to the illiterate by the few who could make out the words. No one was ever found distributing the sheets. They simply appeared. Obviously directed to the attention of the middle-class whites and the blacks, they shouted their message.

BLACK AND WHITE.
ATTENTION!

Do you know you are being robbed of
your birthright by Maximilian Hertog?

Do you understand the gigantic swindle
by which Mr. Hertog acquired Grand Bahama?
This is Crown property. Your property.
The Assembly gave it away.

THROW THE RASCALS OUT.

Force the Pirate Hertog to Return His Loot.

There was no clue to the source of the sheets. In the beginning they were regarded with amusement by the well-established. As tough as old Max was, they agreed, he must be squirming just a little. Later a more sober view was taken. If Maximilian Hertog could be attacked and defamed in this fashion, then no one was safe. For the good of all, they must draw together and present a common front against the assault of this mischief-maker. A check was made of the few printing establishments. All denied having run the leaflets off. Either someone was lying or the printing was being done in Miami or one of the mainland towns. Who was bringing these scurrilous sheets to the island? It was first suggested they were the work of the Progressive Liberal Party. This seemed a reasonable enough assumption until the obvious flaw was pointed out. If the PLP had instigated the attack, it would have identified itself with the leaflets. The brief diatribe had a political propaganda value, but not if its sponsors remained anonymous. Who, then, was the author? The question kept Nassau buzzing throughout the day. Who and why? Throughout the week the handbills continued to make a most mysterious appearance. The text remained unchanged.

186

The first day Carol hesitantly brought one in to Max. She made an exaggerated gesture of holding it distastefully between thumb and forefinger.

"Have you seen this?" She laid it before him.

"Yes. And I'd guess everyone on New Providence has." He eyed the leaflet sourly. "There was one tucked into my Miami paper so I could enjoy it with breakfast. There was another under the windshield wiper of my car."

"They're all over town. I've had half a dozen calls from my friends, who wanted to be sure I didn't miss it." She picked the sheet of coarse paper up, turning it from front to back. "Don't they usually put a printer's mark on something like this?"

"No. Sometimes there's a union label. A printer wouldn't want to be identified with this." He reached for it, read through it again with a scowl, and then crumpled it into a tight ball.

"What are you going to do about it?"

"Nothing." A small grin appeared. "How can I dispute the truth? Hell. I did steal it. I stole it and I'm going to keep it. Someone is sore because he didn't think of it first."

"It won't change things?"

"No. The Prime Minister called me this morning. He may go through the motions of a reexamination of the Out Island Development Act. I agreed that this might make a good impression. There will be no inquiry, and the whole thing will be forgotten. I'll put a lot of niggers to work out there. The first thing you know I'll be a benefactor again. Now"—he leaned back—"what's on deck?"

"Mr. Rich is at the Hotel Montagu. He said he'd be ready when you are. Inter Island Airways has the small amphibian waiting. Will you be back this evening?"

Max rose and reached for the Panama hat he always carried but rarely wore.

"Call Rich and tell him I'm on my way. I'll pick him up. Have Inter Island send the plane to the Harbour Club ramp. I'll be back sometime late in the afternoon. I want to take Rich over Grand Bahama." He started for the door and then turned. "See if you can locate Royal Keating. He was making political speeches on Eleuthera the last time I heard. Maybe Big Maum will know where he is. Get word to him I want to see him. Tell him to come to Windmere."

He was out of the door, across the reception room, and trotting down the steps before she could reply.

The amphibian, a twelve-place job which ducked in and out of the islands carrying mail, passengers and cargo, cruised back and forth over Grand Bahama at five hundred feet. Max and Charles Rich were the only occupants.

"Well"—Max turned from the window and faced Rich—"that's it." He called forward to the pilot. "Take her down, Tom. We'll get some lunch and a drink in West End before starting back." He swung around to face Rich again. "You've seen enough, haven't you?"

"Yes. As a matter of fact, I made an inspection of my own last week. I had all the information I needed and a complete set of aerial photographs."

"Why didn't you say so?" Max was impatient. "We've wasted a morning."

Charles Rich smiled to himself. He was a man of quiet speech and manner and as unaccustomed to having his decisions questioned as was Max Hertog. Because Hertog had what Rich wanted, he permitted the arrogance to go unchallenged.

"I wanted to go over it with you." Rich was undisturbed. "I have already talked with some of our people in New York and Chicago. They are delighted with our arrangement on Paradise Island and are prepared to take my recommendation on any future association."

"All right." Voices had to be raised within the small cabin. Max shouted, "We can talk it over at lunch."

West End lies on a long point of land at the northwest end of Grand Bahama. It is little more than a collection of nondescript dwellings with a small landlocked harbor and a hotel. A balcony hangs over the water, and they had a couple of drinks and lunch there.

Rich boned a hand-sized snapper, crisply fried in deep fat. Only minutes out of the water, the fish was better than any he had ever tasted. He listened while Max Hertog talked, eating and making no comment beyond a nod of the head when it seemed necessary. Most persons reacted immediately and unfavorably to Hertog's arrogance. Rich found it mildly entertaining. This was a picaresque character, a freebooter of another era.

"Just why do you want us in on the development of Grand Bahama?" Rich interposed the question in a break of Max's monologue. "From what I know of you, taking in a partner is not your habit."

"No." Max finished his coffee. "I usually like to go it alone. But the Grand Bahama is going to be two or maybe even three distinct operations. I like the way you and your people do things. Also, you seem to have a hell of a lot of money. It is going to take that to do what I have in mind."

"There is always some unpleasant publicity when our participation in a venture becomes known." Rich lobbed a piece of roll into the air, and a gull caught it in twisting flight. "You should know it will reoccur with Grand Bahama."

"My hide is thick. If it weren't, I would have been cut up long ago. I make my own decisions."

Rich lit a cigarette. "Newspapers thrive on the sensational. We are a large organization with many interests. Our methods of eliminating competition have sometimes aroused unfavorable comment."

Max eyed him with delight. "Standard Oil, in its early days, was accused of a certain ruthlessness."

"Quite so." Rich nodded solemnly. "I hadn't thought of that." His eyes lighted with subdued humor.

Max leaned back in his chair. Rich pleased him immensely. There was this effortless attitude of benign preciseness. He was the headmaster speaking in measured accents to the new boys, explaining with a certain regret how things were and would be. Max wondered how much was affectation, how much habit. The manner was the result of cultivation. Of this he was certain. He was equally sure Charles Rich found it amusing. It entertained him to be what he was.

"What exactly do you have in mind for this?" Rich gestured

with one hand to include all of Grand Bahama. "Where do we fit in?"

This was the part of any deal Max enjoyed. To plan something, to have it take shape in his mind as he talked. He could expand or modify at will.

"To begin with"—he began making vertical lines on the tablecloth with a knife—"I own something over two hundred square miles of Grand Bahama. There are a few squatter claims, but they are unimportant. I'll buy them off or run them off. It doesn't make much difference which. I want to build a town here. Call it Freeport. It will be just that: wide-open, free and easy. You can almost spit the distance between here and the Florida coast. I will have all the mainland to draw from. I want the town laid out up there around where the Pinder Point Light is. A town with an airport, a shopping center, a luxury hotel, nightclubs, bars and whatever goes with them. If the tourists want things we don't have, we'll get it for them. I'll donate the land. You finance the operation."

"How does your end work out?" Rich went immediately to the heart. "Where is Hertog's profit?"

"For one thing I'll have one hell of a lot of land left over. With this place booming, what I bought for around three dollars an acre will jump to five, ten, even fifty thousand dollars an acre. That's where I come in."

While Max was talking, Charles Rich tried to slip in behind the words and find out what he really meant. He must certainly be aware of the Syndicate's interest in gambling, yet a casino had not been mentioned. Why?

"You know, of course"—he spoke slowly, his eyes holding Hertog's—"our primary interest in a hotel on Grand Bahama would be the operation of a casino. We are not"—the smile was thin—"an organization of innkeepers, although we do have investments for the sake of diversification." This was the chairman addressing a meeting of stockholders. "This, I'm sure, has occurred to you."

"Naturally."

"You will have no difficulty in securing a permit for gambling on Grand Bahama?"

190

"No." Max didn't hesitate. "I can take care of that."

"There was no mention of your participation in the casino." Rich probed gently.

"We'll work out something; a deal such as we have with Paradise Island."

"In this"—Rich did not like the careless phrasing—"ours would have to be the larger share to cover our investment."

"There will be plenty for everyone." Max was unconcerned.

"I hope I'm not being misunderstood." Rich underlined his words now. "I'm not speaking of everyone—only the two principals, you and my group."

There was an uneasy suspicion in the mind of Charles Rich. Max was aware of this. He had been overly casual.

"You name what you think is an equitable distribution of the casino profits. After all, I'll be getting a town where there was nothing."

Rich's smile was thin. "We have no real interest in building a community. It is simply part of the overall project. Our organization has a wide range of interests. If we create Freeport, we will expect to have a free hand in it. That means girls, slot machines and other profitable sidelines. We do not know each other too well. I would be unhappy to discover you were squeamish about certain aspects of—shall we say—entertainment and recreation."

Max was growing irritated with this emphasis on the trivial and obvious. Hell, he would expect that the topflight call girls in Miami would find weekends on Grand Bahama profitable. If Rich's group controlled the girls, this was not his concern. As for the other elements of what Rich described as entertainment and recreation, perhaps they were better left unstated.

"I told you I wanted Freeport to be wide-open. I meant it."

"Good." The smile now held warmth. "It is better to discuss these things in the beginning. I'm certain you realize how disturbed my associates would be if, after making an extremely large investment here, there should be any difficulty in securing a gambling permit from the Bahamas government."

191

"That's as good as in my pocket. I think you and I understand each other."

"I hope we do." Rich was thoughtful. "I sincerely hope we do."

Royal straddled a kitchen chair, resting his arms on the back and eating a large piece of chocolate cake from one hand. At the stove Big Maum was turned away, but he could tell from the stubborn set of her body she was disturbed and half-angry with him. The maid, Stella, was setting a single place at the big table. Without turning, Big Maum dismissed her.

"Yo' go 'long now, Stella. Busy yo'sef wid somethin'. I wan' talk wid Royal."

The girl smiled shyly at Royal and ducked past him to the screen door.

"Don' ruin yo' hunger wid dat cake." She still refused to face him. "I fix a steak an' t'ings." She moved with a heavy grace, mumbling to herself.

Royal finished the cake, licked his fingers, and lit a cigarette. Sooner or later she would get to the point of telling him what was on her mind.

Big Maum slid a steak beneath the broiler. "I worry 'bout yo', boy." She turned now to look at him.

"Why, Big Maum?" He smiled at her.

"I hear yo' ain' wuk no more en 'Leuthera. Ef yo' ain' wuk, what yo' do? Lie aroun' wid dat girl yo' gots?"

"The job on Eleuthera is finished, Big Maum. There wasn't anything more for me to do. Now it is for carpenters, masons, plumbers, electricians. They build the houses."

"Then yo' out o' wuk? Th' company ain' gots no mo' job for yo'? What th' other mens do?"

"Oh, they scatter. Some go to one place; others to another. Wherever the company sends them."

"Why don' yo' go wid 'em?" She eyed him sternly now.

"I wanted to stay here." He was uncomfortable.

"Why?" She planted herself before him. "You t'ink I don' know." She gestured with the large fork. "I hears t'ings. People come t' me, an' dey say dis o' dat. Dey say yo' know 'bout yo'

192

boy Royal, Big Maum? All he do now is hol' a meetin'. He talks t' th' people, an' dey rise up, yellin' an' clappin' from th' t'ings yo' tell 'em. You tell 'em black people, 'Rise up an' take from th' whites what belong t' th' blacks.' You wan' git yo'sef killed, boy?" She stared at him, angry now, angry and confused, wanting him to reassure her.

How to explain to Big Maum? How to tell her he wasn't a wild-eyed fanatic preaching blood, fire and revolution? How to explain he was working for an orderly change of government and how he, one day, would be the voice of the black party? She would never understand. Big Maum wanted no change. The whites ran their world. Hers was here, in this house, and she ran it. She had worked for no more than two families in her lifetime. Here, at Windmere, she was the voice of authority. Her loyalty, if she ever thought about it, was to her position and, incidentally, Maximilian Hertog. She had no idea of government beyond Windmere. No doubts nagged at her; no unrest, no dissatisfaction plagued her. She was aware of the black poverty in Nassau and the Out Islands. She knew that to most whites the island blacks were little more than animals to be worked when needed. There was poverty, but then there had always been poverty. How was a black man by the name of Royal Keating going to change those things? He despaired of explaining to her and of linking it with a giddy feeling of triumph and destiny. He had proved to himself and others what he could do. The island blacks listened and were lifted from their apathy by his words. They would vote as they were told in the next general election, and Royal Keating would become the first black Prime Minister in the history of the Bahamas. Of this he was certain. His conviction was so strong he had deliberately tossed away a career in another field. He was convinced now this was not an accident, the result of a chance meeting with the Reverend Whitman. Something had led him to that church; an unknown guide had put his feet on this path. There was no turning from it now. Big Maum would think he was crazy if he said these things. Prime Minister. A black policeman, maybe, she would say. A black policeman she would understand. But even the black police in Nassau weren't native. They were all Jamaicans, imported so they wouldn't be overly sympathetic with the Nassau blacks. She was waiting for him to reassure her.

"Big Maum." He was uncomfortable, squirming as a small boy. The words as he formed them in his mind sounded foolish, the idle talk of an idiot. "It's like I was a preacher going around the islands telling the people how they can make things better for themselves."

"But yo' ain' no preacher." This was pragmatic.

"No, Big Maum. Not exactly."

"Yo' git paid fo' dis wuk?"

"No. Not now."

"Den ef yo' gots no church, yo' ain' no preacher, yo' don' git no pay. Den"—she was triumphant—"yo' out o' wuk. Yo' ain' gots no job."

"Well, yes. If you put it that way."

"So!"

She turned the steak over beneath the broiler. Her shoulders had straightened; the expression of unhappy bewilderment was erased from her face. This was no unfamiliar ground now. A man was out of work. Something could be done about that. It was no disgrace even for a man with her Royal's education. A man lost one job. He found another. In a situation like this, one man, Mistuh Max, could set things right. She was smiling now.

"I 'spec' Mistuh Max hear how yo' ain' wukkin' no mo'. Dat why, I guess, he sen' fo' yo' t' see him heah today."

Royal smiled and nodded. There was no point in telling her Max didn't give a goddamn whether Royal Keating had a job. If Max wanted to see him, then it was because such a meeting would be to Max's advantage.

"I guess so, Big Maum." He agreed because he knew this would please her. "I'll tell you after I talk with him."

"Yo' do so, boy."

She busied herself, slicing a raw onion and a tomato to go with the steak, pouring a glass of milk, setting out a plate of fresh bread from her oven.

"Yo' eat good. When yo' talk wid Mistuh Max, yo' let him

194

do mos' talkin'. Yo' know how Mistuh Max is. He like t' do th' sayin' widout no interrupt. Dat's th' way he muches it."

She brought the steak, arranged everything before him, and then stood back with pride and a glowing pleasure to watch her son eat. She talked easily, bringing him up to date on the affairs of the house.

"Miss Jan an' her new husban' here fo' a few days. She bring him t' me fo' introduce. He pleasan' man wid good manner. I gots feelin' him an' Mistuh Max don' git along so good. Dey don' say t' each oder but jus' look. Miss Jan she like differen' person wid man o' her own. Miss Jan always kinda like my baby, an' I worrit 'bout her. She got dat hunger fo' a man all th' time. I see it en her eye when a man aroun'. It like her sayin', 'Is dis th' one who can do it t' me an' mek it las'?' " She laughed with a soft, rich pleasure. "I bin young. I know th' feelin'. Dere ain' nothin' worse dan t' wan' it good an' have it turn out nothin'. Dis man sure be right fo' her. She ain' starvin' no mo'. Yo' wan' more milk, coffee o' somethin'?"

"No, thank you, Big Maum." He pushed back his chair and lit a cigarette, half listening as Big Maum cleared the table and talked. Despite Max's offer of financial assistance, he had asked for nothing. The general election was in the future. Money would be needed then. It would do no harm now, though, to spread some around among those in the Out Islands who held some small influence. This would be an all-black effort. The poor inbred whites would have nothing to do with the blacks. Their attitude was that of the Southern red-necks; their prejudices were equally as strong and unreasoning. Their hatred ran deep. No. The island blacks would have to look to themselves for their salvation.

"Mistuh Max." Big Maum's words interrupted his thoughts. "He sen' word fo' yo' t' come t' his rooms. It don' do t' keep Mistuh Max waitin'." She laughed, certain of her position in the household. "An' it sure don' do no good ef yo're black. I guess, maybe, I'm th' only black person en th' worl' Mistuh Max don' shout at. He do it onct, but I yell back. Dat dere th' en'. We gots respec' for each oder ev'r since."

Royal mashed out his cigarette and stood up. Mother and

195

son created a striking picture, drawn in great, bold lines. Between them there was an affection never put into words. They were gentle with each other. They had never used the word "love," but it was there. They were inexplicably shy with their demonstrations. A touch of the hand, the light trailing of fingers across a cheek, a smile and a wordless exchange of understanding.

She called now through the open window. "Stella. Yo' come here." She turned to Royal. "I have Stella take yo' t' Mistuh Max."

"Take care of yourself, Big Maum." His hands rested on her shoulders, and he bent slightly to touch his cheek against hers.

"Yo' take care o' yo'sef how yo' talk wid Mistuh Max."

"I will. We get along all right." He released her.

The girl Stella came from the yard and stood before Big Maum, who studied her critically before nodding approval of her appearance.

"Yo' take Mistuh Royal t' Mistuh Max rooms, Stella. Yo' 'nounce him right. Yo' knock on th' door an' when he say who dat, den yo' open it. You say, Mistuh Max, sir. Here t' see yo' is Mistuh Royal." She shook her head, and sudden unhappiness brooded in her eyes. "No." She corrected herself. "Yo' jus' say, Mistuh Max, here Royal." She turned to her son with a small, pleading gesture, asking he understand why the girl couldn't call him Mistuh Royal. To another white, maybe, but not to Maximilian Hertog.

"It's all right, Big Maum. Don't worry. I know Mr. Max pretty well by now."

She watched as he followed Stella from the kitchen. She hoped he wouldn't be free and easy with Mistuh Max, who had no time for black men who didn't know and keep their place.

Waiting for Royal, Max was determined not to make the mistake of that earlier meeting in his office. This time there would be no uncertain maneuvering which had put him at a disadvantage before. He would tell him to sit down, and that

196

would be the end of it. And he would behave as though sitting with a black man were commonplace. This was something to which he would have to adjust his thinking and behavior. He must remember that within the next few minutes a future Prime Minister of Her Majesty's government in the Bahamas might be standing just outside his door.

When the girl brought Royal to the upstairs suite and quickly backed out, closing the door, Max flipped a hand in the direction of a chair. This, he felt, disposed of the amenities of the situation.

"I hear you left the Janis Corporation." It was almost an accusation.

Royal merely nodded an agreement. His glance traveled over the room with an approving interest. Then he seated himself, facing Max. He was in the company of his peer. Nothing more.

"I have a job for you."

Royal was politely interested but made no reply. He was forcing Max Hertog to do the talking. In a subtle fashion this placed the white man in the position of being the petitioner. Max was grudgingly aware of the manipulation.

"I'm going to build extensively on Grand Bahama. I've been in touch with the New York office of Janis. Their recommendation sounded almost as though you had written it."

Royal smiled but said nothing. He could see the small nettle of his studied indifference beginning to irritate Hertog.

"I can give you the job of chief engineer on the project."

"Why?" Royal studied him.

Max checked his temper. The son of a bitch was deliberately needling him. He took time to light a cigar, smothering the temptation to order this smart nigger out of the house.

"Well"—Max was taking his time answering the question— "for one thing you are qualified." He permitted himself a brief smile. "Also, if you're working for me, I can keep track of you. For another thing I think you ought to have the prestige of a big job." He realized he was committing himself to the furthering of Royal Keating's ambition. In a measure he was linking the fortunes of this black man and Max Hertog. He was ready

197

to believe it was going to happen. A black party. A black Prime Minister. "Also"—he picked his words carefully—"an empty-handed messiah doesn't attract much of a following. He has to be able to hand out something or work a few miracles. It is one thing to roam around the Out Islands telling the niggers everything is going to be better. It is another to be able to prove it and give them jobs. If you're supervising the construction on Grand Bahama you will be able to do just that. It ought to create a lot of goodwill and votes for your party."

Royal thought for a moment. He was well aware that Max Hertog had finally come to the conclusion that the Progressive Liberal Party was more than a distant threat to the established order. He was all but saying: "I think you can do this thing. I think you're going to do it, and I like to ride in an open carriage with a winner." Deliberately, Royal meditated, Max Hertog was choosing a side. It was no longer a secret in Nassau that the strong, clear voice of the PLP was a black named Royal Keating. That Max Hertog would engage him as chief engineer on the Grand Bahama development could mean but one thing: Max Hertog was protecting himself.

"Well?" Max permitted a small impatience to color the word. "Yes or no?"

"I think yes. It is a big opportunity. I'm grateful for the chance." There was a shade of good-humored sarcasm in the statement. "I'll do the job. And as you say, every black man at work means a vote for Royal Keating."

They both were aware of what had been said. Royal was stating openly what they both knew to be in the future. The PLP was Royal Keating, and Royal Keating was the PLP.

XII

Out of Bristol, England, in the year of 1650, one Thomas Whaley, son of a prosperous wainwright, cast his lot with a sturdy group who called themselves the Eleutherian Adventurers. Under the command of a former Governor of Bermuda, William Sayle, they made their way to the Bahamas and settled on the present-day island of Eleuthera.

Although young Tom Whaley was never to make a mark for himself as a soldier, politician or merchant prince, he does seem to have been a formidable and active performer beneath the sheets. He sired innumerable progeny by two wives. These, in turn, proved to be equally virile. They rutted freely through the island blacks and whites, and a few even took time away from their favorite diversion to marry. As a result, the family name occurs and reoccurs throughout the Bahamas in almost every settlement.

In general the Whaleys have been honest, law-abiding and unambitious folk in whom the hot, spirited blood of Tom Whaley runs in a cold and thin trickle. The Whaley men have been undistinguished for more than three centuries. They fished, worked small patches of vegetables, hired on as spongers, and in general did no more than was absolutely necessary to exist. A few occupied minor positions in the government service; lighthouse keepers, pilots and customs clerks.

Information on the original Thomas Whaley is sketchy, and

he might have gone forever unnoticed and unnoted save for an unidentified service he performed for an early governor in Nassau, Sir Jonathan Whitehead. There are no details of what Tom Whaley did, but it was of sufficient importance to bring him to the Governor's attention. The Crown's representative, with the authority granted him, showed his gratitude to Thomas Whaley by making him a man of property. A strip of land one-quarter of a league in width and running diagonally across Grand Bahama Island to the points of high tides on both shores was given to Thomas Whaley and his heirs in perpetuity. The grant carried with it no contingent clauses save that it was to remain forever tax-free. There is no record of Thomas Whaley or any of his descendants ever living on this land or attempting to put it to any use. During more than three hundred years the original grant has been overlaid by any number of official documents, faulty transcripts, notices of navigation lights to be installed, statements of seizure and release, and not too surprisingly, in 1853, Grand Bahama was again considered Crown property. Somone either missed or ignored the Whaley award as illegal or unimportant. No Whaley ever came forward with a claim to the land. No attempt was made to settle on it, and it remained a part of the whole. The Whaley strip and the confusion of ownership would have had no present-day importance save for the fact that it lay athwart the land which Maximilian Hertog purchased from the Crown by virtue of the Out Island Development Act.

Acting on Max's instructions, the law firm of Sutter, Tracy and Longworth made a title search of Grand Bahama. This was routine. A clerk was put to the job, and he eventually reported favorably. There were three or four squatter families living on the island, and they claimed their little tracts by virtue of long and uncontested occupancy. They existed in the meanest poverty. Max instructed his lawyers to buy them off or run them off. They eventually accepted a modest settlement and for a few thousand dollars were moved to Little Exuma and Long Island.

The law clerk who had done the title search was satisfied with what he found and reported. Grand Bahama was Crown property. No effort had been made to populate it. He was momentarily disturbed when he came across a stiff and yellowed paper. This was notice of a grant made by the colonial government to one Thomas Whaley in 1675. But by 1780 the entire stretch of the Grand Bahama appeared to have reverted to the Crown. There was no explanation for this. The clerk assumed that Thomas Whaley, unwilling to settle on the land or work it for a profit, had returned it to the government. He could find no confirmation of this, but there was little system in the paper work of the period. England considered the Bahamas something of a nuisance, more a liability than an asset. Clerical work was slipshod. No one really cared what happened to these dots in the Atlantic. England held to them only because they lay across the trade routes of the Spanish and Dutch. In case of a war with either country they could be used as a sallying point against the fat merchantmen. The internal affairs of the islands were noted in a most careless fashion when they were set down at all. Few officials bothered themselves with reports, deeds or grants.

With the all-clear signal from his attorneys Max Hertog pressed the development of the land with his characteristic vigor. He bought and paid for the two hundred and eleven square miles of Grand Bahama. Surveying teams under the direction of Royal Keating had gone to mark off the island and lay out a rough plan for Freeport. Architectural firms in Nassau and Miami put additional draftsmen to their drawing boards. Preliminary sketches, elevations, drawings and plans rose in an ever-mounting stack. A tent community was laid out to house the small army of black laborers Royal brought in from Nassau and some of the Out Islands. These had a disconcerting habit of slipping off on a Saturday evening with a week's pay in their pockets. Native sloops appeared regularly to take them into Nassau with the promise of a weekend carouse. Many failed to return, and the work was always being interrupted. At Royal's urging Max instituted the sale of liquor to the workmen. Girls were brought in and taken back on Sunday night. Such men as had wives and wanted to see them were permitted to have them from Saturday through Sunday. A certain stability was achieved. Light bungalows were constructed to house the white personnel. Grand Bahama roared into life with the sound of the diesels. Huge graders, loaders, tractors and scrapers lumbered like great prehistoric monsters. Grand Bahama was flattened, piled, and graded. Maximilian Hertog strode over the development. Booted, wearing the breeches and old shooting jacket he favored, he was into everything, immensely pleased with the excitement generated by his enthusiasm.

Although much of the expense was being paid for by Charles Rich and his shadowy associates, they offered no intrusion. Rich flew in a couple of times, looked around, and departed. An accounting department for the Grand Bahama development was set up in Nassau. Through this the funds were disbursed. The wages and salaries were paid by employees of the Rich organization, who arrived by plane each Saturday to open the paymaster's windows.

The town of Freeport was staked out. Locations for shops, restaurants, taverns, nightclubs and liquor stores were designated. Plans were drawn for a huge shopping bazaar complex which would be stocked with European imports. All transactions, information, leases and sites for concessions were handled through the Aunt Martha Candy Company, with offices in Nassau, Miami, New York and Chicago. Within six months of the announcement for the proposed development of Grand Bahama, all the business sites had been leased on long-term contracts. Freeport was a boomtown before so much as a single building had been raised.

Not included in the general plans was an area reserved for Maximilian Hertog. Here foundations had been laid, and it was possible to see the outlines of the proposed structure. No one but Max had any idea what was to be built here, and he kept the secret to himself. The work being done was that of an independent crew engaged by Max in Nassau and paid by him so this section of the general development did not come under the scrutiny of Rich's auditors.

Max was building his Oriental Casino, although it was never referred to as such, and he paced the work to keep up with that of Freeport in general so a completed structure would not stand out from the unfinished work in other areas. No actual plan

202

for the operation of a casino apart from the proposed Lucayan Beach Hotel had as yet crystallized in his mind. This left him untroubled. When the time came, he would work it out. That he was deliberately setting up a double cross for Rich and associates didn't disturb him. If he was concerned over the possible consequences, he didn't show it.

Profiting by what he had learned with Paradise Island, Max had the casino's floor plans so drawn that it was practically impossible for a visitor to turn around without confronting a game or a device calculated to separate him from his money. Since the foundation did attract some attention, he explained it away by saying he was building a residence for himself. This was to be a place where visitors of VIP stature could be entertained and put up and where Max might spend a month or so out of the year. This, he pointed out, would no way conflict with the facilities of the Lucayan Beach Hotel to be operated by Charles Rich and his group in association with Maximilian Hertog. For this the plans were already off the drawing boards. It was to be an outstanding example of the complete luxury hotel. Each floor was to have its separate kitchen for room service. All rooms were outside, with lanai types of balconies overlooking a scene of tropical beauty. There were to be acres of landscaped gardens, swimming pools, tennis courts and eventually a golf course. Unless he were determined to indulge in some robust activity such as golf or tennis, a guest at the Lucayan Beach Hotel would never have to move from the shaded and perfumed precincts of the main building. When time gathered heavily on his hands, he could relieve the tedium by a visit to the casino just off the main lobby.

A New York public relations firm was engaged, and Grand Bahama was subjected to an intensive national and international campaign. Beauty contest winners were shown lifting a shovelful of dirt with the Governor of the Bahamas. A fishing contest was sponsored by the Ministry of Tourism. This brought additional photographs and columns of print. An internationally known chef who would be engaged by the Lucayan Beach Hotel syndicated a series of menus and recipes. No small stone of publicity was left unturned. Freeport had achieved an identity long before a single strip of sidewalk or a street appeared. In all the publicity releases there was the discreet suggestion of the operation of a gambling casino. The government had not formally acted on a permit, but it was generally understood that Freeport was to be wide-open. A Certificate of Exemption would be forthcoming when requested.

On the ridge which marks the division between Nassau proper and the miserable slum district known as Over the Hill there is an unpretentious tavern, the Green Shutter. It is a pleasant, homey place, where the food is good, if not distinguished, the drinks are well made, and the service is rendered with an easy friendliness. The butter-yellow cottagelike appearance of the Green Shutter is not something which attracts the tourist's eye. As a result, it is patronized almost exclusively by those who are employed in downtown Nassau. Everyone knows or has a nodding acquaintance with everyone else. The atmosphere is casual and friendly.

At a corner table in the small bar off the dining room Sherry Melnick and Christopher Baildon sat over a preluncheon drink. The meeting was touched by little warmth and considerable suspicion on both sides. Despite the fact he denied it, Chris was certain Melnick had, for his own ends, told Max Hertog what he knew of his operation in the Grand Bahama before the passage of the Hawksbill Creek Act. It was this, Chris felt sure, which had resulted in his being publicly fired and humiliated by Hertog. Now, though, he held a piece of information which could prove extremely valuable. To make it so, he needed outside help. There were any number of persons on Bay Street who would have paid most handsomely for what Chris Baildon knew. Chris was in no humor to part with the information. He wanted this to be a personal thing between him and Maximilian Hertog. But he would need some money. He had no idea how much, but it was well within the reach of Sherry Melnick. For this reason he had arranged a luncheon date, calling Melnick in Miami and setting it up for the coming Saturday.

"How are you getting along with Hertog?" Chris was mildly curious.

"We keep out of each other's way. If it weren't for Jan, I wouldn't see him at all. She set up a routine where we spend part of our time in Miami and part here at Windmere. I'm an aerial commuter."

There was a moment's awkward silence. Sherry spun the ice cubes in his old-fashioned with a finger. Both were aware of the constraint. Both knew the reason for it. Sherry decided to make the opening move.

"I want you to know I didn't have anything to do with Hertog's letting you go the way he did. I mean there was nothing I said." This was not strictly true, and Chris guessed it. "When I mentioned Grand Bahama, he figured you let something slip."

"Forget it." Chris shrugged indifferently. "It wasn't such a hell of a good job. I mean, it could have been a good job if Max Hertog didn't go with it." He paused and then added irrelevantly, "How's Jan?"

"She's fine." Sherry smiled. "I don't think you're buying me lunch just to ask that. What's on your mind?"

Chris hesitated, wondering if he should trust Melnick with the information he had. Sherry might well decide to make a grab for it on his own.

"I have"—he spoke slowly—"Max in a bag, but I need someone to help me close it. That's where you come in."

"Why me?" Sherry was cautious.

"Well, for one thing it is a little on the shady side." He thought for a moment. "Maybe not, though. Anyhow, it is a chance to put our hands on a nice piece of money and screw Maximilian Hertog at the same time."

"I'm fond of money, and I would be delighted to screw my father-in-law. Few persons get the chance."

"We'll need some money."

"How much?" Melnick was suspicious.

"Not a lot, probably. If we keep what we're doing quiet. A few thousand at the most. But I don't have it."

"I do. Let's have the rest of it."

"You remember when we were researching some titles for Max on Grand Bahama?" He glanced about and lowered his voice. "For some reason I didn't think much about it at the time. The whole business of title in the Bahamas is confused and confusing. Then, I don't know why, I went back and had a second look. The damn thing slaps you right in the face. It has been there all the time. I—we—have Max in the damnedest bind you could imagine." He lit a cigarette from the coal of one in the tray. His hand trembled slightly with excitement. "Listen to this. There is a strip of land, a quarter of a mile or so wide, running across the island and directly through what Max is developing. It was included in the whole deal he made with the government. But"—he leaned forward—"I don't think it is Crown property. I don't believe the government had the right to dispose of it. As a matter of fact, I'm damn sure it didn't. What do you think of that?"

Sherry's whistle was low, incredulous. "I think you had better be right or we'll get our tails twisted off in a tangle with Max."

"I'm right. Are you interested?"

"Of course I'm interested."

Rapidly Chris sketched out what he had discovered. The early grant to Thomas Whaley. The complete absence of anything which would indicate Whaley had returned the Grand Bahama property to the government.

"It was to be tax-free." Chris emphasized this. "So it could never have been seized by the Crown for nonpayment. The whole thing is just one of those clerical errors which passed notice for three hundred years."

"Are you sure?" Melnick still wasn't convinced.

"I'm as sure as anyone can be."

"How could Max's attorneys miss it?"

Chris was impatient. "Some clerk simply didn't realize what he saw. He skipped over it the way I did the first time."

"Can you get a photostat of the early grant?"

Chris nodded. "I know a girl who works in records. If I ask her, she'll run it through the Xerox."

"Good." Sherry was brisk, interested now. This was the sort of intrigue to delight him. He was still a little cautious, though. It hardly seemed probable Max Hertog would have been so careless. "Let's go down after lunch and get a copy."

They had another drink and ordered lunch. Over the light meal they grinned at each other companionably.

"Can you imagine what is going to happen when we tell Max he doesn't own that strip?" A note of awe crept into Chris' voice. "It will tie up everything. It runs right through the center of what he calls Freeport. He can't walk around it."

"Let's be sure we have it first. It's not like Max to leave a loose end for someone else to pick up."

After lunch they strolled down the slight incline to the group of government buildings around the post office. Sherry idled about outside while Chris went in to see the girl he knew. It seemed better to have Chris do it alone. The two of them might have given the request an importance in the girl's mind. One careless word could ruin everything.

When Chris came back, he carried a square envelope. "I had a couple of copies made. I told Evelyn I was doing some historical research for the Ministry of Tourism."

Sherry resisted a temptation to open the envelope and study the Whaley grant. It was just too good to be true.

"Let's go someplace where we can read and talk."

They walked back up the hill, turned in at the Royal Victoria's gardens, and then found a couple of chairs at the far end of the swimming pool.

Sherry read through the grant to Thomas Whaley. Then he reread it slowly, word by word. There was no mistaking what it conveyed. The text beneath the seal of the Bahamas government was written in a clear, bold hand by some clerk, dead these three centuries. The copying machine reproduced it sharply.

"You're sure there is nothing in the file to void this?" He looked across at Chris. "No indication of repossession by the government?"

"Nothing." Chris was positive. "I ran down every possible lead. Apparently, since Whaley didn't settle on his grant and over the years no heir came forward to claim the land, the error became established. Subsequent officials and clerks, in preparing new descriptions of the islands and particularly of the Little Bahama Bank, overlooked or ignored the Whaley grant and assumed it was all Crown property. There is no other explanation."

"What about the Whaley family?" Sherry leaned back in his chair.

"There are Whaleys scattered all over the islands. Black and white. We won't have any trouble in locating a Whaley if that's what you're thinking."

"That's what I'm thinking. Let's pick ourselves one. A Whaley in the direct line of descent from Thomas."

"You'd have a hell of a time proving that." Chris shook his head. "I don't think there are any vital statistics before late in the eighteen hundreds. There sure wouldn't be for the Out Islands."

"I don't think it is too important." Sherry pursed his lips and whistled soundlessly. "Any descendant will do. Let's find one on a remote Out Island who doesn't know what is going on or doesn't care." He scowled briefly. "I'd like a legal opinion, but I don't want to ask for it in Nassau. I can probably find out what I want to know in Miami."

"Do we have a problem?" Chris was immediately concerned.

"No. I guess not. I only want to be sure, under English law, any descendant of Whaley can file to establish his claim. I don't see why not, but I'll feel better when I'm sure. In the meantime, you find us a Whaley, a real stupid one who won't ask too many questions."

"From what I hear they are all so inbred they ought to be wards of the Crown. It won't be any trouble to find one who isn't too bright. There's a James Whaley here in Nassau. He's black and drives a taxi. He probably knows about some other Whaleys. I'll ask him."

"Good." Sherry folded the Whaley grant copy and put it away in an inside coat pocket. "I'm going over to Miami in the morning. Call me there when you locate our man. We'll see him together. For God's sake, be careful what you say on the phone. Max would need only one word, the barest suspicion."

"I'll be careful."

Chris walked across Bay Street against the traffic, flipping a hand in a cheerful gesture of acknowledgment of the traffic officer's shrill whistle of rebuke. He looked about him with a sense of ownership. Within his reach now was everything he had always wanted: cars, a boat, recognition, money. Opposite the Hertog Building he slowed his step and then, indifferent to the questioning stares, bowed gravely in the direction of Hertog's office and said, "Thank you, Max."

The trim bungalow had been raised on an elbow of land which jutted out as a small peninsula from the main body of Grand Bahama. A screened porch ran the width of the living room, open on three sides to the sun and the sparkling rush and draining of the sea on a narrow beach. Above the front door there was a neatly lettered sign:

ROYAL KEATING
Resident Engineer

It was Sunday, and the grinding roar and clanking of the earthmoving equipment were stilled. Only the seabirds were noisy, shrilling with a high fury at one another in their ceaseless hunt for food. The island narrowed here. A mile or so to the south of the bungalow the settlement of West End bleached in the hot sun. Few persons were abroad, and the entire community appeared to be locked in for a midday siesta. A sport fishing boat, the white hull and metalwork glittering in the sun and with her outriggers spidery against the sky, picked her way out of the small yacht basin.

On the bungalow's shaded porch Royal lay back on a wide, glider type of couch. He wore only white tennis shorts and a pair of heavy woolen socks. Seated cross-legged within the circle of his arm, Alicia Thatcher gazed down into his face and then gently brushed her fingertips along the curve of his jaw. His eyes opened, and he smiled at her.

"I thought you were asleep."

She shook her head. "I've been watching you."

He half turned on his side. His hand went out and moved upward over the black velvet of her skin, halting at her thigh. She bent toward him with the easy, swaying motion of a reed, her eyes wide and solemn.

"I was but only for a little while." She pressed against his hand. "The weekend is always too short. I hate to waste it sleeping."

Faintly now, carried on a light wind from the opposite side of the island, came the steady muffled beat of jukebox music. At this distance they could hear no melody, only the heavy pounding of the drum.

With Royal's permission and on their own time, the black labor force had built a raised platform for dancing. Royal had induced Max to buy the jukebox. It would keep the men on the island over the weekends. When the girls came on Saturday, the instrument was turned on and with its automatic change of records played continually until Sunday evening. The platform was in constant use, swaying beneath the rhythm of many feet. The commissary stocked beer, a small selection of whiskey and a cheap rum, but no effective system of rationing or of control had been worked out. There were always drunken brawls. Fights were a standard diversion. In an effort to preserve some order, Royal brought over half a dozen of Nassau's off-duty constables. The big Jamaicans laid about them with their clubs, beating the bellicose ones into a bloody submission. No one appeared to harbor any resentment, and a split skull was accepted as part of the price paid for a weekend of fun. Left alone and without too much company supervision, the black men did no real harm. There was some resentment among the West End whites who hated all blacks with an unreasoning anger. They complained of the noise, but no one paid much attention, and there were no open clashes.

Royal cocked his head in the direction of the drumbeat. "Want to go over and have a dance with your soul brothers?" He pulled her down against him, his fingers working at the knot tying the bandeau over her breasts.

Alicia's expression clouded. The note of derision in his voice troubled her. The sound was almost that of a white man. As intimately as she knew him now, she had never been able to pry into his secret heart. How did he actually feel about the island blacks? For that matter, what were his real feelings for her, his mother or any Negro? He had no friends of color and made no attempt to cultivate the intimacy of understanding. Was he really concerned for the welfare of the black island population? Many times, when he was addressing a settlement meeting in the Out Islands, she had listened, critically at first. Then, without realizing what was happening, she found herself caught up in a tide of emotion, swept along on the heady sound of his words until she actually heard herself responding with the chorus of the chanted "Yes! Yes!" which always greeted his more exaggerated statements. At such times she could believe with the others. Here was a man to lead his people. Or—and the answer troubled her—was he? Was he sincere or a charlatan? Was he honest or only using the black people for his own ends? She no longer doubted his will, his determination. He would do what he said could be done: put a black majority into the House of Assembly; give the government a black Prime Minister. Never, since that first evening after the meeting with the Reverend Whitman when it occurred to him what could be done, had he turned from the path selected. Always, though, in his relaxed moments such as now she detected the current of icy cynicism. There were others, the party leaders, the Reverend Whitman, who were also aware of amused detachment when his gaze swept over the crowd come to hear him. Whitman and the others who had welcomed Royal Keating into the Progressive Liberal Party were now forced to stand at the side of the road while he swept triumphantly past with his parade of singing, shouting, sweating black men and women on their way to the Promised Land. They understood it was now within Royal Keating's power to destroy the party or lead it to an almost unbelievable summit. What would be his choice?

Twisting about in his arm, Alicia laid her cheek on his chest. She felt a great pride in this man who was her lover. She was proud of his strength, his mind, his gentleness, his determination. She was also a little frightened for him. White Nassau would destroy Royal Keating if it were given a chance. He walked alone and on a precarious ledge. One careless step, one moment of complacency, and the minority which held the Bahamas to be their own would stamp him to death. They would fall on him if he ever lost his footing and slipped. They would tear him apart. This he must know.

"Why did Maximilian Hertog make you the chief engineer here?"

"Because I'm the best man he could get for the job."

"You know that isn't true." The tip of her tongue ran in a small circle around his nipple. Then her teeth closed gently. She murmured, a drowsy sound. "I don't mean you're not a good engineer." Her fingers marched down his chest, over the tightly muscled abdomen and beneath the tennis shorts. "I'm sure you are." There was a tight excitement in her voice now. "But that wouldn't be enough in a black man for Mr. Hertog, would it?"

"No, I guess not. Maybe he just wants to keep me happy." He grunted sharply as she touched him.

"Why?" She nibbled at his skin, small traveling bites.

"Because he thinks he'll be able to use me someday." His hands moved to cup beneath her taut breasts. The words came with a rising whistle.

"Will he?" The question was gasped.

"Not if I can help it. Do you want me to take your clothes off?"

"Yes." The reply was a tortured gasp. "Slowly. Talk to me. Talk dirty."

He was stripping her. "Do you know what I'm going to do to you?"

"Yes."

"Say it." The command was harsh.

She was naked now, twisting on top of him. "You're going to fuck me."

"What are we going to do to Max Hertog?"

"Oh, my God." There was actual pain in the moan.

"Tell me what we're going to do to Max Hertog?"

"To hell with Max Hertog. Love me. Love me, Royal."

The cry was timed to the jukebox's sound. The slow, heavy beat of the drum. The slap of bare feet beneath a hot and blazing sun. Then her scream hung upon the heavy air, vibrating there, a living, pulsing thing.

212

XIII

The unsteady sections of a dock straggle brokenly from the white beach of a winding cove. The years have bleached the timbers to a silver frosting, and the loose boards rattle with a skeletal sound when trod upon. Barnacles and marine growth heavily encrust the pilings, which seem to brace themselves against the wind and tide with the rickety determination of the very old.

Few persons come here these days, and no one walks on the beach. Back from it a few hundred yards and all but concealed by a heavy undergrowth are the scattered and broken ruins of a sawmill. A fouled and rusted boiler gapes vacantly. The scaled and corroded saws, with gaps in the teeth, are crooked on their shafts. The dock and what remains of the mill are the only reminders that this end of the cay, part of the long chain stretching from Mantilla Shoal to Little Harbour, on Great Abaco, was once a busy, rowdy camp with the saws screaming their way through the fine, seemingly endless supply of logs, slicing them into boards to be loaded aboard the three-masted schooners which could stand off in the deep water. They came in those days. *The Wyefex. The Isabella. The Lady Catherine* and *The Shenandoah* to take the freshly cut lumber.

Well up above the highest high-water mark a small settlement was laid out with a careless hand. It straggled with a drunken abandon in a series of grogshops, eating places, a small hotel with accommodations for no more than half a dozen persons and a barber who doubled as cook wherever and whenever needed. The shacks and even the hotel were of the flimsiest construction, made so deliberately since the frequently savage storms of late October and November could be expected to blow them away anyhow. So the place was rebuilt every few years without any idea of permanency. Its only purpose was to provide housing, food and liquor for the labor force and visiting crews. At one time a loose attempt at a tavern had been made. The construction was substantial, and it offered refreshment and food to the officers of the visiting schooners. Along with everything else, the effort failed and the place decayed. It fell away piece by piece or went spinning through the skies on a high wind. What is left now is a small hovellike structure fabricated from odd boards. The winds worry and whisper through the openings, and a narrow porch, once supported by heavy tree stumps, is flat on the sand. Where there were once windows are now only empty sockets or a hole crisscrossed by dry palm fronds. It seems to huddle in the warm sunshine, drawing itself together as some crone might pull a shawl about herself, trembling with a spell of chill.

On the beach now a man in a faded blue shirt and overalls with their straps fastened by wire stood and gazed vacantly seaward. His hair grew in patches and was pink in color. There wasn't even the suggestion of a downy fuzz on his cheeks, which had never felt a razor's blade. He was lean to the point of emaciation, and his skinny shanks were the blue-white color of watered milk.

Out of the sky he had been studying, a small amphibian took a wide, slow turn, and for a moment the sun polished the wings to a dazzling brilliance. Then it came down on the water with a shower of spray. After a moment's hesitation the beat of the motor again sounded, and the craft taxied toward the shore. The man's head swiveled to follow the plane's course, but the action was without any real curiosity. He did show a moment of surprise when, as the water shallowed, the amphib-

214

ian's wheels came down and it seemed to waddle ashore as some fat and complacent duck. Still, he made no move to walk toward it.

Followed by Sherry, Chris Baildon dropped from the cabin's doorway to the beach.

"You sure this is the place?" Melnick looked about.

"I'm sure." Chris was short. Melnick's habit of double-checking everything was becoming increasingly annoying. He had asked twice whether Chris could really fly before he would board the plane. "That is probably our man down there." He hesitated and then shouted, "Hey! Hello there?"

There was no reply. Chris grinned and shrugged. He and Melnick walked together. Having once settled on their man, they decided to approach him as fishermen and make this their reason for coming to the cay. The true conch is of a suspicious nature, inbred, sometimes, to the point of idiocy, clannish, usually illiterate and with small inclination to be friendly with strangers. In the remote Out Islands he lives in the meanest poverty and rarely leaves his native cay. There had been any number of Whaleys to choose from. As a matter of fact, as Melnick pointed out, there were almost too many Whaleys. From such records as Chris could find, he did trace a rough line of descent from Thomas Whaley to a Joseph Whaley who had settled on this cay. From that point things were a little clearer, for this part of the large family, legitimate or otherwise, had elected to remain here.

On Man of War Cay Chris had found an old woman who told him a William Whaley still lived where the old sawmill once stood. She thought she was some sort of distant relative but wasn't sure, a cousin maybe. Anyhow, if he were still alive, he would be there. "Them Whaley never go off." William Whaley's father was Joseph, and his father had been a Thomas.

Melnick hadn't been disturbed by the vagueness of the connection. "It would take years of litigation before the claim could be proved or disproved. Max Hertog can't wait that long. The nuisance value alone is worth a million dollars to us."

Chris still didn't trust Melnick completely. He could sell

him out to Max Hertog and leave him with an empty bag. There was nothing he could really do to protect himself. He had to go along with Sherry now.

"Hello." Chris spoke again as they approached the lone figure. "We're looking for a William Whaley."

The man stared up at the sky and then down at his bare feet. He watched his toes as they dug into the sand. Then he sucked at a tooth with a hissing sound. He darted a glance at Melnick and then at Chris, and his eyes were a peculiar topaz color. His Adam's apple jumped like a live thing within his throat, but no sound came.

"A woman on Man of War Cay said you could tell us about the fishing here." Chris persisted.

"What woman?" There was skepticism in the question.

Chris lit a cigarette and offered one to the man. He took it without acknowledgment and held it with a pleased unfamiliarity between thumb and forefinger. Chris gave him a light.

"The woman's name was Mercer. Jennie Mercer. She thought she was a relative—cousin or something. My name's Baildon. I'm from Nassau." He offered his hand.

Whaley fumbled with the cigarette and finally managed to thrust limp fingers toward Chris. He withdrew them quickly and stood, peering intently down at the smoldering cigarette.

"I don' know no Mercer. What she look like, say dat?"

Chris checked his exasperation and the temptation to shout: "What difference does it make?" Instead, he smiled his engaging best.

"Miss Mercer's a fine-looking woman to have for a cousin. She said you knew more about fishing than any man in the Little Bahama Bank."

"Where's dat?" Whaley sucked in a mouthful of smoke.

"Well"—Baildon felt himself floundering just a little—"this is it. This"—he waved a hand—"is part of the Little Bahama Bank."

Whaley shook his head. For the first time his eyes displayed an interest. Just a touch of amusement tugged at his mouth. He looked from Chris to Sherry.

216

"You're lost." He made the statement with satisfaction. "Dis ain' never bin nothin' but Hole-in-the-Ocean Cay."

"Maybe so." Chris gave up. There didn't seem to be any point in trying to explain Hole-in-the-Ocean Cay was but a small dot in the long chain of islands. "You live here." He was flattering. "You ought to know."

Whaley's attitude relaxed. He was plainly in the company of fools who might easily be done out of a dollar or two. Anyone who didn't know where he was couldn't be very sharp. He drew tightly on the cigarette.

"Fella," he finally conceded, "come heah now an' den fo' bonefish. Plen'y o' dem. Never un'erstan' why fella wan' bonefish. Can' eat dam t'ing. Gots t' be crazy t' catch t'ing can' eat. Yo' come bonefishin', I 'spec'." He added this slyly and then cackled at his joke.

"By the way"—Chris suddenly remembered the purpose of this visit—"you are William Whaley, aren't you?"

The man nodded. It was a sustained bobbing motion as though his head were set on a spring. He seemed to take a continuing satisfaction in the sound of his name.

"Let's get out of this sun." Melnick was uncomfortable and short.

Whaley regarded him with an air of puzzled dislike. What was wrong with the sun? It was good to stand in. He turned to Baildon for an explanation. Chris said nothing. After a moment Whaley again stared at Melnick. From the beginning there had been this small evidence of hostility. Sherry was aware of it but refused to allow it to interfere with what they had to do. Conversely, Whaley seemed to have taken a trusting fancy to Baildon. A quick glance of understanding passed between Chris and Sherry. Chris would do the talking.

As though he were sensitive to an indefinable conspiracy against him, Whaley turned away without a word and began walking slowly toward the scrub line.

"Hey! Wait a minute." Chris went after him. "Do you want to make a couple of dollars?" He took some bills from his pocket and thrust two at Whaley. "Is there someplace where we can sit and talk?"

"What about?" Whaley took the bills and began folding and refolding them into a narrow strip. "Ef yo' wan' fish."

"Wait a minute," Chris interrupted and called to Melnick, who had remained behind. "Sherry, pick up that bottle of rum in the cabin. We'll find some shade and have a drink." He winked jovially at Whaley, somehow admitting him into a conspiracy. He had also been conscious of the man's immediate dislike for Sherry. Now they were mysteriously in league against him.

With Sherry following, swinging the bottle of dark rum between his fingers, they left the beach and followed a faint path through the clinging underbrush. It ended abruptly at a small clearing and the canted and patched shack which had once been a section of the settlement's tavern. The yard, if it could be called that, was rank with weed and junk; odd pieces of the mill machinery, a dory with half its bottom torn out, a blackened iron kettle and a corroded ship's light. On what had once been the porch before it collapsed to the ground, a woman, an albino, sat in a broken rocking chair and fanned herself with a section of palm leaf. Although she appeared frail and shrunken, she also seemed a thing of evil; tow-white hair, pale skin, eyes of malevolent red, she was a creature more than a person, a spidery thing in a wrapper of faded, dirty cotton. Whaley ignored her, but her eyes followed them with an intent curiosity.

At the rear of the shanty there was a scraggly clump of trees offering an irregular patch of shade. Stretched between two trunks was a bleached hammock of heavy cord which was plainly hand-knit and might once have been a seine. Two old fruit crates were upended. Whaley indicated them to Chris as possible chairs. He picked up a stone jug, shook it lightly, and then spilled out a little of the clear water.

Chris took the bottle from Melnick and opened it. He offered it to Whaley, who drank deeply before passing it back to Chris. He ignored Melnick. Sherry shook his head when Chris extended the bottle.

"What business yo' gots?" Whaley wiped a hand across his mouth and accepted another cigarette.

"Land. Real estate. You understand?" Chris smiled and passed the bottle over. "Right now I'm only interested in fishing."

With the second drink Whaley expanded a little. He even regarded Sherry with a wary but half-amused tolerance. He waved an arm expansively in the direction of the sea.

"Dem flat fill wid bonefish." He mused over this. "Yo' wan' fish today?"

"No." Chris was relaxed. This gaunt and apparently not too bright conch represented a million or more dollars. Chris regarded him fondly and took a swallow of the rum. "We just came down to look around. I'll be back another time."

"I'll take yo' out den. I gots rowboad, flat-bottom. We pole right in wheah fish feedin'. Yo' catch till damn arm gits tired." He laughed delightedly at the idea and reached for the bottle without waiting for an invitation.

Chris glanced over at Sherry, who covertly shook his head. They would, he indicated, play it this way and say nothing about the property on Grand Bahama until a further rapport could be established. To press Whaley into a discussion of land grants, options or sale would confuse and excite him. It would certainly appeal to his naturally suspicious nature if he could be made to understand what they were talking about. No. It would have to come easily, and Chris, alone, was the one to bring it off. When the time was right, he could put the proposition to Whaley as a friend. Sherry would stay out of it altogether.

"I'll be back next week." Chris deliberately left his cigarettes and the remaining rum on one of the crates.

With a pinch-faced cunning Whaley watched to see if his visitors would remember to take the rum and tobacco with them. When Chris' back was turned, he snatched up the pack and hastily stuffed it into an overalls pocket. The rum he put on the ground, half-concealed by the crate. Then he looked about with a bland innocence as Chris turned.

"Yo' come." Whaley repeated the suggestion. "Yo' gets plenty fish."

They walked back to the beach. Chris was curious about the

mill ruins. Whaley said it had been abandoned for years, but he had a small recollection of its operation as a boy. He displayed a childish pleasure in being allowed to climb up into the amphibian's cabin and settle himself tentatively into one of the seats.

"What mek it go?" He looked up at Chris.

Chris pointed forward to the propeller, and Whaley stared at it incredulously and then laughed, indicating he thought it was some sort of a joke.

"Yo' take me wun time?" He slid a hand skyward.

"Sure. Next time I come down. You take me fishing, I'll take you for a ride."

Whaley stood on the beach until the amphibian was out of sight; then he turned from the shore and walked back toward the scrub.

It had been difficult to talk over the motor's sound on the way back, so the discussion of how Whaley was to be handled was delayed until they had returned the rented plane. Sitting now at one of the broad windows of the Coral Harbour Club, they had a drink and tried to see enough of the future to make their plans.

"You'll have to handle it alone." Sherry was reluctant to pull out. "That conch doesn't like me. I could feel it right away."

"He's probably anti-Semitic." Chris grinned. He felt good. Things were working the way they should. Unless something slipped, they'd have Max Hertog by the balls. "I'll handle him."

Sherry nodded with a trace of a smile. "It's a good thing he seems to get along with you. Jesus!" He whistled sharply. "Did you see that thing on the porch? An albino. Imagine waking up in the morning with a hangover and seeing that crawling around."

"She is probably his wife and sister. If they ever got around to getting married. They breed that close."

"Well"—Sherry stretched comfortably—"it's up to you. Go down four or five times during the next couple of weeks. Do some bonefishing. Take it easy and as much time as you need, but don't stretch it out. There is always a chance of something like this leaking. When you have Whaley softened up, we'll give him the business." He made a stabbing motion upward with his thumb. "What we want is an outright buy. No share, no participation. Hell, he wouldn't understand those things anyway. When he's ripe, we'll start counting out a thousand dollars in one-dollar bills and putting them on the table in front of him. If you use old bills, they make quite a stack. Maybe we go to two thousand. In the end, though, bam! It is all ours. How does it sound?"

"To me it sounds great." Baildon was confident. "I'll handle my end."

"Good!" Sherry rose. "I'm going back to Miami this afternoon. Jan and I will be over again for the weekend. She wants to see the old man. It's some sort of a filial complex she's developed ever since she found out she was pregnant. We wallow in sentiment these days."

"Well"—Chris was surprised—"congratulations."

He watched as Sherry walked across the room and out. Jan Hertog a mother. That was a strange one, although maybe it wasn't. She had changed. Sherry had stripped away something brassy and phony, and she stepped out a different person. There was still laughter and gaiety to follow wherever she went, but now it was honest. He had felt this the last time he had seen her on the street in downtown Nassau. He ordered a fresh drink, gazing out of the broad window. Afternoon shadows were beginning to draw a pattern on the water. A cruise-ship, gleaming in white and gold where the late sun struck her, moved sedately out the Northwest Providence Channel. There was no envy in him, as there usually was, for the seemingly carefree tourists. By this time next year he would have a half a million or more dollars in his hand. He could go anywhere with only his fancy to dictate how and with whom. This thing which was so close. It was the pivot of his life. Upon it the entire future turned. What he had learned in Max Hertog's employ he would put to his own ends. With half a million dollars he could begin operating, in a small way at first, in the expanding development of the Bahamas. As you watched Max

Hertog, the whole thing seemed so ridiculously easy. You bought and you sold and you came out with a profit. Never again, he mused, would he have to work for someone else. He'd fix up the old Baildon mansion. It could be a showplace, and it was indisputable background. His dotty aunt and the old man couldn't last much longer. He would renovate the house or build something new and more practical down around Lyford Cay. The discovery of the original Whaley grant had been his. Only damn bad luck made it necessary to take Melnick in. For one or two thousand dollars, which he almost certainly must have, Melnick was cutting himself half of one hell of a big cake. It didn't seem fair, yet Melnick was the only one he thought he could trust with the secret. He lit a fresh cigarette from the butt of the one between his fingers.

Slowly an idea began to take shape in his mind. It wasn't fully formed, but it was there. How could Sherry Melnick, once he had come up with the purchase money, be maneuvered out of the deal? It would have to be a clean operation with Sherry cut away entirely. He would never agree to a smaller share. It was half or nothing. Why not nothing? He could feel the excitement. It was knotting his stomach. All the negotiations with Whaley would be in his hands. Sherry wouldn't be sitting in on a single word. He would have to believe what he was told. So, he summed it up quickly, the whole thing could be broken down into two stages. First, he would establish a friendly relationship with Whaley and eventually ease him into the knowledge he owned a piece of property on Grand Bahama. He would then make an offer to buy, and they would settle on a price. Then, somehow, he would have to keep Sherry out of it. He had to get the money from him without his becoming a part of the final conversation. If he could do this, get his hands on the money and keep Sherry away at the same time, then the transfer of title could be made from William Whaley to Christopher Baildon and to hell with Sherry Melnick. The idea delighted him. He was undisturbed by the unscrupulousness of his plan. He owed Sherry Melnick nothing. As a matter of fact, maybe he did. Maybe he owed Sherry a screwing. He was convinced that Melnick was responsible for Max Hertog's dismissing him. So this would make them even. He felt himself growing in stature by the minute. All his life he had been forced into a subordinate role. He was better bred than any of the persons he had ever worked for. The Baildons, despite their reduced circumstances, were of the island aristocracy. Yet it was men like Hertog who looted and trod roughly to make their fortunes. They showed no pity. Pluckings of conscience never bothered them. They took what they wanted. Well now. Just this once, maybe he would be the aggressor without scruples or conscience. Then, by God, once he held the deed, he would shove it up Max Hertog and listen to him yell. Shove it up and break it off. Max Hertog and Sherry Melnick screaming together. He drained his drink in a single swallow. It would be something to hear, the Hertog-Melnick duet.

In Max's living room at Windmere Jan sat on a corner of the kidney-shaped table he used as a desk and smiled with a companionable good nature as he chewed ruminatively on an unlit cigar.

"How do you like that?" She voiced the rhetorical question with a bright air of amazement. "I was always a cookie for fun and games and nothing ever happened. Then I get married and I get knocked up. How do you figure a thing like that?" She shook her head bemusedly.

Max dropped the wrecked cigar into a wastepaper basket and took a fresh one from a cedar humidor. He frowned at it, breaking open the glass tube container.

"You must have known what you were doing. With all the things they have now. It happened because you wanted it to happen."

"I guess I did, really." She was gravely thoughtful. "And that's a surprise. Why should I want to have a child? It contradicts everything I have done up until now. Hail, blithe spirit. Jan the nymph. In the Bahamas the stars come out at night to spell her name. Jan Hertog the glamor kid."

223

"I always thought you'd get over it." He put a light to the cigar. "None of it seemed worthwhile, and I figured you'd find it out sooner or later."

"Once before"—she was serious now—"I told you Sherry was good for me. He was and he is. That you don't like him is unimportant. Oh, I guess it would be better if the two of you got along, easier on all of us, but it doesn't really matter. Believe me, I didn't get pregnant just to soften you up. We've always had sort of an understanding, and I don't expect you to change now. For the first time in my life I have a feeling of security. It's something you were never able to give me. It is hard to explain. Corny as the word sometimes sounds, Sherry loves me. He's not impressed by you or the Hertog money. He is a man who knew what he wanted when he saw it. Fortunately for me it was I. This thing I feel." There was a soft radiance about her as she spoke, a new gentleness. "There were times, in the convent, I had nightmares. No one was ever going to come for me. I was alone and frightened. I carried some of that with me as I grew older. Now I'm not afraid. A man loves me. I'm secure, out of reach. No one can touch me."

Max grunted impatiently. "Out of all the men you have known why did it have to be this sharpshooter, this Jew? And now I get a little Jew grandchild."

"You get nothing, old man. Do you hear?" The words were icy, brittle, pointed with anger. "Nothing. I'll never let you see my child. There'll be no 'Where's Dranpa?' My God! Is your ego so monumental you can actually believe I'm having a baby so you can have a grandson or daughter? Oh!" She sighed wearily and with resignation. "I ought to know better. Nothing will ever change you. This is an obsession. I try to make myself understand. It's no use really." She leaned toward him. "As for Sherry's being a sharpshooter, I'm not sure what it means. He runs his business as you run yours, and in his limited field, he is quite as successful as you are. As for being a sharpshooter, I have an idea not too many of your fabulous deals would bear investigation." Some of the anger left her. "I'll let you in on a little secret, old man. I wasn't such a hell of a catch. If one looked closely, some of the polish was beginning to tarnish. Jan Hertog heiress to the Hertog millions. Aaah!" There was disgust in the exclamation. "I know another word, but I won't use it. I let myself be handed around quite a bit before Sherry came along. It was all for kicks. A new thrill in every new man. In and out of bed like a grown-up variation of musical chairs. Sherry was the only man who said he was going to marry me. He didn't ask. He told me and I believed him. If you weren't so damned bullheaded, you would see how good he has been for me."

Max said nothing, but he wanted to reach out and touch her. Once they had shared something, understanding, affection, pride. He thought now those were the things involved here. Neither had ever asked more than the other was willing to give. They had had small arguments, but never such a complete disagreement as this. At the root of it all, his refusal to accept and adjust himself to Sherry Melnick, there was jealousy. He was unwilling to share her with any man. It wasn't just Melnick. He would admit this to himself. A man lived with his prejudices, and they became a part of him.

"When do you expect the baby?" He watched as she lit a cigarette. "Are those things good for you? I mean—"

"In my condition?" she interrupted, laughing at him. Half leaning across the desk, she rumpled his hair affectionately. "Do you know something? Underneath that crusty hard shell of a mean old bastard, there is really a mean old bastard."

She slid from the desk and walked to the open French doors and the balcony. Standing there, gazing out across the twilight sheen of the water, she was a sprite, a creation of air and sunshine. He studied her with pleasure.

"When do you expect it?" He was actually embarrassed.

"*It?*" She turned, eyes shining. "*It* ought to be along around the middle of April."

"Well, you take care of yourself. Do you hear?" he rumbled, ill at ease with sentiment. "Where the hell is that husband of yours at a time like this?"

"A time like this," she mimicked him, "is about seven

months away." She turned back to look up at the sky. "He ought to be coming in soon now. I'm going to drive out to the airport to meet him. Want to come along?"

"Why the hell should I want to go out to meet Melnick?"

"Because it might do you good. Blow some of that mean stink away."

He hesitated, interested by her flashes of anger. She had his temper. He screwed up his face and winked broadly at her.

"All right. I just always like to have a reason for doing something."

He heaved himself from the chair and slapped the old Panama hat on his head. Jan watched him with astonishment. He was really going. He was giving just a little. She linked both arms through his and leaned contentedly against him as they walked from the room.

XIV

Freeport, which wasn't a port at all but lay some five miles inland from a newly dredged deepwater harbor, soared on the high crest of a boom.

The magic, of course, lay in the name of Maximilian Hertog. It was inconceivable to those in the money markets, the investors, speculators and conservative banking interests, that this highly imaginative development of Grand Bahama could possibly fail under his creative drive. Everyone wanted in. The Bay Street gang in Nassau chewed enviously at their fingertips and sought to capitalize on the excitement by announcing developments on adjacent islands, Little Abaco, Great Sale and Powell's Cays. Private and chartered planes, bringing prospective investors out of Miami, became so numerous that they created a traffic problem on the single airstrip. Engineers and construction experts came to look, study and appraise. They made their estimates and reported back to their principals. "Get in on this if you can. Hertog is doing what he said he would."

Offers of money were pressed on Max from all quarters. Representatives of banking interests in Boston, Philadelphia and New York sat patiently in the waiting room of the Hertog offices on Bay Street. Max, looking far beyond Grand Bahama and Freeport, overflowed with courtesy and saw them all and to all made the same reply:

"I don't need any financing. If I should, I can get it here in Nassau. But"—and his smile was pleasant and reassuring —"if I ever want outside capital, I'll keep you in mind. When I have finished with Freeport, then I'll open up the rest of the island to the public. Between now and then you're welcome to look around."

Those persons he considered to be of sufficient importance were given the full Hertog treatment. The private plane was sent to bring them over. Windmere and its facilities, as well as Max's clubs, were open to them. There were dinner parties, fishing trips and yachting excursions to the Out Islands. Carol Wainwright, in the role of Max's hostess, saw to it that the days and nights were filled with an entertaining schedule. The Hertog charm was effortless and effective. Later the visitors were taken to Grand Bahama. If Max considered them to be of future use, they were given a Jeep tour by the resident engineer, Royal Keating.

Royal accepted this extra duty with a secretly amused tolerance. He played the part to the full. In the white tropical shirt, shorts, socks and shoes which accentuated his color and size he lent a proper and impressive cachet to the proceedings. There was a semimilitary note in his dress and posture. Here was the engineer of bravura fiction made more spectacular by the fact that he was black. He had a thorough knowledge of all the technical aspects of the development, answering questions with an easy, smiling courtesy and assurance. He did this with an inner amusement, well aware of the effect he created. Now and then, with an invitation from Maximilian Hertog, a private yacht out of Miami, Fort Lauderdale and once even from Long Island, in New York, would put in. They always created a problem since the man-made harbor was usually crowded with freighters unloading building supplies. When it was filled, the private craft were directed around to West End. Max usually advised Royal in advance when he felt a party deserved particular attention. He was at his best with them. He was well aware of their initial surprise in finding him to be a black man. Later they were impressed by his familiarity with all aspects of the huge project. The women were frequently stimu-

228

lated by his size, his smile and manner. That he was black honed the edge of their excitement. He often caught them regarding him with a moist-lipped speculation, a half-sleepy look, with the tips of their tongues unconsciously touching their lower teeth. In the Jeep he would be pressed against with an unmistakable invitation. Invariably he was invited for the cocktail hour and dinner aboard the craft. At such times he was hard put to restrain his laughter since he was certain not one of the party had ever had a drink or sat at a table with a Negro. Because he was amused, he carried off these assignments with an unstudied grace and charm.

In Freeport the streets had been laid and paved. Sidewalks followed. The first of the many bazaars, taverns, hotels, restaurants and international shopping centers were taking shape. Construction of the Lucayan Beach Hotel was well under way. The labor force on the island mounted steadily. It drew all the idle and employable out of Nassau. Additional labor was recruited in the other Out Islands and in Jamaica. It had become necessary to maintain an island police force. These were also brought in from Jamaica. Fire-fighting equipment came to Grand Bahama by freighter, and an experienced corps of firemen was collected in Miami and put on a permanent basis. Every Bahamian employed was made aware from the beginning that he owed his job and high wages to Royal Keating and no one else. A mild form of indoctrination was instituted. Work, such as this, they were assured would be plentiful through the efforts of the Progressive Liberal Party. When the next general election was held, they should vote PLP. There would be men and women on their home islands to show them how. The tent city to house the workers spread over additional acres. Augmenting the resident labor force, chartered planes flew in each morning bringing skilled workmen, all of them white, from Miami. They were returned to Florida in the evening on a commuter schedule. No one, no matter how skeptical, could look around on Grand Bahama and not be impressed by what he saw. It was as spectacular and improbable as Disneyland and just as sound.

For reasons best understood by himself, Charles Rich was a

frequent visitor now. He took a keen personal interest in the construction of the Lucayan Beach Hotel.

Rich had introduced himself to Royal on his first trip over, and as those things sometimes happen, both had been aware of an immediate and spontaneous attraction. They simply liked each other on sight. It was not something to be put into words, and as time passed, neither tried to measure the depth of the friendship. Both were satisfied to allow the relationship to find its own level.

Royal had been outspokenly surprised when Rich told him of the extent of his involvement on Grand Bahama. They were sitting on the screened porch of the cottage. The day's work was done, the clamor hushed, the mechanical monsters herded into their area. A bottle of scotch, glasses, ice and a pitcher of water were on the table. Royal stretched his legs, leaning back in the chair and coddling a freshly made drink.

"I didn't know Max Hertog ever took in a partner."

Rich shook his head. "This isn't exactly a partnership. In exchange for leases and the gambling concession we agreed to build most of Freeport. It was a good deal for everyone concerned. We'll all come out of it with a profit. You probably know we have an interest in Paradise Island."

"I read about it." Royal made the comment dryly. "The papers and newsmagazines were thorough. The Mafia. The Cosa Nostra moves in on the Bahamas. Things like that."

Rich splashed a little scotch into his glass. "We're businessmen. Successful businessmen. That always makes a target."

Royal couldn't resist a small grin of derision. He really had no interest in Rich's organization. The man himself certainly didn't appear sinister.

"Las Vegas," Rich continued, "is supposed to be gangster-ridden. There isn't a more orderly city in the country. The hotels and casinos are well run. It's a family place."

Royal shrugged. "I guess I get my ideas from the movies. But I think it struck everyone as a little odd that Maximilian Hertog went into business with"—he paused—"whatever you want to call it. Organization. Syndicate."

230

Rich smiled. "Those are the more agreeable designations. Thank you."

"In his way"—Royal continued. It was pleasant to sit this way and just talk—"Max Hertog is something of a genius." The admiration was frank. "He translates his visions into fact. Grand Bahama has been lying here for centuries, and no one paid any attention to it. Now"—with a wave he indicated the entire island—"look what is happening. Before he is through, the property he bought for two or three dollars an acre will sell for fifty thousand dollars an acre. The amazing part of it all is that the government let him get away with it. It is the land grab of the century. I'll never understand how he pushed it through. The men in the Assembly aren't all thieves or fools."

Rich lit a cigarette. The evening wind was lifting out of the southwest, bringing with it a new freshness. He was completely relaxed and in company he enjoyed.

"Do you know"—his features were quietly contemplative—"I have been in and out of the islands many times, but I don't think I really saw them until recently? The people. The manners. The customs. The cays with a touch of history on them. How was it to be a boy in the Bahamas?"

"You mean a black boy? There's a difference." There was no rancor in the statement.

Rich's smile was indulgent. "You people can't have all the agony. You'll have to make a little room on the cross for the spiks. The wops. The sheenies. My folks sent me to a military school, Culver. We lived in suburban Detroit. In my rat year I was the wop. It was said jokingly, even affectionately. Then someone found out that my father was Tommaso Ricco. I don't imagine it means anything to you. It didn't to me. But back in the twenties Tommaso Ricco was mentioned in the same breath with Capone. O'Banion. The Purple Gang. It just never occurred to me that my father was any different from our neighbors who were driven to their offices each morning. All of a sudden I was a gangster's kid. My father wouldn't let me quit. He said I should learn to take it or fight back. So I did both. My boyhood wasn't any easier than yours, although not for the same reason."

"It was different for me, of course." Royal half closed his eyes against the lowering sun. "Being black here isn't the same as it would have been in Detroit. The whites who really hate the blacks in the States are those who come into economic competition with them. Here we didn't have that. Oh, there's the Cracker mentality among the Out Island conchs, but not in Nassau. There a black never aspired to a job held by a white. So we didn't have to contend with the fury. Just the same we were never allowed to forget we were black. The Negro slums Over the Hill have festered for years. The whites never really cared. They still don't. That's why this thing in the States can't be solved with money. You can give a black man a job, a duplex apartment, a split-level home in the suburbs, but if you still call and think of him as *nigger,* you haven't even begun to cool the fever. The majority of the whites just don't give a good goddamn, and the black man knows it. They say the riots in the States are senseless. Maybe they are. But the black man knows that because of them, the whites are thinking or trying to think. At least he has found a way to get their attention." He smiled, almost apologetically. "I had it pretty good as a boy. My father was a skilled carpenter. He saved his money and invested in property. We lived in a good house in Adelaide. When my father died, my mother took domestic work. She has been Max Hertog's cook and housekeeper ever since he came to the islands. She saw to it that I had an education and a profession."

They were silent for a few moments. The only sound came from the running sigh of a light surf on the beach and barely audible whisper on the wind.

"What about this PLP you're interested in?" Rich asked the question casually.

Royal turned to him in surprise. "Mon"—he was jokingly serious—"how yo' know 'bout dat?"

"We have a big organization." Rich shrugged. "All sorts of information filters in. Like fishermen, we take out of the net what interests us and throw the rest away."

232

"And the Progressive Liberal Party. It interests you?"

"It could. We've been trying to get into the Bahamas for a long time. Now we're here. Unless something completely unforeseen happens, we're here to stay. But"—he made a small gesture with both hands—"we are vulnerable. We're here by the indulgence of the government. A hostile regime, sensitive to criticism, could close us up, push us out. Naturally, we try to protect ourselves. Tell me, do you really think you can make it?"

"Yes. We can make it." There was no hesitation. "We'll make it at the general election next year. We'll put up the damnedest bloc of black votes anyone has ever seen. Every black man in the islands will vote. We'll roll the election up and carry it away."

Rich was thoughtful. "Do you want any help now? Money?"

"You want to buy a piece of the action also. Everyone is pushing money at me. Max Hertog. You. I could make a good thing out of this for myself if that was all I wanted."

Rich wasn't embarrassed. "We'd just like to try and buy a little goodwill. If you don't make it, we write off the small loss as a bad investment. If you do, then we have a friend at court. It's that simple."

"Some goodwill might be for sale. I'm not. We may need money later. Outdoor rallies with free drinks and food. Transportation to the polls. A few dollars here and there. But"—he regarded Rich steadily—"it won't buy you anything tangible. I won't be your man. If the people get a fair shake out of the gambling concessions, I have no objection. A share of the profits would clean up the slums in Nassau, build some schools for the black children."

"That doesn't sound unreasonable. We've frequently paid more for less."

Royal glanced at his watch. "The mail boat is due in from Nassau. My girl is coming over on it for the weekend. Want to drive down to West End with me and meet her?"

Rich stood up. "I'd like to. Maybe the both of you will have dinner with me. I'm staying overnight at the Cay Club."

"Thanks. We'll see." He laughed with quiet amusement. "I'll tell you something about the Cay Club. When I first came here, I had some trouble there. I went in for dinner with my girl, and they wouldn't seat us. They weren't discriminating, you understand. It was just that everything was reserved. I told Max Hertog about it. Do you know what he did? He bought the club, fired the manager, the clerk and the headwaiter and told me to hire a new staff. I've thought about it many times. It was a strange thing for him to do because he is a real nigger hater."

"Do you know?" Rich was thoughtful. "I don't often hear the word 'nigger' in the Bahamas."

"No. That's true. I use it now and then, but I've been exposed to the outside world and corrupted. A few of the boys who worked in Florida and then came back home use it among themselves, but it isn't common. The black people are exceptionally polite to each other. It is always Mr. Brown or Mrs. Brown."

They walked to where the Jeep was parked and stood for a moment in the silence. The sunset was a great gold and crimson smear laced with thin clouds of purple. Royal was the first to turn away. He climbed into the Jeep and waited for Rich who was reluctant to leave. When he did get into the car his half-smile was just a little embarrassed as though there were something for which he ought to apologize.

"I never actually believe the sunsets in these islands. They are too spectacular."

Royal nodded. "When I was a boy, I picked up odd jobs when I could. For a while I worked for an artist who had a home in Nassau. I carried his easel, stool and boxes when he went out to paint. He finally gave up trying to capture the sunsets. He said there just weren't any such colors."

They drove in silence for a few minutes. The tinny beat of the Jeep's motor was a harsh note in the twilight hour's hush. Royal chuckled and turned to Rich with an explanation.

"I was thinking of the mail boat. It carries a little of everything: things the Out Island people have ordered in Nassau, the mail, groceries, gasoline, candy and ice cream. When it puts in at some of the remote islands, everyone hurries down to the dock and they go on an ice-cream blast. It's the damnedest thing you ever saw. They have no refrigeration, so they have to eat what they buy right away. They go yelling around, clutching as many cones and ice-cream bars as they can hold and stuffing them down before they melt."

West End wanders along the shore without any particular plan. In the brief time before darkness closed down, it was gathered in a golden haze, and the last of the light touched the high cockades of plumes atop the coconut trees. Royal parked at the dock, shut the motor, and leaned forward, arms crossed on the wheel. From the settlement's homes the residents strolled, converging on the piers. The youngsters raced ahead, shouting and tumbling in their excitement. A few hundred yards from shore the stubby little boat thrust her way through the leaden water. Her foredeck was piled high with crates, cartons and steel drums. Her whistle shrilled with a note of cocky triumph. Royal and Rich walked out on the pier and watched as the craft panted her way in.

"There's my girl." Royal lifted his hand in a high salute to Alicia, who was poised on tiptoe on the afterdeck. She raised both arms in an ecstatic reply.

Rich glanced from the girl to Royal. "If"—he smiled—"you decide not to have dinner with me, I think I will understand."

Chris Baildon made a long and awkward cast from the flat-bottomed rowboat, and there was a silver flash as the bonefish scattered from where they had been feeding. Chris knew Whaley was watching him with an amused contempt, but he didn't give a damn. He was hot and tired, growing more irritable by the minute. He didn't care much for fishing. He particularly didn't like bonefishing. The damned things, even the smaller ones, fought like bloody hell when hooked. Maybe some persons got a kick out of it, but Chris Baildon didn't.

This was the third visit he had made to Hole-in-the-Ocean Cay in an attempt to ingratiate himself with Whaley. His only excuse for making the trip was the fishing. Anyone could see he wasn't very good at it. Even Whaley, who didn't seem to be

235

too bright, must be wondering why he insisted on going out. Not only was he unskilled, but he was indifferent to the sport.

"Yo' gots t' git yo' line en sof'," Whaley chided.

The man stood at the stern of the weathered boat and poled the craft gently through the shallow water. The bonefish were all around them. They fed on the bottom, seeming to stand on their heads, and the tips of their tails fluttered above the water. Bonefish were stalked, and when one hit, it was with a streaking fury.

"To hell with it." Chris reeled in and laid the rod in the bottom of the boat. At his feet was a hamper with a bottle of rum, a Thermos of water, some sandwiches and fruit. "Let's have a drink."

Whaley made no reply but laid the pole aside. He might have wondered why so inept a fisherman and one with so little enthusiasm for the sport should pay him five dollars to guide him to where the fish were. Secretly he considered Baildon to be a little crazy and he mused upon this, wondering whether it was something he might turn to his advantage. He seated himself on a thwart and took a plastic cup, half-filled with rum, from Baildon's hand. Chris poured a drink for himself, lit a cigarette, and tossed pack and matches back to Whaley. They were silent. The conch rarely spoke unless it was necessary. They had no range of mutual interest, so these expeditions were conducted with a minimum of conversation.

Chris was exasperated. With anyone else it could have been a simple matter. He could say: "You own some property on Grand Bahama. I'd like to buy it." To say this abruptly would, he knew, start an almost endless series of questions and immediately arouse a native cupidity. Half the time Whaley didn't seem to understand the simplest sentences. To try to tell him he was a landowner with something of value would require patience, a simple approach and tact.

"I don't think I want to fish anymore. Let's go ashore, find some shade, and eat these sandwiches."

Whaley nodded, finished his drink, stood up, and pushed them off the flats into deep water, where he took up the oars. Chris watched him for a moment.

236

"There are a lot of Whaleys in the islands." This seemed to be as good an opening gambit as anything. "You must be kin to them all."

Whaley shrugged. "I hear o' some sometime. Never see wun."

"The family has been here for a long time. Three hundred years or more."

"Don' mean nothin' t' me. I never see wun." With a strong pull he drove the small boat onto the shelving beach. "Dis as good a place as any."

They found a patch of shade beneath the high palms. Chris opened the hamper, passed a couple of sandwiches to Whaley, and put the rum between them. A small rustle in the undergrowth caused him to turn his head. He started with shocked surprise. Half-concealed, resting on all fours, the albino woman was staring at them. Her nose twitched like that of a hungry animal scenting food. Her features were things of evil. The red eyes glared, and the white, stringy hair fell across her face. Chris turned away, pretending he hadn't seen her. Whaley took the sliced chicken from a sandwich, stuffed it in his mouth, and chewed stolidly. After a moment he sailed the two pieces of bread into the brush. The woman fell on them with a howling sound and scuttled as a maimed giant crab out of sight.

"Goddamn woman always hungry. I drown her good wun day. Git rid'n her. No damn good t' me no mo'."

Chris gagged slightly on the rum and lit a fresh cigarette. He didn't think he could take much more of Whaley. He'd say what he had to say, try to make it sound casual and unimportant, and hope it would work.

"I was looking through some titles and land grants the other day and came across the name of Thomas Whaley." This was idle conversation.

"Don' know 'em."

"Probably not. He's been dead a long time. But it just could be he was a relative—a close relative—your great-great-great-grandfather maybe."

Whaley grunted and took the rum bottle, filling his cup. He was unimpressed and indifferent.

"Do you know what a title means?" Chris persisted, trying to break through the ignorance.

"No." Whaley's attitude indicated he couldn't care less.

"Well"—Chris wanted to make it simple—"it's a sort of paper saying you own a certain piece of land." He paused. "What I read," he continued, "says your great-great-great-grandfather owned some land on Grand Bahama, and maybe it's come down to you. Anyhow, I think so."

"No Whaley I know never owned nothin' except, maybe, a boad."

"Well"—Chris persisted—"if it should turn out you own it, I think I might be able to get you some money for it."

A tiny coal of interest began to glow in the dull eyes. Money he could understand, although why anyone would want to give him some was confusing.

"How much money maybe?"

"Well." The reply was cautious. Chris was aware of the awakening interest. "As much as a thousand dollars maybe."

"How much is a thousand?"

A little desperately Chris wondered how the hell he could illustrate a thousand. Finally he took out his wallet and counted ten singles. He placed them on the ground while Whaley watched with an intent and greedy interest.

"Now"—Chris hoped the explanation would work—"this is ten. A thousand would stack up this high." He elevated his hand a few inches above the pack. "A thousand would come to about here."

"Whah two thousand?" Whaley asked the question with a sharp eagerness.

Chris sighed. "Two thousand?" He raised his hand an inch or more. "This would be two thousand."

"I like two thousand." The rum was getting to the man, and he rolled his eyes with an attempt at humor.

"I don't know. I'm not sure. I can try. If I can you'll have to come to Nassau with me and sign some papers."

"I bin Nassau wun time."

238

"You'll be a rich man when you go this time." Chris made an attempt to inject a note of enthusiasm into the dialogue. "I'll come back next week and fly you over to Nassau. We'll have the papers drawn up, ready to sign."

"You have th' money wid you?"

"Yes."

"All right. I'll go." He looked around cautiously. "Maybe I don' come back an' leave damn ol' woman heah t' starve." He was pleased with the idea.

On the way home Chris wondered if he could keep Sherry Melnick out of the final stages and decided it would be impossible. Sherry wasn't going to hand over two thousand dollars without being sure he was getting what he paid for. A lousy two thousand dollars. That was all he needed to pick up a million. He felt abused and cheated. After a few moments he brightened. It would be almost worth giving up a half share just to hear Max Hertog roar. His son-in-law—and a Jew at that—was going to screw Max Hertog as he had never been screwed before.

XV

Mr. Vincent Loring, of Prince and Loring, was a man of gentle speech and disposition. It was doubtful that in his thirty or so years as an adult he had ever used the Lord's name as an expletive or called on Him other than in prayer. Now he stood up, gazed with something close to horror at Christopher Baildon and Sherry Melnick. Then he said it.

"I'll be goddamned!"

Chris grinned and winked at Sherry as he watched Loring's agitation mount. The man made a complete circuit of the room, pausing to look out each window. He halted at his desk. His hands fluttered indecisively over the papers there, and he stared at Baildon almost pleadingly.

"Why"—he all but whispered—"Max will kill you. I mean he'll kill you if he doesn't drop dead of shock first. This is unbelievable, completely, fantastically incredible."

"Will you handle it for us?" Sherry interrupted rudely.

Loring peered at him and adjusted his spectacles. "You? You are?" He actually seemed to have forgotten his visitor's identity. The words trailed away on an unhappy key.

"Melnick." Sherry reminded him sharply.

"Yes. Yes. Of course," Loring stammered. "Mr. Melnick. You are. Oh, my God. You are Max Hertog's son-in-law." Complete astonishment possessed him.

"That's right." Sherry was becoming impatient. "Now will you represent us?"

Vincent Loring pleaded silently with Chris Baildon. His mouth worked convulsively, making the small, popping sound of a gasping fish.

"Christopher"—he appealed to Baildon—"are you sure you want to do this?"

"Of course I'm sure. We want you to ask one million dollars, plus the legal fees. If Max doesn't come up with it right away, then I want you to secure an injunction restraining him from developing one square inch of the disputed property."

Mr. Loring was perspiring. He dropped shakily into his chair and patted at his forehead with a handkerchief. He regarded Chris and Melnick unhappily and with awe.

"You know, of course"—his voice dropped to a whisper— "this will bring everything on Grand Bahama to a dead halt. Max simply can't build around you. The litigation could go on for years."

"We're counting on that." Sherry was pleased.

"Oh, my!" Loring was miserable.

"If you don't want to represent us"—Chris was crisp and undisturbed by Loring's obvious distress—"I'll get someone else."

"No. Oh, no." Loring shook his head. "I wouldn't want you to do anything like that." He almost giggled, and there was a note of hysteria in the sound. "A thing like this can't help leading to international publicity. Mr. Prince and I wouldn't want you to call on other solicitors. We are quite capable of carrying it to the courts if necessary. This will have reverberations. Yes, I think I can honestly say it will have reverberations. Most generally the law is a fusty business. But this. Oh, my! This is going to be most exciting and stimulating. It may well become a legal classic." He leaped up with the agility of a cricket and pumped Baildon's hand enthusiastically. "We shall give it our all, Christopher, our very all."

Outside again, Chris and Melnick stood on the sidewalk and looked about with a proprietary air. They were, both knew, within touching distance of a million dollars. More than that,

241

it must establish them for all time as men of sagacity and monumental cunning. Their reputations in the Bahamas would be made.

Sherry regarded his partner with a bright interest. "How do you feel?"

"God." It was almost a prayer. "I feel great. You know," Chris continued with an ingenuous pleasure, "the calypso boys may even write a song about us. Legends have arisen out of less. I'll buy lunch."

They hailed a cab to take them to the Coral Club. The whole thing had been concluded on far simpler terms than they hoped for. Whaley had been delighted with the plane ride to Nassau. Any suspicion he might have entertained vanished in the excitement and novelty of the trip and the metropolitan bustle of Nassau. He gawked at the people, the traffic, and was childishly pleased when Chris bought him one of the rough plaited straw hats at a stall. All the papers necessary to the transfer of title had been drawn to conform to government regulations. Whaley, who was unable to write his name, made the X mark in the presence of a notary, and the purchase by Baildon and Melnick properly entered the government records. There had been an aggravating delay when Whaley insisted on counting the two thousand dollars. Since he was unable to count beyond ten, the money had to be separated into units of that denomination. The process, with Whaley checking and rechecking, had seemed interminable. Chris tried to induce the man to put the money into a savings account, explaining how he could come and take some out whenever he felt like it. Whaley knew nothing of banks and was reluctant to allow the bills out of his hands. Chris finally bought a canvas zippered bag, and into this Whaley stuffed his wealth. Chris offered to fly him back to Hole-in-the-Ocean Cay, but he refused. The last they saw of him he was idling down Bay Street, clutching his bag of money.

Chris leaned back against the cab's seat with a pleased and cherubic expression on his face. This, he knew, was to be the most monumental screwing to take place in the islands. He laughed aloud in sheer exuberance.

"Are you going back to Miami this afternoon?"

242

Melnick nodded with a grin. "I'd like to stick around and see the fun. But I have an idea I'll be able to hear Max's bellow in Florida."

"What are you going to tell Jan?" There was concern in the question.

Sherry was thoughtful. "I'll tell her the truth. Max was careless."

"She's funny about Max." Chris shook his head. "She calls him a bastard, but they understand each other. There has always been this thing between them, an affection, love. In her way she is proud of him, and this is going to hurt Max. It will cut at his pride. People are going to laugh. Jan won't like that."

"I'm not asking her to like it." Melnick was abrupt. "It is a business deal."

"Well, not exactly." Chris smiled. "Do you think Max will fight us?"

"Oh, he'll probably throw his weight around at first. He'll threaten and pound on tables until he realizes he's in the net. Then he'll calm down and try to figure a way out. When he realizes he can't get away, he'll try to squeeze us, cut us down, make a cheaper deal. Finally he'll pay. He can't afford years in the courts. So we have him where it hurts."

They found a table in a corner of the club's dining room and ordered lunch after a couple of drinks. Every now and then they'd look up and across at each other and laugh.

In the government building's department of records a clerk with an inquisitive nature and time on his hands halted in the filing of some papers. Then he sat down and reread them. After that he went back to the earliest colonial files, read what was there of interest to him. Then he sat down again and felt extremely pleased with himself. He wondered what he could do with the information and decided to wait until his lunch hour. Later, in the main corridor of the post office, he encountered Pierre DuPres, and his question was answered. He and DuPres, who had a nodding acquaintance, walked from the post office together.

"Does a newspaper pay for information, Mr. DuPres?"

"Usually, if it is of value. Why?"

"I came across something today. A real estate transaction which came to records for filing. I think it might be a very big story."

DuPres glanced at his watch. "If you haven't had lunch, have it with me. You can tell me about it then."

Carol Wainwright dropped the telephone's receiver back into its cradle with a puzzled frown. Why, she had to wonder, would Pete DuPres call to ask if she could have dinner with him? Although they had known each other for years, she couldn't recall they ever had a date. So, she concluded, Pete must want something, and that something had to do with Maximilian Hertog. Because her curiosity had been piqued, she said yes, and Pete arranged to pick her up at her home at seven thirty. Also—and she was a little reluctant to admit this—she had accepted the invitation because she was annoyed with Max. She would have denied being jealous, jealous of an island, of all things. Grand Bahama was absorbing all of Max's time and attention. This was something she had learned to expect. Always he turned the full resources of his mind and body into any new project. Until now he always managed to include her in many small ways outside her official position as confidential secretary. She became his confidante, his sounding board. A warm and almost completely satisfying relationship had been achieved. He made her feel a part of the involved transactions, sharing in the excitement of a coup or a complex pyramid of investments. With Grand Bahama he had become close to secretive, jealous of the details. He shared nothing with her beyond the broad outlines of the development. Grand Bahama had become an intensely personal manipulation, and when they were alone, he seemed to avoid talking about it deliberately.

Of late, she had the feeling that her relationship with Max had become a thing of delicate, almost precarious balance. She was neither wholly mistress nor secretary. She had gone to bed with him, as she knew from the beginning she would. He was an exciting man, and the first experience had been full and satisfying. The feeling for him grew, and she found herself, much to her disgust, becoming just a little "nesty," arranging a flower on his desk, wanting to cook and plan dinner. That he was twice her age never seemed to make any difference. He was a man of full vigor, robust and with a hearty animal sensuality. They had an understanding, although it had never been phrased. She had never asked for a commitment. In a way she was proud of her independence. It was Max who now and then mentioned and took for granted the fact that they would be married. The time? Well, that would be arranged. It really didn't seem to be too important. She rebelled at the idea of leaving the office and assuming the duties of a housewife at Windmere. She never pressed him for a wedding date, and Max was well aware of this.

After Jan had married and moved to Miami, coming to Nassau for an occasional weekend, Carol frequently spent the night at Windmere. For reasons which didn't make too much sense she had been reluctant to do this while Jan was living in the house. Oddly enough, Max had supported her in this.

"Most girls"—she was naked and in bed with him, half sitting up within the circle of his arm—"most girls," he repeated, "would be whining around, asking, 'When are we going to get married, Max?' " His hand moved over the curve of her hip.

"I don't whine around. I'm not even certain, sometimes, I want to marry you."

"Of course you do. All girls want to get married. All girls would like to marry a man with as much money as I have."

Somehow, and it was confusing, he could say something like that and not be offensive. She tapped the hot ash from her cigarette on his chest, and he jumped.

"That's for being smug." She put the cigarette in a tray and then turned back to look into his face. "Have you always gone to bed with your secretaries?"

"When they were as pretty as you are. Usually they weren't."

"If I asked you to give me some money, a lot of money, would you do it?"

"To keep you or get rid of you?" He pulled her down on top of him, smothering her laughing answer.

She smiled to herself now thinking about the incident. In his own and sometimes strange way he was a generous man.

But—and she knew this to be true—he rarely did anything unless it afforded him satisfaction or pleasure. She had never asked him for anything. The new car, furs, jewelry, the charge accounts in Miami and New York were hers because it pleased him for her to have them. He made these gestures almost absently. Nothing of Max Hertog really came through with them. Because it seemed impersonal, she never had the feeling of being kept. Her relationship with him had effectively cut her off from the attentions of the few eligible men in Nassau. The selection wasn't large at best. So, in all honesty, she couldn't fall back on the old cliché of having given the best years of her life. These, she knew, had barely been touched. So—and she was brooding—she could terminate her association with Maximilian Hertog whenever she wished. She remained in his employ because it was a challenging, exciting and imaginative job. Going to bed with him. That was one of the fringe benefits and not an inconsequential one. She felt the beginning of a small excitement now at the thought of him. He was rough but somehow gentle. His lovemaking had a fierce urgency which he communicated to her. He had been her first man. Now she sometimes wondered what other men were like.

A small light glowed on her desk. Max was calling. This had been her first victory with him. His former secretary and the other girls in the office responded to a buzzer which sounded with the angry rasp of a rattlesnake. Carol had refused to answer it and had an electrician come in to install this silent bulb. She was certain he knew of this, but he ignored and never mentioned the change, so some of the satisfaction she felt in the minor triumph was dissipated. She left her desk and went to his office, carrying her book and pencil in case he had something of a confidential nature to dictate. The other girls usually took his routine letters.

He looked up from behind his desk, half smiled, and nodded his approval of her appearance. She consciously dressed for him, and she suspected he knew it.

"I'm going to run over to Grand Bahama this afternoon and probably spend the night. There is a lot going on you haven't seen. Want to come along?"

246

"Oh"—she did her best to sound unhappy—"I can't. I just made a dinner date."

"You can break it." He picked up a letter, assuming the matter had been settled. "Answer this, will you? You know what to say." He leaned back in the chair. "Why don't you leave now and I'll pick you up on my way out to Windmere?"

"I have an engagement, Max. I told you." Her voice wasn't quite as firm as she would have wished it to be.

He looked at her oddly for a moment and then nodded. "All right. I didn't think it was that important."

She wanted to say, "It isn't really. I just don't like being taken for granted. No one does." He was watching her, so she said nothing and took the letter.

"Was there anything else?"

For a moment she thought about adding "sir" but realized it would sound ridiculous. They both would laugh, and the posture of independence would be spoiled. Max only shook his head and bent his attention to some blueprints spread out over the desk. She hesitated and then turned, leaving and closing the door quietly behind her.

Pete DuPres made an entertaining dinner companion. He talked easily and well, and since they had known each other from childhood, there was no feeling of constraint. They had driven to the Buena Vista, one of Nassau's dining showplaces. The evening was pleasantly warm and lightly touched with the varied perfumes from the extensive gardens. The tables were arranged out of doors, and there were colored lanterns, swaying and tinkling overhead in the tiny breeze. The scene had a quiet enchantment.

The name DuPres was found among those of the early colonial settlers and Pete—few persons called him Pierre—had taken a second-rate weekly newspaper and turned it into an aggressive daily. His staff was small but competent. Its columns were literate and frequently witty, and Pete DuPres served as editor, publisher and reporter. He had been sent to England and, later, France for his education. His head was filled with amusing trivia and bits of local gossip which filtered to him through innumerable sources. Over the second mai tai before dinner Carol realized she hadn't thought once of Max or wondered why DuPres had asked her out.

"I don't think we ever had a date before, Pete." She bit through a stick of pineapple. "Why now?"

"After dinner. I had a reason, of course. I'll tell you later."

They danced to the calypso band that played from a platform high in a banyan tree and then ordered dinner. Later, with the coffee and brandy, DuPres' light manner changed. He gave her the details of what the clerk in records had told him and what he had later rechecked and substantiated. He followed the possible line from the original Whaley grant to the heirs and the transfer this day from William Whaley to Christopher Baildon and Sherry Melnick. Carol listened incredulously.

"But," she had protested at one point, "it just isn't possible, Pete." She shook her head. "Sutter, Tracy and Longworth checked everything out. I made the call to Potter Longworth myself and told him what Max wanted: the squatters, the squatters' rights, previous sale by the Crown. Everything."

"Well, they missed this." Pete shrugged. "It isn't too hard to understand. The early records were indifferently kept. Also, the grant to Thomas Whaley was to be tax-free. Naturally it never appeared on the tax rolls. Over the years it was just assumed to be Crown property since no one ever laid claim to it. It could easily have happened just that way."

"Max will be wild." She whispered the words.

"I think that is the understatement of the year."

"Jan's husband, too." Her eyes widened. "Max had never liked, never trusted him." She lit a cigarette, and her fingers trembled slightly. "Chris Baildon I can understand. Max was brutal with him. But Melnick." Her whistle of astonishment was low. She looked across at DuPres. "You're going to print the story?"

"Of course. It's the big story of all time out of the Bahamas."

"I suppose so." She agreed reluctantly. "It's going to make Max look foolish. And Sutter, Tracy and Longworth. Max will take them apart, limb by limb. But"—and this suddenly seemed

248

to occur to her—"why did you ask me to dinner? Why are you telling me this? What do you want?"

"Where is Max now?"

"Grand Bahama."

"Can you get in touch with him?"

"I can use *The Witch*'s ship to shore to Royal Keating, the engineer there."

"I know Max. He's going to explode. I can't say I blame him. The story is in tomorrow's paper. Max never wants to give an interview. This time he'll have to say something. I'd like your help in trying to make him understand he should. It's too sensational a story to lie in the aisle. The Miami papers and the wire services will be after him. I want an exclusive, to see him before the others do. That's the reason for the dinner. Will you do what you can?"

"I wouldn't like to have you waste an evening on me." Her smile was brief, saying, we're old friends and can talk with each other this way. "At the moment I'm more concerned about Max. We can't let him pick up the paper tomorrow morning and read what has happened. Will you take me back to Windmere and I'll try and reach him?"

She was silent on the way to Lyford Cay, and DuPres, sensing her concern, made no attempt at conversation. He drove as fast as was safe on the narrow, winding road. Carol, hunched down in the seat, stared straight ahead without really seeing anything.

At Windmere she took the boathouse keys from Max's desk. It was a simple matter then to get a skiff and row out the fifty yards or so to where *The Witch* was moored. She hesitated for a few moments before the ship-to-shore set, finally turning it on and putting a call through to the marine operator in Nassau. From that point the call letters for Royal Keating's cottage on Grand Bahama went winging through the night. She glanced at her watch. It was still early evening. With any luck she might catch Max with Royal.

It was only a matter of half a minute or so before the call was completed and Royal Keating answered.

"Mr. Keating? This is Carol Wainwright."

"Oh, hello, Miss Wainwright." There was no surprise in the reply.

"Is Mr. Hertog still on the island? It's urgent I get in touch with him."

"As a matter of fact he is here, with me. Wait a minute."

The voice then was that of Max. "Carol?" He was surprised.

She glanced almost imploringly at DuPres. How did you tell a man with the vanity and self-assurance of Max Hertog that he would be the victim of a monumental swindle and the butt of laughter throughout the Bahamas in the morning?

"Carol?" This time he was impatient.

"Yes, Max. I—I think you ought to come back to Nassau." She rushed the words. "Now. Tonight."

"You? Jan?" There was immediate concern.

"No, Max. Nothing like that. Nothing has happened to Jan or me."

"Well, what is it then?"

"Look"—she simply could not bring herself to tell him this way—"I don't think it is anything you would want to discuss publicly." All the operator of any boat had to do was to throw a switch and the conversation would come through his speaker. The air was filled with a constant exchange of marine information. "If something is keeping you there, then send the plane for me. No. Wait a minute. Never mind. I'll get a charter out at the field."

He knew her well enough to be certain by now that she hadn't been caught in a sudden panic over some inconsequential development. There was an imperative note in her voice.

"All right." He was decisive. "I'll be waiting at the airstrip."

She sat, staring at the transmitter before hanging it up. DuPres stood nearby. She turned, looked up at him, and tried to smile.

"You don't have to wait, Pete. I'll take one of Max's cars. But thanks for everything. I'll do what I can for you." She suddenly felt weary.

"I'll drive you out to the airport. I'd like to go to Grand Bahama with you."

250

"No. Believe me, Max would be furious. I'll try to get him to see you tomorrow."

It seemed to Carol that the small plane she had engaged at the field was no more than airborne before the young pilot was talking to the tower on Grand Bahama and making a wide turn to come in for a landing on the illuminated strip. As they taxied back, she could see a Jeep drawn to one side. Max was standing beside it. When they were opposite him, the pilot cut his motor.

"Will you want to go back tonight, Miss Wainwright?"

She hesitated for a moment. "No. Mr. Hertog has the Lockheed here. We'll go back in that." She dropped to the ground and waved to him. "Thanks for the ride." Turning, she walked to where Max waited.

Max was unwilling to display any curiosity or concern over her fast trip or the reason for it.

"What happened to your date? Were you stood up?"

Under the circumstances it was a ridiculous question. They were both aware of this. She extended her hand, wanting to touch him.

"No one stood me up. Let's sit in the Jeep. I'll tell you why I'm here."

On the narrow seat she slowly and carefully repeated what DuPres had told her. In the half-light, a pale radiance from a star-filled sky, she could see his features tighten, and a muscle at the corner of his jaw leaped beneath the tanned skin. She faltered just a little in the telling because this wasn't at all what she had expected. Max should have loosed a roar of outrage which would have sounded over the entire Little Bahama Bank. When she finished, he carefully broke out one of his heavy cigars from its container. In the brief glow of the lighter she could see his eyes were bleak.

"DuPres is sure? Positive? There couldn't be any mistake about this?"

"I don't think so. Pete came to me with the story because he hoped I could help him see you after he ran it."

There was just the suggestion of a frosty smile. "I'll see him.

He's a good newspaperman and would have checked it out thoroughly. Chris Baildon and Melnick." He mused on the names. "Chris I won't blame too much. Maybe I was rough on him. But Melnick." He made the name sound as though it were something to spit out. "Melnick is what I have always said he was. A chiseler. A sharpshooter. A tinhorn. My daughter and my house are too good for him."

"What's going to happen now?" She moved closer, and his arm went about her shoulders. "Can they really hold you up?"

"Yes. Everything will have to come to a halt. Even if their claim is worthless, they can stop us from turning a shovelful of dirt until the courts decide. It could take years. I'll have to settle with them and at their price."

"I didn't expect you to take it so quietly." Her eyes searched his features.

"I'm probably a little numb." The chuckle was in his throat. "When I come out of shock, you'll really hear me yell." He turned the ignition key and started the motor. "We'll go over to the club and get you a room. There's no point in going back tonight. Tomorrow we'll find out what the price on this hang-up is going to be."

In the bar of the Cay Club they had coffee and brandy. It was off-season, and there were no other guests. It was a pleasant and relaxing room with the walls finished in native woods and brought to a gleaming polish with repeated waxing. She watched as some of the tension drained away. Anger usually betrayed Max Hertog. This time he held it under control.

He looked approvingly around the room now. "I bought this place. You remember?" He was only making small talk.

"Yes." She smiled, understanding he was creating a diversion for his mind. "I remember."

"They wouldn't let Keating and his girl in one time. They wouldn't serve niggers. They forgot he was my nigger. I fired them all and let Keating put his people in. They have a nigger manager now. Maybe he won't serve white people. That would be a hell of a note, wouldn't it?" He paused and glanced at the bar where the young attendant was absorbed in a paperback. "I think I'm softening up." He made the comment with a cer-

252

tain wonder. "I sat there tonight, in his cottage. We had a drink together and talked. Sometimes I don't even remember he's black."

"Does it make so much difference?"

"Hell, I don't know." He stood up. "Let's call it a night."

Their rooms were adjoining, and both opened on the same balcony overlooking the shore and water. The connecting door between them was open.

"You know," she called to him, "I didn't even bring a toothbrush."

"We can get you one in the morning or you can use mine and I'll take seconds."

"Thanks." She hesitated. "Good night."

She undressed slowly, not bothering to turn on a light. Star points, brighter than she had ever seen them, made darts on the water. The beacon on Indian Cay Rock was a steady guide to the West End channel entrance. No sound was carried on the night. She was suddenly oppressed by a sensation of sadness, of desolation, and wondered at it. She had never known Max Hertog to react to a problem in this manner. He had seemed almost weary, dispirited, and it was all a little sad. She felt pity as she might for a tired and toothless lion.

"Carol?" He stood in the doorway, a formidable figure whose shoulders seemed to touch each side of the frame. Wearing only the bottoms of his pajamas, he held the coat. "I thought you might be more comfortable with this on." He tossed the jacket to her bed. "Good night."

"Thank you."

He had turned from the door, back into his room and out of sight. She smiled to herself. He didn't like expressions of gratitude. They embarrassed him. She slipped into the pajama half, and it fell just short of her knees. The cuffs of the sleeves took two full turns before they rested at her wrists. She was never completely comfortable sleeping naked. Even when they were in bed together, she always got out later and put on a nightgown. This he remembered, and her eyes softened at the small gesture of thoughtfulness. He would do something like this, and it would be entirely out of character with the

Max Hertog most persons knew. She took a cigarette and matches and went out on the balcony to sit on the railing, her head leaning back against a narrow post. A small wind, brief and running on its own out of nowhere, sifted through the dry fronds of a palm fan with a faint, crackling sound. She smoked half the cigarette and then stubbed it out against the rail before reentering her room. Instead of going to her bed, she continued on into Max's room.

He was lying on his back, arms crossed beneath his head. He didn't speak, but she knew he was awake. After a second he released one arm, and his hand pulled down the covers on her side. Without a word she slipped in beside him and his arm locked her close.

"It never occurred to me to worry about you before. I do now, and I'm not sure why. I guess I'm afraid you'll do something rash. I would have felt better if you had stormed around, breaking things."

"I may yet. Maybe not. I don't know. I don't like to be made a fool of. That is what has happened."

"How could you have known?"

"I should have made it my business to know." He was castigating himself.

"Be reasonable, Max. You can't possibly check on every detail of every deal. You hire people for those things."

"I suppose so." He made the admission reluctantly. "After all, it's only money." He made a small whistling sound which almost carried with it a note of admiration. "If I had known Chris Baildon was this smart, I never would have fired him."

She smiled in the darkness. This was the Max Hertog she knew. A sense of humor always saved him. She turned so her cheek rested against his shoulder. It was a long time before either of them went to sleep.

XVI

The story of what could be a multimillion-dollar blunder in the development of Grand Bahama swept over Nassau with the impact of a tropical hurricane. DuPres' paper was on the streets, in the homes and offices early. The story fanned out from the island capital by radio to Florida and the coastal states. There it was picked up and transmitted nationally and internationally. By midmorning it was the talk of the nation's financial circles.

To the astonishment of his employees and Bay Street in general Max Hertog seemed completely unruffled. If there was an area of tranquillity, a calm eye at the storm's center, then Max seemed to sit within it, unperturbed and almost jaunty. Carol watched this unprecedented behavior with mounting wonder.

They had flown back early from Freeport. At the airport they picked up copies of the paper and read them with a silent concentration on the way to Windmere. Max was dropped off there, and Carol went on home to change. Although she rushed through her bath and dressing, Max was in his office when she arrived. He was behind his desk, immaculate in a suit of white shantung silk and radiating the special charm he seemed able to turn off and on at will. One of his heavy cigars rested in a crystal tray, and the smoke made a thin blue spiral. It was further evidence of his imperturbability, for he usually chewed vigorously on an unlit cigar when he was angry.

After a short knock Carol had entered the office and halted abruptly at the spectacle of Max, relaxed and seemingly enjoying the morning, and of Pierre DuPres seated nearby.

Max called to her. "Come on in. Sit down. Pete and I are having a little talk."

Carol nodded to Pete, dropped an eyelid in an expressive wink, and then took a chair across the desk from Max.

"Answering your question"—Max leaned back, stared at the ceiling reflectively—"I'm going to settle with them, of course." The words were directed to DuPres. "Prince and Loring are representing them. They have asked for an appointment." He allowed his chair to drop back to a level position.

"Did they mention a settlement figure?" DuPres was making notes.

"No. But you can be sure they will." He smiled, and the expression was one of genuine good humor. "Do you know"—he addressed both of them—"I am actually enjoying this unsuspected side of my nature? Everyone expected me to roar and tear things apart. Instead, I radiate nothing but goodwill. It must be confusing to a hell of a lot of people."

"He called me," DuPres explained to Carol in an exaggeratedly awestruck tone. "He actually called and invited me over. What the hell do you know about that?" He turned again to Max. "There's a personal angle to this. Probably you don't want to talk about it. I do. I mean your son-in-law, Sherry Melnick."

Carol, watching Max, half expected to see him explode from the chair. Instead, he merely nodded an agreement.

"Let's say"—Max was deliberately being pontifical—"I am impressed by Mr. Melnick's instinct for a fast buck. He is, of course, an honorable man. As my daughter's husband, how could he be otherwise?"

DuPres grinned. "You want me to print that?"

"Why not?" Max was bland. "It sounded pretty good to me."

"It's definite. You won't fight the claim?"

"No." Max was almost indifferent. "It could take years. No.

256

I'll pay off and get on with the development of Grand Bahama. I never leave anything unfinished."

DuPres glanced at his watch. "I'm going back to the office and write what I have. If you don't mind, I'll come back for the general news conference."

"The what?" Carol's voice rose with amazement.

"The damn phone has been ringing all morning. The Miami papers and the news services wanted an interview. So I invited them all to Windmere for one o'clock. You'd better talk with Big Maum and arrange something. I don't know how many to expect." Max had an aura of pleased innocence about him.

When DuPres left, Carol expected an abrupt change in Max's airy indifference. Instead, he continued to act as though the situation had created a monumental joke which everyone could enjoy.

"Charley Rich called from New York. He had heard a broadcast. They have a big, almost unlimited investment. He wanted to know what was going to happen." Max half swung about to gaze out of a window. "I told him I wouldn't let anything interfere with the Grand Bahama development." He rubbed the knuckles of a fist over his nose in a bemused manner. "He wanted to know, and he was precise about it, if I wanted Baildon and Melnick contained."

"What?" Again Carol could hardly believe what she heard.

Max's laughter rumbled deep within his chest. He nodded happily.

"Contained was the word he used. I suppose he means in a block of cement or facedown in a ditch someplace. His associates have a reputation for being direct."

"You're joking."

"No. And I don't think Rich was either."

She hesitated. "Has Jan called? She must have heard or read the story by now?"

"No." He was surprised by the question. "Why should she?"

"I thought, because of Sherry."

"We're not choosing up sides for a game of touch football. She knows me better than that."

"What about Baildon and Sherry?"

"Chris?" He shrugged indifferently. "Nothing, probably. He's a small rabbit and smarter than I thought. He deserves to get away with it if he can. Melnick?" The voice grated now. "This is personal. I'm going to ruin him. Wherever he has a dollar invested, I'm going after it and destroy him. He is high on my list of things to do."

Although the house of quasi-Mediterranean architecture, once so prevailing in southern Florida, was only a dozen or so years old, the grounds and the gardens had been laid out during the boom days more than forty years ago. The area had been among the earliest of the outer Miami development with the result that the trees and shrubbery were sturdy and luxuriant with time, the flower beds solid banks of brilliant color. Sherry's uncle, who had built the place, turned it over to his nephew when he decided he wanted a smaller home on the Keys. Although it was far too large for them, Jan had been delighted with it.

A series of French doors opened onto a flagged terrace. Beyond this was the swimming pool. She stood looking down at Sherry, who was stretched out on a deck chair with the editions of the Miami papers scattered about.

"If I were you"—she seated herself on the arm of his chair —"I'd be looking for a place to hide." She studied a picture of Max in one of the papers.

"Your old man isn't that tough." His hand moved over her hip. "For a girl who's knocked up you're still pretty sexy. How about it, huh?"

"Huh, yourself. You've had your way with me. Also, you don't know how tough my old man is. What in the world possessed you to do it?"

"It seemed a good way to make half a million dollars." He refused to be put on the defensive. "Do you think, if it had been the other way around, your old man would have hesitated to put the blocks to me because I was married to his daughter? He's about as sentimental as an African wild dog."

"I suppose I ought to call him." There was a giggle in the

words. "But I'm damned if I know what to say. Pretend nothing had happened?"

"I'll tell you one thing I wouldn't do, and that's to pretend you were upset. Your old man is quick to spot a phony. So don't give him any 'I feel just dreadful about what Sherry did to you.' He'd vomit."

"Sometimes you sound almost as though you liked him."

"Of course I like him. No." He was thoughtful. "Like isn't the word. He never let me get that close. I admire him for what he is. Tough. Unprincipled. Resourceful."

"He'd love that on a Christmas card."

"I haven't hurt him. He'll just charge another million to Grand Bahama. Anyhow, he doesn't think of money as money. It's something you need to play the game; a stack of chips, a sack of marbles. This thing nicked his pride a little, but when the pain wears off, he'll see it as it is. He might even say, 'You know? That son-in-law of mine is a smart Jew bastard.' It could be a turning point in our relationship."

"I was thinking we might go over for the weekend. Now I don't know."

"Why not?" He brushed aside the doubt. "Half the time we're over there we don't see him." He pulled her to his lap. "Anyhow, I don't think you understand your old man very well. He'd cut my throat in a business deal if he could, but it would be impersonal. Why, look what he did to Willard Harrington over Paradise Island. And, from what you tell me, called him Will while he was doing it. If we should run into him over the weekend, I'd only expect him to be the same unpleasant bastard he always has been."

The broad porch, surmounted by its fringe of ornamental scrollwork, sagged heavily in spots, and when it rained, pools of water gathered there. It was badly in need of repair and paint, as were the wicker chairs which had once been white. Now they were peeled and scabrous, splotched with the yellow of the reeds. No one ever swept it. Now and then a heavy wind would clear it of pieces of palm fronds, dried leaves, berries and branches, but for the most part, it was unattended.

The elder Baildon, gaunt and dry as a bleached bone, was all but concealed in the huge wicker chair. His voice had a high, flutelike sound which seemed perpetually charged with excitement. In a smaller chair opposite him his sister, Chris' Aunt Agatha, had a section of the Nassau paper spread over her thin lap.

"Read that part to me again." Baildon's cane whacked weakly at his sister's legs. His voice was piping with excitement. "Read the part where it says how much little Christopher is going to get."

"I won't read you anything if you don't stop hitting me with that cane, you old fool." She scraped her chair a foot or so away and out of his reach. "You're getting excited again, and when you get excited, you always wet your pants."

"Never mind my pants. Never mind my pants." He thumped his cane on the dry boards. "I'll pee in my pants any time I feel like it. Read that part about the money."

"You're a smelly old man. I can't bear to go in your room anymore. Even the cleaning woman refused to go in. What do you do there?"

"Never mind what I do." The cane swished through the air, barely missing her. "Read the part about the money."

"I will when I feel like it." She was smugly triumphant in the knowledge he had broken his spectacles. She rocked back and forth in silent pleasure. Finally, after she had fully savored the moment, she began to read. " 'It is understood that Mr. Christopher Baildon and his partner, Mr. Sherry Melnick, will ask one million dollars plus legal fees for their claim to the strip of property on Grand Bahama.' "

"Heh! Heh!" The sound was a loony cackle, and the cane whistled through the air. "A million dollars. I always said little Christopher was smart. I wonder where he is now. I wonder what he's doing this very minute. We ought to have a fine dinner for him: a good, red roast, a couple of bottles of claret, some port and cigars. You see to it, Agatha. Have everything nice. I wouldn't want Christopher to think we don't appreciate what he has done. A million dollars. I wonder how much that is in pounds sterling. I don't think anyone in our family ever had a million dollars before."

"We ought to make a list. We have to make a list so we'll know what we're doing." Agatha made a surprisingly agile leap from the chair and trotted into the house.

Baildon regarded her with a mild interest; then he began tapping his cane's tip on the boards. For a moment his eyes had been clear and intelligent. Now they were vacant. He stared out over what had once been magnificent gardens. They were weed-choked and neglected now. Through the high palms on the ridge there was a colored ribbon of the sea. He wondered where Agatha had gone. He was always finding himself alone this way, and although he wouldn't want anyone to know, it frightened him.

When Agatha came back, she held a stub of a pencil and a brown paper sack. She smoothed the paper, stroking it with her hand against her knees. Then, holding the pencil poised, she twisted her head from one side to the other in birdlike jerks. Baildon's interest revived.

"Are you going to draw a picture, Agatha?" The idea pleased him.

She made a sound of exasperation. "You can't remember for one minute to the next what's going on. Sometimes I think you ought to be put away." She eyed him maliciously as he shrank back in his chair. "Did you forget about the money Christopher has? A million dollars."

"No. Of course I didn't forget. It's just that it's vulgar to keep talking about money." He tried to defend himself.

"Now"—she settled herself determinedly—"the first thing I am going to put down is Miss Lacey."

"Who's Miss Lacey?"

"Can't you remember anything?" She spat the words cruelly and watched the tears well in his eyes. "Miss Lacey is my modiste. I want her to make me an entire new wardrobe. I'll look splendid when I take my afternoon's drive in the new carriage."

"Do we have a new carriage, Agatha?" His attention sharpened again. "I haven't seen it."

"Of course not, but I'm putting it down on this list."

"Oh, yes. Of course." He dimly understood. "We must have a list, otherwise we wouldn't know what we were doing, would we? Well." He straightened in the chair.

"Next." Agatha ignored him. "Next I want Bassett's to send a box of Yardley's lavender—"

"No, you don't. No, you don't." He was aroused, understanding what was happening. "It's my turn to have something put down." The cane shook menacingly. "Turn and turn alike."

"Oh, all right." There was little enthusiasm in her agreement.

"Put down to have Trotter and Daley send their man to measure me for new clothes. And"—he hurried this last for fear she would interrupt—"I want Jameson the bootmaker." He finished triumphantly, one ahead of her.

"Trotter and Daley have been out of business for twenty-five years. You're an old fool if you can't remember that." She eyed him with a snarling smile.

"No one told me." He made a weak show of protest. "No one tells me anything. Then I'll have the bootmaker until I can find another good tailor."

"All right." She agreed sourly. "You can have the bootmaker." She made a pretense of printing the name.

"Then we ought to have some spirits in the house. I know it isn't my turn"—he pleaded with her—"but we ought to see to the wine cellar. Do you remember how it used to be, Agatha?" He was wandering along half-remembered paths now, seeking to touch something familiar. Rack after rack of fine wines. The slender bottles of green and brown for the Rhines and Moselles. A cask of Oporto and the sherries from Jerez. "I was very good with wines. Everyone said so. And Father, he had a large brass key which locked the doors. Sometimes he would let me go with him when he selected a wine for dinner. Then, after he died, I had the key; only there wasn't much left by then, and we never seemed to have any money. I wonder why we never had any money, Agatha."

The woman shook her head dumbly, lost in a silent misery. Her fingers fretted with the faded cotton of her dress, and the veins on her hand were blue ridges.

"It will be different now, won't it, Agatha?" He pleaded with her for reassurance. "We'll both have plenty of everything. I'll have my man to draw my bath, shave me, lay out my clothes. You'll have your carriage and pair and your coachman. You'll drive along the sea the way Mother did, and men will tip their hats when you pass. I'll go to my club in the afternoons. I belong to a club, don't I, Agatha?" There was a note of terror in the question. "What is the name of it? I can't remember." He gazed imploringly at her but didn't see the tears as they lay on the lusterless skin or made a streak across a withered cheek. "So very long. I don't think I really want anything. Tear up the list, sister. Nothing fine is going to happen. Christopher isn't going to get them for us. Christopher doesn't come home anymore. He thinks we're crazy. Are we crazy, sister? Sometimes I wonder, and it makes me want to cry."

So the two of them sat, and little by little the sun moved over to flood the porch and bring a touch of warmth to their cold and marrowless frames. They tilted back and forth, their bodies swaying in silent dejection. The rumpled paper sack dropped from Agatha's knee. A touch of wind picked it up, hustling it along the length of the porch. The pencil slipped from fingers cold and nerveless. It bounced and rolled, and the old man and the old woman watched it with unblinking fascination until it fell through a crack and disappeared. Then there was no sound at all but the tiny mouselike squeaks as the reeds of the rattan chairs rubbed together and protested against the endless rocking.

The curtains in the windows of the bedroom billowed out with the fresh wind moving in from the sea. On the double bed Christopher Baildon lay beneath a single light sheet and played with the slender body of an exceptionally pretty blond girl beside him. With her fingers she traced a series of endless designs on his chest and gazed adoringly into his slightly bloodshot eyes. The room was part of a large corner suite in the Fort Montagu Hotel. The service tray with the remains of a late breakfast had been pushed away, while a smaller cart with whiskey, soda and a bowl of ice was within reach.

Chris had tasted the heady wine of public notice. He was a celebrity. People sought him out to shake his hand, slap his back, and buy him a drink. Nassau was suddenly invested with glamor. He was "the man who." He had been interviewed and photographed, flown to Miami for a television appearance. A news syndicate had paid him five thousand dollars for the exclusive story of how he had outfoxed the superfox, Maximilian Hertog. It was this five thousand which made the suite at the Fort Montagu possible, although the manager would gladly have extended unlimited credit since every story about him mentioned the Fort Montagu. The girl was also one of the unexpected rewards of success. Her name was Clarice, and she worked as a receptionist and model for the Ministry of Tourism. She and Chris had dated casually, but she had stoutly resisted his attempts to get her into bed or supine in the back seat of a car or on the beach. Oh, they had played around a little in an exploratory fashion, but it had resulted in little more than some heavy breathing and hard discomfort on Chris' part. Now, though, Clarice was a willing victim of the excitement and aura of wealth and prestige which glowed about his presence. Together they had roved through all of Nassau's tourist traps, leaving a trail of champagne corks behind them. In one masterful sweep Chris had taken her out of a normal orbit and swung her in a new and giddy arc. They had been photographed together in the nightclubs and bars. Calypso boys at the Royal Victoria had composed a song celebrating the mighty deed. She had accompanied him to Miami, where press agents had taken over, showering nightclubs, hotels and restaurants on them. Clarice blossomed and bloomed and considered her shattered hymen well worth the experience of being in the public eye. One of the Miami papers had carried a four-column photograph of them with the caption "Young Financial Wizard and Fiancée." Clarice didn't really expect Christopher to marry her, but designation of fiancée did lend a certain respectability to the adventure.

"Are you really going to take me to New York with you, Christopher?"

"Of course." Earlier he had laced his morning coffee with a

264

stiff dollop of brandy. He felt it now with a sense of power. "First we'll do some shopping in Miami, then a jet to New York."

He pulled down the sheet, wet his fingers in his mouth, and then played with her nipples until they stood erect and hard. Then he bit them gently, and Clarice giggled.

He was momentarily disconcerted by the sound. What he expected was a low, throaty moan of unbridled passion. Still, he consoled himself, she was a pretty thing, and practically everyone in the Ministry of Tourism and the News Bureau had tried to make her. He thought he might take her to New York after a settlement had been reached with Max Hertog. They'd have some fun together, and he would send her home, loaded with expensive presents. He had read how some of the most celebrated European playboys always parted in an amiable fashion with their girls by a few costly gifts. He wouldn't be able to do it in quite the same style. There would be no huge diamonds or circlets of rubies, no Rolls-Royce. Just the same it would be quite an experience for a girl who had never been out of Nassau except for an occasional trip to Miami. After New York he planned to go to Europe, first-class jet all the way. He relaxed with a sigh of contentment.

This suited Clarice, for she secretly thought that the business of lovemaking was highly overtouted. Oh, in a way it was sort of fun and, maybe, a little exciting to know she had this influence over a man, to make him cry out and almost scream. But it was really a little messy and, sometimes, uncomfortable. Christopher didn't seem to get enough. He had awakened her twice during the night with that thing, and the last time she had been quite cross. But then, she told herself, the excitement and attention she received when she was out with him were more than worth the small discomfort. Now he was starting it again just when she thought he was going back to sleep. Well, she'd do her best to please him. After all, he was ever so nice to her. He had pulled her on top of him, and Clarice thought this was a most ridiculous and undignified position. While she fitted herself to him, she wondered if she ought to get a scrapbook, something nice and bound in leather. Then she would subscribe to a clipping service and put all the pictures and stories in it. It would be fun to look at them and remember what a good time they had.

"How is it, baby? Tell me," Christopher urged.

He kept saying things like that, and they exasperated her. She wasn't sure what he wanted. Goodness, she thought, it was difficult enough not to feel a complete fool being on top of a man this way.

"Tell me about it," Christopher pleaded. "Say it. Talk to me."

"My goodness, Christopher." She was really put out with him. "What in the world is there to talk about at a time like this?"

James Lyttleton, law clerk and late of Sutton, Tracy and Longworth, was drunk. He was quite drunk and sat at a corner table in the bar of the Green Shutter staring morosely at his drink. He also had become something of a local celebrity but for quite a different reason from that which had carried Christopher Baildon to meteoric fame. James Lyttleton was the man who had booted the ball into the wrong goal. He had committed the prize boob of all time, and his friends and acquaintances now greeted him with highly vocal derision. He had been within reach of a million dollars but didn't have sense enough to know what he saw. Instead, he had compounded his stupidity by turning in a careless and faulty report to his superiors, who passed it on to Maximilian Hertog. The results had been catastrophic, not only for him but for Sutton, Tracy and Longworth. The firms doors were shuttered, the curtains drawn as they might have been for a death in the family. It was doubtful if Sutton, Tracy and Longworth would ever again function as a trio of solicitors. The staff had been dismissed, and the partners scurried to their homes and sat there fearfully, wondering what terrible wrath Maximilian Hertog would eventually visit on them. Certainly their reputation was in irreparable tatters. Who in all the islands would ever trust them with the smallest task? No. They had to face up to the truth. The good and prosperous years were over, and all because of a stupid clerk. No longer did they represent Maximilian

266

Hertog with his manifold and highly lucrative operations. It was doubtful that Hertog would permit them to practice in Nassau, even if they could find a client. He was a rough man, a fearsome man. The partners avoided one another, their clubs, their friends. Individually they all had thought of some dramatic form of suicide.

James Lyttleton had no intention of doing away with himself, certainly not through the usual channels. He might drink himself to death. The idea filled him with a melancholy satisfaction. He finished the scotch and called for another. He also was faced with the uncertainty of future employment. His reputation at the moment was certainly not one to inspire confidence. The residents of Nassau had little enough to talk about, so they would keep the story of his monumental error green and alive through endless repetition. It was bad enough to be a self-acknowledged fool. He lit a cigarette and drew on it moodily. The thought that he had made someone else famous and wealthy through his ineptitude added additional fagots to the fires which licked about him. That Christopher Baildon should profit and he suffer was almost too much to bear. With just a glimmer of wit he should have seen what Christopher saw in that original grant to Thomas Whaley. It was there, and he had ignored it.

He arose unsteadily, paid his tab, and left without speaking a word to the bartender. It was late afternoon, and the regulars would soon be drifting in. He shriveled at the thought of their mocking laughter and pressed himself against the wall as though to hide himself from the sight of all men.

XVII

   Shortly after the turn of the nineteenth century the home government put an end to slave trading in the Bahamas. Not many years later, with little thought to how they were to survive, some twenty thousand blacks in the island were told they were free.

Turned off the failing plantations of their white masters, unskilled and untrained for little save field work, these people fought to survive in an alien world. The oceans surrounded them, and a new way of living had to be found. Over the years these black men and women with their children moved in a restless tide. Some remained on the abandoned plantations. Others settled in small villages on the large islands of Exuma, Andros, Eleuthera and New Providence. Some found a sanctuary on the innumerable small cays. Slowly they adapted themselves to a different life, this one linked to the sea. Field hands learned to sail the small boats and even build them. That which they had once taken from the soil now came from the sea, and they became fishermen. Some cultivated small plots of yams and beans. Most, in one way or another, eked out an existence. They became native to this island world and multiplied.

On the flat and scraggly land on New Providence outside Nassau three villages, Adelaide, Grant's Town and Carmichael, were formed with an entirely black population. Former slaves, unwilling or unable to bear the lonely terrors of the remote cays, made their way from island to island and eventually to Nassau. From the capital they drifted out to these settlements with their black population. There they squatted. Over the years the huts of wattles were replaced by more substantial structures, and the people were drawn together by a common heritage.

These days Adelaide is a pleasant enough community. It has no particular shape or plan. Paths became roads, and the streets have no names. The houses and small stores are nondescript, but the sun is warm, flowers grow, vines climb and blossom on gates and fences, bananas and oranges flourish with only a small amount of cultivation. Then men and many of the women find employment in Nassau, and they travel the few miles daily in buses which appear to be in imminent danger of collapsing into a heap of rusting steel and molting cushions. The people return in the evenings, and in the velvet nights they call back and forth to one another from sagging porches or sandy yards, exchanging the day's gossip and happenings. The district, although poor, is far removed from the slums Over the Hill. What occurs in Adelaide is repeated in the other black communities on the island. They are the barracoons of a distant time, although walls and guards no longer hold the people in. There is the gnawing of constant poverty, a vague idea that things could and should be better. But there is no real anger. The people, for the most part, are submissive. They have never known anything but this. It was the way of their fathers, grandfathers and the fathers before them. They were free, and yet they were captive to the times and customs of the islands.

The largest building in Adelaide was a garage. The second largest was the church. Neither would hold the crowds which now gathered to hear the speakers of the Progressive Liberal Party. This was true of all the black villages in the islands. Meetings of any size must be held out of doors.

Royal had gone to Max Hertog for the first of the money he was eventually to get. The money, five thousand dollars, was in cash. Royal distributed some of this among the Out Island cadres. Some was spent on the posters and circulars announcing forthcoming meetings, which were taking place through the chain of cays, where the local PLP leaders talked to their people in small groups. The rest was spent on a mobile loudspeaker unit used wherever a large crowd could be gathered.

Royal now was the principal speaker at the Sunday rallies. Sunday was a "nothing-to-do-day" for most of the people. They came to hear Royal Keating as they might go to an afternoon church service: for entertainment. Because of this, the crowds were large, and by the time he had finished speaking they were lifted high on a wave of enthusiasm. Sunday was the only day he could spare from Grand Bahama, and sometimes it became necessary to speak at widely scattered islands. He again went to Max Hertog for money, this time to charter an amphibian. It was the only way he could keep a schedule. Max was making an investment, and as such, he was not inclined to be petty. Royal never offered an explanation. He said simply: "I need this much." Max would give a sealed money-filled envelope to Big Maum, who in turn gave it to Royal when he came to Windmere. Instinctively Big Maum was made uneasy by this obviously shady relationship between her son and employer.

Alone with Royal in the kitchen one Sunday before one of his meetings, she faced him almost angrily.

"What dis between yo' a' Mistuh Max? I ain' no fool." She took a large envelope from an apron pocket. "Dis feel like money."

"It is money, Big Maum." He wouldn't lie to her.

"Den how come Mistuh Max give yo' money dis way instead o' regular like wages. Yo' doin' somethin' wrong fo' Mistuh Max, Royal boy?"

"No, Big Maum." He thought she was entitled to an explanation. How to make it so she would understand? "The money is sort of insurance." He paused. "You know about the PLP, the black man's party?"

"I hear." She grunted sourly. "I also hear 'bout Royal Keatin'. All of a sudden he t'ink he a preacher. He gits all dese islan' people awhoopin' an' ahollerin'. Dey goin' t' mek him king or somethin'. Dat what he t'ink." She was openly scornful.

270

"No, Big Maum. Nobody wants to be a king, but the black people of the islands are going to have a voice in running things from now on. That's what the PLP is for: to bring them together so they will be heard. Now Mr. Max likes to have friends on both sides of the fence. He contributes money to the white party, and he contributes money to the black party. That way no one is mad at him. You can understand that."

"Yes." Grudgingly. "I un'erstan' dat." She put her hand against his cheek. "I jus' don' wan' my boy t' do wrong t'ing. I hear yo' gettin' t' be big man wid all dese islan' mens. Don' let 'em carry yo' too high, Royal boy, 'cause when yo' drop, it a long way back t' th' groun'. I ain' wan' t' see yo' hurt. One more t'ing. Don' mek no mistake 'bout Mistuh Max: He ain' no black man's frien'. Don' believe him ef so he say."

Royal smiled. "I don't trust anyone but you, Big Maum. Now. How about you comin' out to Carmichael with me? I'm making a speech there this afternoon."

"Now why"—her voice was rich with affection—"why would I wan' t' go way t' Carmichael to hear a little black boy, name Royal, whose bottom I spank hun'red time? What he gots t' say Big Maum ain' heard before? Ain' no wise man come among us."

"I guess maybe you're right." He put his arm about her broad shoulders and then laughed quietly. "I guess you're the only one who doesn't think I'm smart."

"Go 'long now." She pretended impatience. "Come back when yo' gets hungry. Politickin' don' put no seat in yo' breeches. I hope yo' still gots dat good job en Gran' Bahama. Yo' gonna need it."

Today's meeting in Adelaide followed the same pattern of enthusiastic response he was finding now in all the islands. After the speech he stood on the platform which had been thrown together for the day, answered questions, and exchanged broad jokes. "When this thing is all over, you may have to let your sister marry a white man. That's what you want, isn't it?" He never made the mistake of dressing down to his people. He didn't try to play the country boy. He wore a white linen suit, shirt and tie. His manner was confident and persuasive. When he spoke, he told them things they could believe, for he was one of their own come among them.

I don't say things are going to be different or better right away. We aren't going to change a three-hundred-year-old system overnight. What I do say to you is that we have a chance at the next election to make a start. If you and all the island black people go to the polls and vote the Progressive Liberal Party, we can have a black government. It's that simple. A black Assembly. A black Prime Minister. Then we can move. Decent schools for the black children. Sanitation. Public health. Clinics where you can go for treatment. A pure water supply. A plan for government help for a black man who wants to buy a piece of land and build a house. For three hundred years a white government has said: "Take what we give you and be satisfied." I'm telling you now you don't have to be satisfied with the scraps from the white table. The power is in your hands. You had better use it now, for if you don't you may never get another chance. The black people in these islands don't need the bloody riots, the looting and burning that are going on in the States. You've heard about them on your radios. There the black people are in the minority. They can't vote in a change. They're helpless at election time. But here you —black men and women—are the most. All you have to do is to walk up to that box with the ballot in your hand. There it is, man. All the black people speaking in a language the whites can understand. Power. There is magic in your vote to make these islands better. That is the black magic I'm bringing you.

The people roared their approval of his words. There was the simplicity of truth in what he told them. They could understand and believe. He told them: "What I have done you can do. A white suit. Good shoes. A shirt and tie. You follow me and I'll carry you to the mountaintop." They believed him.

He was always careful to defer to the local party leaders. They had a place of honor on the platform. When the crowd was large, as it was here in Adelaide, it became almost a holiday occasion. An elaborate barbecue was arranged. A couple of whole pigs and dozens of chickens were done to mouth-water-ing perfection over the pit of coals. Tables were set up under the trees. There were bucketfuls of steaming yams, washtubs of rice and beans. Some rum was circulated among the men, but no one became drunk. The crowd was orderly, eager and childishly happy. Royal made a point of thanking the local party chairman. He did this in a short speech, so everyone could hear, and this created the impression that the picnic was due solely to the local party leader. Everyone's pride was satisfied, and it worked well. He encountered no conflicts of ambition where they might have been expected. There were no jealousies or petty schemes to counter. In a few short months of this intensive effort Royal had created an almost unbelievable unity. He was the accepted leader now of the PLP. Those who might have challenged him earlier or were suspicious of his motives realized they had no choice but to go with him or suffer a defeat among their own people. They followed, hoping to be remembered favorably when the rewards of a black victory were being passed out.

Only a completely insensible man could have been indifferent to the exhilarating sense of commanding power, and Royal Keating was far from a dispassionate man. To have achieved this dominant position, to know his name was being spoken with hope and wonder wherever black people lived in the islands, to realize he was going to do what no black man in the Bahamas had ever done before—this was all but overwhelming. He sometimes laughed at this with Alicia, making light of it and pretending it didn't really matter. The pride was there, and it was reflected in everything he did and said. He was well aware of what he was doing, what he had done. In his mind there was no question, no doubt. The black people would vote in the general election as they were told. The revolution would be stunning but bloodless, and Royal Keating would be asked by the Crown to form a government. There would be no alternative, and Royal Keating would become the first black Prime Minister in the history of the islands.

He was secretly astonished by the seeming apathy of the white Establishment. These people didn't or wouldn't believe what was happening despite the fact that the Nassau newspapers were now reporting all the larger PLP meetings. Pierre DuPres, whose paper sometimes reflected an unwelcome liberal inclination, assigned a man to cover the party's activities. The names of Royal Keating and the Progressive Liberal Party confronted everyone in Nassau who could read. The Miami *Herald,* one of America's outstanding newspapers and sensitive to what was happening in its offshore neighbor's backyard, commented editorially on the miracle which Royal Keating seemed to have performed by welding the Bahamian blacks into a solid bloc. Still, most of the Nassau whites appeared to be undisturbed. It was unthinkable and therefore could not be. When the elections were held, they would tell their servants not to go to the polls. The threatened loss of a job had always been a deterrent to any black initiative. There were a few, though, in the oligarchy of white power who were not so complacent. God only knew what a black Assembly and a black Prime Minister might do to their privileges. The thing ought to be stopped before this black bastard, Royal Keating, did what everyone said couldn't be done. They discussed the situation over their whiskey and soda at the clubs and whispered their suggestions. There must be some way of dealing with this Keating? All blacks were thieves by nature. So they would buy him off. Fix it so he would never have to think of money again. It would be a small price to pay. Put the money in a Swiss bank for him, and let him go and live in France. French women liked black men. He could buy himself a couple. The more they thought about it, the simpler the solution became.

The first thing was to get Max Hertog to fire the bastard from his job on Grand Bahama. Cut off his income. Make him afraid. Bring him down to the black level. That was the way to handle him. He wouldn't find it easy to get another job. Max, it was agreed, might be a rebel, a maverick and a loner, but he was, after all, at the top of the Bay Street power structure. He had as much or more to lose than any of them. A delegation was formed to call on him, but when he found out their purpose, he refused to make an appointment. A few began to wonder if Maximilian Hertog had committed the unforgivable, the unpardonable and unthinkable act of throwing in with this nigger. That word was almost never used by the Bahamian whites of the middle and upper classes, but it was beginning to be heard more and more as a prefix to Royal Keating.

Because the men who sought to rid themselves of the threat of the PLP and Royal Keating were powerful, their apprehensions began to filter down. There was no organized white movement to destroy the PLP, but the smaller merchants, landlords and real estate developers, along with any number of Bay Street's dubious enterprises, began to experience a chill of fear. They saw everything they owned being confiscated by a black Socialistic government. Few had any illusions about what would happen with a black Assembly. The taps of privilege would be turned off.

At the bar of his club one noon Max was finally cornered by three of his Bay Street peers, who did their best to make the meeting seem friendly and filled with a jovial companionship.

"Why don't you get rid of that Keating fellow, Max?"

"Because he's a damn good engineer."

"There are plenty of good engineers around."

Max was enjoying this. He nodded solemnly. "I guess that's true enough, but"—he looked about with an expression of pleased surprise—"I don't know of another one who could be our next Prime Minister, do you?"

That, of course, did it. Max Hertog was either a complete fool—and few persons could be persuaded to believe this—or he was an unspeakable renegade against his class. If anything could be read into his bland indifference to the threat, it was that he had thrown his support to a political party which would have the power and the incentive to destroy them all.

No one really knew what to believe, and no one had any idea what to do about Maximilian Hertog. A lesser man might have yielded to the pressure of social ostracism. Max didn't give a damn about their insular social functions: their dinners, teas and tennis, cocktail and yachting parties and all their old family ties which knit them together into a clan of snobbishness. Also, the men discovered he had champions in unexpected quarters. Several wives came to his defense. Max was a dear. He always contributed generously to their charities.

They refused to strike his name from their guest lists. The husbands huffed and snorted and had no idea that their obdurate wives had at one time and another shared Max Hertog's bed. They looked back now on these afternoons of assignation with a wistful tenderness and would listen to no denigration of a robust and exceptionally satisfactory lover. So the tide of suspicion and resentment never rose any higher than a slight ripple. The truth of the matter was that no one could actually bring himself to believe what was cautiously whispered: that Max Hertog was deeply involved in this revolution of the blacks. It just wasn't credible.

There is among the island blacks, particularly the house servants, a secret form of communication which is as swift and mysteriously effective as Africa's primitive drums. News travels accurately and so fast that the cooks and maids of one household have the details of a marital disturbance in another before the echoes of the angry words have faded. Few infidelities go unnoted. Let there be a whisper at the breakfast table of a minor financial crisis, and the report is winged out and on its way. Many white persons are inclined to scoff at this, putting it down to superstitious mumbo jumbo. Others know it is the inexplicable truth. There is this exchange of gossip, rumor and fact. A breakfast-table scene at Lyford Cay, if it is entertaining enough, is common knowledge in the downtown market an hour or so later and reported in every household of consequence by afternoon.

The kitchen of Windmere was no exception. The gossip came and went, and Big Maum began to hear things which disturbed and made her uneasy, for they concerned Royal and Maximilian Hertog. This, to Big Maum's pragmatic mind, was an unlikely and unholy association. It frightened her.

Big Maum was stubborn in her loyalties. She had run Max Hertog's household for years. Not once had he ever questioned her judgment or asked why a maid had been discharged, a cleaning woman replaced, or trade taken from one merchant and given to another. He paid her the tribute of his complete confidence. In turn, Big Maum accorded him a rare fealty. She would have found it difficult to explain her deep sense of loyalty to this house and its master. It arose out of a complex of emotions. Certainly she felt no affection for her employer of these many years, for he was a rude and sometimes evil-tempered man. But she did owe him respect, and that she gave in its fullest measure. None among the servants was permitted to speak rudely or in scornful anger of Max Hertog in her presence. When, as had happened, a giggling maid came back to the kitchen to whisper of the girl who was naked and asleep in his bed, Big Maum shut off the twittering with a sharp warning or a heavy hand on the rump.

"Who Mistuh Max gots en he bed dis mornin' ain' no business but his. Yo' shut yo' mouth an' take up th' fresh coffee. I hear one mo' word an' yo' gots it good from me across th' mouth."

If Jan and a companion had come home from a party, tight, noisy and amorous, and later made love in her bedroom, not one of the inside help was supposed to be aware of any irregularity. The discipline here was tight and effective, and any breach of it brought swift punishment.

Now, though, Big Maum was on the point of openly questioning her employer's actions. She had never presumed before. There had never been a reason to dispute his judgment. To her own knowledge there existed some secret arrangement between her boy Royal and Max Hertog. She didn't understand Royal's explanation of the money she had been passing to him from Mistuh Hertog, nor could she say why an uneasy feeling persisted. Whatever was happening between them was an out-of-the-ordinary relationship between a white and a black man. To her mind the black man must come off second best in such an association. It was in the nature of things that this should be so. No white man ever did anything for a black unless he expected the action to be to his advantage. This had always been so. There was no resentment in her conclusion. Royal had made light of her questions and concern. So now, with the privilege of an old servant, she took them to the head of the house.

Following the knock on the door and his command to enter,

Max looked up with unmistakable surprise as Big Maum filled the doorway. He couldn't remember ever seeing her on the second floor, although he was certain she must have made a regular inspection of the quarters.

"Big Maum?" There was a question and small astonishment in the tone. "Well, come on in. Don't stand there. What's on your mind?" He was curious and friendly. "I don't think I ever saw you up here before."

She half smiled. "Th' bref don' come so easy no mo' for clim'in' steps, but I gets up reg'lar. I come t' talk a min'it 'bout my Royal." She moved into the room, seeming to fill it with a stately presence.

She stood resolutely now, waiting for him to speak. He didn't tell her to sit down, and she didn't expect him to do this. They understood each other well.

"What about Royal?" Max was still in his pajamas at his cluttered work desk. He pushed some papers aside as though to clear it for a new problem. "He's not in any trouble, is he?"

"Dat what I don' know. What I come to ask. I worrit now. T'ings I hear. T'ings I know. What yo' doin' wid my Royal, Mistuh Max?"

"Oh"—he relaxed and smiled—"I thought we had a crisis in the house. Royal?" He paused as though considering the name. "I'm giving him a little help where he needs it."

"Why?" The question was abrupt and close to an interruption.

Hertog's smile faded, but his tone continued, reasonable and reassuring.

"It looks as if Royal is going to be a big man in the islands. You ought to be proud of him."

This was an evasion of the question, and they both knew it.

"I am proud t' him, but I don' wan' no big mon en th' islan'. I don' wan' no big dead mon neither. I jus' wan' Royal like he is. I wan' you t' let him alone, Mistuh Max, please. Leave him be."

There was something dangerously close to a command in the words, although they had been carefully phrased as a plea. Both of them were well aware of this, but Big Maum did not waver or shift her gaze. The attitude was not one of defiance but, rather, of resolution. In all her life Big Maum had never ventured quite this far in speaking to a white person.

Hertog's anger was swift. It rioted within him, seeking a release in violent words or action. He fought to control his emotion and to lead them back, step by step, from this dangerous cliff. What he did and said now would certainly be reported back to Royal. He couldn't risk a break with the man. Too much of value was involved. He stood up, pushed away his chair, and walked toward her. She regarded him steadily. Then he did a surprising thing. A hand went out and rested with an affectionate gesture on her shoulder.

"I'm not pushing Royal into anything, Big Maum. You're worried over nothing. Royal is going to do what he will. He's made up his mind. I couldn't stop him if I tried. I give him some money now and then because in politics it needs to be spread around where it will do some good. You've been with me for a long time. Royal's your son. That's why I'm helping him." For a moment he was almost ashamed of the cheap effort at piety.

"Th' white mon don' he'p no black 'less he do good for himse'f. Yo' know dat, Mistuh Max. So do I." She refused to take the easy way out and retreat.

"All right." Max curbed his impatience. Big Maum was on the fine point of open insolence. Both wanted to avoid this. "I help Royal now because I may want a favor sometime. Royal knows this. That's the way things are in the world. One hand has to wash the other. It's expected."

Big Maum experienced a feeling of helpless misery all blacks knew when they attempted to talk with a white. It was like speaking into an empty barrel. What came back was only the echo of their own words. The whites always held the advantage. They would tolerate the expression of a difference of opinion for only so long. Then their attitude of polite interest faded, and the door to their attention was closed in the black man's face. It was so easy for them. She could sense the man's impatience. Max Hertog was shutting the door.

"I'm afraid fo' him, Mistuh Max." She was as humble now

279

as her nature would permit. "Yo' know th' whites ain' goin' t' take no black mon t' sit over 'em. It ain' never bin so. They kill him firs'. Dat what scare me. If yo' don' he'p him, maybe he quit."

"No one is going to kill anyone." He was surprisingly gentle again. "This is Nassau and not what you hear on the radio about what goes on in the States. We don't have that sort of violence here."

"You don' really believe dat, Mistuh Max?" She wanted to be convinced.

"Of course I do." He was hearty, reassuring. "The white people don't like what is happening. They'll fight Royal's party, the black party as hard as they can, but no one is going to be killed."

"Yo' could stop him, Mistuh Max." She was begging now. "Yo' already give him dat big job en Gran' Bahama. Now yo' say, 'Royal, git on wid th' wuk heah. I out o' patience. Yo' gots no damn time t' be runnin' 'roun' mekkin' speeches. Yo' do th' job I pay yo' fo', an' stop dis politickin' business.' He gots t' listen t' yo', Mistuh Max. He proud of he wuk an' what he learn. He won' wan' t' give it up."

Max shook his head. "He'd just laugh, Big Maum. He'd laugh and walk away. He's too close to something he wants. It smells good. He won't let it be. Believe me."

Big Maum nodded dumbly. Misery was deeply carved into the lines about her eyes and mouth. She didn't believe a word of what the white man had said. Black persons who worked for Mistuh Hertog never said no to him. Royal, with all his education, was an island black inside, no matter what he showed outside. If Mistuh Max told him to stop doing something, he'd do it, but Mistuh Max didn't want Royal to stop now. There was something good in it for Max Hertog. That's why he wouldn't let Royal quit. She started to speak again but realized nothing would be changed. Royal and this white man would do what they started. If anyone were hurt, it would be the black man.

She made the smallest gesture of helplessness and then turned away. She walked from the room straight and proud.

280

The small bell on her ankle chain tinkled with a barbaric sound, and her step was firm until she was out of sight on the staircase landing. Then she bent a little and held tightly to the bannister railing on her way down.

XVIII

Within the beach-fringed circular haven of Hope Town's harbor on Elbow Cay the cabin cruiser barely rocked in the slight wash as the tide lifted her gently. A few hungry gulls circled her gleaming length hopefully. Their cries were the only sound.

Beneath an awning over the afterdeck four men lounged comfortably in the canvas slings of their chairs. A low table with whiskey, soda, ice, cigars and cigarettes was within reach. Now and then there would be a slight movement: the rasp and a spurt of flame as a match was struck to light a fresh cigar. The men, save one, seemed cut to a pattern or cast in similar molds. They were tanned, slightly paunchy from too little exercise, manicured and barbered "ten times o'er." Their manner was self-assured, and they smiled infrequently. They all were in their middle fiftes, graying a little here and there about the temples. They wore off-white linen shorts, light shirts and sandals on bare feet.

The odd one, Sir Stephen Simon, seemed strangely out of company here and alien to the surroundings. His skin, which had not felt the direct rays of the sun for many years, was the claylike color of an oyster. His belly lopped over the waistband of the shorts in a doughy fold, and his hairless legs were thickly drawn with the thin blue tracings of clotted veins. Lying there, without moving, he somehow gave the impression of ponderous effort. The fat-layered flesh seemed to tremble continually as though it were set in motion by some inner rumbling. His teats, with their madder-tinted nipples, hung as flat as a hound's ears against his chest. He sighed audibly now, and with the sound his companions turned hopefully with bright, inquisitive expressions.

With a finger Sir Stephen probed at the pink socket of his navel as though something of value were buried there. Finally he raised his glance, and his pale eyes had the innocence of childhood in them.

"Why don't you just have the son of a bitch killed?" The question was a liquid whisper.

The men in the chairs drew their breath as one in a small, collective, whistling sound. The word was finally out. For hours they had talked, mumbling uncertainly. The three-man crew had been sent ashore. The privacy was complete. All, save Sir Stephen who listened, indulged themselves in harmless euphemisms, shrinking away from the words which Sir Stephen had just uttered with a deceptive mildness. At various times it had been suggested "he be taken care of" or "something has to be done." They all understood what these pointless maunderings were supposed to mean, but none, save Sir Stephen, had the courage to speak what had been in their minds from the beginning.

Strangely enough, these were men of little conscience. So it was odd they now sought a delicacy of speech to cover their intentions. In their daily pursuits they were ruthless, savage and predatory. That was business, and they operated out of their Bay Street offices with a relentless ferocity. The reward was money, and they never tired of the contest or seemed to get enough of the prize. Other men had met financial disaster through their manipulations. One or two had even committed suicide rather than face complete ruin when they were caught short in a deal. These things left them unmoved. Murder, though, was an unfamiliar word, harsh and frightening. Silently they tested it.

Arthur Creighton stared at the long silver ash on his cigar

and then tapped it off on the edge of a tray. He looked about the circle of chairs.

"Sir Stephen is right, of course." The heads of the other men jerked up at the sound. "We've been talking around it, but we all know what has to be done. That is why we are here, on a boat in this empty harbor. I won't be a party to trying to buy him off. I don't think he can be had that way. Second, it is a form of blackmail. I'm against that on principle. So"—unconsciously he lowered his voice—"I agree with Sir Stephen. Let's have the black son of a bitch killed. Because if you don't"—the words were precisely stated—"this Royal Keating is your next Prime Minister and with him a black Assembly. Get rid of him and we put the old fear back into the hearts of the blacks. There is too much at stake for temporizing."

"How?" The man on Creighton's right voiced the question they all were asking themselves. "It is a little outside my experience." He laughed nervously.

Sir Stephen was kneading the roll of belly fat between pudgy fingers. It oozed beneath the pressure as thick cream. The skin began to show red splotches as though a fever burned. As he caressed himself in this fashion, he stared out past the others to the settlement and the hill where a striped lighthouse stood. His lips were pursed into a thoughtful pinch.

"Am I to assume I am being consulted professionally?" The eyebrows lifted to accent the question, and he looked from Creighton to the others.

"Yes. Of course," Creighton answered for them all. "We wouldn't think of moving without your advice."

"Good." There was a vague flutter of a hand as though he were giving them his benediction. "It is best to understand these things at the outset. My fee in this case will be one hundred and fifty thousand." He gazed at them benevolently. "That makes a nice division among you. Fifty thousand apiece."

"I—I don't know." The third man spoke hesitantly, drawing away from the commitment. "I just don't know."

"What is it you don't know, dear boy?" Sir Stephen's question was tipped with venom.

284

"Well, I mean—" The man looked helplessly at the others. Sir Stephen folded his hands on his paunch, lacing his fingers. His lips formed a rosette, a pink blossom of petulant evil. The eyes were cloudy as is absinthe when touched by water. He was indifferent to and oblivious of their presence.

Arthur Creighton spoke again. "Jim is all right, Sir Stephen. He—"

"I should hope so." The interruption was sharp. "For if he isn't, we are all placing ourselves in considerable jeopardy by discussing this in his presence."

"I only meant"—the man called Jim ventured unhappily— "that I—well"—he ended with a rush, anxious to be rid of the thought—"it isn't so much the money. It's the—" He floundered.

"The involvement?" Sir Stephen spoke the words with a wet, dripping sweetness. "My dear boy, you can't hope to avoid that. Can you now?"

"The fee for your consultation and advice, Sir Stephen, is not in question." Creighton spoke again. "There is no argument. For one, I have no idea how a thing of this sort is handled."

"My dear boy"—Sir Stephen mellowed slightly—"that, of course, is why you have consulted me." He placed his fingertips together with small, precise motions. "I have sources of information. I shall avail myself of them. When I have put everything together and the arrangements can be concluded, I shall be in touch with you. There will be, you understand, an additional fee for the person or persons who carry out the actual assignment. My participation is only as an adviser and an intermediary." He smiled benignly on them all and lay back, seeming to dissolve into a mound of shaking flesh.

For at least a full minute no one spoke. Creighton and the other two avoided looking at one another. All understood they had taken an irrevocable step. Oh, it was still possible to pull out, but each knew the decision had been made. All of them had assumed privileged rights in the Bahamas which had made them wealthy and powerful. A black government, determined to reform, eager to overturn the established order, could ruin them overnight. Everything they owned could be swept away by a bunch of black fanatics. They might be killed, their homes burned and families murdered. Actually, they were only protecting themselves. No one could deny a man this right. They began to feel better. The rationalization was complete. They were only taking a sensible precaution. There was a general easing of tension. They glanced at one another with small noddings of agreement.

Creighton stood up and stretched. "Let's get the crew back. I don't know about the rest of you, but I'm ready for a good lunch."

This talk of safe, commonplace things such as lunch had a reassuring effect on them all. They were back on familiar ground. They added fresh ice and whiskey to their drinks, not because they wanted them, but because this involved simple, everyday motions. They wanted back in, out of the chill of the unknown and the cold fears raised by what had been said here. Their voices were a little louder than necessary when they spoke to one another.

He was a most undistinguished-appearing man, thin and with slightly stooped shoulders beneath the ill-fitted jacket of a ready-made suit. The cheap Tyrolean hat with its cockade of red feathers seemed to have been put on his head by mistake. He stood at a gate in Miami's International Airport Terminal and clung tightly to the worn handles of a bulging canvas zippered bag. At every unexpected sound—a voice over the loudspeaker, the backfire of a car—he started nervously, and there was fear in his eyes. When the gate was finally opened, he thrust his boarding ticket out for the attendant's inspection and all but ran across the tarmac toward where the big silver plane waited with its boarding ramp down.

Now the stewardess was eyeing him with troubled curiosity. He was slumped down in his chair staring fixedly at the back of the seat in front of him. The canvas bag was wedged in at his side. He had refused her offer to put it in a rack and seemed to hug it to him. She studied him now, asking herself: *Another nut or just a worried, nervous man?* She couldn't make up her mind. All the airlines had been plagued by a series of sense-less hijackings and bomb threats. Now you never knew if the jumpy ones were threats or just another cuckoo with a gun who wanted to be flown to Havana. She ducked into the galley and took a quick draw of a cigarette and then went forward to the pilot's compartment. The crew looked up as she entered.

"I don't know." She didn't like to cause unnecessary trouble. "I wish you'd come back and take a look at him, Captain. He's scared and jumpy."

The pilot nodded, spoke to the tower, and then left with the girl. He nodded pleasantly to the passengers. At the man's seat he bent, using the fastening of the seat belt as an excuse.

"Are you all right, sir?" The words were quietly spoken.

"Yes. Of course." The man jerked out the reply.

The officer sat on the seat's arm. His attitude was pleasant and confidential. The other passengers were unaware of anything unusual.

"Wouldn't you like to have your bag checked and get it out of the way?"

"No. It's all right. Why don't you leave me alone?" He started to rise.

The captain's hand tightened on a thin shoulder. "I'll have to ask you to let me look at that bag." He was friendly but firm.

The man started to protest and then shrugged. "All right, but hurry. I have an important business appointment in Nassau." He moved out of the way.

The zipper slid easily, and the bag gaped open. The captain peered inside. It was stuffed with ledgers, thick manila file envelopes, checkbooks. Office stuff. With his hand the pilot searched underneath and then closed the bag.

"Sorry to have troubled you. We have to be careful. You understand?"

The man licked at dry lips and nodded wordlessly. The pilot regarded him for a moment and then laid a reassuring hand on his shoulder and went forward.

After they were airborne, the stewardess brought a little bottle of brandy, a glass and some water on a tray. He swallowed the brandy in a gulp and nodded his thanks. Then he lit a cigarette, and his hand no longer shook. After a minute or so he began to take an interest in the sheen and the color of the water below. He peered down at the small cays of dark-green foliage with their circles and crescents of sheer white beach.

At the Nassau airport the man was met by Max Hertog's chauffeur and a car from Windmere. His manner was easier now, almost jaunty. He allowed Hertog's man to take the bag and then settled himself in the car's deep cushions. He could smile and relax. He was out of reach. Nothing could touch him. This was the sort of break he had been waiting for all his life. He had the promise of a good job and a bonus of five thousand dollars. These things for bringing with him all the records of Melnick Enterprises, where he had been employed as bookkeeper and accountant for the past fifteen years. On this Sunday morning he had gone to the offices on Flagler Street and emptied the files and safe of every record, check and financial statement, correspondence and memorandum he could find. He didn't have the slightest idea why such a man as Maximilian Hertog would have an interest in these things, but he had long ago learned not to ask questions.

He leaned back against the gray whipcord upholstery and glanced with approving envy at the sterling silver appointments of the compartment, the beautiful wood paneling of a cabinet built into the front seat's back. Marveling a little at his assurance, he opened the cabinet's door. There were two cutglass decanters of whiskey, glasses, cigarettes in a gold box, fat cigars in glass tubes. He glanced at the chauffeur's back and then selected a cigar and poured himself a short drink. How was it, he wondered, to be able to surround one's self with this luxury? The fragrance of the tobacco made a cloud about him, and the whiskey was a warm puddle within his stomach. He half closed his eyes. In his fancy he was a financial wizard, a tycoon, an industrial giant. After an exciting week in Wall Street, when he had dominated the trading in the world's market, he was now on his way to the magnificent home he maintained in the Bahamas. He had flown down in his private plane, of course, accompanied by at least two beautiful secretaries who alternately shared his bed. Tonight, in his home, he would be the host to a gathering of beautiful women and attentive men, who regarded him with fawning awe.

"Yes, sah."

He was jolted out of this blissful reverie by the chauffeur's words. They had stopped in a broad driveway before the house, and the man was holding the car's door open. Reluctantly he stepped out and looked around.

"Mr. Hertog?"

"Yo' fin' him en th' front terrace, sah. Right 'roun' dat path. I bring th' bag."

On the broad sun-swept terrace he approached the man at the table diffidently but with a curious feeling of disappointment. If the man was Maximilian Hertog, then he certainly didn't look the part. He wore a broad-brimmed ragged hat of plaited straw and bathing trunks. Spectacles were perched on the tip of his nose, and he looked over them and nodded.

"You're Parsons. Sit down." Max spoke but did not rise or offer his hand. He motioned to the chauffeur who had followed, carrying the bag. "Put it over there, Dan." He studied Parsons with something close to mild distaste and then leaned back. "Did you bring what I wanted?"

"It's in the bag there, Mr. Hertog." Parsons felt cheated. Somehow he had expected Max Hertog to act as though they shared a common guilt and were intimate companions in a conspiracy. Instead, Hertog gave every indication of finding his presence offensive. "I brought everything I could find. There wasn't even a blank sheet of paper in the files when I left." He was eager to demonstrate his thoroughness and willingness to serve and be of value.

Max grunted and shoved an envelope across the table. Parsons picked it up, pressed its thickness quickly. He caught himself with a guilty start. He had been on the point of opening it.

"It's all there." Max was amused. "Five thousand."

"Oh, I didn't—" Parsons tried to speak. His mouth was dry. "I wouldn't."

Max refilled his cup from the coffeepot on the warmer. "There's a room for you at the British Colonial Hotel. A car will pick you up there each morning and bring you here." He indicated the bag. "I want you to go through that stuff with me until I know as much about Melnick's business as he does. I want everything. The deals he is in. How much money he owes. Who holds his paper. What his financial setup and condition is. Where he is overextended. If he is. Everything. Do you understand?"

"Yes, of course, Mr. Hertog." Parsons was ingratiating. "I'm familiar with all the details." He made an attempt at a confident smile and then tried an airy approach. "You sound as though you were going to buy Melnick out."

Max stared at him for a moment. "No. I'm going to run him out."

Charles Rich stood in the Jeep Royal had lent him and studied the building. It was, he thought, the damnedest-looking thing he had ever seen. Finished in a smooth stucco, with conical towered minarets and oval domes and raised here on the western side of Grand Bahama, it suggested a motion-picture set with harem girls, sheiks and soldiers of the Foreign Legion. There was an excavation for a long, narrow pool leading to the entrance. When finished, it would bear some faint resemblance to the one which fronted on the Taj Mahal. The construction of this pseudo-Oriental architecture was the mental eruption of Max Hertog. It was apart and distinct from the other buildings on the island. Max had designed, ordered, and paid for it, and the architects had figuratively held their noses while they worked on his plans.

After dropping down from the Jeep, Rich walked across a sandy stretch. Work was, apparently, temporarily halted. There was no one about. Inside, it was coolly damp. The floors had not yet been laid, and the interior walls were rough plaster. Rich moved down a long corridor and into what was obviously designed to be the central room. There he stood and tried to reconcile what he saw, this single broad area of rectangular shape, with what he had been told. This was Maximilian Hertog's personal project: a private pavilion where his guests on Grand Bahama would be housed and entertained. *Well,* Rich thought, *the guests might be entertained here, but*

they most certainly would not be housed. There was no indication of provisions for living quarters, rooms of apartments.
Walking through the soft, clinging sand, Rich paced off the
area and whistled softly to himself. And after a while an all
but incredulous expression was on his face. He knew what he
would use this large room, when completed, for, but the notion that Max Hertog held the same idea was difficult to accept. He simply could not be such a complete egomaniac to
believe he could get away with it. Yet instinct told Rich what
logic denied.

Driving back to Royal's bungalow, he discovered that instead
of being disturbed and even angry over what he suspected, he
was actually amused. He held a high degree of tolerance for the
frailties of all men. He was entertained by the notion that
Max Hertog would deliberately try to outmaneuver the organization he represented. It was naïve beyond belief.

He parked the Jeep in the shade and went on to the screened
front porch. Royal was at a table studying a topographical plan
which was spread out and tacked down to cover the entire
table. He looked up as Rich crossed toward him.

"You're back early." He glanced at his watch.

"I only went to have a look at that mosque or whatever it is
Max Hertog is having built. What the hell do you suppose he
is going to do with it?" He dropped into a chair and lit a cigarette.

Their talk sometimes covered a ranging variety of topics, and
there was respect on each side for the opinions held. Rich, although he never discussed his associates, was well aware that
after the publicity attendant upon the opening of Paradise
Island, Royal understood the connection. They never discussed
it.

"I know"—Royal answered the question—"what I would
do with it."

"So do I. That's what puzzles me."

Royal rose, went inside, and came back with an elevation
drawing backed by a stiff board. It had been executed in brilliant color and showed the blue pool, flanked by ornamental
urns filled with tropical blossoms, the building with the con-

ical gilded domes. Beneath what were presumably date trees, camels and their drivers rested. Scantily clad girls in harem costumes were posed in attitudes of dreamy abandon. He handed it to Rich with an appreciative grin.

"The construction crew call it the house of the golden tits."

"I walked inside." Rich barely glanced at the drawing. That's one hell of a big room. You could make a couple of tennis courts out of it."

"Or bowling alleys." Royal knuckled his nose to hide the smile.

"Or a skating rink maybe."

They both had arrived at the same conclusion, and it amused them now to approach it in this oblique fashion.

"He could make a dance hall out of it," Royal suggested.

Rich nodded. "But if he didn't want a dance hall, there's plenty of room for some dice, blackjack and roulette tables."

"I wonder." Royal leaned back and stared at the ceiling. "I just wonder if Maximilian Hertog ever thought of that."

"If he hasn't, he will." Rich was no longer smiling. "And that would create a situation. The interests I represent would be decidedly upset if such a thing should happen."

"I should imagine so."

"Our investment here is large. It was made because we were assured a gambling permit would be issued to us. This was what brought us into the operation." He took a small gold penknife from his pocket and trimmed a broken fingernail.

"It's hard to figure Max Hertog." Royal was thoughtful. "I don't think he is a brilliant man, brilliant in the sense he recognizes opportunities other men can't see. He relies on guts and gall and bulls his way through any situation. If he scents the profit, he'll take the chance. The maestro can do no wrong. The ego is beyond all measuring."

Rich was coldly analytical now. There was no trace of banter in his words.

"It would be unfortunate if he should believe we can be manipulated. Many things have been said about us." The smile was thin. "But it has never been suggested we are not efficient in the removal of obstacles. The methods are not quite

292

as crude as those of the nineteen twenties, but the results are much the same. We make our deals and keep our contracts. We expect the same from Maximilian Hertog."

"Whoa!" Royal made a pretense of backing away. "I only work here. I didn't like the way you looked at me when you said that."

"Of course"—Rich was relaxed again—"I didn't expect you to carry a message to Hertog. If it becomes necessary, the words will be loud and clear. He will not misunderstand."

"Do you know"—there was a certain admiration in Royal's tone—"I don't honestly think Max Hertog can be intimidated, scared off something? I wouldn't put it past him to try some group screwing with your organization after you have built Freeport for him."

Rich's expression brightened. "In that respect we are still virginal. No one has ever screwed us successfully." He closed the knife with an emphatic snap.

"Maybe that's what makes the idea so attractive to Max. I've heard he's partial to virgins." He stood up. "It's lunchtime. If you're not flying back right away, come and have it with me at the club." He stretched and looked at the sunshine outside. "I can't get too worried over Max Hertog on a day like this."

XIX

What had seemed completely without purpose or reason in the beginning now began to shape itself into a recognizable pattern. As the design became apparent, it supplied the answers which had eluded Melnick from the day the removal of the files had been discovered.

For a couple of weeks after the bookkeeper, Parsons, had disappeared, the police had conducted an indifferent search for the man and what he had apparently looted from his employer's offices. Then all the material was returned. It was neatly boxed and delivered by a Miami parcel service. It was a routine operation. Neither the driver nor the dispatching clerk knew more than that the box had been prepaid and left at a branch office. There was no trace of Parsons and no explanation of why he had taken the books in the first place. No real effort was made to find the man. He lived in a two-room apartment in a dingy building. Nothing in the room indicated he had been subjected to violence there. A couple of cheap suits, shirts, underwear, socks and handkerchiefs were in a closet and bureau. Since Melnick had filed no charges, the police displayed little interest in his whereabouts, and the small investigation was dropped.

Thereafter things began to happen in rapid succession, and they supplied all the information Melnick needed. Only someone who had gone over the books and records with minute thoroughness could have so quickly spotted some of the weak spots. Land which Melnick Enterprises needed to complete a large subdivision on Florida's west coast was bought out from underneath them. Tracing the transferred deed, Sherry came up with a familiar name. The Aunt Martha Candy Company had acquired the property. So Parsons had taken the books to Max Hertog. This was obvious. Next, Melnick Enterprises was notified that its lease on extensive office space in a Flagler Street building would not be renewed. Then a bank in Sarasota which held a large amount of Melnick Enterprises' paper routinely notified Sherry that his notes had been discounted and purchased by the Aunt Martha Candy Company. Construction of a large low-cost housing development near Homestead ran into building inspection trouble. Minor infractions were blown up into major problems. Fires, obviously the work of an arsonist, broke out. There were jurisdictional strikes among the unions. The delivery of material to several other projects became uncertain. Old clients, owners of office and apartment buildings who had retained Melnick for years as their agents, suddenly withdrew their business without explanation. Fat commissions grew thin. Long-term credit suddenly became a problem. Sherry, in the beginning, had been inclined to laugh off Max Hertog's intrusion into the affairs of Melnick Enterprises. Now he began to feel uncomfortably crowded. Max, without ever leaving Windmere, was able to reach out and trip him in widely unrelated fields. The strength and variety of his connections, the pressure of his influence were all but unbelievable. The quiet malevolence with which he exercised them unrelenting.

"Your old man"—he brooded aloud to Jan one afternoon—"is roaming around with a big scythe trying to cut me off at the knees."

They were on the terrace overlooking the long stretch of waterway leading to the Keys as it ran between the beachside and the Miami mainland. It was the period of brief twilight. An arrowhead flight of ducks was inked against a cloudless sky. Jan leaned back in her chair, cupping a brandy and soda with both hands. Her face was half turned away from Sherry. She didn't want him to see the small flutter of a smile.

"What did you expect?" There was no rancor in the question. She had refused to align herself on either side. "You and Chris diddled Max out of a million dollars. He is not accustomed to being screwed. If he yells 'Ouch!' in one way or another, it is only the natural protest of a virgin."

Sherry scowled, annoyed by the lightness of Jan's reply. There was, of course, truth in what she said. A little grudgingly he admired her for remaining neutral. She was the old man's daughter all right and would stand off to one side and watch with a spectator's interest. He made a fresh drink for himself, pausing on the way back from the portable bar to bend and kiss her. She reached up quickly and touched his cheek with a gentle hand.

"That entire project over near Aripeka blew up in our faces when the Aunt Martha Candy Company bought the tract we needed." He wanted to chew on it. "That's a hell of a name for a mangy wolf like your old man. The Aunt Martha Candy Company." He snorted disgustedly and took a long pull on his drink. "He's costing us a lot of money. He's a one-man Mafia. How the hell he ever made all these connections I'll never know. There doesn't seem to be anyplace where he can't stick in a finger and stir up trouble."

"Maybe you shouldn't have tangled with him on this Grand Bahama thing."

He turned, regarding her with honest surprise. "Don't you think he would have done it to me?"

"Of course."

"Well?"

"Well"—she regarded him steadily—"the difference is you're not Maximilian Hertog."

Resentment flared and was gone before she was certain it had been in his eyes for a moment. Now Sherry rubbed a thumb knuckle against the tip of his nose, studying her with a quizzical interest. Suddenly he grinned and nodded.

"You're right. That's the difference. When you take on the champ, it's the main event. You're not fighting one of the preliminary boys. You take your knocks."

"I love you for that." She reached a hand to him. "It's honest and the way things have always been between us. Honest. I wonder why so many persons think you're a con man."

"There's a touch of it in me. Otherwise I wouldn't have taken on your old man."

"Let's go over to the islands for the weekend. Nassau. Windmere."

"You want to get me knocked off?"

"Max wants your blood because you took some of his. He wouldn't expect me to avoid him or take sides. You don't want him to think you're yellow, do you?" She rose from the chair with an easy, graceful motion. "Besides"—she touched her abdomen—"I want him to see how the baby is getting along."

"How is he, by the way?"

"I think he's going to be a jockey. He just booted me."

While Carol watched with open amusement, Max sat on a corner of his desk, aimed a dart, and with a snap of the wrist sent the missile flying to the target. It sank into the cork with a thud and quivered there, well within the center rings but off the bull's-eye. He smiled and grunted his satisfaction.

This, Carol thought, was the only really childish thing she had ever seen him do. He had ordered the target hung on the wall and then confided to her that its name was Melnick.

"Mr. Melnick," he amended quickly. "Mr. Melnick. He isn't the sort of man with whom I would want to get too familiar."

Thereafter, whenever he felt he had struck successfully at Melnick Enterprises, he put another dart in the target. Almost a dozen were impaled there.

"When I really get him," he told her, "I'll put a dart right in the center of the board and we can have it taken down."

"Why don't you squeeze a little clay figure together and stick pins in it?"

He looked at her with an expression of astonishment. "What makes you think I haven't done that?" He slid from the desk. "I'm through for the day. Come have lunch with me. We'll go to the club."

"You're not through." She was unusually brisk and efficient. "There's a luncheon engagement with Sir Stephen."

"Oh, yes." He was disappointed. "I wonder what he wants?"

"Not just your company. You can be sure of that."

He reached, taking her elbows and drawing her close. Her surprise was apparent. He was rarely demonstrative and never, certainly, in the office. Once she had made the mistake of a playful gesture. Bending to put some letters on the desk before him, she had brushed his cheek with the lightest touch of her lips. Somehow, in that instant she realized it, everything they shared and enjoyed together was reduced to the shoddy level of a furtive officetime affair between employer and secretary. He held her at half an arm's length.

"Come to Windmere for the weekend?"

"I usually do." The absence of enthusiasm was deliberate.

His interest sharpened. "Something wrong?"

"No. Of course not."

It was a juvenile evasion of the truth. She had no honest answer to the question. What was wrong? Something. It was to be felt, if not named. Was she tired of the arrangement? The answer had to be no. To break with Max would create an unendurable vacuum. What they shared was exciting. *A damn sight more exciting,* she had told herself, *than it would be if I were his wife and left behind at Windmere every morning.* Did she really want the respectability supposedly inherent in marriage? She wasn't sure. It was, she thought, more a matter of pride. She actually wanted to hear the words. She wanted Maximilian Hertog to ask her, "Will you marry me?" Damn him. He wouldn't do it. Instead, he told her, "One of these days you and I are going to get married." She rebelled against this assumption and was irritable now.

Max lifted her chin with a finger. "If there was anything wrong, you'd tell me?" There was concern in the question.

"Of course." She forced a smile. "It may be a long lunch with Sir Stephen. Don't come back here for me. I'll meet you at Windmere." She slipped from the light touch of his hands.

He watched as she crossed the room and closed the door. A damn fine-looking girl and smart. One of these days. He lit a cigar and stood in front of an open window, wondering what

298

Sir Stephen wanted or had for sale. He thought he was one of the few persons who actually enjoyed Sir Stephen Simon's company. The air of ingenuous candor with which he surrounded himself and made light and a sort of playacting of all villainy appealed to Max. Sir Stephen truly made of his world a stage, and his continuous performance delighted him. Max thought he must strut a little even in his sleep.

On a rubbing table in the elaborate steam room built into the basement quarters of the house, Sir Stephen was prone. He loomed in an incredible mound of pink flesh and made soft, cooing sounds of pleasure. A tall, almost unbelievably handsome young man with a towel knotted about a lean, muscled waist switched Sir Stephen roughly with an elastic bundle of leaf-heavy birch and pine branches. They were shipped to Sir Stephen from Canada by air each week, and there was the fragrance of the deep north woods in them.

"That will be enough, Kyle." Breathing heavily, Sir Stephen relaxed, face buried in crossed arms.

The young man called Kyle gathered up the loose wet towels from a damp floor and tossed them into a pile. He moved with the easy grace of a professional athlete. His taffy-white hair grew almost to his shoulders, but there was nothing effeminate in manner. His speech was the lilting one of a Scandinavian country. Taking a huge robe of white terry cloth from a wall hook, he stood waiting.

Sir Stephen heaved and rolled with a heavy, elephantine motion until he rested on his knees. The belly sagged to the boards of the table. Kyle draped the robe over him and then arranged a pair of rope sandals in position. Sir Simon slid backward, feetfirst, from the table in the sliding motion of a bull walrus skidding down a wet boulder. Feet in slippers, he tied the robe's cords and took a towel from Kyle, winding it about his neck.

"We'll forget the ice water, dear boy. I don't feel up to it."

"Very well, Sir Stephen." There was courtesy but no subservience here.

"I'm not at all certain any of this does me the least bit of good. The steam. The kneading and pummeling. I'm afraid I am what I am, and nothing, no amount of effort on your part, will alter my ponderous figure one jot." He puffed with the effort of speech and studied Kyle's fine body with unembarrassed admiration. "You are a beauty, are you not, dear boy? It is too bad." He spoke with a wistful honesty. "I am not queer for young men. What an adventure in the erotic we could make of it."

Kyle Hendricks only smiled. He was accustomed to the extravagant speech and manner, and they no longer confused him. He went about his duties here, in Sir Stephen's household, with an assured competence. He was a towering and amiable youth who had been a rubber in the New York Athletic Club. Sir Stephen had encountered him in the shower room. They had talked, and a few days later Sir Stephen invited him to dinner. Over the table Kyle was offered this job in Nassau. In the beginning he was certain of and waited for the approach. The hand or the word. This fat man who all but lisped when he spoke had to be a fairy. Kyle had no feeling one way or the other. He had attracted deviates before. The experience left him unmoved. His behavior was motivated by curiosity. How would the fat man reveal himself? Now and then his employer mentioned with obvious regret he was not homosexually inclined. This could have been an opening, but it wasn't. Sensing Hendrick's suspicions, Sir Stephen referred to them only once.

"I suppose I am a little queer in my own way, dear boy. But aren't we all? In my fancies and dreams you do not appear. So"—there was a touch of the regal in this—"I advise you to relax before your Fabian attitude becomes tiresome and objectionable to me. I do not lust for you."

Sir Stephen seated himself now on a low bench. Hendricks ducked in and out of the shower, pulled on a striped Mediterranean shirt, slacks, wool socks and tennis shoes.

"I think"—Sir Stephen spoke abruptly—"you once told me you had some knowledge of boats and boating."

"Yes." Kyle looked up from tying a lace. "My grandfather

300

had a yard in Norway for the building of small boats. I learned to sail when I could walk. Later there were powerboats."

"Splendid. I think I shall want you to undertake a commission for me. It is quite possible it will require the knowledge and skill to navigate and operate a power cruiser. I believe that is the proper description."

Hendricks smiled briefly but made no reply. None was expected.

"A meeting is being arranged in Miami. I, of course, shall not attend it. You will represent me and have the authority to complete arrangements. For this and whatever part you may be required to play as the situation develops, you will be generously compensated. Yes. Most generously compensated. May I count on your cooperation?"

"Of course, Sir Stephen."

"Aaah!" It was a sound of complete satisfaction. Sir Stephen rose from the bench. "I am forced to be honest. You will become involved in what, for the moment, I shall only call a situation. But then this should serve to guarantee a prudent behavior on your part later. I repeat. Your compensation will be generous." With a gracious nod he moved away and down the corridor to the elevators which would take him directly to his rooms on the second floor.

Hendricks looked after him with admiration and amusement. He was a queer one all right, with his young girls who came and went continually. He was certainly queer, but not in the way most persons used the word. Underneath all that quaking blubber, the perfumed and powdered fat, the sometimes mincing manner there was a blade—a thin, deadly blade of finely tempered steel. It was rarely revealed, but Kyle sensed its existence. He felt a sudden chill of uneasiness and shook it off with difficulty.

The magnificent robe of royal purple, heavily worked through with thread of gold, billowed in the light breeze, threatening to balloon into a dazzling show of color. Sir Stephen wore it with a thick yellow tasseled cord belted about his girth. On his feet were sandals of soft golden leather. His toenails, showing through the openwork, were tinted with a pearl lacquer. Watching him with a sly amusement he was certain they both shared at the moment, Max Hertog thought only a laurel wreath on the brow was missing. With that Sir Stephen would have been one with the Caesars or Borgias.

The table was set in the warm shade beneath a striped awning at the pool's side. The luncheon had progressed through a *pâté* and paper-thin toast with a fine bottle of Bernkasteler to a *glace* and champagne. Each course had been as perfect as the hands and knowledge of a great chef could make it. For the past two hours Sir Stephen had chatted of many things. He was, when it suited his humor, the most charming and gracious host, maliciously witty and a storehouse of anecdotes.

"I remember quite clearly, although it was many years ago during my first experience as Prime Minister here. He was a most odious person. An industrial tycoon who wished to invest heavily in the Bahamas. The Governor asked me to be especially nice to the man, an American. So I really put myself out. I received him here, at my residence. He not only drank too much but had not the slightest idea or appreciation of what he was being served. He even attempted to become tipsily familiar with one of my wards—a lovely child, incidentally. Then, in a moment of passably sober conversation, he said something about a 'British accent.' Well! That did it. I fixed him with what I like to think of as a cold and pointed eye and said, 'My dear fellow, there is no such thing as a British accent. There is, I grant you, an American accent.' Aaah!" Pleasure spread across his face at the recollection of the riposte. He belched happily and then beckoned to the black man, who waited at one side, to refill their glasses.

"No more for me." Max shook his head.

"Ah, yes!" There was appreciation here. "The clear head. The steady hand. I forget you do not have my capacity." He patted his belly affectionately. His gaze roved over the treetops as they swayed lightly. "A most pleasant interlude. I enjoy your company, dear boy. I truly do. But that, dear Max, is not why we are here. Is it?" He turned a bright and inquiring gaze on his guest.

"I don't imagine so, Sir Stephen."

"Of course not." Fingers wiggled at the servant with a gesture of dismissal. Sir Stephen waited until the man was out of sight. "I hesitate to speak of what is in my mind in the presence of a black. They have ways, you know. Ways and means." He made this cryptic remark sound sinister and then placed a finger against his lips as an indication of caution. He glanced about to be certain a black man wasn't hiding in the pool or beneath the table.

Max lit a cigar. It was a pleasant day. He was in no hurry. In good time Sir Stephen would come to the point of this luncheon.

For a moment or two Sir Stephen swung the heavy tasseled cord. He hummed a few notes which seemed to have no connection with one another or even, for that matter, with the diatonic scale. He nodded to his guest as though in appreciation of something said.

"You must know, my dear Max, I entertain the highest regard for you. You possess qualities I greatly admire. Courage. Determination. Now"—he crossed his arms on the rounded ledge of his abdomen—"what I am about to do is regarded as reprehensible by the legal profession. It is called a conflict of interests or clients. At the moment I represent a faction, a small group, whose aims and intentions are inimical, it may be, to yours. This disturbs me since I hold you in such warm affection."

"Of course." Max felt a word of agreement was called for here.

"As I was saying, I have been retained by certain persons to give them counsel and assistance in a matter of extreme delicacy."

"And," Max interrupted pleasantly, "you think it would be to my advantage to make a similar arrangement so you would be representing all parties?"

"Oh!" The pain was acute. "How cruel your thrust, my

303

friend." Tears actually gathered in the wide, pleading eyes. "In what low regard you must hold me." The head was now bent, and shoulders trembled visibly. "How crass a man I must seem to you." He drew a handkerchief from somewhere within the robe's folds and touched at his eyes.

"I'm sorry, Sir Stephen." Max was moved by the performance. It was admirable in all respects. "I misunderstood. I apologize."

Sir Stephen shook his head bravely. The wound would never heal. His eyes lifted with a piteous expression, and then he nodded his unhappy forgiveness.

"It was my fault, dear friend. My phrasing was awkward. It was natural you would misunderstand." He shuddered over the enormity of the moment. "Ah, well." He bounded back to the subject. "Let us forget and proceed. I shall state certain truths well known to us both. First, I know you are contributing financial support to this black Progressive Labor Party." He held up an admonishing hand as Max started to speak. "I have done the same thing in the past and will continue to do so in the future. But with more discretion than you have shown. You have been unnecessarily flagrant. I regard my contributions as premiums on truly doubtful insurance. Second, the strong man of the PLP, the only one with intelligence and strength, is one Royal Keating, now in your employ as chief engineer on Grand Bahama. Also, his mother has been in your domestic service for years. I am correct in stating these things, am I not?"

"Hell"—Max was brusque—"those aren't secrets."

"Good." Sir Stephen nodded. "Now we come to a most delicate point and a question which only you can answer. Upon what you tell me I will base all future activity on behalf of my clients."

"What do you want to know?"

"Simply this, dear Max. Is your interest in Royal Keating and the PLP merely a precautionary one, or do you have the party in a bag? Is Royal Keating your man? Is he locked in? My decision rests on this. I will accept your estimate. Has Keating been bought? Will he stay bought? How can you be

304

sure? I accept the probability that he can become the next Prime Minister. When he is in the seat, will Max Hertog be holding him on his knee as a ventriloquist's dummy, or will he suddenly begin to speak in his own voice? It is most important we know these things."

"I wish I could be sure." Max was honest.

"But, my God, man"—Sir Stephen was horrified—"you have to know. It is a common suspicion you are giving the PLP and Royal Keating more than token support. You are deliberately alienating strong men and combinations in Nassau on the assumption the PLP and Keating will win and you will be rewarded for your aid. My dear friend, the expectation of finding gratitude in men is a most fragile reed upon which to lean."

"I'm certain Keating and the PLP will sweep the next general election." Max had the uncomfortable feeling of being lectured by the headmaster.

"Max. My dear, dear boy." Sir Stephen regarded him with pity. "If you don't have this man bought, if you don't have some hold on him other than support for his ambitions, you are courting utter disaster. Once in office, he and the other blacks will lump you with all the whites, while the Nassau whites, the Establishment, will despise you as a renegade."

"What are you suggesting?" Max had been secretly troubled by much the same thoughts and reasoning. "I don't give a damn who goes in at the next election. I only want to be on the winning side or, at least, have friends there."

"One does not dispose of a threat by taking it to one's bosom. The black majority in these islands pose a danger to you, me, all of us who have fattened so well on privilege. You cannot expect to share your bed with them. If you try, you will end on the floor while they are warm beneath your blankets. You think about it, my dear friend."

"Who came to you? What do they propose?"

"Propose?" Sir Stephen's eyebrows lifted. "Why, my dear boy, they propose to rid themselves of the son of a bitch. They want him dead. So do I. So should you."

Slowly, deliberately, Max opened the tube of a fresh cigar. He had no difficulty in adjusting himself to a new alignment.

It had always been his practice to do what was expedient. Sir Stephen was right, of course. He had been deluding himself with the idea Royal Keating had been bought for a few thousand dollars and an important job. The nigger had probably been laughing at him all the time. The only sure, the only safe, way was to get rid of him, break the back of the PLP, destroy the pockets of black leadership in the Out Islands. Once these things had been done, the general election would be uncontested as before. The United Bahamian Party would continue to run things as they had been managed by a few for the past three hundred years. The same old, complacent and compliant political hacks would be in. They could be had and counted on as always. Keating was the unknown. The X. The threat. It had been idiotic to believe for a minute he could be handled once he was in office.

A small question nagged at him. He turned to Sir Stephen. "Why were you so interested in learning what I knew, my arrangement, if any, with Keating?"

"My dear boy." Sir Stephen was relaxed. He had the answers he needed. "If you had been able to assure me Keating had been bought, securely nailed down beyond any possibility of his wriggling out, I would have gone along with you. I would have found it impossible to work with the group, the three men, who approached me. I also like to be on the winning side. Together we should have worked openly to ensure the victory of the PLP. Once in power, the black majority can stay there, and Keating would be our man. Since this is not the case, we join now to rid ourselves of him. You agree?"

"Yes. Of course."

"It is such a pleasure to deal with you, dear Max, a man of little conscience. We are much alike, untroubled by small notions of honor or scruples. Honesty of purpose is a clear, fresh wind. I find it bracing."

Max tried to hide the smile through an intent study of his cigar. He frowned at it and then laughed. Sir Stephen regarded him with an alert and pleased interest.

"You are amused, dear boy?"

Max nodded. "How do you intend to get rid of Keating?

306

Somehow"—he chuckled—"I just can't picture you as a finger man for the mob."

"Oh, I am not without imagination. Naturally, I don't propose to do it myself."

"I didn't think so."

"I have certain reservoirs of talent upon which I may draw. Now"—he returned immediately to a more practical aspect—"those who requested my assistance in this matter each contributed fifty thousand dollars toward my fee. I do not regard this as excessive, and I shall be most happy to find your check for a like amount with my mail when it is delivered in the morning. Please don't concern yourself with details. Always, when possible, relegate that which is unpleasant to someone else." He sighed contentedly and allowed a benevolent gaze to rest on his companion. "We see things as they are, do we not, and make no attempt to disguise them with pretty words? It is most refreshing."

Upon this happy note of amity Sir Stephen concluded the luncheon. He bestowed on Max his most benign and fraternal smile of approval. They understood each other.

He made no attempt to rise when Max left. A small crooking of his little finger was an accolade. Alone, he sat for a few minutes in contemplative silence before shaking the small silver bell on the table. When the manservant came, he indicated to him the box on a ledge.

"Bring me the telephone, Morgan. Then find Hendricks and say I wish to speak with him."

When the servant was out of sight, Sir Stephen put in a call for a number in Miami.

XX

Bunches of artificial red and purple grapes hang from a latticed ceiling intended to simulate an arbor. Paper roses, clumps of wisteria, a little faded and dusty now, bloom from the tarnished wall light fixtures. The walls are pink. The tables and chairs blue and white. Over everything is the odor of beer, cheap wine, fried shrimp and slices of beef and pork, pounded thin and cooked with peppers and oil.

La Favorita. It is one of the many small cafés which have sprung up in Miami over the past fifteen years. Its clientele is exclusively Cuban, the refugees who fled before Castro's advance and, later, his occupation. They came by the hundreds and then thousands in boats, ships and planes, pouring into Miami. Doctors, lawyers, dentists, merchants, politicians, soldiers, writers, artists. They flooded the city, finding the climate much to their liking. Some had money. Most had none. They took jobs where they could find them—driving a taxi, washing dishes, working as maids, cooks, porters, bellmen and day laborers—the menial and unskilled openings which were already contested for by whites and blacks. Others took the American dole and spent their days and nights in such places as La Favorita playing their noisy games of dominoes, drinking cheap rum, arguing interminably. They spun elaborate schemes for liberating Cuba, assassinating Castro, returning in gaudy triumph. They formed juntas and then promptly fought

308

over who should be the leader. They effected a tenuous and mysterious association with Miami's criminal element and spoke boastfully of an alliance with the Cosa Nostra which would assist them with money and arms to retake Cuba. The Mafia would help, it was explained, because it wanted to re-open the gambling casinos in Havana. Oddly enough, there was some small truth in this. No great investment was ever made, but sums did trickle in to the more militant refugee leaders. This was an exploratory move to see if there was any real strength or leadership. A couple of powerboats and guns were supplied for an abortive attempt to land commando raiders on the Cuban coast. This rowdy and vocal element was a constant source of annoyance to the Miami police, the State Department, the CIA and the FBI. The plots of the ineffectual juntas fermented constantly. They erupted as does the gas in swamp waters, bubbling to the surface, breaking there, and disappearing without trace.

Some of the refugees adjusted themselves to a new way of life. Others lived in discontent. Born of the latter was a generation which had been children when their parents arrived in Miami. They were grown now, young men and women. Some, speaking English fluently, integrated themselves into a simple hardworking society. Others, of an antisocial bent, frequented the street corners, the cheap bars and such places as La Favorita. They were the young whores and their pimps, the car thieves, the muggers, the gangs of hoodlums who would hit two or three gas stations in a night and disappear. For the most part they pursued their occupations among their own kind. But an outsider with the proper credentials had no trouble in finding a young girl, a knife or a gun for hire. These were the "quick tricks," and no lasting association was formed. The girls took their money and left the dingy rooms. The young men closed their knives and hid their guns. All waited hopefully for additional commissions.

In a corner of La Favorita's central room Juan Cepeda sat at one of the scarred tables. Before him was a plate of boiled shrimp, a saucer of pepper-flecked oil and vinegar, and a bottle of cold beer. Methodically he peeled away the shrimp's transparent shells and dipped the pink meat into the sauce before tilting back his head and dropping the morsels into his mouth. Cepeda was a slickly handsome youth. His father had been an officer in Batista's army. When Castro came down from the mountains, Captain Manuel Cepeda hurried his family into a car, drove to the yacht club basin at Santiago. There, at gunpoint, he commandeered a cabin cruiser and fled to Miami. The United States gave him political asylum. Juan had spent most of his twenty years in surroundings of violence. In Miami he scorned school and alienated himself from his parents. At the age of seventeen he had an unimpressive police record of petty crime: street fighting, window smashing, car theft and statutory rape. From these things he spent some eighteen months altogether in the Dade County prison. Now he had progressed. Most of his time was spent in and around La Favorita. He had three girls hustling on the streets for him. The money they turned in helped keep him dressed in the style he admired and provided a cheap but flashy secondhand car. He was known, where such knowledge was useful, to be vain, spiteful, quick-tempered. But he could be also depended on to carry out an assignment. He had gradually worked himself into the leadership of a small gang whose talents could be called on. He was the middleman for those who wanted a husband or wife beaten, a rival chased away, a job of arson done on a neighborhood store. There had even been a couple of murders which further elevated him in the eyes of La Favorita's patrons. He was known as a punk but a reliable one.

Seated opposite Cepeda, Kyle Hendricks traced a design with a finger on the frosted side of his beer glass. He was unmoved by the Cuban's efforts to impress him by suggesting a bone-chilling, sinister nature, a man of steel nerves and quiet ferocity to whom violence was commonplace. He thought Cepeda's slick hair was greasy and dirty, the pointed two-tone shoes ridiculous, the tight trousers and flared Edwardian jacket silly. Also, Cepeda was overextending his role as a mastermind. He sneered when he spoke, playing the gangster of the old movies he watched on television. He made offhand references to dark deeds. He was a chain smoker, and Kyle noticed his fingernails were dirty. His speech had the faintest trace of accent, which, for the purpose of adding a dramatic note to his character, he deliberately exaggerated.

The meeting in La Favorita was the result of the telephone call made by Sir Stephen Simon to what he referred to as a source in Miami. From there, as a favor, the word was passed down from the highest echelon until it reached the Cepeda level. Juan would have liked to have Hendricks believe the word he had received was a request. Actually, it was an order. He smarted a little beneath it. His dignity and self-importance were offended. He had been told to go nightly to La Favorita and wait at a corner table. Sooner or later he would be approached by a blond man whose name was Hendricks. He would be given an envelope. Inside there would be a thousand dollars, instructions and a name. Cepeda could then subcontract the job or do it himself. It was, however, to be done. There was no mistaking this. Cepeda would be held responsible. There were to be no loose ends, nothing left to chance. It was to be clean and with nothing left behind. Hendricks was unaware of the actual assignment.

"You took your time getting here." Cepeda was unnecessarily truculent. He wanted an excuse to assert his position. "I been here every night."

"Like you, I came when I was told to come."

Cepeda glowered at this. It placed them on the same level. Servants doing what they were ordered to do. He didn't like it.

"Where are we going?" He made a gesture of contempt. The whole thing was beneath him.

Kyle swallowed some of his beer. "The Grand Bahama. Didn't the letter tell you?"

"No. It said you would take me there, like a chauffeur or something, I guess." He felt better. This reasserted his position.

Hendricks smiled. These loud ones were the same the world over. He had known kids on the Bergen waterfront who would have taken this one apart without even getting out of breath.

311

He wondered why Sir Stephen would employ him for anything. He was also curious about the mission but refused to ask any questions.

"When do you want to go?" Kyle finished his beer.

The letter had instructed him to be on Grand Bahama any day but Saturday or Sunday. This was Sunday evening. They could go any time. Cepeda pretended the choice of a day was a problem with which he must contend. He frowned and then shrugged.

"Tomorrow or the next day."

"Tomorrow is all right. I have a boat at Clayton's Yard on the river. *The Spindrift.* You meet me there tomorrow morning."

"I don't like boats. Why can't we fly?"

"Because I was told to take a boat and you were told to go with me. Stop trying to make a big pin out of yourself. I don't impress worth a damn, and I don't like your company."

This, Cepeda knew, was the moment, the opportunity to assert himself. This squarehead should know without any more fooling around who gave the orders and made the decisions. He started to rise, was halfway out of his chair when something in Hendricks' expression halted him. He remained fixed in an awkward position, bent over, hands resting on the table.

"Keep coming," Hendricks encouraged him softly.

Cepeda pretended to misunderstand. "I gotta take a leak." There was little conviction in the statement.

Hendricks watched as he crossed the room. In his confusion he had left the envelope with its note on the table. Earlier he had made a small production of taking out the money, riffling through the bills with a smirk, hoping to impress Hendricks as he fitted them into an imitation alligator leather wallet. Kyle unfolded the paper. "Royal Keating, chief engineer, Grand Bahama. Bungalow on southwest side. Alone except on weekends." He replaced the note and leaned back in the chair. So they were going to see a man by the name of Royal Keating. Mentally he shrugged. There had to be more to it than that. The arrangements were too detailed, too secret.

It didn't take much imagination to figure Cepeda. A cheap hood. A killer, maybe, but only if it had been well set up and fairly safe. Kyle Hendricks was a man of sluggish temperament and small curiosities. He was almost totally devoid of interest in the lives, angers, hates or loves of others. Satisfied to walk his own path, he was content to allow others to choose their way. It seemed almost certain Cepeda was being sent to kill Royal Keating. Somehow—and this puzzled him—it led back to Sir Stephen Simon. What was the connection? With one finger he fished the note from the envelope and after a moment's hesitation put it in his pocket. He was well aware of his involvement in the situation. It remained only to determine if it was worthwhile. He decided it was. He liked his job with Sir Stephen and hoped to make more of it in time. This connection had to link him closer with his employer. If there was, as he suspected, more involved than a social call on this Royal Keating, then he was determined he would share the dangerous secret with Sir Stephen. At the proper time it could be turned to his advantage.

During the morning he had gone to the boatyard and presented a letter to the superintendent. The man glanced through it and nodded.

"I had a call from Mr. Quayle yesterday. He said you'd be coming down. His boat, *The Spindrift*, is in the number four slip there." He pointed to where a thirty-eight-foot Matthews cruiser was moored. "She's all tanked up, fuel, water and ready to go."

"Thanks. I'll go aboard and look around."

The superintendent fell in step beside him, handing over a loop with four keys on it.

"You'll need these. Engine. Hatchway. She's a fine boat. Going fishing? She'll take you anywhere and back. Mr. Quayle doesn't use her much."

"We're going outside, maybe over to the Bahamas and around the Keys. Two or three days."

The man left him at the slip, and Kyle went aboard. He checked out the fuel and water. The lockers were open. There was plenty of canned food, beer, rum, whiskey. At least they wouldn't go hungry. He snapped the blower switch on and let the fan clean out any gas fumes before starting the motors. He synchronized them to a steady beat. Satisfied, he cut the switches, locked up, and left.

He looked up from the table now. Cepeda was coming back. The man dropped into his chair, drummed indecisively with his fingers. Finally he reached for the envelope. Kyle watched intently. Then, without looking to see if the note was still inside, Cepeda tore the paper into small pieces, filling an ashtray. He put a match to the pile and watched it burn.

"I'll see you tomorrow morning at the boatyard." Kyle stood up. "You know where it is?"

"I'll find it."

"It's *The Spindrift*. Can you remember that?"

"I can remember anything you can." Cepeda was snarling. "You keep pushing, don't you? A real wise Dutchy."

Kyle turned away. When they had finished whatever it was they had to do, he thought he might just beat the hell out of this spik. The idea pleased him immensely, and he was smiling as he walked through the noisy crowded room.

Junkanoo. The origin of the word dates back to the early days of slavery in the Bahamas. It is buried somewhere in the years. It is the whites' spelling of a black man's word, spoken out of one of the many African dialects. No one is sure. No one is certain this is a reliable verbal translation of a sound.

In Nassau the Junkanoo is a time of revelry, of costumes and dancing, of parades and colorful floats, of calypso bands and mummers not unlike the Mardi Gras of New Orleans. In the sparsely populated Out Islands the spirit is the same, but the preparations are less elaborate. The costumes and masks are whatever can be pieced together, and the result is that of children dressing up for Halloween in adults' clothing.

On Grand Bahama, Royal made of the day a weekend celebration. He provided transportation, bringing the people in from Nassau, Eleuthera, Great and Little Exuma and the small settlements on the scattered cays of the Little Bahama Bank from Great Abaco to Spanish Cay. There was money to spend now, and it came from several unidentified sources to him for the Progressive Liberal Party. He used it for the maximum effect, loading the faithful in chartered sloops, ketches and powerboats. Everything was free, and the man to thank was Royal Keating. There were large galvanized-iron tubs of strong iced rum punch with slices of pineapple, lemon and banana floating; great kettles of rice and peas; serving tables heaped with freshly fried fish; racks with chicken and pork from the barbecue pits. The sun was warm an' the lovin' easy. Three calypso bands, alternating or playing together as the fancy pleased them, beat out the rhythms on their steel drum instruments. The guests and those who worked on the Grand Bahama project brought or sent for their girls and women. Those who had no costumes managed to create the effect of one with scarves of bright purple, green and yellow. They were bare of feet with blouses pulled down over glistening shoulders, and when they danced with their men, they were in a sinuous, hip-snapping movement from head to toes. Often, as though on signal, there would be an impromptu parade which snaked in and around the tents and down a newly paved street. Laughter and voices were warm and rich, hands reached out for hands, and no man was stranger to another. This island in its tranquil sea was a continent removed.

Alicia had come over from Eleuthera the day before, bringing with her a costume. It was a vivid creation of short, ruffled skirt, off-the-shoulder blouse, a yellow turban wound high. On her ankles were circlets of small bells, which made a tinkling music when she walked. Royal joined with her in the spirit of the day, improvising his dress with knee-length white ducks, a red shirt with the tails knotted outside, sandals and a broadbrimmed, roughly plaited straw hat. Today there was no "mon," no boss. With Alicia clinging to his hand, he walked and danced with the crowd, halting to eat a freshly fried crisp hot fish and washing it down with the icy punch which seemed to grow stronger with each refilling of the tubs from five-gallon wicker-covered jugs.

They halted before the platform raised for dancing. It swayed with the pounding of many feet, and the jukebox blared

315

its rivalry with the calypso drum. Arm linked with his, she leaned against him, finding excitement in the touch of his lean, hard body. He was, she knew, enjoying himself in the noisy, demonstrative natures of the people. *His people.* She said the words to herself with surprise. *He really thinks of them now as his.* He had a majesty, although he would have been embarrassed to have her say such a thing, majesty and the secret of leadership springing from complete self-confidence. She wondered if he had ever doubted himself. Today he managed the paradox of seeming to be a man of the people, while at the same time standing aloof. The men and women recognized this, and their greetings were sometimes shy but not obsequious. They would call out "Mon!" and the word was an affectionate greeting and a tribute. When he danced with Alicia, they would press about the platform and watch with the smiling interest of children seeing an adult unexpectedly at play.

They strolled across an open area to where several palm-thatched shelters had been hastily raised for the Junkanoo. Here women suckled their babies or rested from the picnic. Men with a little too much rum and food in their bellies snored contentedly. There were tables made of boards and sawhorses, but most persons seemed to prefer to eat and walk about. Royal lifted her easily to one of the tables and took a seat beside her, lighting cigarettes for them both. Beyond the shelter stretched a colorful panorama: the new city, Freeport, without its inhabitants; the great hotel shimmering in the clear air; the stretches of undeveloped land; the great yellow hulking monsters of earthmoving equipment; the tent city raised to house the workmen; the bands; the crowds in an ever-shifting pattern; and, above all, the sound. It had the roll of the sea, a muted thunder.

Junkanoo falls on the day after Christmas, and it is somehow an extension, radically altered to meet different conditions and temperament here in the Bahamas, of the motherland's Boxing Day. To most of the Out Island people, Junkanoo on Grand Bahama was Christmas. Money in the remote settlements was hard to come by, and what little there was could not be spent in celebration and gift giving. This weekend here had released them from the sometimes pitiful efforts to make something bright and exciting out of what was, after all, just another day. They were making the most of it, and the occasion would provide a topic for excited reminiscences for the coming year. And they would remember who had been responsible for the magnificent excursion. The "Mon." Royal Keating and the Progressive Liberal Party. Their knowledge and interest in politics were vague, but this they were sure of now. If Royal Keating and the PLP could do this, then they could be expected to do more in the future. They would not have to be driven to the polls at the general election. There was also a sense of obligation, of dignity and of what was proper. Small jealousies and fancied wrongs were forgotten. The few men who drank too much of the punch and became quarrelsome were quickly hustled out of sight and kept under guard until they were sober and repentant. There was little need for the big handsome Jamaicans who made up Grand Bahama's police force.

A group of women and children passed the shelter where Royal and Alicia sat. They ducked their heads and called with shy smiles. The children stared with wide dark eyes.

"You're Santa Claus today." Alicia pressed her cheek against his shoulder. "Tell me, Santa. Am I your girl?"

"You're my girl all right." He laughed softly.

"Is it that funny?"

"I was thinking of Big Maum. She asked me once if I had a girl on Eleuthera. I told her yes. She wanted to know what kind. A fo' marryin' girl o' jus' lyin' en th' grass girl."

"What did you tell her?"

"I told her a fo' lyin' en th' grass girl. Ouch!" He yelped as her small fist dug into his side. "I didn't mean it."

"I think you did." She was half-angry. "And anyhow, who taught me about this lyin' en th' grass business?"

"That's just doing what comes naturally."

"Is that all there is to it?" She searched his face with her eyes. "I've wondered."

"Nooo. I guess there's more. We've had something pretty good going for us. I think we ought to keep it. What I'm getting around to is, I want to marry you."

317

"I hoped you would. I guess no girl is ever really satisfied with an arrangement. She may pretend. I'm not the same away from you. It's a different feeling. I'm not sure of so many things when I'm alone. When we're together, something of you shines on me. There is pride. Pride in you and myself. Pride, even, in being black because we have come so far with so little in so short a time."

"We're just beginning to clear the road ahead. You'll see. I'll show you."

"I'm not sure." She was doubtful. "I mean about the PLP and the elections. I like what is on that little sign above the bungalow door. 'Royal Keating. Resident Engineer.' Isn't that enough? Can't we be satisfied with it? There's a whole world where you can build things: roads, dams, bridges, buildings. I'm frightened for you here. You know yourself it is an unnatural situation, a black government in these islands."

"No." He shook his head. "It's unnatural only because it never happened before."

"All right." She made an effort to smile an agreement and then grinned with a quick return of humor. "Let's get back to that marriage stuff. When?"

He looked over the crowded area. "Now if you want it. There must be a dozen frocked and unfrocked ministers in this crowd." He slid from the table and with his hands at her waist lifted her easily. "Want to go find one?"

"No." She shook her head emphatically. "If I hadn't been your lyin' en th' grass girl, I might say yes. It would be fun. Now, though, I want it at home with my mother and all the aunts crying and my father looking embarrassed. I want an organ playing, bridesmaids, orange blossoms and a wedding cake. I'm going to wear a virgin's white, and we'll pretend this lyin' en th' grass never happened."

"All right." He took her hand. "But you know? If you wait a little while, you could be marrying the new Prime Minister in Nassau. That's a pretty big step for an Out Island conch girl."

The smile and laughter in her eyes disappeared. In their place was a deep concern. She stared up at him almost pleadingly.

318

Tomorrow I'll tell him they changed their minds. He thinks I'm alone."

Cepeda grunted. He straightened up and sat on the bunk's edge, lighting a cigarette.

"I don't want to be seen by no one. Later you got to go ashore. No one will think anything if you want to walk around and stretch your legs. There's supposed to be a bungalow on the west side of this crappy island. I gotta know how to get there. How long it takes to walk it and back."

"Well"—Kyle emptied the bottle, spun it in the air and caught its neck—"if that's what you want to know, when it gets dark, start walking. West is over there." He motioned with a thumb. "I brought you over here, and I'll take you back. That's all I'm paid to do. Who's Keating?"

Cepeda jerked himself upright. "How do you know about him?"

"You left a note on the table. I read it when you went to the can."

The Cuban sank back against the cushions. "You can get your nose sliced off, sticking it in someone else's business."

"In a way it's my business, too."

"Yeah." The agreement was a smirk. "Like what they call an accessory. What are you getting out of it?"

"Enough." Hendricks whistled meditatively. "You don't act like a *numero uno* to me. I think your guts are running right now at the idea of killing someone. What's Keating done?"

"How do I know?" He was boastful, trying to impress Hendricks. "It come to me as a contract from up top."

"Up top doesn't know you're alive."

"You know"—the Cuban rested on an elbow, scowling—"you're a real, wise squarehead with a big mouth. If I didn't have this other thing on my mind, I'd shut it for you."

Kyle stood up. "We'll have lots of time later. I'll remind you."

He dropped the empty bottle into a trash basket and then ducked out of the companionway, closing the hatch behind him. Pulling up a chair, he settled himself in the stern well.

Through half-closed eyes he watched the sky change with the turn of evening. Long gray streamers of clouds turned red and then purple, and a deep hush settled on the island and the surrounding sea. Untroubled by what he knew was going to happen to this man Keating, he began to wonder who he was and what he had done. How did a man like Sir Stephen get involved with a Cuban punk and a man on Grand Bahama? His imagination simply wouldn't stretch that far. There would seem to be no possible connection. He had seen his employer for only a few minutes before the taxi came to drive him to the Nassau airport.

"Your part is simple. You will meet this man and take him to the Grand Bahama. This is necessary because he would be noticed if he flew in. When his business has been transacted, you will leave but not in haste. There must be nothing suspicious in your behavior. As I promised, you will be generously compensated upon your return. You will discover I am a man of warm disposition to those I can trust. I hope to number you among the few. Now, dear boy, one more thing." His hand had rested on Kyle's shoulders. There was surprising strength in the fingers. "Experience has taught me never to leave a loose end dangling. Someone inevitably will pull at it out of curiosity."

Hendricks now lit a cigarette. He wondered if he were supposed to read more into this seemingly casual remark. Would the Cuban be a loose end once the job was done? Was he supposed to rid himself and Sir Stephen of a loose mouth, a push over the side in the night on the way back to Miami? Or— And the thought surprised him. His mouth half opened, and the cigarette dangled from the lower lip. Was he also that loose end as far as Sir Stephen was concerned? Was the Cuban supposed to get rid of him? Cepeda could have no knowledge of Sir Stephen Simon. So only Kyle Hendricks could point the finger, swear to the involvement. Sir Stephen wouldn't be happy with this knowledge. He would certainly take whatever measures necessary to protect himself. What had seemed like a cozy arrangement with his employer and maybe an opportunity for a touch of blackmail later now had become a black and frightening pit over which he leaned, ready to be shoved. His mental processes were usually slow and deliberate, but this required little effort. The more he thought about it, the less attractive a return to Nassau became. He had been stupid and should have asked for more than the two hundred dollars Sir Stephen advanced for expenses. He had no obligation to the man and less to the spik. To hell with them both. The thing to do was to get out of this without losing some skin from his ass. He wondered if he should go to this Keating and try to make some kind of a deal: money and a chance to get clear in return for information which might save Keating's life. He shook his head. It was too damn involved, and he would probably end in jail. The thing to do was to get back to Florida, out of the islands and Sir Stephen's reach. He was, he had to admit, a real dumb squarehead. The knowledge only increased his growing panic.

Night came with a silent rush, and small lights began to prick West End's darkness here and there. He went forward and called softly to Cepeda. "I'm going ashore."

"Go screw yourself." The reply was bitter, scornful.

As he stepped across to the dock, Kyle Hendricks thought that was exactly what he had done. He had screwed himself out of a soft job. But, he asked himself stubbornly, how could he have known Sir Stephen had murder in mind? His instructions had sounded innocent enough, and no one could have figured Sir Stephen for a deal like this. You could never really tell what someone was like inside. A fat swish. Like hell he was. He walked on down a sandy path in the direction of the Cay Club. There were lights in the windows, but only darkness surrounding the low building.

At the club he went to the bar and settled himself on a stool. No one questioned his presence.

"I'm tied up in the marina here. Can I get a drink? Scotch and water."

"Yes, sah." The Negro bartender smiled.

"Pretty quiet around here."

"Yes, sah. It dis way till after New Year." The drink was placed before him.

Kyle drank half of it. "Can I get some supper?"

"Dining room open at seven, sah. Drink all right?"

Hendricks emptied the glass. "It will be if you fill it up again."

He stared at the amber liquid in the shot glass and then tossed it down straight. At the moment he was scared and feeling very much alone. The more he thought, the worse it became. Suppose the Cuban punk bungled the job? This Keating could be hard to handle. Suppose he laid Cepeda out cold and then called for help. When the spik came to, he would run off at the mouth because they would be beating the hell out of him. Suppose? Jesus! There it was. They would trace Cepeda back to *The Spindrift,* and there he, the squarehead, Kyle Hendricks would be, waiting to be knocked off the limb like a pigeon. He lit a cigarette and watched his hand shake. The answer came as it had to. He'd get the hell out of here tonight and leave Cepeda to handle things if he could. There wasn't any other way. He sure wasn't going back to Nassau or Miami. Before leaving, he had studied a chart. The Lake Worth Inlet and Palm Beach were only a little more than fifty miles from Grand Bahama. He had plenty of fuel. All of a sudden things began to look better. He took a deep breath. It was an audible shudder of relief. The barman turned.

"You all right, sah?"

"Yes. Sure. Caught a little cold, I think."

A white-coated waiter looked in at the bar. "Dining room open, sah."

Hendricks nodded. He was no longer hungry. He wanted out and away. Things began to fall into place. He would give this Cepeda ten minutes away from the boat, out of sight and sound of it. Then he would get out of West End. Let the bastard take care of himself. He'd put the boat in at the West Palm Beach municipal dock and then lose himself in a hurry. What happened to Keating and Cepeda here he could read about in the papers someplace a hell of a long distance from the Bahamas or Florida. He felt better and ordered another drink.

There was no hurry. Cepeda would wait until the evening or night was well along before he showed himself.

For the first time that day—and it had been a long one from sunrise on—Royal was relaxed. He sat on the screened porch, closed in by the darkness and blessed quiet. From here he could watch both of the flashing lights on Settlement Point and Indian Cay Rock. They winked at him in six- and four-second intervals, and he found them almost hypnotically soothing. He had a tall drink in his hand. A bottle, ice and water were on a nearby table. He laughed softly to himself and lit a cigarette. The whiskey was warm and assuasive in his stomach. The bite of the cigarette's tobacco was pleasant in his mouth.

It had sure been one hell of a day. He hadn't expected to get any work out of his black laboring crew. In this he had been right. He made a leisurely Jeep tour over and around the Freeport development and was met with a disconcerting series of sheepish grins and hangdog expressions. One or two groups made small flurries, pretending to be engaged in some purposeful activity, but this fooled no one. The real job, that of getting the Out Island visitors into the waiting boats, was being completely ignored. There were knots of milling, shouting women and wailing children. The men lounged, hands in pockets, staring into the distance as though they were completely unrelated to the noisy confusion. With a few explosive words Royal had set them to the task of separating the Out Islanders and assigning them to the proper craft. He straightened out family arguments and wiped the noses of squalling youngsters. Some of the Out Island people had come over in their own sloops. These were inclined to a show of independence, attempting to prolong the holiday and elect their own time of departure. Family by family, couples and individuals were finally loaded and waved away. Then the chartered powerboats were checked off with their full complements of passengers. From the shore he had watched the craft string out into a bobbing, weaving line and thought with a grin that it was the damnedest-looking regatta he had ever seen. He couldn't help wondering if they all would make it home that day.

The skilled men—mechanics, plumbers, electricians and masons—had been flown in on the morning planes as usual. They were at their jobs, independent, for the most part, of the black labor force. Royal had made a wide tour of the area and discovered that the celebrants had recovered enough to clean up an incredible amount of litter. The dancing area and the barbecue pits were in neat order, and the latter would be filled in during the day. The chairs, benches and sawhorse tables were out of sight. All refuse had been burned or carted away, papers gathered, empty bottles and cans disposed of. Standing up in the Jeep and studying the site, Royal thought this was as much as anyone could expect. At home now he stretched out his legs and took a long, reflective swallow of his drink. They would talk about this Junkanoo in the Out Islands for months to come. It would not be easily forgotten, and in the forthcoming general election their loyalties would be to Royal Keating and the PLP.

Sitting in the darkness, he wondered at what point he had stopped playing to his audiences and succumbed to his own words. When had the mountebank been replaced by the man of sincere purpose and conviction? He could ask himself this question without laughing. When he spoke to the people now, he believed what he told them. There was a better way for the island blacks, and it lay with the PLP and Royal Keating. He understood that the old party leaders were still uncertain of his purpose and unhappy with his dominance. He refused to reassure them. They were forced to follow where he would lead. He smiled a little. Alicia also had her reservations. Was he a fraud, a gammoner, an opportunist? She still hadn't quite made up her mind. Thinking of her, he laughed out loud, and the sound was deep and filled with sudden humor. She really meant to come to the wedding night as a virgin. He thought he might send her a telegram saying: "Don't forget to say ouch!" The decision to marry hadn't been an impulsive one. She had beauty, poise, breeding and education and would make a damn fine wife for a Prime Minister. She would understand

326

the responsibilities of the position, for she was all black as he was, the black of which the island people must learn to be proud. She would give them pride by example.

He poured another dollop of whiskey into the glass and added ice. For a moment he thought about going over to the Cay Club for dinner and then, almost immediately, dismissed the notion. He didn't want to talk with anyone. He had had enough to do with people for one day. There was plenty of food in the cottage. Later he might fix a steak. A half dozen deviled crabs from a Miami restaurant had come over on one of the morning planes. What more did he want? He went to the bedroom, stripped, and took a shower. Then, in pajama bottoms, he fixed another drink and ate two of the crabs as a starter. Tomorrow he would be Royal Keating, resident engineer. Tonight he would just be an island man upon whom the bounty of the Lord had unexpectedly showered. He laughed again, a hearty, booming sound of sheer pleasure at being alive.

It was a little after ten o'clock before Cepeda, fortified by three stiff drinks of rum, forced himself to leave *The Spindrift*. Throughout the long and seemingly endless evening he had remained within the cabin hoping the squarehead would come back. He had decided to offer Hendricks a couple of hundred dollars if he would come along. As the night wore and his nerves began to shriek, he raised the imaginary offer. They would split the thousand between them. Cepeda was untroubled by the idea of murder. It was impersonal. Someone he had never seen. If everything went well, it would be over quickly. Even those who disliked Cepeda admitted he was a good man with a knife. He was apprehensive here because he was on unfamiliar ground. Dangers of which he had no knowledge must surround him. This was a hell of a lot different from a job in a dark alley. *Cristo!* He could even get himself lost on this rock and sand pile and not be able to find his way back to the boat and safety. If he weren't afraid of certain, swift reprisal from a frightening source in Miami, he would abandon the job and go back. Those who had contacted him and gave him the hit demanded perfection. They were intolerant of failure. To return with the contract uncompleted might very well have him end facedown in a drainage ditch somewhere along the Tamiami Trail. If he hadn't been greedy, he would have farmed the job out and taken a ten percent agent's cut. No. He wanted it all, and now, by God, he had it.

When he had finally drummed up enough courage to leave the boat, he had first thrust his head out above the hatch with the movement of a cautious turtle. There was no one on the dock or shore. *The Spindrift* was the only craft in the slips. He padded away in rubber-soled sandals, making not even a whisper of sound and clinging to the shadows whenever they could be found. There was only one source of light, and that came from the Cay Club. The small scattered and weathered houses with their paths bordered by polished conchs were dark. West End went to bed early, and not even a dog's nervous bark disputed his silent passage. There was no moon, but the stars were almost too bright here. He halted beneath an inclining palm tree and lit a cigarette with care, hiding the light within his hands. Some small measure of reason began to assert itself. He had been worrying himself into a panic. He had as yet done nothing and was as free to stroll here as any man. Suppose someone did see him? The sight of a man walking down the road would cause no alarm. Even if he passed someone, there would only be a glance of casual curiosity. His presence at this hour might be remembered later, but by that time he would be off the island and away. He was getting wind in his guts for nothing.

He crossed the narrow spit of land separating the yacht anchorage from the beach and open water. The cottage was not hard to find. It stood alone near the shore.

Now Cepeda hunkered down and watched intently. He lit one cigarette from the coal of another and kept the glowing tip shielded. His eyes never left the bungalow's trim lines. There was no sound other than a small constant murmur of the waves. No light showed. If there had been a dog, it would have sensed his presence by now and barked its alarm. So he stubbed the last cigarette into the sand and straightened up. Now he must go for it. There was no turning back. What was to be done swiftly and in silence could no longer be delayed. He was cold now and without nerves. He cocked his head with an animallike gesture to catch and identify a sound. It was gone. From where he stood, the yacht basin was hidden from sight. So in this moment he could not know that *The Spindrift*, without her running lights, was slipping away through the channel between West End Point and Indian Cay Rock as silently as a ghost ship. The motors were just ticking over, giving Hendricks only steerageway at the moment. That was all he needed, and he did not look back until he was well past the flashing light. Then he laughed. His shoulders straightened confidently. Whatever happened now, he was out of it. If the spik killed and was caught, no one could pin any of it to Kyle Hendricks. His hand moved toward the throttles which would blast the cruiser into a roar of life. He was in no hurry. He was enjoying his last sight of Grand Bahama. By tomorrow the Cuban would be running like a frightened rabbit from the dogs and finding no place to hide.

Each step, as he took it now, was carefully tested and calculated in advance. He had no stomach for an encounter. He wanted his man asleep in bed. The screen door was unlatched. Cepeda opened it an inch at a time, fearful of a squeak from an unoiled hinge. He turned his body to slide through the narrow opening. The porch was vacant. In the starlight the chairs and a swinging couch were humped shapes. He had been certain no one slept there before trying the screen. Now he stood on the porch, and an excitement gripped and knotted his guts and then ran swiftly to his nuts. Sometimes it was almost like having a woman, this feeling of power, of mastery. Depending on what he did now, a man would die or live. His mouth was suddenly dry. Slowly he allowed the screen to close behind him, checking it with his fingers. In the final half inch his carelessness almost betrayed him. The light frame slipped away and closed with a soft, barely audible snick of the latch. He held his breath. In the silence the sound had seemed as loud as the cocking of a heavy pistol.

He moved from the porch with a single flowing glide and

was in the bungalow's living room. It was much darker here, and he could hear a light, rippling snore. The bedroom door was open, and the oblong cleft was gray-black against gray-black. As he approached the doorway, the snoring stopped, and Cepeda flattened himself against the wall to one side of the opening.

Royal lay, eyes wide, wondering what had awakened him. He stared at the ceiling, listening. The house was without sound, and yet he had the feeling someone had entered. Who? Why? There was nothing of value here. Day and night the doors and windows were never locked. Besides, no one employed on the Grand Bahama project would have thought of coming to the bungalow uninvited. Just the same he could not rid himself of the conviction he was no longer alone.

"Is anyone there?" He sat up in bed and called.

Even as he waited, he had to smile. If anyone were in the house, he would be a damned fool to answer. For a moment he was tempted to drop back to the soft pillows and then, inexplicably, changed his mind. Having tossed off the light covering, he strode toward the door which led to the living room.

There was no time to check his stride or to take a defensive measure. He half whirled to confront the man, and then this terrible, streaking fire raged through his body. The heavy-bladed knife had gone in and up at an angle beneath the rib cage, and Royal Keating was dead. His mouth opened, but there was no sound; only the crimson flood of a massive hemorrhage poured out to cover the rough grass carpeting with a black stain. As he pitched forward, Cepeda stepped away, and the body fell clear with a heavy impact which shook the light building to its foundation. Then there was no sound until a few seconds later the screen door's latch caught with a faint snap. After that only silence.

XXI

Fear now swept through the islands, and it was stamped on the faces of all men. Would the murder of Royal Keating incite the predominately black population to an uprising of terror and violence without precedent in the Bahamas?

White families grew increasingly nervous in the presence of their servants. Some of the large houses were hastily closed, their owners flying to Miami or safe and neutral ground abroad. The anticipated flow of tourists was shut off almost overnight. Winter cruiseships, with Nassau as a port of call, changed their courses and bypassed the Bahamas. The Ministry of Tourism frantically sought to place reassuring stories with the wire services and North American newspapers. There was no real cause for alarm. No one really believed this.

The black settlements on New Providence set aside days of mourning. Bands of funereal black appeared on shirt and dress sleeves, and little wreaths were hung on doors or appeared in windows. Special evening services packed the churches. Those who could find no room inside stood in the sandy yards and lifted their voices in a chanted threnody of lamentation. In the Out Islands the black people gathered in small groups to offer their prayers and cry their anguish, for Royal Keating was remembered not only as someone who promised them a better way but as a good man—a good, black man. The loss was personal, and the old hymns took on a new, fierce rhythm of challenge when they were sung. Few of the men and women reported for work at their regular jobs. The luxuriously appointed clubs and hotels were without cooks, waiters, maids, gardeners, caddies and boatmen.

In Nassau the Premier and Governor called on all the people to exercise judgment and restraint. Few listened. The native hat stalls by the piers, where the women gathered daily to gossip and plait their wares, were deserted. The fringed-top surreys, a tourist attraction with their top-hatted Negro coachmen, no longer clopped through the streets. The black drivers of taxicabs were absent from their accustomed stands, and the pedestrian traffic on Bay Street appeared to move with a cautious step. It almost seemed as though the people, black and white, held a collective breath, for no one could say what might happen. Most felt it would take only a small racial incident to touch off a riot of murder, arson and anarchy which could reduce Nassau to smoking and bloody ruins.

The whites may have wondered and whispered their opinions to one another. They were cautious, talking only with trusted friends. Was the murder really such a mystery? The blacks knew better. The whites had killed Royal Keating because he and the PLP threatened their comfortable monopolies and way of life. These things they said aloud and defiantly. A few of the more militant hoped a white man would hear and protest.

Within the sun-flooded patio by the swimming pool Sir Stephen Simon lay back on the heavily padded lounge chair. With an indulgent smile his gaze followed the noisy antics of his two wards as they arced their graceful bodies from the springboards or chased each other as sportive mermaids through the dappled water. What exciting little creatures they were, surprisingly inventive for their years and with rare streaks of really savage cruelty beneath this outward display of childish innocence. He adored them, and they were so happy here, surrounded by all the luxury he could so well afford. They were practically naked, burnished by the sun to the color of cured tobacco. Small bands of silk only seemed to accentuate the swell of breasts and mount of pubes. The little points of nipples seemed ready to burst as blossoming flowers. It was really too bad they never lasted but sooner or later grew tiresome and stupidly mechanical in their efforts. He would have to send them away, but not for a couple of weeks or so. Until then they were really charming. Half listening to their chatter, he thought of other things.

He had read, of course, and listened to the commentators on radio and television of Royal Keating's murder. A foreman, troubled by the technical problems on a job of construction, had gone to the bungalow. No one had seen Mr. Keating during the morning. Usually he was out early, driving the Jeep to the different sites, talking with the men, straightening out small difficulties. Having opened the unlocked screen door, the foreman said, he had walked from the porch to the living room. There he found the body. The physician who was in charge of the clinic and first-aid station examined the body. Death had resulted from a knife wound. No weapon was found. Without a postmortem it was impossible to say when death had occurred, but the doctor suggested sometime between ten and twelve o'clock the preceding night. The sergeant of the Jamaican police force employed by the Grand Bahama project suggested that the murder was the work of a disgruntled laborer or someone with a fancied wrong. There was no indication that robbery was the original purpose and that murder came later. Nothing of value—money, watch or small jewelry—seemed to be missing. Because of the growing concern, the Nassau Commissioner of Police sent his deputy to the area for the purpose of interrogation. It wasn't explained how one man was expected to be able to question the several hundred persons employed on the island, any one of whom might be considered a suspect. Tension increased, but in Nassau it was Pierre DuPres' paper alone which demanded a thorough investigation.

Sir Stephen half closed his eyes. The sun's warmth folded about him as a fragrant cover. The cries of his nubile wards were those of happy children. Surely the world of Sir Stephen Simon was a most delightful place. He did feel a slight twinge

333

of regret over the loss of Kyle Hendricks, a beauty of a lad. But, as Sir Stephen well understood, time might prove him both tiresome and dangerous. Kyle knew too much, and as he must have found out by now, a little learning can be an unfortunate thing. The paraphrase caused Sir Stephen to smile. He was a man with a real passion for neatness. It would have been untidy to allow Kyle Hendricks to remain alive. It had been made unmistakably clear to his "sources of information" that Hendricks was not to return ever, anywhere. In this situation he was expendable. How and in what manner he was disposed of were of little interest to his patron. He was, in fact, a loose end which must be snipped off before it called attention to itself. Since Kyle had not returned to Nassau, Sir Stephen felt confident his instructions had been carried out. It was too bad, really too bad, for he was a dear boy.

His reverie was interrupted by the approach of his man-servant, Morgan, who carried a telephone with its long cord trailing.

"Mr. Hertog is calling, Sir Stephen." At his employer's nod he put the instrument on a table and left.

"Hello, my dear Max." Pleasure was in each word. "How good of you to call." He cushioned the receiver to his ear. "I have been reading and listening to the radio and television. Such a tragedy and no solution. I know how completely you depended on this Keating for the success of Grand Bahama. He was, if I recall, your resident engineer on the project."

He was silent for a moment, nodding slowly as Hertog talked. Then he became keenly alert, all but heaving himself from the lounge.

"Of course. Of course." This was an impatient interruption. "I know. All Nassau understands you feel a personal loss, particularly since his mother has been in your employ for years. The people of the Bahamas are well aware of your open heart, your kind and generous nature, your devotion to justice. But" —the voice sank to a dry, whispered rasp—"I would most earnestly counsel you against offering a five-thousand-dollar reward for the apprehension and conviction of Keating's assailant. Someone might find him, dear Max. I most emphatically caution you against such a foolhardy gesture." The receiver was dropped back into its cradle.

Leaning back against the pad again, Sir Stephen was the picture of complete exhaustion. His eyes were closed, his breathing heavy. The bloody goddamned fool. What in hell was Max Hertog thinking of? Did he imagine that by offering a reward, he could still the whispers that Bay Street was somehow involved? The bloody, bloody idiot. Couldn't he guess that five thousand dollars would send every pimp and whore, every bum and tout, every hustler and small-time thief in Miami to sniff around? Sooner or later a careless word would achieve a frightening importance and be fashioned into the first link of a chain which might secure them all. My God! He took a deep breath and felt himself growing calmer. Men of small imagination made dangerous companions. They were incapable of seeing beyond the moment. Max Hertog wanted only to do what was good for Max Hertog. If necessary, he would have to be contained.

Time and the bush have worked together to reclaim the land, and the winds play through the rubble and stunted trees. Here, on Little Exuma, the effort to create an extensive plantation ended in heartbreaking failure. The shell of the manor, its pillars wraithlike in the moonlight, still stands at the end of what had been a long driveway bordered by ornamental shrubs. Spotted over the acres are the ruins of cane-grinding machinery, warehouses, a small building for the curing of tobacco, barns and a forge. They are squat sentinels of the night.

To this southern tip of the Exuma Cays Joseph Keating brought his family, together with all his worldly goods, in the year of 1782. Here Joseph Keating lived, and here he died, as did his wife and several children. They are buried on a small knoll, and the modest headstones of marble are remarkably clean, free of erosion and growth. The names, sharply cut, are easily read: "Jos. Keating. Infant Son. Died 1784. Mary. Beloved Wife of Arthur Keating. Died 1798. Jos. Keating, Sr. Died 1799." There are others, and the plots were once squared by a fence of wrought iron in a picket design. Only rusted stubs show now. Beyond the warehouses and what were once the fields are the graves of the Keating family's slaves. Here the black people were buried. On boards, long since rotted and blown away, their names were cut: "Josh Keating. Sarah Keating. David Keating. Saul Keating" and so on. These were also Keatings, and they had no names other than the African tribal ones which their white owners could not be bothered to pronounce. Now there was little left of the white Keatings save their name as it was perpetuated in color. What had once been their plantation had been recently bought by a syndicate of Canadian businessmen. Within a few years a resort hotel, golf course and yacht club would be built here, and these would rise over the bones of the Keatings, white and black.

Through a vague claim of inherited squatters' rights but more because of an indulgent attitude on the part of the new owners, the black Keatings on Little Exuma now occupied what had once been the overseer's house. The stone building with its thatched roof had stood firmly against the years. Part of its wide chimney and square fireplace had been repaired from time to time. The thatching had been renewed. The walls and floors, though, were thick, solid and enduring.

Few of a once-large brood were left. The grandmother, as shrunken and twisted as an old piece of leather left in the rain and sun, was carried outside each day. Her son, Dwight Keating, and his wife, Dodie, shared the never-ending task of taking care of her pitifully small wants. The ancient one ate little but liked a bit of rag soaked in milk and sprinkled with snuff. It was kind to her toothless gums. The children of Dwight and Dodie were grown now. Cleo and Nina had steady jobs in nearby Rolle Town. James worked on the hand-operated flatboat ferry by which Little and Great Exuma were connected. Curtis remained at home and helped his father with the garden plots of beans, squash, yams, tomatoes, corn and peas. He tended the chicken run, fed the sow and her litter, and with a hand net took fish from the sea. They all lived together in the five rooms and were deeply rooted to this soil. On this land their parents, grandparents and great-grandparents had been born.

336

Once the slave cabins had stood in two short rows at the north end of the field. There the black Keatings were born, reared and died. Those who came after them had never known any other home.

Big Maum, eldest daughter of the old woman, had been born in one of the slave cabins. On the abandoned acres of the plantation she had worked, raced, played, and finally loved. Her husband had been a distant cousin, a Rollie Keating. By him she had had four sons. Royal had been the youngest. Now, in her misery, she brought him back to be buried in this Out Island earth. His grave, freshly turned and marked with a stone, lay with the other black Keatings. Big Maum could not have said what had drawn her to this remote cay or why she wanted her son buried here. She rarely visited her family and felt no kinship with the old woman or her brother, Dwight. Old memories reached out to touch her with unsteady fingers: the time of growing up; the time of marriage; the time of birth and death. Two of her children had died, and the blood of her womb was in this soil. So she brought her joy, her pride, her Royal, to this old place. Now he was a part of the land and of all that had gone before.

She worked these days, the big, silent woman, beside her nephew and her brother-in-law in the garden plots and sometimes went with Curtis to the ocean, and they would haul a short net together and pick out the shining fish. She did these things because she must keep busy; otherwise, a wild hysteria would take her by the throat. Now and then she would sit in the warm sun with the old woman, but they did not talk, for they were strangers in time. Once the old woman had thrust out a clawlike hand and run the bony fingers over Big Maum's face. She drew it back with a sharp gasp, as though she had found something frightening there. Big Maum did not know, nor did anyone ask, if or when she would go back to Nassau. Room was made for her in the cramped quarters, and she was absorbed without questions. They did not speak of her long residence on New Providence or the Nassau they had only heard in the talk of Out Island boatmen. It would have been discourteous, a breach of good manners.

Long after the others were asleep Big Maum would lie on her bed, eyes open and stark with pain. It seemed as though time would never erase the hurt or soothe the ache. At such moments she laid a heavy arm across her head in an effort to block out the memory.

From one of the kitchen windows at Windmere she had seen the official car with the Superintendent of Police come up the long driveway and thought only that the officer had a breakfast appointment. She had Stella prepare another tray and waited for Mistuh Max to ring. Instead, he had come to the kitchen. This, in itself, was unprecedented. She could never remember his ever making such a concession before. When he wanted to speak with a servant, he sent for him. Now his face and manner were grave, and she could recall thinking there was something dishonest in the way he looked and spoke. An instinct for which she could not account warned her. This man was an evil something and a liar. Then he told her what had happened but not why, and she stared at him. Her features graven. A Congo mask, dark, cold and a little frightening.

"We're having him—the body—brought back to Nassau." Max almost faltered beneath her stare. He was uncomfortable, and to hide this, he became impatient. "If there is anything you need. Anything I can do."

She spoke then for the first time. "I guess yo've done fo' Royal jus' 'bout all yo' can do, Mistuh Max." Her eyes were level. They did not waver. She stood straight and with a brooding majesty nailed him there with a bitter scorn.

Max met her challenge and then nodded briefly. He turned away. The Superintendent of Police hesitated. It was as though he felt some word of gentle understanding should be spoken. Big Maum's head lifted a trifle higher, and she stared past him. He turned and followed Max Hertog from the room.

As the door closed behind the men, Stella and the other two maids began to slap their hands together with an ageless gesture of lamentation, and their keening wails rose on a slowly ascending note.

"Hush yo' faces. You Stella. Mimsey. Dora." She cuffed them with a heavy hand, but there was no anger in the blows.

338

The girls backed away snuffling and meekly set about their morning tasks. Big Maum went again to the windows and stood looking out and seeing nothing. Now and then one of the girls would dart a timid glance in her direction. The back and shoulders were straight, but when they looked closely, they could see the awful trembling. Big Maum cried for her baby, her son, her man. It was as though a mountain were rocking.

Jan and Sherry were at breakfast when the announcement came with the morning television news. They both listened without comment, and then Sherry reached across the table and laid his hand on hers. She thought it was a surprising gesture for him to make.

"I suppose you want to go?"

She nodded.

"There's no plane now until this afternoon. I'll get one for you. A charter. Right away?"

She nodded again. Always he would do these unexpected things, the gesture of understanding, of sympathy. She thought they should no longer surprise her. They always did.

"I love you." Her eyes were shining.

"Ah!" It was a sound of rejection, but he winked. "You're just crazy about my money."

She hadn't called Windmere to say she was coming but took a taxi from the airport. Instead of seeing Max first, she went directly to the kitchen, and somehow, it did not seem at all unnatural to find Big Maum about her quiet supervision of the household. She had not shut herself away, and a magnificent dignity held at a distance the outside servants who came to offer their sympathy. She knew it was in the nature of these black people to be demonstrative in their joy or sorrow. Big Maum, through her own example, had shut this off.

"Big Maum." Jan hesitated in the doorway, feeling as though she should ask permission to enter. "I came as soon as I heard."

The black woman's smile was weary as though it had been forced too many times this day.

"Yo' look pretty, chil'. Dat mon yo' gots mus' treat yo' good." She eyed the girl critically. "Th' baby come pretty soon now." She was trying to evade the unavoidable.

"About Royal?" Jan was confused.

"Ain' much t' do 'bout Royal now. Dey bringin' him t' Nassau. Den I take my boy back home fo' buryin'."

"Home?" Jan was surprised, confused "Why, I always thought—" She halted, uncertain of what she thought. Then she realized it had never occurred to her that Big Maum or Royal might have a home apart from Windmere. "Where?"

"Royal born like me en Li'l Exuma. We go back now. Him fo' th' las' time."

"Max." Jan was forced to make the correction. "My father will have everything taken care of. He'll do what he—we— can. You know that."

"No. Dis a t'ing I do myse'f. I hire a boad an' take my boy home on it."

"No." Jan shook her head. "I won't let you do it that way. You have no right. I mean. I want to help. This is family. You can take *The Witch* with Spindle or Major. Or we can get a plane if there's a field or airstrip on Little Exuma."

In the end she prevailed on Big Maum to take Royal's body to Little Exuma aboard *The Witch*. She did not go down to the dock but watched from a window as Big Maum went aboard and thought it strange and a little touching that she took with her the parrot, Sir Rupert, perched on her shoulder.

Now, as she had done since her return to Little Exuma, Big Maum walked on the beach alone in the late afternoon as the sky took on its smoky, amber tint and the curious but familiar hush descended upon the world. Here she had often romped and strolled as a girl. She was bare of foot now, as she had been then, and the damp sand was cold between her toes. The golden bell at her ankle played a tune for dancing with its bright tinkle. Here, in the silence, she made up her mind. It was time to go, to leave Little Exuma with its memories and Royal. There was nothing for her here but sorrow. The days of open mourning were over. So, she decided, tomorrow she would send Curtis over to Rolle Town where *The Witch* was moored and tell Spindle they would be going back to Nassau.

Having turned, she retraced her steps, marveling a little at

340

how quickly the imprints erased themselves as the millions of tiny grains came together to fill in the depressions. Now and then she would stoop to pick up a bright shell. She did this now and in rising glanced down the stretch of beach. It had been empty a few minutes ago. Now the figure of a woman, a girl, was there. As she approached, Big Maum understood the girl was waiting for her. She had not followed. She made no move now. It was as though she said, "I won't force myself on you. If you stop, I would like to talk of things. If you only nod and pass on, I will understand."

Only a few feet separated them. The girl made no gesture, and Big Maum used the few seconds to study her. There was beauty and dignity here. Big Maum halted and waited.

"I'm Alicia. Alicia Thatcher. I heard." She was not confused. The short sentences came unhurriedly, spoken as they were because there was no need to say more at the moment. "Miss Hertog told me you were here."

"I don' know yo', girl." The statement was abrupt but not hostile.

The smile was brief, understanding. "I think you do." The correction was gentle.

Big Maum thought this over. "Yo' were my Royal's woman?"

"Yes." There was no embarrassment.

"He tol' me onct." Big Maum watched her and wondered. "He say t' me onct he have a fo' lyin' en th' grass girl en 'Leuthera."

The smile came quickly, and Big Maum no longer wondered. She didn't need anyone to tell her. This was a black girl of rare pride. She wished she could have seen her walk with Royal. It must have been something, the two of them, as if they owned a piece of the world.

"Royal told me what he said." Alicia was not pressing. "Then it changed. I was his girl. We were going to be married."

"Royal never say t' me." The denial was without antagonism.

Alicia smiled again. "I think it came over him all of a sudden. He would have told you."

341

"Yes." Big Maum nodded. "He woulda tol' me." She considered the girl for a second or two and then made up her mind. "Yo' wan' walk wid me?"

Without answering, Alicia bent and slipped away her shoes and then her stockings. Resting on one foot, she teetered a little off-balance, and Big Maum's hand reached out to steady her shoulder. Alicia glanced up, surprised. The smallest of smiles rested for a second around the woman's mouth and eyes. They walked, and the only sound was the ankle bell. Across the western sky the long clouds were strung out in pennons of violet and saffron. The wind had died completely, and the waves barely had strength enough to drop on the shore.

"Dat Royal. He was a somethin' man." She wanted to talk. "At a diffrun' place an' time he coulda been a king. I know dat th' day he bin birthed." Her features softened as old memories soothed the pain. "Wid th' oders I had t' strain an' push. Dat Royal! He fight t' get out. He couldn' wait." She turned suddenly to face Alicia. "Why didn' yo' stop him befo' it got too late?"

"I tried. He just laughed and wouldn't listen."

Big Maum nodded. The explanation satisfied her. "He was dat way. I say onct th' whites don' let no black man sit 'bove 'em. No one pay no mind. So dey kill him. Th' black people know how it was. The whites too; only dey don' say it aloud. Dey scared."

They followed a winding path leading up over the low hills and across what were once the Keating fields. Big Maum slowed her step but did not halt.

"Yo' wan' see wheah Royal at? Th' buryin' place?"

Alicia shook her head quickly. "No."

Big Maum nodded her approval. "I don' go dere myse'f no mo'. It jus' a pile o' dirt. It ain' wheah my Royal at. Don' do no good t' look. Yo' gots a place t' stay th' night?"

"Yes. I have a cousin at the Ferry. Tomorrow I'll go back to Eleuthera."

"Tomorrow I go too. Ain' nothin' fo' me heah but sadness. Th' next time I come dey'll be carryin' me t' lay neah Royal. Mos' all th' Keating, white an' black, bury here."

342

They halted at the intersection of two paths. One led down to the small, neat community called the Ferry. Big Maum reached out with gentle hands and turned Alicia so she could look into her face and then touched big, spatulate fingertips to a cheek.

"Yo' would make fine woman fo' Royal. Yo' both had dat somethin' what make people glad when dey look at yo'. Now good-bye an' take care o' yo'se'f. We don' see each oder no mo'. It bes' we don'. What we say t' each oder? Only Royal t' talk 'bout. I gots no tears lef'." She dropped her hands, turned away, and walked across the stubbled land. Alicia stood watching, and by some trick of the lighting, the stunted, twisted trees forming a background, Big Maum seemed to grow in stature. She strode now with an effortless movement, looming in the short twilight as the huge, primordial black mother of all black men.

In the coffee shop of the Greyhound Bus Depot in Waycross, just across the Florida line in Georgia, Kyle Hendricks sat on a stool. He had finished a large breakfast of ham, eggs and hashed brown potatoes. Now he nodded assent as the waitress came with fresh coffee to refill his cup. At the side of his plate there was a copy of the Jacksonville *Florida Times-Union*. It was turned and folded at the second page, and Kyle now reread the story for the third time.

> NASSAU, Bahamas (AP) The Commissioner of Police here today issued a statement concerning the mysterious man who was discovered hiding in the heavy undergrowth of Grand Bahama two days after the murder of Royal Keating, leader of the black Progressive Liberal Party and resident engineer on the Freeport construction work for Maximilian Hertog. The man has been held incommunicado for the past week while the authorities here and in Miami checked out his story. He is Juan Cepeda, twenty-one, son of a Cuban refugee family who gave a residence address in the "Little Havana" section of Miami. He was found by the police on Grand Bahama when they made a tip-to-tip search of the island, looking for possible clues to Keating's assailant. Cepeda insists he came to Grand Bahama on a

343

fishing trip with an unidentified companion, who, for obscure reasons, seems to have abandoned him on the island. He denied knowing the man's name, saying they had met casually in a bar. "He was a big blond Swede or something. I never did know his name. He asked me to go fishing. That's all. I don't know why he left me there." He [Cepeda] also said he couldn't remember the boat's name. When asked why he was hiding, he said he heard some laborers talking about the murder while he hid in the underbrush. "I was a stranger on the island. I was afraid the police would try and pin the killing on me. I thought maybe I could stow away later on one of the transport planes which bring the workmen over from Miami." The police in Miami say Cepeda has a record of juvenile delinquency, auto theft, assault and extortion. He was once held on a murder charge, but the indictment was dismissed. Part of his story was substantiated by the dockmaster at the West End Cay Club, who said a cabin cruiser had been assigned a slip. He didn't pay any attention to the name or registration number since this information is not required for boats which lay over for less than twenty-four hours.

There was more, two full columns; a recapitulation of the murder, the career of Royal Keating, and his association with the large development taking place on Grand Bahama. The correspondent also reported that it was generally believed in Nassau that Keating's murder was politically motivated.

Hendricks shoved the paper away. He had no interest in what was happening in Nassau beyond the fact that he was not identified by Cepeda, who really didn't know his name. He thought they would probably turn the spik loose. He wouldn't have been stupid enough to leave anything behind which could link him to the crime. The burden of proof would be on the Crown. In a week or so the whole thing would probably simmer down to nothing. After all, who had been killed? This Keating was just another dinge. Despite this reasoning, he was determined to get as far away from Nassau as possible. He didn't trust Sir Stephen one damn bit. He was half swish at least, and those old bags had long memories and were real bitchy.

Glancing up and into the wide mirror spanning the wall

beyond the counter, he caught the girl watching him again. She was separated from his side by a single stool. Twice before he had raised his eyes and met her speculative gaze. This time she smiled diffidently. She was a pretty thing, seventeen or eighteen, maybe, with long brown hair which looked as though it had just been ironed. She didn't look like the ordinary pickup. There was a fresh and innocent air of excitement about her.

Kyle took his cup and check, moving to the seat next to her. She pretended a deep absorption in the lunch counter signs.

"Hello." He shook out a cigarette and lit it.

"Hello." The reply was barely audible. She didn't turn to look at him.

"You waiting for a bus?"

"Yes." She relaxed a little.

He offered her a cigarette, and she shook her head.

"Thanks, but I don't smoke." She was a little surer of herself now. "I was watching you in the mirror. I guess it looked like I was a pickup."

"I didn't think so." He lit his cigarette, watching her.

"I'm not, really. It's just that you have about the blondest hair I've ever seen." She pronounced "hair" in two syllables as *hy-ah*. "It's almost white."

"It turned white because I worry about pretty girls like you."

A quick smile dimpled her fresh cheeks. "That's crazy." She was pleased.

"Where are you going?"

"Back home. Quitman. Quitman, Georgia. I guess you never heard of it."

"Of course I have." His leg touched hers beneath the counter, and she did not pull away. "Quitman, Georgia, is the capital of the world. Everyone knows that."

"That's real crazy." She was delighted and leaned toward him so their shoulders touched for a moment. "Where are you going?"

He thought for a moment. Why not? He had to go someplace. He had nothing to lose. This just might be something special. She watched him.

"Oh"—he was casual—"I guess I'll go to Quitman, too."
He slid off the stool and walked away.

Puzzled and a little hurt, the girl turned to watch him. Disappointment was in her expression. He was a so good-lookin' boy, who would be fun to know. She continued to follow him with her gaze as he went to the ticket window. When he returned, he put a pasteboard tab on the counter before her.

"What does that say?"

"Quitman! You really meant it." She was excited by the novelty of it all. "It's a real crazy thing. Comin' to Quitman just like that because of me. Or"—she hesitated—"I guess that's why, isn't it?"

He nodded, reached for the ticket, and put it in his pocket. Quitman, Georgia. Who the hell ever heard of Quitman, Georgia? It would be the last place Sir Stephen would think to find him. He didn't have to stay there, but it sure would be safe. Besides, it had been a long time since he had had a girl like this one. It began to look like a good deal all around.

XXII

As the days following the assassination of Royal Keating were counted into weeks, some of the easy, careless rhythm of life in the islands slowly reasserted itself. Most of the people had a small capacity for sustained emotion, and soon the sinister implications of the murder were all but forgotten.

The carriages and taxicabs reappeared on the streets. At the hat stalls, near the docks, the women were back at their weaving and gossip. The handsome black police lost their worried frowns and smiled again at a pretty girl as they deftly handled traffic on crowded Bay Street. House servants returned to their posts with vague and mumbled excuses for their absences, and the angry militant gangs of young men in the Negro settlements fell apart. They had no cause to serve beyond stirring up discontent. Few persons were in the mood to listen. The first of the winter cruiseships ventured into Nassau's harbor, and the boys dived from their rowboats for the coins tossed down by laughing tourists.

With the return to almost normal conditions the whites forgot their nervousness and fears of a black revolt. Their institutions and privileges were safe. There wasn't to be a time of crimson fury, after all. Most of the large homes, hastily closed, were reopened. In the hotels the white managers were no longer

hesitant about rebuking a porter or bellboy. This was the tourist season, and everyone had better be at his smart best. No
dawdling, mind you. Look sharp. Act sharp. On your toes
every minute. As the fear of riot passed, the old white attitude
of half-amused tolerance again displayed itself. These blacks
were really happy, carefree children, who had been manipulated
into a rebellious state by the political agitation of this Progressive Liberal Party. That fellow Keating, or whatever his
name was, undoubtedly had taken his money and instructions
from Moscow. Well! The islands were damn well rid of him,
and what happened ought to be a lesson to the other blacks.
They should remember their places and leave the business
of governing to those who, by birth and position, were fitted to
conduct the islands' affairs. A damned outrage to have this sort
of thing happen. It hurts business no end. There were now
open warnings to cooks, porters, bellboys, maids, boatmen,
butlers and waiters not to take an unhealthy interest in the
forthcoming general election. After all, it was pointed out,
good jobs weren't easy to find. Anyone could be replaced without difficulty. This was something to keep in mind when outside agitators came around, urging them to vote for some black
man. The islands had been orderly for a couple of hundred
years, and in them, people, black and white, knew their places.

In the Out Islands the leaders in communities and larger
villages found themselves adrift and with no sense of direction
or purpose. They went through the motions of holding rallies,
but there was no real enthusiasm in the people and they knew
it. No one held a torch with which to rekindle a dying fire.
They watched apathetically as a once-bright flame grew dim
and threatened to flicker out. Such men as the Reverend Whitman gave the impression of pathetic helplessness. They had lost
the skill for leadership. For too long they had been carried along
on the drive of Royal Keating's personality. Their will had
been subordinated to his. Now they floundered where they
should have walked boldly and were without purpose. When
they tried to address a community gathering, their speeches
were more apologetic than inspiring. There was no iron in
their words. The Progressive Liberal Party seemed to be on

the point of complete disintegration, and no one knew how to halt the slow decay.

On Grand Bahama, Max Hertog had replaced Royal with a white engineer, who seemed unable to cope with the many small racial problems which arose daily. There was always some minor trouble and bickering between the Bahama blacks and those brought in from Jamaica. Royal had settled such things quickly, with a smile and a sure instinct. The quarrels dissolved, and the men chuckled and laughed among themselves. The "mon" stood for no foolishness, and they knew it. Now there seemed to be constant friction. There were annoying delays, which took time to adjust. But the work progressed, and the development of Freeport into a glittering resort community became something of a construction miracle.

Freeport was no longer just a vision. Bars, restaurants, nightclubs and hotels were packed. Two American motel chains had bought property and were in operation. An electronics firm had purchased a site on the island at its east end and was building. Other concerns were making applications for purchase. The possibilities of Grand Bahama were just being realized. The Lucayan Beach Club, the ultimate in luxury, was all but complete. Charles Rich and his associates were more than happy with their investment. The mysterious Oriental temple which Max Hertog insisted on calling his guest house rose in its bewildering splendor.

One of Freeport's outstanding attractions was the International Center. Here a group of speculators and financiers had created a shopping and entertainment area which was proving to be the island's greatest tourist attraction. Freeport's deepwater harbor was complete, and vessels from Miami, cruiseships and excursions from Nassau arrived daily. The International Center was a collection of theatricallike bazaars. The shopping and entertainment areas were modeled on European and Asian districts. There were the mews and pubs of old England, complete from the roasting joints on a spit and pewter tankards to saucy, full-breasted serving wenches. Montmartre and the shops of Hong Kong. A street in Berlin or Manila or an alley in Rio was faithfully reproduced. The wares and

349

products, food and entertainment of the cities to which the districts were native were a magnet for the visitors.

Max had been eyeing the International Center with a greedy speculation. He had extended the franchises to the promoters on the most favorable terms. Now he was experiencing the unfamiliar pain of witnessing an unexpected and overwhelming financial success in the hands of someone else. He wanted it back. Finally he had Carol make a luncheon appointment for him with Sir Stephen.

They met at the Lyford Cay Club which was a considerable distance from Nassau proper. Sir Stephen had insisted on this. He had recently become infected with a physical culture virus. The illness resulted in frequent steam baths and the pummeling by a huge Negro masseur, who was thorough but lacking in Kyle Hendricks' expert touch. Sometimes Sir Stephen thought wistfully of Kyle and wondered in what manner he had been done away with. Concerned now with the improvement of his "figgah," Sir Stephen considered the ride to Lyford Cay in his Rolls in the nature of a health-giving exercise. He explained this to Max over the luncheon table.

"You ought to think more of your health, dear boy." Sir Stephen touched disapprovingly at his bulging midriff. "I am losing pounds." He beamed approvingly. "Now, dear boy, what happy circumstances bring us together? I always enjoy these luncheons with you."

Briefly Max sketched out the details of the International Center. The franchises. The remarkable success of the venture.

Sir Stephen nodded and made small, clucking noises to indicate sympathy and understanding.

"So"—he was bright and airy—"someone else has stuck in a thumb and pulled out a plum and says what a good boy am I! That's it, isn't it?"

Max inclined his head with surly agreement. "I thought you might have some ideas."

"Oh, but I do. I do." Sir Stephen was transported. "I shall explore them." He clasped his hands with an attitude of devotion. "I do sometimes envy your single purpose mind. Nothing seems to divert you. Girls. Drink. Little fat boys. Before your eyes is always the golden sovereign. What a contented man you are with never a principle to nag at a wayward conscience. By the way, have you driven that son-in-law of yours to the wall yet?"

Max smiled for the first time. "No. But he's getting close. I'm costing him a lot of money. Now"—he was impatient— "let's get back to Grand Bahama."

"Oh, I am certain we can resolve things. I will give it my full attention." He reached across to pat Max's hand. "As you know I do so like to be paid while I am thinking. In this case my fee will be twenty percent interest in what I recover for you."

"That will run into a hell of a lot of money."

Sir Stephen belched happily and gazed raptly out of the window.

"All right." Max gave in. "I'll have the papers drawn up."

"Do that, dear boy, and then we shall compare them with the ones I shall have my clerk prepare. No doubt they will coincide." He allowed the fingers of one hand to dance across the table's edge in a silent arpeggio. "Has it ever occurred to you, my dear Max, that you are constantly adding to the number of persons who would be delighted to have you dead?"

"I can take care of myself." He was unimpressed.

"I sincerely hope so, dear boy. I find you a most agreeable companion. We understand each other. You dislike me for what I am and what I cost you, and I see through you quite clearly. We do complement each other. Just the same. I must remind you that murder might not be too far away from the minds of many persons. You are putting together quite an impressive list of enemies."

They finished luncheon on this note. The result of Sir Stephen Simon's thinking brought screams of outrage and muttered threats of violence from the investors in the International Center. Their franchises were abrogated through the legal manipulations of Sir Stephen. It was held that they violated Bahamian law by employing non-Bahamian shopkeepers and personnel. Also, they were importing their merchandise direct from the countries of their origin, instead of dealing with a commission agent in Nassau. Since the cartel held no lease on the land but only a franchise to operate, they were quickly squeezed out. Max then negotiated new franchises with some of the most powerful Bay Street merchandising interests. In these Max held a substantial interest for himself. It was a financial coup of truly magnificent conception. He was immensely pleased.

There was only one outspoken critic in Nassau of Maximilian Hertog: Pierre DuPres' newspaper. DuPres was now following Max's maneuvers with an amused interest. Never had such a pirate walked on the island shores. He said this and other things in the columns of his paper, but the stories were written without acid comment. What DuPres wrote in effect was: "This Maximilian Hertog is a highly diverting fellow. The question is: Can we afford him?" Nothing Max did escaped the paper's attenton.

"What the hell is DuPres trying to do to me?" Max growled the question to Carol in the office.

"I don't know." She concealed a smile. "Do you want me to ask him?"

He grunted and looked up sharply. "I didn't know you saw him."

"Oh, he calls and takes me to dinner now and then when you are away. I think he regards me as some sort of occasional widow. My illicit relationship with you invests me with a certain glamor or possible availability. Old gentlemen, in particular, eye me moistly and with feeble longing."

He stared at her for a moment and then grinned. "You're pretty fresh for a hired hand." He hesitated and actually seemed embarrassed. "You and I are getting married in the spring and going to Europe."

She nodded without enthusiasm. "Remind me when spring is here. 'Light again. Life again. Leaf again. Love again. Oh! My wild, little poet.' Something like that. Keats. Shelley. Byron." She made a dancing twirl which carried her to the door. There she dropped in a deep and graceful curtsy and left him staring after her.

He reached for a cigar and scowled. He was always suspi-

352

cious of amiable women. They usually had just sharpened a knife. Was Carol getting mixed up with that fellow DuPres? And, damn him, he was becoming a nuisance. All this unwelcome publicity. He wondered if he could be bought off. He would look into the paper's financial condition. With some pressure it might be closed down. Everything he did now seemed to fall under DuPres' sarcastic eye. The paper was beginning to devote itself almost entirely to the activities of Maximilian Hertog.

He chewed angrily on the cigar and spat the shreds onto the carpet. Earlier in the week the Assembly had quietly passed a bill authorizing a Certificate of Exemption for gambling on Grand Bahama. Ordinarily this would have attracted little attention or comment since it was generally understood that a casino was to be part of the Grand Bahama development. The certificate had been granted to the Aunt Martha Candy Company. It was this which intrigued Pierre DuPres. He made some inquiries, put out some feelers, and came up with the information that Max Hertog was Aunt Martha. He printed this without editorial comment, but the ironic touch was in every line. The little old lady, Aunt Martha, padding about in her tennis shoes and making pans of fudge was no other than Maximilian Hertog. All Nassau laughed, and Max found the sound unpleasant.

On an impulse now he reached for the telephone and had the switchboard put in a call for DuPres.

"This is Max Hertog."

"Yes, Mr. Hertog." DuPres' voice carried surprise. "What can I do for you?"

"Nothing. I'm going to the toilet now. I thought you would like to know." He clicked down the receiver before DuPres could reply.

He began to smile and actually hummed an off-key tune. It had been a damn silly thing to do, but just the same it made him feel better.

In an office, part of a large suite, high above the street level and overlooking the shimmering expanse of Biscayne Bay,

353

Charles Rich sat at a desk facing the broad windows. It was a pleasant room, done in the subdued tones of gray with deep chairs of soft leather. The furnishings reflected both taste and money.

At his hand was a stack of newspaper clippings. They were prepared for him daily out of all the important newspapers in the United States, delivered by a clipping service messenger and then sorted by a secretary and two assistants. They were required reading, for the organization had a wide variety of interests. Shipping and trucking lines. Automatic laundries. Many of the trade unions. Real estate. Theaters. Airlines. Loan offices. Country clubs. Office buildings. Gambling. Narcotics. Prostitution. There was little within the field of human endeavor which was considered outside the Syndicate's spheres of influence and investment.

Rich read again through a clipping from the Nassau *Sentinel,* and a perplexed frown drew small furrows across his brow. It was DuPres' report of a granting of a Certificate of Exemption for the operation of a gambling casino on Grand Bahama to the Aunt Martha Candy Company, and Aunt Martha was Maximilian Hertog. It had been well understood by all concerned that a gambling permit would be forthcoming and that it would be issued to the Lucayan Beach Club. This, now, was quite obviously not the case. Max Hertog held it.

Long ago Rich had accepted the fact that Max's Oriental monstrosity had been designed and built as a casino for gambling. He had not been particularly disturbed by this. When the time came for opening of a second casino on Grand Bahama, Max and Rich's organization would come to mutually agreeable terms. It was unthinkable that Hertog would attempt to move into the field alone. He simply could not be that innocent. He must know he was not dealing with a group of timid businessmen who would pull out of the operation on Grand Bahama, rather than engage in the rough-and-tumble of a conflict of interests. Yet here it was, and the sheer effrontery of Hertog's move evoked a certain wry admiration from Charles Rich. Did Max really believe he would stand to one side, wringing his hands, while this brazen double cross was attempted? Rich was disturbed because he honestly liked and, in a way, admired Max Hertog. They both had the same direct approach to a problem and a complete disregard for the obstacles in their way. Both were ruthless, but Max had no conception of the truly global power of the organization he was preparing to defy. The elimination of Maximilian Hertog, if such a move seemed desirable and necessary, would be handled with such swift efficiency that Max would never have the time to know what was happening. Rich understood Max did not believe this. Within his sphere he was so important that it was inconceivable to him that he could be erased from the scene without causing international reverberations.

Rich pushed the clippings aside, lit a cigarette, and turned in his chair to stare out the window at the all but unbelievable spectacle of Miami Beach. It seemed impossible that less than fifty years ago that golden shore with its towering hotels was a snake-infested mangrove tangle that even the mainland natives shunned. With Grand Bahama, Max Hertog was performing a similar miracle. Why the hell couldn't he be satisfied with what he had? Rich discovered he was becoming irritated by Max's foolhardy disregard of all consequences. He reached for the telephone, changed his mind, and touched a button on the desk. When his secretary entered, he told her to call the airport and have the plane ready to take him to Nassau. The best chance of resolving the situation was a frank talk with Hertog. It was no time for vague threats. They would only anger the man. He was not easily intimidated, but Rich was determined he must listen to reason.

Big Maum surveyed her kitchen with a critical eye. On the surface, at least, everything was in order. Stella and the other two girls waited at one side of the room in an apprehensive knot. Relief flooded their faces when Big Maum gave a short grunt of approval. She had been away for just a day or so short of a month and had expected to find chaos.

"T'ings better dan I expec'. Set me some coffee en th' table, Stella. I eats later." She walked to the windows overlooking the backyard. The parrot, Sir Rupert, hung upside down from a vine. "Dat Sir Rupert glad t' be home. He don' like dem Out Islan'." Her eyes clouded with the memory of Little Exuma.

The day they left, the boy, Major, had placed a chair aft for her. She sat there, staring back as *The Witch* ran up the long string of cays. When Little Exuma was no longer more than a smudged penciling on the sea's chart, her head dropped slightly, and her lips moved in a silent prayer. All her deep love, her pride, bright hopes and faith were buried back there with her boy. Now she was just a big old woman, and what happened to her was unimportant. Within her were the terrible ache and a black anger. She wanted to strike out at them, at all whites and particularly Mistuh Max. She was certain nothing happened in these islands without his permission. If Royal had died with a knife in him, it was because Mistuh Max had let it be so. The white men had killed Royal. The blacks of the islands knew this, and they whispered among themselves. It was the old story. When a white and a black man met on a narrow path, the black must stand aside.

"Coffee ready, Big Maum," Stella called to her.

Big Maum nodded and took her place at the table. Her fingers, by long habit, touched at the shell of transparent porcelain with a caressing pride. She reached in her apron for one of the long dark cigars, and Stella quickly held a match.

"Yo' have no trouble wid me gone?"

"No'm, Big Maum. Mistuh Max he away mos' o' th' time. Miss Jan stay heah an' her husban' come over twice. Dey don' have no special party o' nothin'."

The door between the serving pantry and the kitchen swung open, and Jan came in. She wore pajamas and a robe and shook her head when Big Maum started to rise.

"No. Stay where you are. I saw *The Witch* and knew you were home."

"Yes'm. Spindle brung us en las' night. Yo' have some breakfas', Miss Jan?"

"No. Just coffee." She dug into her robe's pocket for cigarettes and a lighter. "You're all right?"

"Yes'm."

356

"I'm glad you're back. Now I can go home. I thought some-one ought to be here, but Stella and the others are good girls." She smiled at them. "Just the same everyone missed you."

Big Maum stared at her coffee. She wanted to hate all whites. After what happened to Royal, she sometimes just wanted to go crazy, to yell and pound her big fists into their sick white faces. Yet there was no hatred in her heart for this girl.

"Mimsey"—Jan put down her cup—"you come up and put a few things in a bag for me. I'll go back this morning." She halted abruptly, and her expression was one of astonished amazement. Her eyes grew wide, and for a moment, her lips were compressed into a tight line. "No." The word was half-gasped. "I think I'll just go to the hospital and have my baby instead."

Big Maum rose from her chair. Gently she put a heavy arm about Jan's waist, supporting her easily.

"If dat's what yo're goin' t' do"—she spoke soothingly—"we go upstair now an' call th' doctor. Don' worry. I take care o' yo'."

XXIII

A heavy fog swirled out of the northeast and over Lyford Cay, wrapping Windmere in a soggy blanket of dirty gray, and the water dripped with a steady monotony from branch and eave onto the sodden ground.

In Windmere's kitchen the lights were bright and warm, and the room was filled with the teasing scent of hot bread, coffee, fried ham, beans and rice. The men and three girls at the long table bent their heads over steaming mugs, turning to glance or smile sideways at one another when they spoke. Their talk and laughter had a new sound of freedom. The accents were rich and fell pleasantly on the ear, and the people were without constraint or self-consciousness. Now the men lit their cigarettes and cigar stubs with an exaggerated casualness which betrayed their unfamiliarity with this new privilege. A couple of the men involuntarily glanced cautiously in Big Maum's direction as though fearful of her disposition. She stood near the windows, peering out into the murk. Her shoulders were squared, and her back was straight as though she braced herself against this desecration of her kitchen, the breakdown of order as she had maintained it here through the years. She pretended to be unaware of the sudden laughter, the sly jokes and innuendos which had laced the morning's meal. She resented the familiarity which was tinged with insolence for the man who owned this house and whose wages they took. In her heart there was hatred. In their empty conchie heads, she thought, there was a furtive contempt which would quickly dissolve into a meek submission in Maximilian Hertog's presence. They were bold here because she permitted them to be free with their talk and behavior. Everything she had held to be inviolate—the dignity of her position, the discipline of the household, the stout loyalty she had once given this house and its master—was crumbling into ruin. Intentionally and with a brooding anger she had allowed this to happen. She wanted to pull Windmere down on them all. She only half listened now to the gossip in which Stella and the other two girls were joined and thought how quickly they had scented out and taken advantage of this loosening of authority. In her presence they were respectful, but their attitude toward their duties had changed. Once they had been proud of their places. To work and live at Windmere set them apart from most house servants. They walked with heads lifted. Now they frequently appeared with a soiled apron, where once they would have changed quickly at the appearance of a spot. Their hair was often untidy and their manner slovenly, their carriage a slouching step. Once they realized these lapses of conduct did not bring Big Maum's wrath and quick punishment down on them, they experimented and discovered the big black woman no longer seemed to care. The knowledge that they were somehow safe in this open defiance of all regulation excited them to further experiment. They stole small things now from the rooms. A cigarette lighter. A silver ashtray. Stockings from Jan's wardrobe, which she still maintained. Food. Tobacco. An occasional bottle or half bottle of whiskey. These things were small and would hardly be missed. The girls took them spitefully and with a senseless cupidity.

On the second day after her return from Little Exuma, Big Maum, as usual, allowed the outside men, along with Spindle and Major, to come to the kitchen for their breakfast. At the meal's conclusion and while they all were finishing the coffee, she had astonished them.

"Yo' mons smoke ef yo' wan's t'." She had turned abruptly away as though angry at herself.

359

There was complete, stunned silence for a moment. Those at the table glanced at one another, wondering if this was a joke or some sort of trap aimed at their expulsion from the house.

"Yo' mean dat, Big Maum?" One asked the question for all.

"Suits yo'se'f. It don' mean no matter t' me." She refused to discuss or explain.

Cautiously, puzzled by what was happening, they lit their tobacco and drew on it. But on this first morning they were uncomfortable with the novel privilege and did not linger over their coffee. With the succeeding days they quickly fitted themselves into this new order. Big Maum watched with a tight scorn how, with one breach of an established code of behavior, they began to abandon all pretense of courtesy. Once they had come to her kitchen with shy smiles of appreciation. Hats in hands, they had ducked their heads in her direction and murmured their "A good-mornin' t' yo', Big Maum." They had taken their places at the table with the bright, polished look of children at a party. Now, confident in this new license, they drifted in carelessly, tossing a curt "Big Maum" her way. They hauled their chairs out with an unnecessary clatter, slouched in them, and directed leering, intimate jokes to the girls, who giggled and preened themselves.

Against these familiarities Big Maum turned her back. She would not permit anyone to see the angry shame consuming her. The collapse of all decency, of courtesy and pride here in her kitchen and house stabbed at her heart. They were dirtying her place, and she encouraged them.

On this morning with the fog heavy but beginning to lift, they left the table reluctantly and shuffled outside. One or two remembered to say, "T'ank yo', Big Maum." The others mumbled indistinctly. She kept her back to them and did not reply. When the men were gone, she took her place at the table's head and did not rebuke Stella when it was carelessly set with loosely arranged silver and an improperly ironed napkin. The girls knew this and waited for Big Maum's voice of outrage. Always they kept testing to see how far they could go.

Big Maum ignored the setting, and by her silence she almost seemed to give her approval to what was happening. She watched indifferently as Stella poured her coffee and slopped some of it into the saucer. The girl hesitated, was about to get a clean cup and saucer, then changed her mind. Big Maum said nothing. Calmly she lit one of her cigars. Stella smirked and tossed a hip defiantly as she moved away. The other girls smothered their giggles.

The room indicator on the wall rasped with its sharp, commanding whir, and the small plaque indicated Maximilian Hertog's rooms. Ordinarily his tray would have been ready, and one of the girls would have hurried upstairs with it, for he did not like to be kept waiting for his morning coffee. Now Stella indolently began to set a tray, but Big Maum surprised her. She crossed the room and detached one of the wires from its terminal, silencing the alarm. Then she returned to her chair and sat smoking thoughtfully. The girls stared at her and then at one another. Now they were truly puzzled and a little frightened. They waited apprehensively. The wall clock's hands moved silently, covering five, ten and, finally, fifteen minutes. When the door was slammed open with a force that almost tore it from the hinges, the girls, in a huddled knot, yelped in fear.

Max, in pajamas and with the untied cords of his robe trailing, planted himself in the doorway. His bristly reddish hair was on end, and he had the appearance of an infuriated cockatoo. He glared at the girls and then at Big Maum, who rose from her place with a deliberate slowness.

"What the hell is going on down here?" Max shouted at them all. "I've been ringing my bell for half an hour. Why the goddamned hell doesn't someone answer it and bring my coffee?"

Big Maum was astonished. "Ain' no soun' from th' bell, Mistuh Max." She was concerned, puzzled.

"I tell you I've been ringing it. There's something going on around here. I can feel it. What the hell's the matter with all of you?"

"Ain' no bell ring, Mistuh Max." Big Maum repeated the statement with a maddening complacency.

Max glared at her and then strode across the room. He snatched at the loose wire and then shook it accusingly.

"No wonder it doesn't ring. How did this come off?"

Big Maum shrugged. "Mus' shook off, Mistuh Max. Or maybe it got rubbed off when th' girl clean dere."

"How the hell could it shake off?" The roar thundered. "Well, maybe," he conceded, unable to believe there was any open defiance, "it could have been pulled off." He turned to Stella. "Get me some coffee, whatever the hell your name is." His glance fell on the table with its soiled dishes for a dozen or more persons. He stabbed a finger in their direction and spoke to Big Maum. "Who the hell do you feed here in the morning: every goddamned nigger on Lyford Cay?"

Big Maum's expression did not change. "Jus' th' house an' yard people, like always, Mistuh Max."

"By God, they must be bringing their relatives. I don't have that many niggers working for me." He whirled about and slammed the door behind him.

There was complete silence for a moment, and then the girls sniggered.

"Whooee!" Stella shook her head admiringly. "I never see him so mad before."

Big Maum went back to her place at the table and put her cigar to one side in a tray. Mimsey brought her a slice of fried ham, hot bread, rice and red beans. She slid the plate in front of Big Maum, instead of placing it there. As she was about to turn away, Big Maum's fingers closed about her wrist with a crushing force that went deep and painfully into the bone. Mimsey half screamed and twisted her body in agony.

Big Maum stared coldly at the girl. "I give yo' all a lot o' leave because I gots t'ings on my mind. But lemme tell yo'. If yo' be lax wid me dis way, if yo' git smart, an' I mean all o' yo', den I split me some heads en dis kitchen. Now you take dis away." With her free hand she swept the dishes to the floor. "An' bring me my own china, my silver, my linen like always. An' yo' set dis place like you bin taught an' yo' say, 'Yes'm, Big Maum,' an' 'No'm, Big Maum,' an' yo' mek th' curtsy t' me o' I goin' t' beat th' livin' hell out o' all yo' three. Un'erstan'?"

"Yes'm, Big Maum." Mimsey's face was twisted with the pain. "Yo' breakin' my wris'. Please, Big Maum, lemme go. I didn' mean nothin'. I jus' forgot."

Big Maum released her hold and gave a shove which sent the girl sprawling. From the floor she stared up at the woman with wide-eyed terror.

"Yo' ain' forgot." Big Maum was not to be placated. "Yo' keep inchin' an' inchin' t' see how far I let yo' go. Now yo' know an' yo' keep it en min'. Aroun' me remembuh yo' manner o' I beat yo' t' death right en dis room. Now bring me my t'ings like dey should be an' some fresh coffee."

All three girls jumped at the command, frightened and confused by her unexpected outburst of fury. Lately she hadn't seemed to mind how things were done, and everyone was careless and impudently indifferent. They were unable to understand she was destroying Windmere and Maximilian Hertog in her mind. To further this wish, she permitted house and yard servants unheard-of liberties. Let them foul the place and make it stink of decay. But—and this the girls hadn't understood—here in the kitchen they would serve her with the same respect and courtesy as before.

Max had his coffee and the day's first cigar on the balcony. The sun burned away the early fog, and the wind was fresh and steady now out of the south, sweeping up through the Exuma Cays. He smoked thoughtfully and stared at the tripod-shaped light tower on Goulding Cay without really seeing it. He was deeply troubled. Something was happening, not only here, in the house, but outside it as well. Slowly he was being ringed by confusion. Instinct, intuition warned him of this, and they had always served him well. He was being quietly but relentlessly tracked by a disaster which refused to assume a shape. Angrily, impatiently, he reached out for it, and his fingers closed on nothing. He grunted. This was a witch woman's thinking, nigger talk of the white-eyed, pink-skinned duppies who plagued a man and stole away his strength at night. A man couldn't fight the duppies. When

363

they came, he might as well give up. Well, by God, he wasn't afraid of the duppies whatever and wherever they were.

He grinned a little at the notion of Maximilian Hertog chasing little, naked pink men. The idea cheered him momentarily. He would find out what was going on outside and, maybe, kick a few asses here in the house. Where to start? The black humor returned to envelop him. A man couldn't fight what he was unable to see. This was a thing of mood, not of substance. He could almost swear that this business with the kitchen this morning had somehow been planned. But why? Who in the goddamned hell would want to do something like that?

He refilled his cup with the hot coffee. If he had been a superstitious man, he would have said things had begun to go wrong with Royal Keating's death. He winced inwardly, pulling away from the word "murder." Yet it was there, and he had been a willing party to the deed. Willing, hell! He had paid fifty thousand dollars to have it done. There was no escaping this. From that moment, almost, things began to go wrong. At least he felt they were out of joint. The talk of a white conspiracy against Royal Keating and the PLP had grown bolder, and for one of the few times in his life he was uneasy.

Also—and this was a part of the syndrome—there was the matter of a Certificate of Exemption for Grand Bahama. In the ordinary run of things it should have been granted quietly and the necessary legislative approval passed unnoticed. Instead, DuPres sniffed around and came up with Aunt Martha. Why, he had asked editorially, why not Maximilian Hertog or the Syndicate? Why the subterfuge? What was being concealed?

Charles Rich also wanted an answer. He did not call for an appointment. He simply appeared on Bay Street, walked past the page boy, the receptionist and Carol. Strode into Max's private office and closed the door with authority. There had been no preliminary sparring, no exchange of meaningless amenities. Rich was as direct as Max Hertog.

"What are you up to with this Aunt Martha Candy Company and the gambling permit?"

364

Max's first inclination had been to roar his disapproval of this intrusion. Then he decided Charles Rich wouldn't be impressed by theatrics. His rudeness had been deliberate. It was what Max Hertog would have done. They understood each other fairly well by now.

"Sit down, Charley." The invitation was a sarcasm since Rich was already seated. "Cigar? A drink?"

"No. Just an explanation, Max."

Hertog was too crafty to attempt an evasion with someone he considered equally shrewd. He took an unnecessarily long time, opening his cigar and lighting it. This usually disturbed an adversary. Rich ignored the elaborate byplay.

"Well"—Max was being patient—"I didn't want it issued in my name. The Aunt Martha Candy Company is a holding device. I use it for a lot of things."

"That's not good enough, and you know it." Rich shook off the too-pat explanation. "The certificate should have been issued to the Lucayan Beach Club. Not to you. Not to me. Not to Aunt Martha or anyone else. It is permission for the Lucayan Beach Club to operate a gambling room or rooms on Grand Bahama. That was our original and, of necessity, oral agreement. In return for this, we have invested something more than fifty million dollars in Freeport and Grand Bahama. I'm not saying it isn't a good investment. It is. But we did not go into Grand Bahama for the purpose of developing it. Our interest is the gambling concession, and you know it." Not by the fraction of a decibel did the voice raise or did Charles Rich betray an anger.

"Oh"—Max was tossing it off—"things change, Charley. You can't always blueprint a project of this size. It has to be kept fluid. What is decided one day may not be practical the next." He smiled at Rich with an engaging, ingenuous air.

"I'm not interested in your semantics, Max. Neither am I impressed by your Little Boy Blue act of innocence. In simple words I can understand, tell me what you and Aunt Martha propose to do with the gambling permit?"

"Oh, that?" Max was genial. "I'm going to open the Oriental Casino on Grand Bahama. You know—the place they call the house of the golden tits. We'll work out a small percentage for your people. Later I'll find a way you can operate the Lucayan Beach Club. I just don't want to press too fast for another certificate. It will take a little time."

"The Lucayan Beach Club will open on schedule as advertised, Max." Rich was precise. "The Aunt Martha Candy Company will sign over its certificate of permission for gambling to the Lucayan Beach Club, and it will do that without delay." Each word was as cold and hard as a diamond point.

"I don't see how that's possible, Charley." Max was regretful. "I have already made my plans for the Oriental Casino. Wait until you see it." He expected Rich to share his enthusiasm. "I'm going to have harem girls behind the bar. Belly dancers as cocktail waitresses. Camels and camel drivers. Foreign Legionnaires as doormen and security guards. Sheiks for stickmen at the dice tables." He recited these things for Rich's approval.

Rich lit a cigarette. Over it he stared incredulously at Hertog and then shook his head.

"I don't believe it, Max. I just don't believe any of this." Thoughtfully he tapped a knuckle against his teeth. "Don't you really know what you are doing? Have you no idea of the organization you are planning to try and freeze out of a deal made in good faith?"

"Oh, you hear things, of course." Max tossed it off airily.

"Max"—Rich was earnestly trying to reach him—"I'm not talking about an old movie on television. Rat-tat-tat-tat-tat goes a machine gun, and everyone falls dead. I am speaking of a worldwide syndicate with assets in the billions. It is stronger, wealthier and more powerful than any corporation you can name and, for that matter, most governments. Its investment on Grand Bahama can be written off today without causing a ripple in the financial structure. What can't be erased, Max, is your commitment, your word, our agreement. These things become a matter of principle. Our record of defending this is one hundred percent. We do not permit anyone to renege or default. And that applies to a bagman in Harlem or Maximilian Hertog on Grand Bahama."

366

"Come on, Charley." Max was close to being patroniz- ing. "You don't really think I scare, do you?"

Slowly, carefully, Charles Rich stubbed his cigarette out in a standing tray at his chair. He watched the coals glow brightly and then turn black. He looked up again at Max Hertog.

"Max"—he was actually pleading—"let's stop playing with words. Hear me while I say one, small, simple thing?"

"Sure, Charley." Max was friendly, agreeable.

"All right." Rich nodded toward the telephone on the desk. "If I pick up that telephone and put a call in to Miami or any of a dozen other cities, you . . . are . . . dead." The last three words were evenly spaced. "It is no more involved than that. It is as certain as two and two are four. And, Max, if the Lucayan Beach Club doesn't get its gambling permit on time, that is exactly what is going to happen."

Hertog's features hardened, and his shoulders hunched bel- ligerently as he leaned forward on the desk. Eye to eye, neither he nor Charles Rich blinked.

"I don't like threats, Charley. I don't pay any attention to them. If I could be scared off something, I would still be a pick-and-shovel day laborer. I don't spook worth a damn."

Charles Rich nodded and rose a little wearily. He had done his best to make this stubborn man understand. "Think it over for a few days. Be sure you know what you're doing. Take your time. There will be no pressure unless you turn the handle first." He had nodded in a friendly manner and left the Hertog offices on that note.

Musing here on the balcony now, Max began adding up the score and discovered it had become a little lopsided. Things, large and small, were happening. Or actually, he was permit- ting them to happen. This was contrary to all his experience, his philosophy. You moved the chessmen. They didn't move you. Then—and the memory of this galled him more than anything which had occurred or was occurring—there was the incident with Sherry Melnick at the Coral Harbour Club ear- lier in the week. *Only a Jew,* he thought savagely, *would have so little regard for common decency as to precipitate a public scene.*

He had been at the club's bar having a preluncheon drink with Walter Mase and Tom Barron. Both men wanted to buy in on some Grand Bahama property. Someone shoved roughly in beside him, and he had turned quickly to find Melnick there.

"I want you off my back, Max." The voice was deliberately raised to carry throughout the room. "You've had your blood. Be satisfied with that. Because if you aren't, if you keep pushing me, I'll kill you."

It had been, of course, nothing more than an idle threat and made for no other purpose than to create an embarrassing scene. There had been complete silence as Melnick walked away.

"Well"—Max fought the rage within him and tried to keep his tone normal—"if you find me dead some morning, you'll know who to look for. The gentleman, in case you don't know him, is my son-in-law."

Thinking of Melnick, he was forced to admit failure or, at least, an empty triumph. He had hurt him, of course, in places where Melnick Enterprises was vulnerable. He had been forced to make hasty adjustments in his financing, expansion and credit. But he was certainly far from any real disaster. The truth was that Melnick had proved to be both smart and elastic. He bounced when he should have played dead. When he was really pressed and needed fast help, he had been able to get it from several sources beyond the reach of Maximilian Hertog. He was shrewd and a skillful operator. Under other conditions Max would have jumped at the chance to hire him at almost any figure Melnick cared to name. He had the cold nerve of a professional gambler, of a Maximilian Hertog. After the first wave of anger had swept past, there had been no real pleasure of trying to wreck Melnick Enterprises. Actually, it had taken more time than the game merited. Even if he had succeeded in breaking him completely, one ironic fact remained. All the fellow had to do was wait. Sooner or later Jan would inherit the vast and complex Hertog fortune. Much of this would pass through her husband's hands.

Jan dropped in at Windmere only occasionally now. There

had been no open rupture in their relationship. With rare common sense she had refused to side with either Sherry or her father and was outspoken in her opinion that they both were behaving like a couple of spoiled and petulant brats. Melnick, Max knew, had an interest in a development on Governor's Harbour. He and Jan were dividing their time between Nassau and Miami. They had rented a house in the Cable Beach district, and when she was in the islands, Jan frequently called or drove out to Windmere. Often they had lunch together, and something of the old warmth and understanding they had always shared was rekindled. Max had yet to see his grandson, and on this point Jan was adamant.

"If you want to see him, then you'll have to forget your quarrel with Sherry and come to our place. David is a fine, strong boy, who appears not to resemble you in the slightest." An engaging grin robbed the words of any bite. "So why don't you forget your grudge, your prejudices? Come to the house and play Dranpa; coo and make funny faces. David will be delighted with you. He is too young to recognize a real mean old bastard." She was sitting on the edge of his chair and with a sudden gesture of affection pulled his head close to her side and held it there for a moment. "Why do you work at it so hard, being a bastard, I mean?"

He arose and stretched and for a moment thought about taking a swim before breakfast. But he had no real interest in going down to the beach alone. Too many memories walked with him there. If he wasn't so stubborn and stiff-necked, he'd make the first gesture to Melnick. Well, maybe. He'd think about it.

Carol put aside the pen. Resting elbows on the small desk in a corner of her room, she stared out of the windows, past the plumed fans of the tall palms to the sharp brilliance of Nassau's harbor. A Swedish cruiseship lay just off the channel. Her passengers had been discharged earlier and were now trooping up and down Bay Street in an eager confusion of purpose.

She picked up the letter, and there was a shadow of unhappiness in her eyes. It had been difficult to write; almost impossible to put into words what she knew must be said. She had made several false starts. "Max, dear. Dear Max." Finally she had settled for "Max."

This is a sort of Dear John letter. Also, in its way, it is something of a love letter. I am not sure how it should be written. What is there to say at the end of a love affair where love was never mentioned? I'm not certain what we had. Affection. Respect. Those things certainly. I refuse to think of it as simply an office affair. The boss and the eager secretary. There was more to it than that. At least I hope so. Whatever it was, though, seems to have been lost somewhere along the way. Maybe we were both careless with it. If not lost, then it has, as someone once said, "ripened into apathy." I am saying good-bye, so long, this way because I am a coward, but there is no bitterness in me, as there is no real room in your heart for a woman. This is something I always knew but refused to admit. So, dear, darling Max, I go. To Miami this morning and then, maybe, to Spain and Italy. I have more than enough money saved to keep me well for a year or more. I am certain that will be your first thought upon reading this. (I guess there is a little bitch in me, after all, or I wouldn't have written that.) Anyhow, I am certain you will understand why I am leaving and, after the first shock to your ego, even be a little grateful to—

CAROL

Slowly, carefully, she folded the letter, sealed it, and wrote the address. Then, with a tight fierceness, she spoke aloud.

"Damn it. I will not cry over you."

As she knew she would, she dropped her face to arms folded on the desk and wept quietly, and her tears stained one corner of the envelope.

XXIV

In the sandy churchyard, spotted with wind-twisted pines, scraggly oleanders and clumps of pink and white phlox, the boy Major waited proudly beside the polished station wagon. The chords of the final hymn rolled from the white frame building in a soaring wave.

Sunday was something special for Major. During the week he worked with Spindle around *The Witch,* the speedboat and the boathouse. On Sunday, though, he was allowed to drive Big Maum and two of the girls to the church in Adelaide. He slipped out from a last-row seat in the congregation a few minutes before services were closed. This permitted him to be seen by all as he held the car's door open for Big Maum and bowed her in with a fine flourish, chauffeur's cap in hand. She always sat in the front with him. The girls took one of the rear seats. This morning the big woman was a figure of eye-compelling dignity. A purple bandanna was wound in a high swirl about her head. Large gold loops were in her ears. Her dress of bright yellow fell to a scant inch above the ground. As a concession to the solemnity of the day, she wore sandals. The bell on her ankle tinkled as musically as always. As she crossed the yard with a free stride, Stella and Mimsey were all but forced to trot to keep their places at her side. They were in their best dresses of flowered print and held prayer books in hands covered with white cotton gloves.

The routine on Sunday morning varied only with the girls

who attended with Big Maum. One always had to remain behind at Windmere to answer Max's early ring for coffee. This morning it had been Dora's turn to stay at home. She had been sulky about it, muttering under her breath until Big Maum had cracked her smartly across an ear with her hand.

"Yo' take yo' turn like th' res'."

The trips to and from Adelaide were special events. Big Maum knew this. Church was a time for singing, gossip and small flirtations with the boys before the services started. The girl who was on duty in the kitchen frequently had no bell to answer. Max sometimes slept late. Often he wasn't at home at all over the weekend. None of the servants dared intrude into his quarters to see if he slept. So often the girl only sat in the big kitchen, listening to the radio, waiting for his summons, feeling abused and lonely in the big silent house.

Now, from her place beside Major, Big Maum bowed with a stately majesty to casual acquaintances as they passed. To those on a more intimate footing, she would speak a few words of greeting or inquiry, inclining her head with a grave smile to the child of a friend. When Major drove slowly from the yard, most heads turned to follow the Windmere servants. They were the only ones who came to church in an automobile. Big Maum and the others knew this, and their postures were ramrod-stiff with pride. Once out of sight, the girls relaxed, lolling on the seat, chewing a stick of gum, giggling and whispering together. Big Maum was tolerant of their youth, even though Sunday was a solemn day to be observed with quiet reverence. Once in a while she relaxed and told Major to take a roundabout way on the way back to Windmere.

This morning she was unusually silent and sat staring straight ahead with unbending concentration. Major, conscious of his temporary position as chauffeur, took the liberty of lighting a cigarette, watching Big Maum out of the corner of his eye. He was a man with responsibilities on this day and showed it in the way he drove with one hand while using the dashboard lighter with the other. The woman pretended not to see, but the smallest of smiles quirked about the corners of her mouth.

"Yo' a good mon, Major. A good driver, too." This was the accolade and her permission for him to smoke.

They skirted Lake Killarney and the airport to pick up the road to Lyford Cay. Sherry Melnick, in Jan's Triumph roadster, fell in behind the station wagon and followed it through the Windmere gates. Jan had asked him to drive out and get a couple of sweaters she had kept with other clothing at the house. She had done this, not because she had any real need for them, but with the hope Sherry and Max might meet casually. Alone and without the necessity of striking an attitude, they just might come to a plane of understanding. She had the feeling neither of them still harbored any real animosity and needed only the opportunity to effect a degree of tolerance on both sides. She didn't believe her father and husband could ever become close friends, but they could at least learn to acknowledge each other's presence without a baring of teeth.

"Good morning." Sherry included them all in his greeting but added, "Big Maum," singling her out.

"Mistuh Nick." Big Maum had never mastered Melnick. If she thought about it at all, it was as two names, Mel and Nick, both of which sounded ridiculous to her ears. "Good mornin' t' yo'."

They walked toward the kitchen door at the rear of the house. Major and the girls followed at a respectful distance.

"Mrs. Melnick wanted a tan and a blue sweater. She said they were in one of the bureau drawers. The girls would know where."

"I have Stella get 'em. Yo' like some breakfas' o' lunch, Mistuh Nick?"

"No, thanks. I could use a cup of coffee."

Big Maum preceded him into the brightly lighted kitchen. Dora stood up hastily as though caught in something shameful. She held a magazine behind her back.

"Mistuh Max ring yet?"

"No'm, Big Maum."

The woman nodded, turning to Sherry. "I have some fresh coffee en a min'it. Th' girl bring it t' yo' en th' dinin' room o' en th' terrace. Wheah yo' like."

373

"That's all right. I don't want to be any bother. I'll have it here."

Sherry was being friendly, informal. It didn't occur to him he was encroaching here, taking a liberty and much for granted. Persons ate in Big Maum's kitchen by invitation.

Big Maum half smiled. He was a nice enough man. "Like yo' wan', Mistuh Nick." She turned to Stella. "Miss Jan wan' two o' her sweater, if yo' girl ain' already stole 'em. A tan an' a blue." As Stella started to leave the room, Big Maum called, "Take a quiet peek an' see ef Mistuh Max asleep en his room, or maybe he don' come home las' night like sometime."

Sherry lit a cigarette and took a chair. Big Maum set the girls to setting a place for him, putting a kettle on, and measuring coffee for the drip pot.

The scream rose to a high, ear-piercing note and was sustained there by the terror behind it. The sound wailed and quavered, seeming to fill the house with frenzied echoes. It grew in volume, rising and falling in treble notes of wild hysteria, and the sound fixed everyone in the kitchen into a state of immobility. Then the door was slammed violently inward. Stella was framed on the threshold. Her eyes were bulbs of fear, and her mouth opened and closed with a gasping, sucking gargle of sound. She stared at Big Maum and tried to speak, only to have a mounting scream shut off the words.

Big Maum grasped Stella's arm roughly and slapped the palm of her hand across the girl's mouth. The girl did not struggle but pleaded silently as some of the horror drained away. Big Maum released her hold.

"Mistuh Max." The words were gasped. "He lyin' dead up dere, an' his head is all bloody."

With a twisting motion she wrenched herself free and raced for the back door, choking on her vomit. For a stunned moment, no one moved, and then, by common assent, they turned to Sherry and not to Big Maum.

"You'd better come with me." He spoke to the woman. "The rest of you stay here."

Up the sweeping staircase and down the long hall. Sherry was conscious of the bell on Big Maum's ankle as she followed.

374

The door to Max's sitting room was open, as were the French windows leading to the balcony. Sherry went through to the bedroom and halted.

Max was supine upon the bed, both arms outflung. One leg was drawn up at an angle. On his forehead there was a thick, black clot, and beneath it his skull had been crushed with the force of one, deadly blow. To Sherry's untrained eyes it seemed that Max had been struck by a club or an iron bar. He held an untrained finger on Max's wrist. He could feel no pulse, and the flesh had the chill of death upon it. He turned away and glanced at Big Maum.

She stood at the end of the bed, gazing down at the body of Maximilian Hertog. In her expression there was no horror, no sorrow or concern for the man. If she felt anything, her face did not betray it.

Sherry looked about the room. At the bedside a chair was drawn up in what seemed to be a confidential position. It was as though someone had sat there, talking intimately with Max. That, or the murderer had occupied the chair after the deed, waiting patiently to be quite certain Hertog was dead. There had been no fear of apprehension, no haste.

"I'd better call the police." Sherry's words came mechanically.

When he was connected with police headquarters, he said only that there had been a serious accident at Windmere. They had better send someone at once.

He lit a cigarette and noticed his hands were shaking. He looked at Big Maum. She had not moved. Her hands were clasped lightly. Her features betrayed nothing of what she felt. She stood erect, and with an unstudied confidence, looking down upon what remained of Max Hertog.

For the first time Sherry wondered about the murder weapon. Despite the horror on the bed he half smiled to himself and thought he was unconsciously making like a detective. There was no sign of a struggle. It would seem that someone had entered the room while Max was asleep and gone to the foot of the bed. Awakened, Max had sat up. His recognition of the intruder must have been his last conscious act. The blow had been struck. It had been heavy and coldly deliberate. Behind it there had been no murderous frenzy; no savage pleasure in repeated blows. This had been an act of retribution. As he walked slowly about the room, Sherry was aware that Big Maum's eyes were following him. Now that the shock of discovery was subsiding, he found he was gathering certain, obvious facts into focus. Any number of persons would be happy to have Max Hertog dead, but few, if any, would have risked murder. Whoever had killed him had been familiar with the house, and, perhaps, even with Hertog's habits. So. He stopped and whistled softly, turning to look at Big Maum. The woman had made no outcry nor uttered a single word of regret. It was unnatural, for all the blacks he had known became highly emotional in the presence of death. They cried, wept, sang and shouted at the bier and held chanting vigils. It was understandable that Big Maum would not have felt real sorrow. It had not been easy to like and almost impossible to love Max Hertog. But his death in this manner should have moved her to some expression. She met his gaze now with the same impassiveness with which she had looked upon the body.

He walked away, to the other side of the room. Without realizing it, he stared fixedly at a three-paneled ornamental screen. It was beautifully and delicately made. In bold strokes the artist had drawn long, pinioned storks flying across a sky of saffron-colored silk. It took him almost half a minute to realize he was no longer studying the screen. His attention was held by a smudge at one corner of the ivory frame. Even as he walked toward it for a closer examination, he was certain of what he would find.

The print was a rusty-black color now. It was that of a thumb, a large thumb, larger than his own, larger than that of the average-sized man. It was as large as the thumb on Big Maum's hand. Of this, now, he was positive. Maximilian Hertog had been one with those who had conspired to murder Royal Keating. For this he had paid with his life.

The thumb print had no significance to Big Maum. She watched with a mild curiosity as Sherry went to the bathroom,

376

wet a handkerchief at the tap, and came back to wash away the incriminating smudge.

Sherry spoke without turning to face her.

"You'd better go down to the kitchen and wait. I'll stay here until the police come."

He walked out on the balcony, and the tinkle of the ankle bell told him the woman was leaving. He lit another cigarette and drew upon it with a hungry nervousness. He was confused by what he had done. Why? What was Big Maum to him? Was he trying to protect her because he had disliked Max? No. It wasn't that simple. The motive lay deeper. Maybe it had something to do with justice. He found himself thinking of the big woman with compassion, and he was not by nature a compassionate man.

"Sah." The word caused him to turn.

The constable held his white helmet beneath one arm. He was a handsome man, as most of the Nassau police were, and stood at stiff attention in his white tunic and blue trousers with their red stripe. He waited as Sherry came in from the balcony.

"I am Constable Adamson, sah. Someone telephoned. An accident was reported."

Sherry indicated the bedroom doorway. "I made the call, Constable. Mr. Hertog is in there, murdered."

"I see." Constable Adamson did not lose his fine attitude of professional detachment. "In that case, sah, I think it would be better if I telephoned headquarters and spoke to the sergeant, who will undoubtedly want to communicate with the commissioner. This"—the faintest of smiles touched his darkly polished features—"this is hardly constabulary duty."

CORONER'S JURY RETURNS
VERDICT IN HERTOG MURDER
by
Pierre DuPres

A coroner's jury today returned a verdict of murder by person or persons unknown and so brought to conclusion the first phase in the mysterious slaying of Maximilian Hertog.

The questioning of witnesses was exhaustive, particularly

in the case of the servants at Windmere. Six Negro men and four Negro women are employed on the lavish estate in a permanent capacity. They occupy quarters some distance from the house. There is a dormitory for the men and a small cottage for the women. Other men who work on the grounds are brought in by the day and leave at about five o'clock in the afternoon. The principal witness or, at least, the one who occupied most of the jury's attention was a Mrs. Refa Keating, housekeeper and cook at Windmere, known as "Big Maum." She is also the mother of Mr. Royal Keating, the former resident engineer for Mr. Hertog on Grand Bahama, who was mysteriously slain several weeks ago. This tragedy is still on the books as unsolved. Mrs. Keating is a large, colorful and stately woman, slow of speech but with a sharp mind. She answered all questions freely. She told the jury that the doors at Windmere were rarely locked and any prowler would have easy access to the house. Robbery, incidental to the murder, was ruled out early in the investigation by Colonel Arthur Moberly, Commissioner of Police. Nothing in the house was taken or disturbed. The unidentified assailant was on the Windmere estate with only murder on his mind. It is understood the authorities have not ruled out the possibility that the crime was committed by a woman.

Mrs. Keating testified that Mr. Hertog had dinner served to him in his suite and that this was not unusual. A table tray with a conch salad, light turtle soup, broiled lamb chops and creamed potatoes was taken to him by one of the Windmere maids, a Miss Mimsey Taylor. Mr. Hertog called down to the kitchen a few minutes later and asked for two bottles of ale. An empty glass left on the suite's balcony contained a small amount of Scotch whisky. It is assumed that Mr. Hertog drank this and that he was alone since only one glass was found.

Mrs. Keating said that about 8:30 P.M. Mr. Hertog called the kitchen and that another maid, Stella Moates, went to the suite and brought back the tray and the remains of dinner. She subsequently testified that Mr. Hertog was in his pajamas at that time. Mrs. Keating then said she and the maids had their dinner. The kitchen was cleaned, and she and the three girls then left. This was their habit unless Mr. Hertog had guests or had one of the girls remain on duty.

Mrs. Keating then told the jury that she and two of the girls went to church in Adelaide, for the ten o'clock services

378

the following morning, leaving a Miss Dora Hunter at Windmere in the event Mr. Hertog wanted breakfast. This was also the normal routine. Upon returning from church, Mrs. Keating sent Miss Moates upstairs to see if Mr. Hertog was still asleep or if he had spent the night at Windmere. He was frequently away. It was the maid, Miss Moates, who discovered the body.

The medical examiner had already testified that Mr. Hertog died sometime after midnight and that he had been struck on the head by a heavy instrument, a hammer or, possibly, a crowbar. The murder weapon has not been discovered.

There was a small flurry of excitement in the courtroom when Mr. Sherry Melnick, Mr. Hertog's son-in-law, was called for testimony. It had been reported that Mr. Melnick had threatened to kill his father-in-law during an altercation in the Coral Harbour Club Bar. Mr. Melnick was almost immediately cleared of any suspicion when witnesses testified he and Mrs. Melnick had attended a party at the residence of Mr. and Mrs. Roland Hartwick. He and Mrs. Melnick did not leave the Hartwick residence until approximately 3:30 A.M. and went directly to their rented home in the Cable Beach area. Mr. Melnick dismissed his threat as an idle one, pointing out that if he had planned to kill Mr. Hertog, he certainly would not have made his intentions public.

The murder has created international excitement, and it is understood the Nassau authorities have requested assistance from the Miami Police Department's homicide bureau and detectives are expected to fly over tomorrow morning.

One person who might be expected to shed some light on possible suspects is Miss Carol Wainwright, Mr. Hertog's confidential secretary. Miss Wainwright, however, flew to Miami earlier in the week en route to Madrid. Authorities say that she telephoned Nassau from Spain but could add nothing to what was already known. It is most doubtful she would be asked to return.

Following the hearing, Mr. Hertog's daughter would reply only briefly to questions. "My father," she said, "was a difficult and sometimes violent man. He made few friends and a great many enemies, but murder is not something done lightly. Whoever killed my father did so believing the act justified. It is hard to conceive it would arise out of a business disagreement. This was something far more personal." Mrs. Melnick contradicted rumors she was engaging private detectives. "I have confidence in the Nassau authorities. I believe they are doing everything possible. There seems to be a complete absence of clues." She added she would probably close Windmere with the idea of putting the estate up for sale at a later date.

So, within a matter of weeks, the Bahama authorities have been baffled by the murders of two prominent men. Mr. Hertog was, of course, a financier of international reputation. Mr. Royal Keating was the leading spirit and drive behind the Progressive Liberal Party. It seems almost certain the party would have been victorious in the forthcoming elections. Mr. Keating would have been asked to form a government as the first Negro Prime Minister in the history of the islands. Many persons are inclined to believe the two slayings are somehow linked.

The big house at Windmere was enveloped in an uneasy silence, and those who moved about it or worked outside whispered at their duties and wondered how a man as big and powerful as Mistuh Max could have been beaten over the head until he lay without life in his blood. Jan had called both yard and house servants to the living room. For the yard and boatmen, this was the first time any of them had been inside. They made small, shuffling movements with their feet and darted apprehensive glances at one another, wondering what was going to happen. Watching them, Jan was almost tempted to laugh despite the circumstances. This was something out of a Civil War movie. The young mis'ress calling in the faithful blacks to warn them of the Yankees. She smiled reassuringly at them and lit a cigarette.

"I'm going to close Windmere." She spoke with a sympathetic understanding. Good, steady jobs on this scale weren't easy to find. "I'm not sure I will ever open it again. If I do, it won't be for some time. All of you have been here for years. I am going to do what I think my father would have me do. All of you will receive a year's salary. Arrangements have been made at the Inter Island Bank to pay you your regular wages weekly instead of all at once."

They understood this to be another example of a white person's humor and smiled cautiously.

380

"Even," Jan continued, "if you find other jobs, the money will be paid as though you were still at Windmere. Each Friday you go to the bank and get your wages." Her glance traveled down the line. "Are there any questions? Anything you don't understand?"

"No, ma'am, an' t'ank yo'." They managed a small chorus. There was a reflection of pleasure and relief on their faces. This was more than they had expected. "T'ank yo' again."

Jan nodded. "Until I close Windmere, the house servants may remain in their quarters. Good luck to all of you."

They waited a moment or two, not certain they had been dismissed, and then moved as a single rank in the direction of the kitchen.

"Big Maum," Jan called. "I'd like to have you wait."

When they were alone, Jan studied the woman and wondered why a relationship which had always been easy, almost affectionate, was now somehow changed. She could find no hostility in the big black woman. She wasn't defiant but withdrawn and remote, cold.

"Would you like to come to Miami and work for me?"

"No, Miss Jan. I don' know no place but th' islan's. I don' t'ink I would like Miami, wherever dat is."

"What will you do?"

"I t'ink I go back home, t' Li'l Exuma."

"You have been here longer than any of the others. You have always had the responsibility of Windmere. I'm having the bank set up a pension. You know what that is?"

"It money."

"Yes." There was a note of exasperation in Jan's voice. Big Maum wasn't being insolent, but there was something. "I have arranged for the bank to pay it to you for as long as you live."

"No, ma'am. I don' guess so."

"Why not?" She was really irritated now.

"I save my money. I don' need no help. T'anks, jus' th' same." She smiled for the first time. "It don' take much t' live on Exuma. I got plenty fo' as long as I'll be 'roun'. I got my boy bury dere, an' so I'll jus' go home." She did then what was

381

to Jan an inexplicable thing: She untied her stiff white apron, rolled it into a ball there in the Windmere living room, and held it in her great hands. "I don' have no mo' need fo' dis."

Of all the Bahamas the Exuma Cays are the loveliest, and in many places man has yet to put his hands on them. They are now as they were. So, if it is your mood, you may stand where no one has walked before and hear no sound save that made by a gentle movement of the sea. They start with Hog Cay, in the south. Then there is Little Exuma, Great Exuma and for almost one hundred miles they stretch northward to Sail Rock. Over them the winds whisper endlessly, and the seas and beaches are of an almost unbelievable color and whiteness.

Where the Keating plantation had been so bravely laid out, there is little left but the ruins and the graves of the Keatings, black and white. One is kept fresh now and the flowers, sometimes only in a can or bottle, are simply placed upon the mound which covers the remains of Royal Keating.

At night, at times, a big black woman walks in her loneliness upon a curving beach. Memories move with her here: the time of being a young girl, the time of love, the time of being married and the time of birth and death. The sharp edge of hatred has been dulled. No one has ever asked why she came back to Exuma. She talks rarely and now finds a curious peace in sitting with the old woman in the sun. That they are mother and daughter spins no real kinship between them. The old one is lost in vague imaginings of things only dimly remembered. She has even forgotten her daughter's name and is untouched by anything happening beyond this cay. So Big Maum and Old Maum sit and feel the warm sun on their faces, each confined in a private world of her own. Once Big Maum said a man had gone to the moon. She heard it on a small battery-powered radio. The old woman asked why and Big Maum had no answer.

The winds of change run ceaselessly over the Bahamas, and man, with his insatiable greed, hacks and gouges, drains and fills on the remotest of the island chain. Splendid hotels and yacht havens crowd the white beaches where once an Arawak Indian girl may have walked or rode laughingly upon the back of a lumbering sea turtle. A primitive silence, broken only by a bird's lonely cry, has been shattered forever. Something rare and of great value has been lost to a world in noisy turmoil. In its place are the fine marinas, the swimming pools, the golf courses, the fishing clubs, the angry whine of outboard motors and the endless beat of calypso steel drums. Now all the cays are beginning to look alike, and no one seems to mind. In the counting houses the stacks of dollars mount. Who would want to peer beyond them? Here the rapist and the ravaged are in happy communion.

In Nassau the name of Maximilian Hertog is rarely mentioned. A stranger with an inquiring mind and questions on his tongue senses a conspiracy of silence. Now and then he hears a whisper. A word is dropped, an opinion voiced. But no one there really knows and, as the years turn and are folded upon each other, it seems, sometimes, that no one really cares.